Praise for *Jubilee*

'An amusing and fast-paced saga sure to please fans of classic space opera.'
Publishers Weekly

'SF fans will enjoy this adventure that takes a look at the future of humans in space. Stanford's debut pushes his characters to the brink while making statements about our current world.'
Booklist

'Loved *Jubilee*. Absurdly fun, smart science fiction.'
Anthony W. Eichenlaub,
author of *The Man Who Walked in the Dark*

'Quirky, witty, and wild sci-fi fun.'
Zabé Ellor, author of *Silk Fire*

'Sharp with flawed-yet-relatable characters.'
Jennifer R. Povey, author of *The Lost Guardians* series

'A wild adventure across worlds.'
David Dvorkin, bestselling author
of *Time and the Soldier*

STEPHEN K. STANFORD

STARS LIKE US

Jubilee Book Two

This is a **FLAME TREE PRESS** book

FLAME TREE PRESS
6 Melbray Mews, London, SW6 3NS, UK
flametreepress.com

US sales, distribution and warehouse:
Simon & Schuster
simonandschuster.biz

UK distribution and warehouse:
Hachette UK Distribution
hukdcustomerservice@hachette.co.uk

Publisher's Note: This is a work of fiction. Names, characters, places, and incidents are a product of the author's imagination. Locales and public names are sometimes used for atmospheric purposes. Any resemblance to actual people, living or dead, or to businesses, companies, events, institutions, or locales is completely coincidental.

The cover is created by Flame Tree Studio working with the artist Dominic Bugatto. The art is © Dominic Bugatto 2025.
The font families used are Avenir and Bembo.

Flame Tree Press is an imprint of Flame Tree Publishing Ltd
flametreepublishing.com

A copy of the CIP data for this book is available from the British Library and the Library of Congress.

1 3 5 7 9 8 6 4 2

PB ISBN: 978-1-78758-965-0
ebook ISBN: 978-1-78758-967-4

Printed and bound in Great Britain by Clays Ltd, Elcograf S.p.A.
Represented in the EU for product safety and compliance by Authorised Rep Compliance Ltd., Ground Floor, 71 Lower Baggot Street, Dublin, D02 P593, Ireland. Contact at www.arccompliance.com

MIX
Paper | Supporting responsible forestry
FSC® C018072

STEPHEN K. STANFORD

STARS LIKE US

Jubilee Book Two

FLAME TREE PRESS
London & New York

Part One

Chapter One

"Wake up, lazy bitch," cried Sana. "Your babies are about to drown in their own poop."

"Where's Col?" grumbled Danee, surfacing from out of our bedroom, yawning, bed hair a tangle. "Is he ever planning on being more than a sperm donor dad?"

Grossly unfair. I spent at least as much time taking care of the girls as she did.

"Don't blame Col!" shouted Sana. "*You're* the one turning into a crack mother."

This is how the girls jibed each other. Funny, though it did get a little tiring sometimes.

I emerged from the bathroom. "Sorry, Danee, I'm about to go on duty – want me to call the robo-nanny?"

She yawned and patted down her hair. Today was a rostered day off from her job at the Intelligence department, but Sana's joke did have a ring of truth. While never much of a 'girly girl' to start with, Danee was putting even less time into her personal appearance these days since the twins were born. "Nah, just kidding," she said. "Wanna kiss the bubbas goodbye?"

In the nursery, Lila and Anjali (who we called Lala) were crying lustily. We each picked one up and, indeed, a wafting smell of something rich and nasty filled the room.

"Goodbye, gorgeous," I cooed, planting a kiss on Lila's cheek. She stopped crying instantly, her face and eyes still puffy and red.

"Dadda," she gurgled with a shy smile, the kind of smile that turns a father into squishy Play-Doh.

I leaned over and kissed Lala.

"Bye bye, Dadda," she said softly, turning that Play-Doh into melted ooze.

They say in ancient times on Old Earth, humans were divided into distinct races within which, most people's physical characteristics were similar. Nowadays of course, we're mixed up and kids pop out with any combination of skin tone and bodily feature.

But even so, the difference between *our* girls was startling. Anjali was exactly like her mother; blonde and blue-eyed, strong of frame, and a hearty eater.

Lila, in some twist of fate or karma, or whatever, was tiny and birdlike with dark skin and hair, and black eyes. She was lighter than air and ate no more than two spoonfuls of food per day. When we were all out together, people naturally assumed Sana to be the mother – then you could see them having strange thoughts when they realized I was father to both girls.

My domestic life *is* rather complicated!

I grabbed Danee for a group hug.

"Will you be all right?" I asked, handing Lila to her.

Danee leaned over and kissed me slowly on the mouth – triggering an instant hormonal response. "Hurry home," she said – and after a nice smooch like that, who wouldn't?

"See ya, Sana!" I cried, heading for the door.

Only silence from the adjoining apartment, she'd probably gone back to sleep.

Was it weird, having my ex-wife live right next door? Yes and no. On the one hand we'd all fallen rapidly into a stable domestic routine, Sana joining us for meals, or just as often doing her own thing, pursuing the many and varied projects that seemed to have sprung up around her on Jubilee. She loved the twins and they in turn adored Auntie Sana, spending as much time as they could with her. She and Danee caught up for afternoon teas and went out together – even after the girls were born. Amazingly, they had become best friends. And as for me, Sana had morphed back into my life in this new capacity – almost like a whole new person – and after a while it grew hard even to remember she had once been my wife.

Though sometimes, just occasionally, when we would share a joke, or remember something from the old days – or if I became aware of her keeping intimate company with members of the opposite (or same) sex – I couldn't help feeling that a small spark was still there, still smoldering somewhere deep down, even if scrupulously suppressed.

Anyway, it all seemed to work somehow. Us one big, strange family – me for my sins surrounded entirely by females, cheerfully drowning in a sea of estrogen.

I took the lift up to Concourse, Jubilee's famous main drag. Douglas, the eccentric AI who ran this place had installed us in the depths of sector twenty, on level seventeen with the other families. Naturally, a strict quarantine was in place to prevent sensitive young souls being exposed to the red-light zone.

It was early 'morning' and I watched the crazy artificial world of Jubilee coming to life from the window of my transit car.

Danee had fallen pregnant during our mission to Grendeva. Her birth-control nanos glitched – happens occasionally – which would normally have triggered an alert on her kom. But of course, her kom was uninstalled for the mission and like most modern women, Danee wasn't aware of the signs. I agreed instantly to co-parent, and she carried the girls to full term herself – a rare thing these days.

At Sector Fifteen I decided to jump off the transit, take in the 'morning air'. Why not? At Sector Eleven the hologram of my old friend Zhang the poet waved from his black box. Zhang was tortured to death by the Movement, but Douglas had installed this facsimile of him as a poem-writing attraction on Jubilee, a tribute of sorts, I guess.

"How're you doing, Donny?" he asked. He still called me by this fake name he'd known me as, even two years after I'd explained.

"Not bad, Zhang. How were the crowds last night?"

"Oh, you know, the usual. Handed out 1,563 poems. Close to a record."

"Good work, buddy. Let me know if you see anything, eh?"

"No worries, Donny, have a great day!"

I turned to walk on. Just a few blocks more to my office in Sector Nine, where I worked as head of security for Jubilee. But a voice called from behind. Zhang's voice, sounding strange.

"COL!" he cried, "*BEWARE* THE IDES OF MARCH!"

I turned around. "What's that, buddy? Beware *what*?"

Zhang was standing frozen, arms at his sides, a faraway look in his eyes. "Beware the Ides of March," he repeated quietly.

I went to speak to him. The hologram flickered for a moment then righted itself. "What were you saying just then?" I asked. "*Beware the tides of March*?"

Zhang laughed. He seemed himself again. "Beware the *ides* of March," he corrected me. "Where did you get that from, Donny? That's Shakespeare. *Julius Caesar*, Act 1, Scene 2, the soothsayer's warning. No one knows that stuff anymore – except ancient history buffs, *and* poets, of course."

"You said those words to me, just now."

Zhang made a wry smile. "You're shitting me, right?"

"I swear, just moments ago, you said that line, twice."

Zhang looked blank for a moment, then laughed. "Donny, I think you might have been smoking a bit too much of the old..." He did an impression of someone toking on a long joint. "Would you like a poem?"

I shook my head. "Not today, thanks." I didn't think I could take any more of Zhang's enigmatic claptrap. "See you soon."

"See you, Donny."

I turned and walked on. No further interruptions this time. What the hell was that about? Who would know when it came to Zhang?

Concourse was filling fast. The permanent residents having their morning power walks, mixing with the desolate and bedraggled who'd been up all night playing the tables or diving through the innumerable fleshpots of Jubilee. What fresh dramas were in store for today?

I paged Douglas. "Anything new?"

"Mornin', Col, just the usual. Eleven muggings, twenty-one stabbings, and a bunch o' health crises. Nothin' we couldn't handle." These weren't real stabbings or muggings of course; an enormous security infrastructure stood poised to intervene at the first sign of trouble, enforcing the golden rule of Jubilee: do whatever you like here, but never harm another person. At Tenth Avenue, I stepped over the prone bodies of an amorous couple, half naked and sleeping in each other's arms, when the lights went off.

Just like that.

Total blackness. Of a kind you can only experience in a place that has no windows or natural light. Someone right next to me started screaming. I tried Douglas but my kom was dead. Thumps and bashing sounds came from all around, people starting to panic and crash into things – crikey, it didn't take long.

"Calm down, everybody!" I cried out in a voice as loud and authoritative as I could muster. "Very shortly the—"

At that moment, the lights came back on – some of them anyway. Emergency lighting that cast a silvery gray wash. The stores and streetlights and all the fancy holos were still out though, and without them Jubilee suddenly looked tawdry and cheap, like the big heap of space junk it really was. I stepped across to a nearby air vent, put my ear to it and heard a faint hiss. Good, at least we weren't all about to asphyxiate. I dashed across Tenth Avenue, trying Douglas all the while.

The girls!

Hot panic clutched my heart. I called Danee, then Sana. Nothing.

What to do?

Head to the control room – closer than my office and the best place to start. I galloped along Concourse, weaving my way around the stunned and the stoned. But when I reached it, the elevator was out. Of course. Couldn't even page it on my kom.

Stairs.

Had to be stairs, but where? I'd never used them before, not once, never even looked for them. The elevator stood closed fast in front of me. It was on the corner of a small alley; I took a few steps around the corner and spotted a door. No sign, but worth a try. The handle turned and it opened inward without any trouble, stairs running down into the gray gloom. I took them four at a time, then told myself to be calm – I'd be no help to anyone with a broken ankle.

How many flights?

Who knew? But not many. The control room was situated in the dead center of Jubilee. It was the first thing they built all those years ago, so it couldn't be too far below Concourse level. After two flights there was a door with a sign: *Control Room*. There you go. I pushed through, emerging into the familiar space, calling out, "Douglas!" But it all seemed uncannily empty, lit only with the same pervasive gray light.

There were the rows of dusty old desks and holo-screens now lit up. I'd never seen this before in the many times I was here. When Douglas came online centuries ago, the manual systems were disabled, though not permanently it would seem. These must have all been left operational as a fail-safe. I sat at one of the screens, which was blinking, 'log on'. But how, what was the code?

I keyed in 'DOUGLAS' – maybe that would get him back online?

No change, the log-in field went back to blank.

Fuck. I had no idea whatsoever.

I tried 'JOHN HUDSON' – the name of Jubilee's founder who Douglas loved. No good. Then 'JOHN', then 'HUDSON', then crazily, my own name, 'COL'. Nothing. Could be any combination of letters and numbers. How many tries before I was locked out?

OK, think. Think. Did Douglas ever mention anything?

A memory came. All of us sitting in the control room; Danee and Sana and me, along with Douglas (or one of his robot avatars, to be more correct). "What goes on with all of this?" I asked, waving at the screens.

"Ah, ye won't be needin' any of that with me around. Just as well coz John put no bleedin' security on anything."

No bleedin' security.

What did that mean?

I hit enter – no password – and the room came instantly to life. Bingo. The holo-screens now showed meaningless swirls of 3D code. A genius like John Hudson would know what to do with all that, but me?

A bank of security cameras filled the wall to my right; I'd never noticed them before. They were much older, cheaper models than the state-of-the-art equipment we had in the security center, but they blinked to life and started showing vision from all over Jubilee, switching perspective every few seconds. The scene was everywhere the same; gray monochrome light, people stumbling around in confusion. From a view along Concourse, I saw one of Douglas's avatars frozen in mid-stride and reflexively looked over to the bank of equipment where he was hosted to see a field of unblinking red lights. That had to be bad.

It was around this time that I saw the looting start. First one person, tentatively, then others following. Then everyone all at once. A mob, breaking into shops, upending gaming tables. Within moments, uproar exploded across the public spaces of Jubilee – and surely this was only the *beginning* of what was to come. We had to get Douglas back online.

What about the girls?

I slid across to a nearby console labeled *cameras*, which seemed the logical place to start. Typed in the coordinates of our home. One of the screens nearby switched to a view of the common area inside our apartment where it connected with Sana's. I sighed with relief; there they were. Danee's expression fixed and grim, Sana boggled-eyed, the girls pattering around oblivious, and all bathed in the same sickly gray light. There was an old-fashioned microphone in front of me with a button labeled *speak*. I pressed it.

"Danee, Sana, can you hear me?"

They looked around, startled. I released the button.

"Col!" cried Danee. "What the *fuck* is going on, where are you?"

"I'm in the control room. Douglas is offline, God knows why. I just logged the old manual system on, but I've got no idea how to use it. This is an intercom we're talking on."

"We need someone in there who knows how to operate that old system. I think I know a guy at the department."

"What's his room number? I could call him on this thing. Hell, it probably does a Jubilee-wide page if you know how."

"Don't know his number but I know where he lives. I'll just go get him," said Danee. "He's two floors up."

"Be careful, it's getting rough out there."

She glared at me through the camera. "Remember who you're talking to!"

Indeed. My sweet wife could more than take care of herself. In fact, I pitied the looter who tried something with her. "Take a blaster anyway. For me."

Danee scowled but doubled back to the bedroom. She emerged moments later with her weapon, then bolted out the door, still in bed clothes.

I've thought back to these events many times. Obviously. Of all the things I might have done differently, getting Danee to take that blaster was not one of them.

"You OK, Sana?"

"Sure, it's a bit scary, but the girls seem OK—"

There was sudden movement on the screens. I looked across and what I saw made everything crystal clear. Horrifyingly so.

"*Holy shit!* Sana, we're being *invaded*!"

The security system must have had AI built into it, because the cameras were switching over to shots where new action was occurring. If I had access to the main system, I could have seen a schematic of what was going on, but visuals told the story well enough. Outside, in the space off Jubilee, a fleet of warships had appeared. Massive, brooding hulks bristling with weapons.

Warships.

Who has warships? The Sirrelian Insurrection was the last major battle of any kind, and that was ten thousand years ago. More appeared, winking into existence. Ominously, transports as well. Were they planning to storm Jubilee? Who the hell was doing this? In my mind it had to be the radical retrogressive group, Movement 4 Morality, or M4M, who'd previously kidnapped Sana and tried to take over my home planet, Brouggh.

Who else?

And we were defenseless. A giant casino and flophouse, all our security was focused inward to stop bad behavior. Danee and I had tried to warn Douglas over the years, but he was dismissive. "We got our ways of lookin' out for ourselves," he'd say. "Don't ye worry about that."

Well, he should have worried. They must have taken him offline in their first strike of what was clearly a well-planned operation. Software first, then hardware.

But how did they get here? Jubilee existed in its own parallel universe point zero eight seconds removed from our own. You needed a special jump code to synchronize with the local stars' weird gravity waves to leap over.

They must have figured it out. Must have observed and experimented – the Aurelian AI would have been involved. If John Hudson had been able to work it out back in the day, then they could too. On camera, more ships arrived by the second; the space around Jubilee teemed with them. Boarding us now. The cameras switched to shots of the landing docks, airlocks opening, armed troops entering. They'd commandeered the docking codes as well.

What to do?

Come up with a plan, obviously. But my mind spun in neutral.

Why would the Movement go to all this trouble?

They hated Jubilee, of course, and everything it represented: 'loose' morals and freedom from any jurisdiction and control of course. But also, Douglas had helped defeat them on Brouggh and maybe worst of all, had been instrumental in Sana's rescue. I noticed something in one of the far cameras. Another landing party, a phalanx of troops bursting into a landing dock with a tall figure at its center giving orders. Thin with long dark hair, dressed all in white.

Gilham, the self-appointed leader of M4M looked perfectly relaxed. He scanned the room, black eyes glittering, walked up to the camera and looked directly into it – directly at *me* it seemed – and smiled warmly as if greeting an old friend, palms together in his trademark 'namaste' sign. Could he sense me somehow, know I was watching? Did his powers extend that far? A second later the screen went dark.

This was personal.

"What's going on!" cried Sana. "What do you mean we're being—"

"Gilham's *here*. Here on fucking Jubilee!" I told her what I'd just seen as the semblance of a plan finally started to form. Not much of one, but better than nothing. "Jubilee is lost Sana, we can't save her, they're here in huge force. You have to grab Danee and the girls and get to an airlock. I'll give you the number: 19-14B. Can you do that?"

She looked up, eyes blank with panic. "I don't understand, what are—"

"Sana, we have to *flee*. There's a small flyer in that dock – Danee knows all about it. We gotta get you all out of here. It's our only shot."

She looked around weakly, decisive action never one of her strong suits.

"Say it back to me, *lock 19–14B*."

"19-14B," she said distantly.

"OK, grab stuff for you and the girls. The second Danee returns, run like the wind. I'll meet you there."

"OK." She teared up. "Col, I'm scared."

"Sana, it will be all right," I lied. "Just do what I said, get to 19-14B, and then we can—"

I was cut off by a huge explosion that blew in the unlocked door of the control room. Blaster fire poured through the haze of dust and debris, followed by a squadron of troops.

Chapter Two

"I love it!" said Douglas.

The rest of us looked at him skeptically. All except Sana, of course, in mid-gush about her latest art project – *Dance of the Robots.*

"...it will be a juxtaposition of the organic with the synthetic, human born with the constructed. Perfect symbolism for life on Jubilee." She looked pointedly at the secbot Batum, who'd become part of our little pod after joining us on the rescue mission for Sana.

"Forget it," he said. "Under no circumstances will I participate in a fucking *dance show.*"

It had been a grand night; Danee and me, along with Batum, Douglas, Sana, and her new best-friend-forever, Domenic. He had been her manager while she was enslaved on Rethne as Gilham's domestic, and unwittingly saved the rescue mission. A closeted gay man, he'd lived in constant danger on the Movement's home planet until Douglas arranged his escape to Jubilee.

We were eating at **P U H O L**, one of Jubilee's top establishments, rated 467th in *The Galaxy's 10,000 Best Restaurants.* Though calling what we were doing 'eating' was a gross exaggeration. Endless tiny courses arrived, involving foams and sprays, strange decanters to sniff, and plates of food that turned out to be holograms – more of a magic show than a meal. Sana and Domenic were ecstatic, and of course Douglas relished it all with the usual lip-smacking enthusiasm. But I'm more of a meat and potatoes guy. I was hammered from all that wine on a half empty stomach and fantasizing about a burger on the way home.

Danee and I exchanged looks, time to wind up. Neither of us were exactly party animals, and even less so these days. We waved our goodbyes and left them to it. I had a bad feeling for Batum. No way was he getting out of being in Sana's new show.

Which soon gathered unstoppable momentum. A venue was found – the largest on Jubilee, belonging to one of the casinos – and a casting call put out. Droids and bots of every shape and size showed up and were warmly accepted, though Sana did have one condition: all the mechanical cast had to be running from operating systems that were independent of Douglas. Like Batum for example, and in the end, I think Douglas wore him down with the offer of an upgrade. Sana's apartment turned into a nerve center with laughter and chitchat running to the wee hours. It was amazing how quickly she'd become a person of note on Jubilee, wrapping everyone up into her plans and schemes.

Life rolled on for Danee and me, caught up in our routine of work and children. One afternoon toward the end of shift I found myself in the upper reaches of Sector Two and on a whim decided to visit the Swami. I found his quarters in a state of uproar; boxes stacked to the roof, a stream of people moving equipment and furniture. I spotted the friendly receptionist from my last visit, waved, and shrugged.

"We're moving out," she explained, "but Swamiji's around if you want to say goodbye?"

She showed me through to a side room where he sat in a high-back chair, deeply engrossed in a game of chess.

"Is that Douglas you're playing?" I asked.

He swiveled around. "Yes, oh *hullo*, Col! I'm going to miss playing him. Actually, I'm going to miss a lot of things."

"What's happening?" I asked. "Where are you going?"

The Swami sighed and pointed to a chair. "We're moving on."

"Really? To where?"

He laughed ironically. "*India*, believe it or not." He pointed to one of the many pictures on the wall showing a village lying on the bank of a beautiful turquoise river labeled, *The Ganges at Rishikesh*. Looked ancient, maybe somewhere on Old Earth?

"Never heard of it. But why? I thought you liked it here on Jubilee?"

"Yes, yes, of course." He seemed distracted. Then he took a breath and looked at me directly. I found myself falling into his eyes, a bottomless ocean. "It's been a while, Col," he said finally. "I thought we might see you again, much sooner?"

I sighed. "Been somewhat busy, I guess." And I told him about recent events. "I kept meaning to drop around, but you know..."

"Fair enough." He smiled, eyes crinkling. "I guess we'll just have to catch up another time, another place."

"But why leave? Don't you have everything you need here?"

"Yes." He sighed. "Let's just say I got an offer that I couldn't refuse."

The buzz for *Dance of the Robots* grew exponentially. Domenic was conscripted to do costumes and became a constant presence at Sana's side. A famous composer, now retired and living on Jubilee, came forward with an offer to write the score, and by opening night excitement was at fever pitch. Danee and I, feeling somewhat out of place, surveyed the red carpet from a safe distance and were just about to start down it when Sana rushed out from somewhere, took us both by the arm and guided us through the gauntlet of paparazzi.

We took our seats in the front row alongside Douglas, who was jumping out of his skin with excitement. "I ain't never seen nothin' like this!" he said, grabbing me around the shoulder. Douglas was, of course, participating in *and* watching the show – probably from twenty different angles using just a few of his countless avatars. I scanned the crowd in fascination; seated all around us were the great and the good of Jubilee society, waiting expectantly and dressed to the nines. To our right, a single row of seats centered in front of the stage remained unoccupied, the last empty seats in the house. Must be for VIPs, but who?

The question was answered moments later when Jade Kamala entered with entourage.

That's right, *the* Jade Kamala, pan-galactic pop sensation. I heard a rumor she was living on Jubilee, there was a suite of apartments Douglas had told us to be extra vigilant about – and now confirmation. Danee nudged me and giggled. There were gasps and kom flashes as she walked to her seat, wearing a spangly black outfit and sprouting trendy androgynous facial hair. I guess that meant the show could now start.

On stage, a vacuum-bot was busily cleaning nonexistent dirt while the orchestra made tuning-up noises. Jürgen, the composer, had put together a traditional orchestra, like something from Old Earth, with violins and cellos and all those other ancient instruments I'd only ever seen on TV. Astonishing. These players must have all been living on Jubilee.

Time passed and the crowd started to fidget. *Dance of the Robots* was scheduled to start at 19:30, but things seemed to be running late. The house lights were still up, and now another droid, a domestic, was on stage doing finishing touches. Fluffing the side curtains, rearranging things. The stage curtain was closed but furniture and props had been positioned in front of it: a lounge, two couches and side tables suggestive of a human sitting room.

I had a sinking feeling in my stomach. Had Sana done anything like this before? Not that I could recall. Did any of these robots have the capacity or programming to put on a show?

Another domestic droid joined the others on stage. They all stood around looking a bit confused and out of place, positioning and repositioning props as if in a loop. The orchestra all the while tuned up endlessly. A titter of laughter swept the crowd, and behind me, a lady I recognized – some famous critic – leaned back in her chair with a smirk.

Something was wrong.

I noticed some in the crowd getting up to leave, but most stayed glued to their seats, murmuring and laughing aloud. A *debacle*, what fun!

But now there was a subtle change from the orchestra. A melody formed, coalescing gradually out of the random tuning sounds, becoming more apparent with each beat. On stage the robots started swaying (a little clumsily) to the music as one by one the house lights dimmed.

The orchestra began to pick up time and the robots on stage moved together. The three domestic droids in front made a dance formation, the vacuum-bot behind, zooming back and forth, nozzle swooping to the music.

Then one of the droids leaned down and with a single 'hand' picked up a couch, twirling it on its finger like a spinning top. The audience gasped. Surely this was not physically possible? Those droids might have super-human strength, but the power-to-weight ratio was all wrong for handling something that massive. A mini gravity engine must have been built into it somehow to create this trick. Clever though. The first robot tossed the couch through the air to another droid, who flipped it over its head to the third. A juggling act. The robots picked up other pieces of furniture, dancing with them in precise formation, perfectly in time.

The audience watched, enthralled now. We'd been tricked by the opening, pleasantly so. I guess it was making some sort of statement about human attitudes to robots and their unacknowledged labor. Sana would have put it far more eloquently.

And then the curtains opened, and the full stage was revealed, a rainbow world lit with brilliant color and light. Filled with dancing robots of all shapes and sizes, including Batum. Performing tricks, leaping off shoulders, doing somersaults. The vacuum-bot reappeared, wearing a dazzling glittery costume, and Douglas, grinning like mad, descended from a rope and leaped onto the stage to cheers from the crowd. *Everybody* loved Douglas. The music and dancing built to a crescendo. Glitter bombs exploded, lasers flashed, and the audience went wild.

But that was just the opening stanza.

The lights dropped, the orchestra shifted to a minor key and human dancers appeared for the first time. Now for the narrative. Something about a little girl lost in the woods. Facing many dangers, saved by a benevolent robot, and transported to a magical land where they all lived together. Something like that; I got lost after a while. It all finished with another huge set piece with more flashing lights and glitter, the stage filled with humans and robots dancing together. The crowd stood and cheered for five minutes and finally, Sana appeared, grinning and beaming, pointing to the cast for their curtain calls. A triumph.

At the after-party, Sana made a beeline for Danee and me, steering us through the throng, and making sure we were at ease. This was Sana at her best, considerate and generous. I plucked some champagne flutes from a passing serving bot, and we toasted, the ladies magnificent in their evening gowns, hair piled up.

"You're a very clever girl," said Danee, affectionately.

"That means *so* much coming from you," replied Sana, hand on heart, "and I just want to say—"

Something we'll never know, because a scrum of media swept her away, all asking questions at once. I caught a snatch of the conversation…

"…oh, they all *loved* it!" she said. "They've even set up a private comms channel so they can keep talking and stay friends afterward. It's been such a…"

You get the picture.

A tall, redheaded lady dressed all in black had been holding court in the center of the throng. I recognized her, *Kat Blair*! Danee and I had seen the opening of her art exhibition when we first came to Jubilee. O B F U S C A T I O N S, it was called. She now strode through the crowd, which parted like the sea.

"Congratulations, darling!" she said in a booming voice. "*Strong* work."

Sana glowed at the compliment, beamed, and drew her into a hug.

Years before when we were first together, Sana schooled me on the lingo of the art world. "People never say what they really mean," she explained.

"Same in the cop world. You should see what the crims come up with!"

"No, not like that!" She grinned. "For example, if someone comes up to you and says your work is 'interesting', that means they actually *hate* it."

"Why? You're not allowed to just say you hate it?"

"Absolutely not. That's being *negative*."

"But if you call it 'interesting', don't they know you hate it anyway?"

"Certainly, but you didn't actually say it. That's the important thing."

"OK…got it," I said skeptically.

"And if they *really* hate something, they'll say it was…'brave'."

"We also have a different use for *that* word in the Services."

"I'm sure."

"But now I'm confused, what if someone actually *likes* it, what do they say then?"

Sana laughed. "Well in that case they say, '*strong work*'!"

There were many 'strongs' bandied around that night, which I think of now as the high point of my life on Jubilee, with only one discordant note: Domenic. He was nowhere to be seen. Surprising, given his major role in the show. The costumes were remarkably good if you like that sort of thing.

"I had a headache," he said to Sana the next day. "Didn't want to bum anyone out, so just took myself home."

A few months after the show, he called for a favor.

"Sure, how can I help?" I asked. We were sitting at a café on Concourse, among the daily throng of people streaming past all caught up in the thousand adventures of life on Jubilee. Domenic had paged me earlier, the first time he had ever initiated contact, so I was intrigued. There'd always been something about him that pinged my radar as being a little off. For one thing, a subtle but permanent expression of surprise or distaste, like he'd *seen something nasty behind the woodpile*, as my hometown buddies in Jerbet would say.

"Firstly," he said, "can you please not tell Sana about this conversation?"

"Sure. I mean I guess so. What's this about?"

Domenic put sugar into his coffee and stared at it, stirring for too long. "This is hard to say so I'm just going to come out with it." He finally looked at me. "I need to get back to Rethne. Can you help?"

I tried not to react. Rethne had been hell for him and would be especially dangerous now after living on Jubilee. "Return to Rethne? Didn't you—"

"Yes, yes! I know what you're going to say." His voice trembled. "But really, it's my home, much as I love Jubilee. And now my mother is ill. I need to get back, and I don't want people judging me. Can you arrange it?"

I looked at him warily. "OK, I'll see what I can do."

"*Please*," he begged, as we parted, "don't tell Sana. I know she's going to be devastated."

"But you'll be back, right? Assuming they let you?"

"Of course!" he said. But somehow, I knew that was a lie.

It took a full two months, but Domenic's passage was finally arranged. It was even harder to organize than I expected, such being the ever-growing paranoia of the Movement for Morality. I walked with him to the dock, carrying one of his bags. He looked terrible, downcast, and teary. If he really felt this bad about it, why leave?

"Tell Sana I'm sorry," he said from the airlock as it began to cycle.

"*Domenic!*" I said, exasperated. "I'm sure she'll understand, particularly if your mother is sick?"

He looked stricken. He turned away, then back to me, tears in his eyes.

"I'm sorry, Col, they have my family."

The doors closed, and that was the last I ever saw of him.

Chapter Three

Blaster fire arced across the room, equipment exploded into flames and debris rained down. Part of the ceiling collapsed, filling the room with dust, and sparks danced through the opaque air. I dived to the floor and crawled under the desks away from the entrance but seconds later a full squadron of troops was standing over me – twenty blasters aimed, trigger fingers quivering. One of them lifted his helmet and stared coldly. Squat-shaped, dark skin and hair, and with blue eyes – Rethnian from a mile off. A holo image rose from his kom: my face, emblazoned with the words *wanted dead or alive.*

"Col Perolo," he declared triumphantly, "you are arrested for the crime of Debasement of Public Morals, the punishment for which is death. You have been pre-tried, found guilty and may die immediately in the heat of battle like a man, or face extradition to Rethne, where you will be tortured to death like a dog. *How do you choose?*"

Such great options.

"What do you say, Perolo?"

I could feel fingers tightening on triggers.

Everything felt surreal. Just an hour before I had kissed my girls goodbye on the way to work. I raised my hands, stalling for time, looking around the room for God knows what – anything that might give me leverage.

There was movement behind the ring of men, over in the far corner of the room. Something unnaturally quiet and fast, a silvery shape that I recognized.

Salvation.

"Captain," I croaked from the floor, which was covered in a dense layer of dust, "I do have something to say, two things actually." I sat up, trying to summon as much dignity as possible. "Firstly, this charge is bogus and you know it. We're all Services guys here, right? C'mon?" I looked up at the men, searching for a sign of humanity. The returning gaze was only steely and hard.

The captain smiled smugly. "The Tribunal of Elders has spoken and—"

"OK, OK I get it," I said. "Then my second point is this: if you want to live longer than the next – I dunno – minute or so, you should lay down your arms and surrender right now."

The captain smirked; there was a ripple of laughter through the men. "As well as being a degenerate, you are obviously mentally unsound, Perolo, though I'm sure the two go easily together. We have twenty blasters trained on you right now. What possible threat do you pose to *us*?"

"Captain, I say this with all sincerity from one Services guy to another, if you don't back off right now, you and all your men are doomed."

The captain stared at me sourly. "Your choice, Perolo, get ready for the next world."

"No, Captain," I said sadly, "this is *your* choice." Then to the silvery shape, "*Now!*"

Batum swung into action, releasing some kind of flying knife weapon. It whirled through the air at hypersonic speed slicing through armor and soft flesh, severing heads and arms, splitting bodies apart in geysers of red. A couple of the men managed to turn and fire, even getting a few shots away – but it was all over in seconds. Body parts strewn, the captain lay pinned to the floor, the flying knife at his throat.

"Shall I kill him?" asked Batum coldly, spattered with blood. I realized that for all these years we'd been acquainted, I'd never actually seen him in action. It was a terrifying sight.

"Captain," I said, "there's been enough bloodshed. I'm going to immobilize you and then—"

"Fuck you, Perolo, and your vile *newtech*." He spat at Batum. A gob of saliva attached itself, then slid down the robot's face.

An unwise response.

The knife twitched, and that was that for the captain. More noise came from outside, and Batum directed a stream of blaster fire at the roof above the door, bringing down a pile of debris. "That should hold them," he said. "Come." I followed him through the shattered remains of the control room, everything blood-splashed and ruined, including the equipment that once hosted Douglas. Jubilee would not be coming back online anytime soon.

We jogged through the stasis chamber where I first met John Hudson, to an open hatch at the far side of the room. Batum pointed for me to go ahead. I clambered through and down some stairs with the robot following, pulling the hatch closed. At the base of the stairs a grimy corridor ran off in a straight line, directly underneath Concourse. Access for the Services, I guess.

"We'll head to your apartment," said Batum. "Grab the girls, then go to your ship, agreed?"

"Yes, perfect."

I was crouched over, trying to run as fast as possible in this low corridor clearly designed for someone, or more likely something, much smaller. "But how do you know about the escape ship given that the comms are down?"

"DOTR network," he said, then stopped in front of a hatchway set into the floor, consulting with himself for a moment. "This is it. Might be a bit tricky, though." He looked at me directly. "You all right with that?"

I gulped. What did 'tricky' mean for a droid like Batum? "Of course."

He opened the hatch, slipped onto the edge of the hole, then leaned down into it. He grabbed something and swung off into the darkness. Faint footsteps could be heard now, tromping along the corridor, many pairs of them. Could be close or far away, hard to tell in a space like this.

Through the hatch was only blackness, not even emergency lighting down there. A torch flicked on, coming from Batum's head, partially illuminating a huge empty space, maybe sixty meters deep – just as well I don't suffer from vertigo. Batum was hanging by one hand from a rail fixed into the roof. "We have to get over to the ladder. It's thirty meters that way." He pointed with the other hand into the gloom.

I swung down into the hole, grabbed a rail with both hands, body dangling. The hatch was just behind me, still open. "What about that?" I cocked my head. From Batum's wrist a metal tendril shot out through the opening. It coiled around the hatch and pulled it shut with a clang that reverberated in the huge space.

My arms were starting to burn already. I put in a lot of time at the gym but hanging like this was not the kind of exercise I'm good at – unlike Sana, say, who could scurry up a climbing wall faster than a spider. She weighed about ten kilos, all of it muscle and sinew.

Batum set off, hand over hand, into the dark and I followed. The pain in my arms grew with every second – how much farther? I tried to focus on the activity: reach out, grab the next rail, swing over. Reach, grab, swing. It was agony in the arms now. *Think about something else.*

It had to have been Domenic.

That made sense. The Movement hadn't *let* him go; they *sent* him to Jubilee as a spy. He obviously felt bad about it, but not enough to sacrifice himself, or his family – or whatever it was they had over him. He must have given them a huge amount of intel for this invasion.

Including the location of our apartment.

My arms were growing numb, hands losing power. I could see the wall now wavering in the light of Batum's torch. Only a few meters to go, maybe five. Ten handholds. Reach, grab, swing. Reach, grab, swing. There was a ladder running down the side of the wall. Batum leaped at it with robotic agility then instantly dropped a few rungs to make space for me. In agony I reached across from the last roof rail, put my foot onto a rung and tried to step across. But my hands were numb, the ladder wet and slimy. I slipped off, flailing into the abyss.

Chapter Four

Batum caught me in his arms, a hook cable deployed around the ladder securing us. He held me like a baby as I shivered in shock.

"Recover," he said.

I tried to slow my racing heart. "Thanks, need to get some feeling back in my arms."

"Sorry for that. This was the best way, through the old settling tank. We can get six levels down without being detected."

Clever move, this place would not be on any Movement maps – certainly none made by Domenic. Jubilee was cobbled together one piece at a time from random space junk, a crazed patchwork of construction, redundant elements plastered over by the new. Douglas kept building this way even after amassing an immense fortune. I think it gave him a perverse pleasure. This giant tank had probably served a useful purpose once, hundreds of years ago but now lay disused, a giant, rotting hollow just meters below the gleaming façade of Concourse.

"What's going on out there, do you know?"

"The invaders are converging on your apartment; we're trying to head them off."

I slapped my arms a few times, reached up and grabbed the ladder. "Better keep moving, Batum, I've got a bad feeling."

We clambered down the old ladder, moving as fast as we dared. At the bottom lay a foot or so of turgid black water. We sloshed through it to the far wall, where Batum opened a partially submerged hatch and kicked at something. There was a crunch and then the sound of water splashing somewhere.

"Through there," he said.

I grabbed the top of the hatch and swung through. Landed jerkily in one of the residential corridors, probably Level Eight by the look of it. The hole I came through was near the top of the wall just below the ceiling and brown water poured from it. A door opened nearby, and a man stepped out dressed only in tracksuit pants and a stained t-shirt. Ravaged face unshaven, hair long and scraggly, he looked down at the brown water lapping at his bare feet.

"What the fuck is going on?" he rasped. The voice of someone who'd spent a lifetime gargling hard liquor.

"Go back in your room and wait for instructions," said Batum tersely, in war mode now and even less disposed than usual to indulge human niceties. The man put his hands on his hips, ran his eyes up and down the both of us and seemed to reach a conclusion.

"Fuck that, you two are up to something."

Batum raised his arm menacingly, went to shove the man back in his room, but I stepped in. "It's OK, Batum. Sir, we are working on the lighting problem that you have no doubt observed. If you will just wait quietly, I can assure you—"

"Bullshit!" The man laughed wheezily, then doubled over in a coughing fit. Batum let him go and jogged off. "This way," he said.

Other doors were opening, people standing around dazed, rubbing their eyes. Jubilee staff, many of them working 'night' shift. This would be the middle of their sleep cycle. I followed Batum, sloshing through the water, nodding at the residents as we passed. We were in the dead center of Jubilee here. My apartment was in Sector Twenty, ten kilometers away laterally, then down another nine floors to Level Seventeen. From there we would need to drop a further three levels to find the airlock that was our destination. That was a lot of traveling to do without being detected.

We jogged a kilometer or so till the flooding water was far behind, the endless corridor stretching ahead into the gray gloom. I heard a sound and turned to see the man who confronted us earlier. He was puffing and red-faced but following close behind.

"Sir," I said, "this is *very* dangerous—"

"Listen," he said, grabbing my arm, out of breath, "I can tell something bad is goin' down, and no one seems to know nothin' about it except for you two jokers. So, *I'm comin' with*!" He pulled out a blaster from the waistband of his tracksuit and waved it around. "Trust me, I'm a very *useful* guy in a tight situation."

I made one of those split-second decisions. The kind you look back on and think, *what possessed me?* "All right, you can come with us. But you have to keep up."

"Big mistake," said Batum grimly. He'd circled back to see why I'd stopped.

"You're the mistake," spat the man. "Fuckin' *tin can*, what would you know..." Still barefoot, in bed clothes, he waggled his gun provocatively in Batum's face. A blaster tube emerged from Batum's forearm and trained itself ominously on the man. How many instruments of mass destruction were packed into that body?

"Enough," I said, stepping in before the man was turned into a pile of steaming meat. "I've got a feeling this guy could be a help, let's move it."

Batum glared at him, unblinking – a look to melt space-grade duraplaz – then turned without a word and jogged off.

"Let's put the blaster away, shall we," I said to the man.

We ran along the corridor, more people emerging all the time. I wished I could help them, but how? In the distance, the sound of firing and explosions. Batum stopped before a large hopper door, hinged at the top, labeled *Hard Rubbish*. I'd forgotten about these things. Douglas installed a few dozen of them around Jubilee for people to throw away their big stuff, like old furniture. Batum pushed the door open and jumped in.

"Follow me," he said. "I will slow our speed near the bottom."

He disappeared down the chute. The man gestured, *after you*, so I jumped inside, and before I could think better of it, pushed off. I spiraled down into the darkness with terrifying and ever-growing speed – if you've ever ridden one of those giant theme-park slides, you'll know what I mean. Every few seconds there was a jarring thunk as I slid over a join in the metal. This thing was meant for old crap having its last ride, not smoothed out for human comfort. Behind me came grunts from the man and ahead the sound of metal on metal from Batum.

After what felt like hours, I heard a skidding sound and moments later collided into Batum, who had his arms stretched out to catch me. The man behind me slammed into my back and we all screeched and slowed, finally coming to a stop. The light in Batum's head flicked on, showing we'd ended up near the terminus of the giant chute where it flattened out, a graveyard of old junk and furniture beyond, all piled up and smashed together – end of the line.

"*That's* what I call a ride!" said the man.

A vibration thrummed through the slide, and a swooshing sound came from far above – something coming! People amaze me sometimes. Here's Jubilee in the middle of getting stormed by enemy forces and someone decides it's a good day to *chuck out their old stuff*?

"Quickly," said Batum, pulling us to our feet. It was only meters to the end of the chute, but something was coming at immense speed. I started to run on the slippery surface and in the same moment the man tripped and fell hard, landing face down. He tried to get up, groggy with blood running down his face, but fell again. Batum snatched him up like a rag doll, slung him over his shoulder and jumped.

It was close. There was a three-meter drop at the end of the slide. Batum launched himself sideways and landed on his feet, squatting low to absorb the energy of the jump. I dropped straight down. Seconds later came a roar as a huge object tore down the ramp and zoomed over my head. It crashed into the pile of junk, wreckage flying high into the air. By the looks of it, an old leather lounge suite.

A motorized door ground open and an automated forklift entered. It started gathering the broken trash and pushing it all into the maw of a large hole, steel teeth grinding everything to sameness. This latest addition must have triggered a clean-up cycle.

"This way," Batum said, running to the door, the man still slung over his shoulder. We were deep in the bowels of Jubilee here. An emergency light pulsed red, conveyor belts and giant machinery stood empty and quiet. Part of the vast complex of loading docks keeping

Jubilee supplied, which normally ran day and night. Looked like everyone had fled.

"Still happy you brought this guy?" asked Batum as I followed him weaving through the dock. The man roused himself, waving. "Arigght, put me down!" He slapped Batum's side and we stopped. He leaned back against one of the giant machines, shook his head and rubbed his face, smearing it with blood.

"Thanks," he said begrudgingly to Batum, "I'll be all right now. Name's Yonny by the way, though everyone but Mum calls me *Chook*." He held out a hand to shake, covered in blood.

"Pleased to meet you," I said, squeamish for a moment, then took the proffered hand. I guess by some reckoning we were blood brothers now. "I'm Col, and that's Batum."

"Pleasure's all mine. What's the plan, boss?" He looked at me calmly, ready for instructions, seemingly unfazed that the whole universe was collapsing around us.

"We're collecting my family in Sector Twenty, then getting the hell out."

"And all this, it's an invasion, *right*? Do you know who's behind it?"

"Movement for Morality."

Chook swore a string of oaths. "Mother*fuckers*, I got history with—"

"*Hurry up,* jump on," called Batum from a gravity sled he'd produced from somewhere. It was humming, ready to go, hovering a foot off the ground. "Things are heating up."

We clambered aboard and the sled took off. Normally these things only go about twenty klicks an hour, but Batum must have overridden something in its gizzards for in no time we were flying through the rabbit warren of corridors and caverns at dizzying speed. We passed the odd dazed-looking person in blue worker overalls, but most of the staff had run off somewhere. We zoomed up a ramp, over a giant unpacking machine, then through a long tunnel, and emerged into a residential corridor, Level Nineteen by the look of it. Two floors below my apartment.

The speed was terrifying down here so close to Jubilee's chaotic outer surface where the corridors weren't nice and straight like those above.

The sled dipped and almost flipped as we went around each minor turn, Batum calibrating with robotic precision.

From nowhere a squad of enemy troops appeared. We turned a corner and there they were, in arrow formation with blasters drawn, waiting for us. In that same instant Batum unleashed a volley of blaster fire and pulled us off the sled, sending it flying into the squad at hyperspeed.

Chaos reigned. Blasters fired in every direction as ceiling and wall panels flew, dust and debris filling the corridor. Chook and I rolled along the floor, then flattened ourselves while Batum ran straight into the conflagration, weapons emerging from every part of his body. There was a blizzard of firing for a few seconds and then total silence apart from the *tick tick* of cooling weapons.

"All clear," called Batum.

We picked ourselves up and stepped gingerly over the pile of dead soldiers. Chook's eyes lit up. "You bewdy!" he crowed, rummaging through bodies seemingly without a care in the world. He passed me a gun after wiping it clean of blood on one of the dead soldiers' pants. "Here you go, plenty more where that came from."

It was difficult to comprehend the carnage created here in just a few seconds. Body parts mixed with collapsed roof and walls, a huge opening in the floor exposing the loading dock below, some of the giant equipment down there on fire already – and what about the hull? Using high-power energy weapons so close to Jubilee's outer skin was insanely dangerous. I motioned for Batum and Chook to be quiet, and we all stopped for a moment to listen.

And there it was.

A loud hiss, unmistakable. Three or four levels down, so it had to be large if you could hear it from here. "The hull is breached," I said, "and the repair bots run off Douglas' operating system." In other words, this was not getting fixed. You would think a hull rupture would not be conducive for fire, but in fact it was usually the opposite.

"The breach will draw air flow, stimulating the fires," said Batum. "Everyone down here will be incinerated."

"*Cheerful* prick, isn't he?" muttered Chook to himself.

"Do we have time to fix it?" I asked.

"Not if you want to escape," said Batum. "I've reached a maintenance bot through the DOTR channel. It will try its best." He turned and started off down the corridor. "Come, we will have to run. The gravity sled has been destroyed."

I stared at the scene below, and for a moment considered doing the noble thing, putting out the flames and patching the hull – what would it take, forty minutes? An hour tops. How could I leave millions of lives in peril? And then, selfishly, I thought of my baby girls. Their faces swam before me, innocent and trusting.

We took off after Batum, hopeful the maintenance bot would fix the hull and douse the flames. Chook had strung half a dozen looted impulse rifles around his body like a *bandido* from some holo-drama. Batum kept a cracking pace, silver legs like pistons, and soon we were panting as well as leaving a trail of discarded guns behind us. We came to a corner and Batum stopped suddenly and ushered us to the wall, finger raised for silence. A tendril appeared from his body and peeked a millimeter around the corner, then withdrew and wrapped itself around my wrist.

"Soldiers there," said a tinny voice inside my head. *"I am speaking to you sub-vocally. Reply in the same way if you hear this."*

"Roger that," I said silently, mouthing the words.

"Me too," said Chook. A tendril must have reached him as well.

"They're guarding the elevator that leads to your apartment," said Batum.

We were close, therefore. Made sense, we'd come a long way. Around the next corner or two this corridor would run into a blank wall, the far end of Jubilee. "We can't storm these guys," Batum said. "They've deployed a dead-man trigger. The squad we destroyed must have got a message off, even though I disabled their koms in my first round of firing." He brought up a holo image. One of the soldiers clutched a small box, finger holding down a button. If released for any reason, that button would trigger a massive explosion. Their strategy was evolving.

"How do we get past them, Batum?"

"I'm working on it."

In other words, no idea. This was a clever tactic, a conundrum. We'd probably have to run back to the last elevator in Sector Nineteen, a kilometer away.

"I know what to do," said Chook. *"Hold this."*

He passed his last remaining rifle to me and, rubbing his face, smearing fresh blood, staggered out around the corner before we could stop him.

"Arrgggh, help me, please help!" he cried from around the corner. "Oh my *God*, help *please*!"

Batum brought up a mini-holo showing the scene: six soldiers, all jumpy with impulse rifles trained. One guy in the middle held the dead-man switch. "Stay away," he called, "or we'll fire."

"Arrgh, you don't understand!" cried Chook. "See what they did to me? Look!" He staggered toward them, bouncing and spinning off a wall, clutching his bloodied face.

"Take him out," commanded the soldier holding the box, probably squad leader. But there was no firing, not immediately. They all seemed a bit stunned.

"Please, you don't understand, *mercy*!" moaned Chook. He fell to the floor, dragging himself forward like a dying man. He reached up, groaning, imploring the soldier holding the box, tugging at his pants as the man tried to shake him off. Then with lightning speed, Chook snatched the box and rolled away. Cue Batum.

In a flash of silver, he was around the corner, multiple weapons firing at once. Six soldiers dead on the ground, the leader's face frozen in surprise. "That was foolish," the robot said, ripping the box out of Chook's hand, then doing something to disable it.

"Did the trick though, didn't it?" Chook crowed, rummaging through a soldier's jacket. "Well, looky here!" He brandished a small flask, flipped the top and sniffed, then emptied the entire contents into his mouth. "Jeez, fuck, that's *strong*!" he said admiringly.

Movement troops were carrying booze on them. During an offensive operation. I'd observed a surprising level of ill discipline in their forces when I was on Rethne, and here was evidence of more. A vulnerability. The lift pinged, called by Batum. We leaped in as Chook stuffed flasks of booze into his pants. It seemed to me that he had a more than passing familiarity with hard liquor.

"Batum, what's waiting for us up there?"

The robot's mechanical eyes were inscrutable. "I'm not sure. Some kind of field has been deployed. It's concerning."

"Right then," I said, pulling out my blaster. "Chook, this is my family up there. We have to get them out and down to the escape ship. *Without killing them* in the process."

"Got it," he said. He emptied another flask down his throat and tossed it away, then brought out two giant blasters, one for each hand, and flicked the safeties off in a well-practiced action.

"Bring the bastards on!"

Chapter Five

The lift pinged. We flattened ourselves to the walls as the door opened to an empty corridor. Batum stuck a tendril around the corner – all clear. Outside, everything was lit in the same monotonous gray, and strangely still. This area was normally full of life with people coming and going and children playing. Now it was deathly silent. We moved out, fingers poised on triggers, Batum in the lead. My apartment lay one hundred meters ahead on the left and as we approached, I could see already the front door was wide open. We crept forward silently, keeping to the wall.

A door opened next to me, and a small boy stepped out. He was holding a stuffed toy and looked up with large black eyes, tugging at my leg. "Where's my mother?" he cried, shockingly loud in the empty corridor.

I shushed him and took his arm, motioned for the others to wait, and led him back through the door. "Your mother will be home soon," I whispered, leading him past some bedrooms to a living space where there was a mess everywhere. A chair had been pulled over to the kitchen bench, food and utensils strewn.

"Does she normally go to work during the day?" I asked.

"Yes, she leaves before I wake up." His eyes widened. "There were soldiers here, *in the house*. But I could tell they were bad, so I went to my hidey place." He pointed to a cupboard behind the holo-screen. "Then they went away again. Actually, they didn't try very hard to find me."

Smart, this kid. Those same soldiers appeared to have taken everyone else in the area.

"How old are you?"

"Seven and a half."

"Shouldn't you be at school?"

"I don't *go* to normal school," he said with a slight air of superiority. "I'm in the advanced stream, so I do it here. With Tina."

School for the staff children was on Level Sixteen. For all I knew, the Movement had rounded them up already. "Is Tina your robo-nanny?"

"Yes, but she's *not working*," he whined.

Of course. In the corner lay a cheap-looking robot, collapsed and clearly offline, like everything else powered by Douglas. I'd need to keep this kid occupied for a while if he wasn't going to get in the way of saving Sana and the girls.

"Want something to eat?"

He nodded. "I'm hungry."

"OK, I'll fix you something." Fingers trembling, I grabbed some bread and fillings, rapidly put together a sandwich, then handed it to him. I cleaned a dirty glass from the sink – obviously his own, decorated with action figures – and filled it with milk, still cold despite the lack of power. How quickly events had unfolded!

A deep, subsonic rumble passed through the floor, rattling the plates and cutlery on the hard kitchen bench top. The gravity lurched heavy, then light, then back to normal again. No, not quite normal. There seemed to be a tilt now, as if the gravity engines were running a touch sideways or skew-whiff. Then I noticed the milk. The liquid was slightly higher on one side of the glass than the other.

Gravity engines damaged, perhaps. Or being played around with by the Movement. Either way, not good. We needed to get the hell off Jubilee, and fast.

I handed him the drink, which he snatched greedily. "What's your name, son?"

"Sheng," he mumbled between slurps.

"Sheng, I need you to do something for me. Very important."

The boy nodded.

"In a moment I have to go, but I need you to wait here in your home and be very quiet. Dangerous things are about to happen outside, so you have to stay far away, OK?"

"When will my mother come home?"

"She'll be back soon. Do you have any toys to play with?"

"Nothing's working."

"I can see some blocks over there. Maybe play with them for a while?"

The boy nodded again; he was a serious little thing. My heart broke to leave him, but what could I do? I waved goodbye, putting a finger to my lips for silence, and stepped back outside. To find the corridor empty, Batum and Chook gone.

Vanished.

I looked left and looked right; the corridor ran off in each direction, merging into the gloom, totally deserted. What to do?

Continue on, I suppose. What else?

But my mind reeled. How could they have just disappeared? Surely, they wouldn't just leave without waiting for me.

But if there'd been a struggle, I would have heard it.

One thing I'm usually pretty good at, is not charging forward blindly. Always best to stop and consider if possible. Something was not right. But what? It had to be a trap of some kind.

Stop, think, observe.

I looked around the area carefully, at the roof, the walls, the floor. What could I observe that might be amiss?

The air.

Just a meter in front of me, something was glimmering very faintly. A field of some kind running across the corridor. Batum had hinted at this. Or was it just my imagination?

OK, test it then.

I reached down and rubbed a hand across the sole of my dirty shoe and blew some dust into the air. It spread out in a cloud for a few moments, then sparkled as it hit the perimeter of an energy field running across the corridor just in front of me.

Gotcha.

Some kind of field or beam I'd never heard of. The Aurelians, or maybe their AI, must have come up with it. *Newtech.* Fine, so long as it was theirs. But what to do? And was that a faint whiff of smoke in the air now? Yes. More than a whiff. And what about the floor level, did it feel like the corridor in front of me was running ever so slightly uphill? It did, like a ship listing to one side – or rather, heaving on a swell – this corridor ran lengthways, so that meant Jubilee was leaning 'backward' along its length, along Concourse.

I felt a wave of despair, surely this was a hopeless situation. Taken by surprise, completely outgunned, how could we possibly make it to the escape craft? Maybe it would be better to just walk into my apartment and turn myself in. Get taken off Jubilee by the invaders. I would be tried in their kangaroo court and probably executed, but it might be the only way to save the girls.

I looked around dejectedly, searching for something, anything. I looked up to see a pair of robotic eyes staring down at me through an air grill in the ceiling. Which was moved quietly aside, another pair of eyes added to the first. Then another.

"Join us," came a message on my kom. *"We've just given you access to the channel."*

"What channel is that?" I sent back.

"DOTR network."

A cable dropped down with a foothold at its base. I stepped in and was hoisted into the ceiling to find the narrow roof cavity filled with robots of all kinds, mainly domestic models, all staring at me intently. Some of them were familiar, how?

From Sana's show, *Dance of the Robots*. Of course.

Then I got it. The cast had set up their own private channel to stay in touch after it was all over. *The DOTR network.* Sana had insisted they be units that ran off their own independent operating systems so they would still be functioning even now with Douglas offline.

"Sorry, we didn't know what that field did till Batum got caught in it. We're not very experienced at this sort of thing."

These guys were mainly low-level cleaning or service models, not built for war like Batum.

"What does it do?"

"Some kind of immobilizing thingy. It wrapped up Batum and the other man and dragged them into your apartment."

"Who else is in there?"

"Lots of people. Sorry, we don't know them all."

"Describe."

"Sana and two infant humans, Batum and the other man who was with you. The enemy humans."

"And Danee, is she there?"

"Sorry, we don't know her, is that the blonde lady who came to opening night?"

"My wife, yes, though technically Sana is still my legal wife of course, but we're not together anymore – anyway it's a long story. Do you know where she is?"

"Might be a few levels up, that's what we heard."

Where *was* Danee? It was more than an hour since I spoke to her from the control room. Surely, she would have found that person we were looking for and returned by now? It might actually be better if she remained in the wind, though it was a loose end. Something to be factored in.

"What else can you tell me about the enemy humans?"

"There is a very tall man, dressed in white. Seems to be in charge."

A tall man in white? Surely it couldn't be…*had* to be? Gilham. Ridiculous for him to be here *in person* in my home, supervising and gloating probably. But what a nutjob! Leaving it to the professionals would be far better – but maybe I could use that?

"There's also a technician operating the field and the rest are soldiers, six of them. Your apartment is very messy. It will need a lot of work to make it sparkling again!" A robot to my right wagged its nozzle in a friendly way.

"Is that you, vacuum-bot, messaging me?" During the show it had come on stage wearing a diamanté vest.

"Yes, we really want to help. We love Sana so much!"

Even here on Jubilee among a bunch of domestic robots, Sana was still the queen of networking; everyone always wanted to do things for her. A plan began forming. A crazy one, of course, and it would rely on Gilham's arrogance and narcissism for it to work, though you'd have to think that was a reasonably safe bet. The fact that he was here, in my apartment himself spoke to that.

"What happened to all the people in this area?"

"Taken away by soldiers when they set up the beam."

They missed one, the little boy Sheng.

"And have you seen how it works, is it running throughout the corridor?"

"It spreads outside your apartment on each side. Triggers when someone touches the end then sucks them inside."

"What about in the middle?"

"If you're on the inside, it doesn't seem to touch you."

A kind of tractor beam, therefore, triggered when the perimeter edge was broken and set as a trap for us. That was a working hypothesis anyway.

"Do you have weapons?"

"Sorry no, but we brought a bunch of other stuff."

"OK, let me have a look, I think I have an idea."

I crawled through the ceiling space surveying the assembled robots. A hundred or so, many of them butler-bots who'd worked as ushers or backstage workers. They'd do fine. There was a large box full of props and other items from the show. Almost charming that they thought to bring this stuff along. They were domestic droids, not made with the highest intelligence; the show would have been the high point of their mundane lives.

"OK, everyone," I messaged, "*listen up, here is the plan…*"

Minutes later an air grill above the front door to my apartment slid aside. I was lowered down, landing without incident, and not trapped by any beam. So far, so good. I gave a thumbs-up and the cable retracted, the grill silently slid shut. I patted myself down, took a breath and before I could have second thoughts, turned and strode through the open door.

Chapter Six

I walked through to the common area linking Sana's flat with ours, dread rising with every step. Thank God there'd been no time to stop and think, because I never would have been able to stroll so nonchalantly into that room to find them all lined up on the floor immobilized; the girls blessedly asleep – probably knocked out with some drug or potion – Gilham seated, looking bored, scrolling his kom while a dozen soldiers reclined against the walls in varying states of unreadiness. They all did a double take when I entered the room, snapping to their feet with impulse rifles aimed and quivering. Overkill as always. A single shot from just one of those things would unleash carnage in this confined space.

"Mr. Perolo!" said Gilham, standing abruptly, covering his surprise with a wry smile. "Finally joined us!" He put his hands together in greeting and I thought for a moment would trot out his signature line, *I welcome you with love.*

"Can't say it's a pleasure to find you in my lounge room."

It felt like I was hallucinating. Here were my loved ones lying paralyzed on the floor of my home surrounded by troops brandishing guns. How could this have happened?

Gilham smiled warmly, as if to an old friend. "I beg to differ, Col, things got off to such," he paused to think, "a *rocky* start last time, don't you think? Why don't we call this a *reset*?"

He seemed totally at ease, as if this were his own lounge room we were standing in. He motioned to a guard, who bounded over and patted me down, took my blaster and gave it over to Gilham, whose casually held out a hand. I chanced a look to the others; Sana and Chook wide-eyed but frozen, clearly awake and following events, Batum slumped against the wall. I prayed that he was merely suppressed, not permanently deactivated by whatever field had gotten to him.

"Yes, *the gang's all here!*" said Gilham, who must have seen my gaze. "Well almost, just waiting on, what's her name, not Lady Darmley, something else?"

I held his gaze, reluctant to provide any satisfaction by speaking her name aloud.

"Begins with a *D*, I believe."

"Danee."

"That's right, Danee *Hasum*. I expect she'll be along shortly." Gilham was showing off. He knew our real names, knew they were different to the assumed names we used on the mission to rescue Sana. "Always full of surprises, aren't you, Col? Here you are entering this room freely despite the beam and all our preparations. Well done. Futile of course, but nevertheless mysterious. *How was that possible*, Puram?" He shot a quizzical look toward the man seated in the corner, operating the equipment.

The man looked nervous. "The system is functioning correctly, sir."

Gilham seemed different from three years earlier when we'd met on his home planet, Rethne. Those jet-black eyes had always been opaque, but now they appeared disconnected. Un-present. There was no need for him to be here, no need to be on Jubilee at all. Waiting in the middle of this trap would mean dispensing with all but the core of his bodyguard. There'd be others on standby somewhere, but not instantly available. A foolish risk, taken for illogical reasons. Probably to demonstrate he was on top.

I reminded myself of my own advice from three years before: Gilham was a *wrong crystallization*. On some fundamental level he was weak. He would be disturbed by the fact that I'd blithely walked in without triggering his device but would want to play it cool. I had to engage, keep him talking rather than having me immobilized like the others.

"You've gone to a lot of trouble, Gilham, for a catch up."

"No trouble." He shrugged. "Is it, guys?" The soldiers stood stiffly, gripping their guns tightly as if they might be ripped out of their hands. "It's nice to see what you really look like, Col," he said gently, "and Sana looks *terrific*. Life on Jubilee must suit her."

"More than being enslaved on Rethne."

"*Now, now.*" He smiled, clearly enjoying the repartee. "All good things must come to an end."

While this chitchat was going on I scoped the room using peripheral vision as I was trained for. The technician operating the beam had a small black box sitting to his right. Looked like the controls to whatever mechanism was imprisoning Batum – who I tried reaching out to through the DOTR network:

"Batum, can you hear me? Are you online?"

"Col! I'm active, but my systems are inhibited."

"Are your sensors working – do you know where you are?"

"Last data was from the corridor outside your apartment. Then everything went blank."

"You're in my apartment. You were dragged inside and are being held by some sort of field. We'll try to release you shortly and when we do, go after the soldiers, but careful of the girls and don't touch Gilham."

"Gilham is here?"

"Yes, stay tuned."

I figured the controls to the immobilizer holding Chook, Sana, and the girls frozen wouldn't be with the tech guy in the corner. Gilham would want to have that himself, keep the power in his own hands. I just needed to keep him talking a little longer.

"There's a lot of people here on Jubilee, *millions*," I said reproachfully. "It's going to get ugly."

"It already *is* ugly, Col."

"So the answer is what, destroy everything? You're supposed to be a religious person. Isn't religion meant to be about *love*?"

"Col," he looked at me tenderly, "you need to think of all this as an act of *mercy*. The people here are suffering. They may not be consciously aware of it, but they are, and to leave a person in that state is perpetuating cruelty, it's not being compassionate. Sometimes true love means providing *release*. That's my mission." He smiled gently, holding my gaze without blinking.

The guy had gone nuts. Obviously. But he wanted to keep on talking and talking, which was fine by me.

"Let's say a child is about to do something dangerous like run in front of an oncoming train. A loving parent will use *strenuous measures* to keep her from harm. No sane person would allow that child to act as she pleased in some misguided notion of individual freedom. Wouldn't you agree?" He gazed tenderly at my two baby girls for a moment, lying unconscious on the floor, then did one of his dizzying about-turns, fixing me with narrowed eyes. "Time is running short. We need to know where Ms. Hasum is located, otherwise, however unfortunate, strenuous measures will be required."

"I don't know where she is."

Gilham sighed. He cocked his head to one of the guards and pointed at Chook. "This gentleman here is surplus to requirements I'm afraid."

The guard moved into position before Chook with his rifle raised, looking back over his shoulder at Gilham for a signal to fire.

"Truly, I don't know where Danee is. We needed to find someone, or at least we thought we did, so he could operate the manual controls." I was trying to keep the conversation flowing to delay as long as possible. "That was before we realized Jubilee was being invaded, so she went off to find them about an hour ago. I don't know which direction she—"

"We will start with this person, who is obviously a degenerate. Then we can move on to more valuable targets, like say…the girls." Chook lay frozen like a statue, but his eyes burned.

Would the robots be ready yet? According to the timeline they needed another three minutes, but that felt a long way off– unless I was prepared to sacrifice Chook.

"Do you really intend to let Jubilee burn down?" I asked, stalling some more. "You know there's been a rupture in the outer wall, and a fire's started below in Sector Fourteen, and now something seems to have gone wrong with the gravity. All those lives are in your hands. Do you know what you've taken on?"

"Not your concern, Mr. Perolo." He sighed again. "Jubilee is a stain on the moral fabric of the galaxy. I suppose here in your own little private universe you believed you were immune from the laws of karma. But you thought wrongly. *Now*, back to business." He raised a finger to the soldier, who clenched his weapon and aimed directly at Chook's head.

"Information, *please*. I'm asking nicely."

He crooked his finger a little as if to say, *not yet*.

"She said the person was four levels up from here," I lied. "We didn't know the exact address so she was going to see if she could find it."

"Closer to the truth, I'd say. Location?"

"Honestly, I don't know."

"*So* sad, oh well." Gilham dropped the finger and nodded to the soldier. "Fire when ready."

I chanced it.

"Now!" I sent through the DOTR network and the next instant there was a clunking sound out in the corridor as something large was caught in the beam. It banged and clanged through the corridor of my flat and into the living room: the vacuum-bot. I stared in faux surprise; the soldiers stiffened even further, which I thought impossible, training their guns, as though this were a troop of assassins.

"Room service!" cried the robot cheerfully.

There was more clunking, and another two robots were dragged in brandishing cleaning equipment. Butler-bots. I looked at Gilham and shrugged. "Housekeeping." He waved at the technician. "Deactivate the spider beam, no need for it now."

Spider beam, perfect name. As I hoped and prayed, Gilham had ordered it to be turned off, which meant it was time for phase two. The three robots started cleaning: manically spritzing and wiping, daintily vacuuming around the captives on the floor. One of the soldiers tried to block the path of a butler-bot. It sprayed and wiped down his rifle, chirping, "Very good sir, thank you, sir."

Gilham frowned. "Get rid of them!" Then he stopped at a new sound coming from outside in the corridor.

Music. Very loud, pulsing through the thin internal walls of our apartment. The climax, I knew, to the prologue of *Dance of the Robots*. There were muffled thumps as the robot cast went through their routine, leaping and somersaulting. Gilham pointed and half the guards rushed out to see what was going on. I tried to look nonplussed, avoided Sana's gaze.

"Report," said Gilham sharply.

"*Dancing*, sir, there's a bunch of robots out here in the corridor, *dancing* to music. Pretty good show, actually."

Then a huge *kaboom*, a shriek, then laughter.

"What now!"

"A glitter bomb, sir."

None of this was part of the plan, and he must have sensed things starting to go awry because for just a moment Gilham looked confused, glancing downward, bringing his hands halfway up to his head. Just a moment was all I needed.

"Now!" I messaged through the DOTR network. *"The black box."*

What happened next took place within…I'm not sure exactly, but let's say, a couple of seconds. I'll break it down for you:

The vacuu-bot darted across the room, striking at the black box with its cleaning nozzle, and striking *surely.*

Point zero five seconds.

Batum released, leaped to his feet, and exploded with precision blaster fire at the five remaining soldiers. Then disappeared in a flash of silver.

Let's say another point zero five seconds.

Simultaneously, I reached out and snatched the blaster from Gilham's soft hand, grabbed him by the collar and thrust it into his shocked face.

Altogether, two seconds.

"Give me the immobilizer!" I screamed at Gilham, and by the time these words were out, all five soldiers were convulsing on the floor.

The room had been transformed in an instant, filled with dust and smoke, the horrific stink of burnt flesh and the moans of dying soldiers. One of them slid slowly to the floor, leaving a trail of blood on the wall. Outside in the corridor, Batum made short work of the remaining soldiers.

Gilham looked at me, expressionless, slowly raised his hands, then tilted his head. Right pocket. I let go of his collar, and keeping the blaster trained with my left hand, rummaged through the loose pocket of his robe. There it was!

I clicked the device off, and now there was a second eruption: hysterical shrieking from small children in distress. Sana tried to comfort them while Chook, wild-eyed, leaped to his feet, looking for something to kill, settling on the technician cowering in the corner.

"Don't kill him, Chook!" I shouted, not daring to move a muscle, eyes fixed solely on Gilham.

Chook grabbed the operator, shook him like a rag doll, then slammed him backward into the wall. The two girls shrugged off Sana and ran to me, crying "Dadda," clutching my pants. I kept my blaster trained on Gilham, reached down, and patted them both on the head.

"Don't cry, darlings, I'm here now and everything's going to be all right."

I caught of flicker of amusement in Gilham's eyes.

"You think not?"

He shrugged. "Jubilee is encircled, there is no chance whatsoever of you escaping – but by all means try, you're just going to get your little girls killed."

I stared at him coldly. He seemed totally relaxed, annoyingly unfazed by events.

"Do as you will with this body," he said, "but that will not change the outcome."

I squinted at him. "Gilham, you'd be wise to keep your mouth shut for a while."

I was already planning our escape and, in that moment, realized it could possibly work. So long as we moved quickly.

"What now, boss?" called Chook. He bounded over to Sana and helped her off the floor just as Batum returned, body spattered with blood and glitter. "The enemy has been neutralized," he said, somewhat unnecessarily. Then the room filled with robots of all types pouring in from the corridor. They mobbed Sana, who stood shocked and mute in their midst while errant glitter floated about. The noise was deafening.

"OK, quiet!" I called. "Robots, thank you, please wait outside for now. Batum, can you give Chook access to the DOTR network, and also keep guard here?"

The robot joined me, a blaster emerging from his forearm, which he trained on Gilham. "With pleasure."

I scooped up a girl in each arm, clutching them in relief. For a moment, I held their tiny bodies, felt their quick hearts beating. Cries rapidly died away to sniffles – how quicksilver, the emotions of children.

"Girls, listen. We are going to run away now, get on a ship and leave. But it's very dangerous so you have to be good and do whatever Dadda says, OK?"

They looked at me gravely, eyes still watery. Then I pulled Sana in and we all hugged; she was shaking like a leaf. "Good work, calling the robots. It might be the one thing they didn't plan for." She said nothing, just clung to me. "Do you know where Danee is?" She shook her head mutely, in shock probably.

What to do now? At any moment more troops might fall upon us, though we did have the ace card of Gilham. If only I knew where Danee was. *"Robots,"* I sent through the DOTR network, *"shortly we will move out to Level Twenty. Please try and find Danee. We need her to join us there."*

"She was on her way to Level Fifteen," said Sana through the network.

"Could someone please scout there, see what's going on?"

"Already on it," came a reply.

Good, surely they'd find her somewhere? What next? Leaving for the escape ship right away might result in Danee getting left behind on Jubilee, but the longer we waited the less chance we'd have. I agonized. I had to decide.

What would Danee want?

That was an easy one: save the girls.

"Sana, did you pack a bag?"

"In the bedroom. The girls will need changing."

"OK, we'll do one each." To Chook and Batum, I said, "Two minutes."

Sana and I raced to the bedroom with a twin each. How was it I could still be disgusted by feces despite my home being full of freshly murdered bodies? Lala gurgled and laughed, squirming on her changing blanket, spreading poo all over her back and legs. The automated nappy system clearly wasn't coping, so I had to step in and clean her manually. By the time I was done, Sana was ready at the bedroom door, quietly cuddling her minute doppelgänger, Lila. She looked a bit more with it now; maybe this familiar routine had helped snap her out of shock.

"You OK?"

She nodded. "Yes. OK as you can be, I suppose."

I patted her shoulder. "Stay close, I have a plan."

A super half-baked plan that only a crazy person would have any faith in. But a plan, all the same.

"OK, listen up," I said loudly. "Batum, you lead the way. Chook, guard this one." I pointed to Gilham. "Watch him like a hawk. Sana and I will have the girls. We want a bunch of you robots ahead of us and a bunch behind us as well. We are going to move out along the corridor then down to the airlock. If anyone hears from Danee, tell her to join us en route."

"Think I'm a degenerate, eh?" said Chook, grinding his weapon into Gilham's head. He gave me a wink. "Don't worry, boss, I won't kill him." Then, to Gilham, "'Just as well I have a highly forgiving nature."

Gilham stood erect and silent, seemingly oblivious.

"Better take the emergency stairs," said Batum.

"There are emergency stairs down here?" I'd never needed to use them, didn't even know they were there. Three years running security and it still felt like I'd barely scratched the surface of Jubilee in all its byzantine complexity.

"Yes, follow me there."

I switched to the DOTR network and messaged him back. *"I assume you've dealt with Gilham's kom?"*

"Yes, his signal is suppressed, though I can't vouch for the first point five eight nanoseconds after I was released from the beam."

Best to assume Gilham had gotten some kind of message out – which meant their back room team would now be working up a plan. What would I do in their shoes? Somewhere during this trip down to the airlock an ambush of some kind would be hastily arranged. They'd have to be super careful though, given we were holding Gilham.

"What about this shithead?" said Chook, gesturing to the technician. "Can I at least kill him?"

I've always abhorred violence, and here was my home despoiled by it, filled with the stench of death. That operator was a loose end, but a relatively harmless one. "There's a better way," I said, striding over to the man and pointing the immobilizer. I clicked *capture*, then left the device on a chair in the middle of the room. The man would be stuck in plain view of the tool that could release him, but with no means of reaching it. Maybe one of his own troops would find it and let him free? If not, then he would suffer the same fate as everyone else on Jubilee.

Outside, the corridor was filled with carnage; bodies and blood-spattered walls, glitter swirling as we tramped through it. I could smell smoke even more strongly in the air now, especially out here. After we walked only a few meters I called a halt. Agonized for a moment outside the half-open door faced with yet another painful decision. "Give me one minute," I said, and marched into the apartment.

The boy was where I left him, in the lounge room playing with blocks, a stuffed toy clutched in the crook of his elbow: *Timsy*, the Tiger. That had been my brother's favorite when we were kids, though I never could stand the too-cute buggy eyes and high-pitched gurgling laugh. There was a smear of peanut butter on Sheng's chin; he looked up with wide, trusting eyes.

"Hello!" He got to his feet and ran to me. I squatted down to his level.

"Sheng, have you heard from your mother yet?"

He shook his head.

"How long ago was it that she left, can you tell?"

He thought a moment. "She always leaves when I'm sleeping. Tina looks after me when I wake up."

"When does she normally come home?"

"Lunchtime. We always eat together."

In another hour or so. She would have been on duty when the invasion started.

"Do you know where she works?"

"A hotel."

"Have you ever been there?"

Another headshake.

"What does she do there, do you know?"

"She makes drinks for people."

"What's the name of the hotel?" Maybe I could get a message through the DOTR network.

"It's called the Shangrila – *see*?" He pointed to a drink coaster on the kitchen bench. It was printed with the hotel logo and embedded with a holo of a sophisticated-looking bar filled with beautiful, well-dressed people, happily drinking and playing gambling machines.

The Shangrila was twelve kilometers away. A huge, swanky joint (swanky enough to have human barmaids) with at least a dozen bars. Which one of them did she work at, and who would we even ask for, *Sheng's mum*? And even if we found her, what then? How could we get her back here?

"Sheng, I'm going to ask you to make a choice. It's really not fair to do this to you, but I'm doing it anyway."

He stopped still, expressionless. Brown eyes coolly appraising.

"Something bad has happened. Some very…*bad* people have come here to Jubilee and they are trying to destroy everything."

"Like on *Galaxy Raiders*," he said flatly.

"Yes, exactly." No idea what that was, though it was easy enough to imagine. "It's highly possible your mother will not be able to come home for a…long time. You could be left here all by yourself. Do you understand? But me and some other people are leaving. You can come with us if you want."

He looked at me coldly. "But I want my mother."

"I know you do, Sheng, but—"

"I *want my mother*!"

I was asking the impossible of this kid. "Your mum might have been taken by these bad people already. If you come, there's a good chance we can escape. Then later on we can try to find her." Sheng looked away, then back. His eyes bored into mine. "I know this is very difficult, but I'm trying to help you."

His face screwed up. He stood and ran back to his blocks, threw himself on the floor in a rage. "Go away!" he cried.

"There's not much time. If—"

"Leave me *alone*!"

"Sheng, I—"

"*Bugger off!!*"

It must have been the worst thing he'd ever heard an adult say. I thought about grabbing him, taking him with us anyway, but how could I manage another squirming child? Besides, it wouldn't be right to bring him against his will.

So be it.

"Good luck, Sheng." I stepped back outside where Sana waited with questioning eyes. "Long story," I said, feeling hollow. Poor Sheng. But then again, what about all the other Shengs that were about to be stranded on Jubilee?

We moved off in a long column, Batum in front, followed by a bunch of the robots, then Chook with Gilham, and Sana and me with the girls. More robots took up the rear. We arrived at a nondescript panel that Batum kicked at, exposing a stairwell heading down into the gloom. The emergency stairs. That panel was probably supposed to blow out in the event of an emergency, which meant there was not enough smoke yet to trigger it. Something, at least.

The stairwell rang with robot footfalls, metal on metal. No other noise, not even from the girls, who'd become uncharacteristically quiet. Up ahead Batum must have called a halt. We all paused, then the line started forward again. This was a large and slow crowd to move. Maybe taking all these robots was more of a liability than an asset?

I heard a cry from behind, farther up the stairwell. Followed by muttered shushing sounds from the robots and then quick light steps running down, stopping just behind me. I turned to find Sheng. Wearing day clothes, not pajamas anymore, and carrying a fully stuffed backpack. In his right hand was a toy blaster and clutched in the crook of his other arm the lime-green tiger. He looked up at me with big serious eyes and I held a finger to my lips.

"Is that the 'long story'?" messaged Sana.

"Yes, I couldn't leave him without at least trying."

She reached out and took my hand, gave it a squeeze. Lala held the other. A moment later the line started forward again.

Chapter Seven

We reached the bottom of the stairwell, the very last landing. On the other side of this floor lay only the vacuum of space. Out in the gently undulating corridor, a long line of robots stretched ahead of us with Batum leading. Down on this lowest level there was no giant machinery or infrastructure. Much of Jubilee's passenger traffic poured through here and the corridor was studded with exit doors to the transit lounges and private hangars. Our destination was one of these, a kilometer ahead in Sector Nineteen.

"We've located Danee," came a message through the network, no sender ID. *"She's with a group of people. They're going to rendezvous with us at Sector Nineteen."*

Relief overwhelmed me. I thanked all the gods of all the religions and messaged back, *"Good work – how many are with her?"*

"Seven adults and a couple of robots."

Too many to take in our little flyer. A problem. Hopefully there would be other craft in the hangar, though none would be so well equipped as ours. Deal with that later when the time came, concentrate on getting there safely first.

"Can you get Danee online?"

"Negative. The network is partially down. We think the enemy are suppressing it somehow. This message was brought by a scout traveling ahead." The Movement was catching up. Maybe Gilham did get a message out to his troops in those nanoseconds before Batum took control of his kom? He walked ahead of me calmly at an even pace, Chook's blaster trained just inches from his head. *"This is Batum, by the way. We can only message between the people on this floor at the moment."*

"Thanks for the heads-up. I can see sender ID has also dropped out, so we should sign off every message. Col out."

"Agreed. We will meet up with Danee's group in around three minutes. Batum out."

Lala rode on my shoulders, already tired from walking, her sister was being piggybacked by Sana. Both were surprisingly quiet, tuning in to the gravity of the situation the way kids do. Whatever had gone wrong with Jubilee's gravity was creating the effect of an uphill slope in the long corridor before us. I kept swiveling my head, looking around and up; there could be a squad of troops around every corner, behind any door. Intersections with other corridors were what spooked me the most. This place, normally thronging with people, was eerily quiet. I caught a glimpse of a transit lounge through an open door with just a few people in there camped out. Someone dozing on the carpet peered up as we passed.

"Col, bring your group to me, we're about to meet up with the others. Batum out."

Ahead, Batum had stopped, letting the robots in between us pass him by. He turned and held up a robotic hand. *"I'm getting telltale signals from around here somewhere. Suppressed, but there's a signature. Be on guard, Batum out."*

A smaller corridor intersected ours a few meters ahead. Around half the robots had crossed it and were waiting on the other side, the others behind us. Batum stepped quietly to the wall and sent a tendril around the corner, then gave a thumbs-up and waved us forward.

I took Lala from my shoulders and held her hand as we started walking. Sana and the others followed. At the intersection I looked left, then right – *to see Danee*! Running toward us with a ragtag group, blaster in hand. She waved and grinned and my heart lit with joy.

"Mummy!" cried Lala, slipping her hand from mine, and bolting away. Lila writhed out of Sana's arms and did the same. The two little girls scampered to Danee with lightning speed, grabbing a leg each.

And then the world fell in on us.

Part of the ceiling collapsed and a phalanx of troops in hardened battle armor dropped to the floor.

In my mind, I've replayed the next crucial minutes a thousand times. Replayed and analyzed them, sought to find a different outcome. It's a pointless exercise of course, and the more you do it, the worse it feels. It's a trap, an infinite mirror maze of *what-ifs*.

We'd taken a few steps into the branch corridor when the enemy landed more or less in our middle. Gilham stepped to the side as if the whole thing had been choreographed in advance, then walked calmly into the body of troops, which formed a circle around him. Chook looked on frozen, blaster in hand.

Neatly done.

Batum unleashed fire at the troops but it washed harmlessly off their hardened armor – God knows why more of them weren't equipped this way. He took a concentrated stream of blaster fire in return. His body glowed bright red as the walls around us convulsed and collapsed. Smoke and dust filled the corridor and flames erupted. The roar of explosions and firing was deafening, and shock waves slammed our bodies. I caught a glimpse of the girls through the swirling smoke, huddled on the floor with Danee, silently screaming just meters away.

The rest of us threw ourselves on the ground, though not Sheng, bless him. He stood firing at the soldiers with his toy blaster, shots ringing all around. I dragged him down, pulling him into my body for protection.

"Everyone, swarm," came a message through the DOTR network – had to be from Batum – and robots poured in from around the corner, piling onto the soldiers. Butlers, cleaner-bots and domestic droids of every shape and size threw themselves in, engulfing the enemy in a wave of thrashing metal. These machines were all unarmed, but they still had metal hands and hoses and pincers. They'd be hard to shoot at close range.

But even more soldiers emerged from the roof and walls. Not sporting hardened armor, I noted, but deadly enough.

"Quick, to the hangar!" I messaged, grabbing Sana's hand, picking up Sheng and waving for Danee to follow. We started running in a crouch just as more soldiers dropped from the ceiling, falling in between our group and Danee's. They formed a circle and started shooting in all

directions as Batum launched a massive barrage. Those without armor fell like ninepins.

"*Danee, come! Danee!*" I screamed, everything a dream now, unable to hear my own voice. I waved for her to follow, but deadly fire was flying in all directions and one single shot would be all that it took. She picked up the girls, trying to shield them, and sprinted back down the branch corridor from which she'd come. Away from me. The wrong direction.

For a second I thought of trying to follow, but a boiling mass of fighting and laser fire now lay between us. Danee and the girls became hazy shapes, then disappeared into the gray fog.

Somehow, I found myself back at the intersection of the two corridors. Then I was around the corner. Something tugging my sleeve, trying to pull me away from danger. Sheng. Far away already, Sana and Chook were small figures in the gloom, running toward the hangar and I was shouting something, the same word, mindlessly over and over.

Danee!

The tugging grew more insistent, dragging my arm down. Batum backed himself around the corner into our corridor, laying covering fire behind. I had to keep moving, hope that somehow Danee and the girls could still find their way to meet us at the hangar.

I took Sheng's hand and we ran, but too slow at his child's pace, so I scooped him up and swung him onto my back. I tried to shout *Hang on*, but whether my voice had gone, or my ears or both, the words were inaudible. Up ahead a hundred meters or so, was a small sign with an arrow, normally illuminated:

14B.

★ ★ ★

"Just meet me there," chirped Danee. "It's going to be a blast!"

The call had been audio only, but I well knew the tone, knew the cheeky smile that would have been playing on her face as she tortured me by withholding tantalizing titbits of information. Danee was up to something. My mind spun with a thousand possibilities as I took the lift down to minus nineteen.

She'd called out of the blue, 'mid-afternoon' on a workday for both of us. Wanted me to come and 'check something out'. Plotting an *afternoon delight* perhaps? A delicious possibility since things had been rather dry in that department lately, the girls going through a bad sleeping patch. We could have put the robo-nanny on night duty of course, but Danee had strong opinions about the value of human parenting. Opinions that I felt might be set aside a little more often than they were.

So it was with disappointment that my destination turned out to be an ordinary-looking hangar. Danee stood beside the open airlock, pointing and smiling wryly. "*Ta-da!*" she crowed.

I stepped warily through to find myself inside a medium-sized flyer. I looked around to see what the fuss was all about and… *Whoa!* This was a craft like nothing else. The roof, walls, and floor, all were melded together, made out of one single piece of duraplaz. Not metal, but metallic certainly. The pilot chairs emerged out of the floor as if they had grown from it, and the flight controls were stripped down to a single screen and joystick. It was a complete reimagining of flyer design, doing away with ninety percent of the clutter and hard edges, all beautiful curves and stunning geometry.

"Wait till you see what she can do!" said Danee, slipping into the pilot's seat. "Douglas, let's go!"

"In a jiffy, madam!" came the answering voice, emanating from everywhere and nowhere.

I sat dutifully in the copilot's seat as the flyer door slid shut, heard the airlock cycling then cutting off seconds later. Other than that, there was no feeling of motion or flight as we moved off from Jubilee. Danee did something – though I didn't see her touch any controls – and the walls became totally clear as though we were flying in a translucent bubble. We sped across the 'underside' of Jubilee, so close it felt like we could touch it, flying 'upside down' (though of course in space there is no such thing), but sitting inside the ship's artificial gravity, it seemed as if we were flying 'above'.

"She's built from a single piece of programmable, intelligent material that forms itself out of nanoparticles. They've been quietly working on it for ages."

Douglas cut in. "Whaddaya reckon, Col? She's a killer!"

"*Amazing.*"

"And if you open this floor," gushed Danee, "there are more levels downstairs with everything: six berths, a galley – even a porta-ICU." A section of the floor next to us retracted, revealing steps down to a large space. The ship was roughly pyramid-shaped then, and we were seated at the apex.

"What are you going to do with the technology, Douglas?"

Danee replied, "So far we've only got this one ship. We're going to use her in my department." As a spy ship, therefore. "Watch this." She pulled back on the small joystick and we flipped away from Jubilee at enormous speed, executing a turn so sharp as to be almost a right angle. "The gravity drive has been rejigged to allow total freedom of movement, and as you can see, there's not the slightest sense of motion within the cabin." It was true, as Danee continued her startling maneuvers we felt nothing. If it weren't for the vision on the monitors, I would have thought we were in a simulation, sitting at home in our lounge room.

"All this has been theoretically possible for years, centuries!" bellowed Douglas. "Fuck knows why nobody thought to use the gravity drive like this."

I laughed. "Douglas, that's why we pay you the big bucks!"

"Now watch this," sang Danee, eyes shining like one of our twins with a new toy. Jubilee exploded into light as we circled around from the dark underside. The sunlit surface glinted and sparkled, made from a thousand different shapes and shades of metal, a wild collection of space junk bolted and welded together, festooned with cables and antennae, while farther out, a halo of ships waited their turn to dock. Our flyer approached one of these, a large passenger liner, and we zoomed within meters of the nose, where the pilot's bridge should be. I waited for the proximity alarms to sound, the angry booming message, but there was nothing.

"She emits practically no energy signature even at full power and the hull is fully stealthed, you can barely see it with the naked eye. Even just meters away!"

"Douglas, forget the sex, drugs and rock 'n' roll," I said. "You need to go into business selling *these* things."

"We got plans, mate! Don't you worry about that."

Danee took her 'up' and away from Jubilee till it became a bright child's toy suspended in space. She brought us to a standstill, then scrolled through the monitor's display options. The hull could be made fully or partially translucent, from 'surround' – flying in a bubble – to fully opaque. You could set certain panels to 'view', similar to a standard flyer, or run them in any combination you liked. The ship was also jump-capable and ran off Danee's kom, the only active control being the joystick.

"Here, I'll set you up," she said, and moments later a message appeared on my kom, advising I had full access. "You should take her home, get a feel for the controls."

We sat together in silence for a few minutes. Danee yawned and stretched and leaned back in her chair, dimming the cabin lights as we drank in the magnificent panorama; local sun the size of a beach ball, the intense wash of stars unblinking in the hard vacuum of space, and Jubilee gleaming in the middle distance.

"So," I said after a while, "she's fully shielded. What about the comms, can you turn *them* off as well?"

"Sure, super easy."

"Why don't you do that."

"No problem – there you go, *done*."

"Nothing coming in or out?"

"Not a thing."

"So right now, just for argument's sake, Douglas cannot see or hear anything that might be going on in this ship. We have total privacy?"

"Total." Danee looked at me with wide eyes, a smirk playing across her cheek.

"Here we are then."

"Indeed."

A lock of blonde hair had come loose from her ponytail while she was flying the ship. It drifted across her forehead in a most adorable way.

I raised my eyebrows suggestively, "Would be a shame, don't you think, to not do something useful with all this marvelous privacy?"

"What did you have in mind?"

"Not entirely sure. Got any ideas?"

Without breaking my gaze, Danee brought a hand to her throat and unzipped her one-piece uniform, slowly…very slowly. "I think I may have a suggestion."

I crossed the space between our two seats in an instant, and for the second time that afternoon had an experience of beautiful curves and stunning geometry.

★ ★ ★

The last hundred meters felt like running through molasses, a marathon in slow motion. Sana and Chook looked back for an instant, then disappeared inside the hangar. More troops arrived, small figures in the distance but closing fast. We were pincered now as they moved in from each direction. Blaster fire hit a wall nearby with a mighty boom, flames bursting out into the corridor. The hangar door was ten meters away, then five, then just as we came abreast Batum arrived, laying covering fire. His body, normally shiny silver, was pockmarked and glowing ruby red. It gave off a fearsome heat.

"You and the others board," came a message on my kom, *"I will hold them off till the ship is ready."*

The noise was deafening, the air filling with smoke and flames. The enemy would be upon us in moments, and I should have turned immediately and ran for the ship, but instead found myself rooted to the spot.

Where was she now?

Did Danee get away, slowed as she was by the girls? Seemed unlikely. I tried to imagine myself breaking out of this closing ring of soldiers, searching for her, bringing her back to escape with us.

Madness. Suicide.

But how could I just leave?

"Where the fuck are you, Col?" Another message, probably Chook. Without me they wouldn't be able to fly that ship. The corridor sizzled with blaster fire through the dust and smoke, but I stood frozen, the chaos around me fading to nothing.

Beautiful Danee, love of my life.

Lala and Lila, my very heart.

I could leave them behind and escape now…or die. *Surely death would be better.*

I felt something dripping on my foot, and I looked down. Blood. Pooling on the floor, lots of it. Gushing from somewhere, but I felt no pain, no sense of being hit (often the way in a crisis). I swung Sheng off me, still oddly pain free, then saw why. It was him. He'd been shot in the small of the back, blood running down his body, bubbling from his mouth. Still alive then! But not for long.

My body acted without me. I picked Sheng up and ran through the gate, past the departure lounge and into the airlock, turning the ship on from my kom as I ran. I had to remember how it worked; I'd only used it just the once and that was months ago.

"I'm seconds off," I messaged. *"The boy's hit, someone has to get him into the ICU downstairs immediately."*

"Where are the stairs?"

Shit. How did you open that hatch to the lower level?

I charged through the airlock, explosions and shooting just outside in the departure gate as Batum retreated his way to the ship. Chook snatched Sheng – a limp doll covered in red – out of my arms as I dived into the pilot's seat, frantically scrolling my kom. There it was!

The lights came on as the ship woke up, and next to me the floor slid open, revealing the stairs. Chook raced down them with Sheng lifeless, slung over his shoulder. He messaged, *"Where's the ICU, what do I do?"*

"No idea, never been down there."

"Fuck! Shit! OK I'll figure it out!"

I started the launch sequence; it would only take seconds, but a new problem!

"Batum," I messaged, *"how do we close the airlock door?"*

Dear reader, I know we're right in the middle of the action here, but please indulge me for just a moment. Perhaps you've never been in space? – no shame in that! I read somewhere that over eighty percent of us have never even been off-planet.

Or maybe you travel a lot, and, in that case, you might never have noticed the marvel of engineering you step through every time you enter a spaceship. Fixed in design by galactic treaty for a thousand years, your ship's airlock fits perfectly – to a hundredth of a millimeter – with the mating craft's door. A mechanical sensor (mechanical because electronic things invariably fuck up), tests the air on both sides and if it reads full atmosphere, the outer doors of both craft open together. Then the trick's repeated for the inner doors. So simple, so commonplace – yet the smallest failure could lead to a catastrophic blowout, killing everyone.

Which is why, when you undock, the system is expressly designed to release your craft *only* when both outer doors are securely closed.

And on Jubilee, that function was performed solely by Douglas.

"Strap in," came the return message, *"this is going to get tricky."*

The last time Batum described something as 'tricky' it was nearly fatal. I looked at Sana and pointed at the copilot's seat, strapping myself in as I ran through the controls. The ship's engines were running up to speed, ready to leave in moments – *if* we could disengage from Jubilee. Outside in the airlock, a continuous stream of fire poured into Batum as he backed his way toward the ship. A black shape ejected from his body, flew through the air and exploded with a chest-rattling subsonic *whumph*. A shaped charge, directed into the departure gate. The shock wave snapped my head sideways. There would be no living troops in that room now.

Batum backed into the ship's airlock, moving creakily, I could see. The cumulative effects of the battle had clearly worn him down. But how astonishingly lethal he was! A one-man army, now limping to the end of battle. He stood on the join where our ship's floor met Jubilee's, and something emerged from his back, long and thin. Some newfangled, never-seen-before weapon?

A laser tool, emitting an intensely blue/white light. Fusion-powered then. Its beam struck precisely at the place where the two airlock doors met, cutting apart the seal holding us to Jubilee. The beam worked its way down one side of the door with agonizing slowness, metal bubbling where it touched, fumes from it mixing with everything else (smoke, dust and cooked flesh). I turned up the air filtering and tried not to gag.

The beam burned its way across the floor at a perfectly even robotic pace. Outside in the gate, there was noise, shouts, and thumps. It would be a charred hellscape in there, bodies strewn against walls, everything smoldering hot. But a minute later, as new soldiers arrived, the first shot bounced off the airlock wall, making a crater of molten metal, pinprick hole at its center. The fools were firing into an *airlock*; what did they think was going to happen?

"Got any more of those charges?"

"That was the last. Get ready, we'll have to pull away early."

The burner worked its way up the other side of the door, reached the top and started across the roof. We were joined to Jubilee by only the roof of the airlock now. Then suddenly it was full of Movement troops firing like morons in every direction. Shots rang off the airlock walls, opening new holes, bouncing off Batum and exploding into the cabin.

"Pull away, pull away!" messaged Batum, firing volleys into the advancing soldiers and directing more shots into the airlock walls themselves. There was a hurricane shriek of escaping air, and my kom lit up with warning flags.

Now.

I summoned the movement control and pulled sideways on the tiny joystick. The ship pulled away with a screech of metal as Batum fired continuously at the airlock roof. Part of it remained stuck to our door as we came unstuck from Jubilee, and with our port open to space there was a howling rush of air.

The ship depressurized instantly.

Chapter Eight

Sana and I were sucked violently toward the open door, saved from being blown out into space only by our harnesses. Those belowdecks were safe, but for us upstairs we had mere seconds left. Seconds before the vacuum of space started bubbling our bodily liquids into vapor. I remembered the training, touched Sana's arm, and mouthed, "Breathe out." I exhaled a long slow breath so there'd be no air in my lungs to suddenly expand and rupture them.

Eight to twelve seconds.

It doesn't sound like much time, and it isn't. But time seemed caught in aspic, slowing, stopping, crystalline in my memory.

Eight to twelve seconds before deoxygenated blood started being delivered to my brain, causing hypoxia, followed by death.

Sound drained away with no air to carry it. Bodies spilled out of Jubilee's open port in a continuous stream. They shot into space, and I have an image of one, a soldier, his face frozen in shock as he flew by. But that's impossible surely, a trick of memory.

Batum braced himself and kept cutting. The top section went fast now, the remaining piece of roof joined in only a few places. He fired again and slung the last piece of Jubilee away – we were finally free – and with lightning speed, he slammed the control panel next to the airlock door, which closed instantly.

Sana and I lay gasping as air flooded the cabin, everything spinning. I'd be suffering from space shock now for sure, but there was no time for that. I hauled myself up in the seat, activated stealth mode and pulled back on the stick. We zoomed away from Jubilee twisting and turning, carving a convoluted course. Sana lay back in her seat, eyes closed but breathing. Looked like she'd be OK.

Half a click away loomed a huge black hulk, one of the Movement battleships, part of the ring of force surrounding Jubilee. I could see no civilian craft. Where were they? Many would have been detained at MGNA#12 back in the 'normal' universe, but what of all the other craft that were leaving or arriving at the time of the invasion? There were a few ships at dock, but all the others must have been cleared away.

The giant ship grew closer in our screen, bristling with weapons: rail guns mounted on turrets, ship-busting lasers and giant missile tubes with yawning open mouths. The galaxy had been at peace for so long – millennia – where had these things come from? How could they have been built without anyone knowing, and anyway, who even had the skills these days to make them? I prayed that Douglas's technology held up. Danee claimed this ship emitted almost no energy signature, but I didn't like the *almost* part. I kept her moving at a consistent, medium pace and held a course running straight between two warships.

I barely breathed as we sailed ever closer to the ominous hulks. We could be turned into a cloud of random electrons by any of those weapons. But there was no sign of activity.

The Movement boffins would be scrambling. One minute you have a small ship at dock, one you'd taken little notice of. Your targets board it, pull away from Jubilee while still attached, killing God knows how many of your soldiers, and then next minute, it suddenly vanishes from your screens.

Not supposed to happen.

There'd be consternation, red faces. Orders barked and harried officers hunched over their stations. A response would be required.

And there it was. A fusillade of nano missiles streamed out from the nearest ship, looking like sparkling dust on our monitors. They spread out in a deadly bright swarm, randomly switching course, and filling the space around us like a cloud. I assumed the other warships would be following suit.

OK then, that was it for medium pace. I pulled viciously back on the stick, and we shot 'up' and away from Jubilee at dazzling speed. No feeling of movement within that amazing ship, and in seconds Jubilee and its attendant warships were mere points of light. I set an elliptical course that would take us to the far side of our nearby star. ETA one hundred and sixty-eight minutes. We could regroup there, with the sun in between us and Jubilee and try to figure out what the hell our next move should be.

"You OK, Sana?"

She nodded, dazedly. I slipped out of my harness to find Batum collapsed on the floor behind me. He looked up through eyes that, had they been human, I would have said were weary.

"How about you, Batum?"

"Had better days. Going to need some time in the shop, I'd say."

Every part of his body was burned, twisted, and gouged by battle. "I'll be back. I want to check on the boy."

Down below, Chook lay sprawled on a flight chair, holding a blood-soaked cloth to his arm. He too had seen better days. He pointed behind him without opening his eyes. "In there."

Sheng's tiny body lay inside the glass cylinder of the ICU, which looked absurdly oversized – obviously designed for adults – tubes and wires hanging from everywhere. A readout displayed a dozen different squiggly lines with a warning message glowing red: *Critical / Stable.*

"He'll be OK, I think, once that machine gets enough nanos into him. Bloody hell, what the *fuck* happened to you!?" Chook stared at me in shock – not that *he* looked wonderful, face and every part of his body cut and bruised and covered in blood.

"Space shock, the upper cabin depressurized when we pulled away from Jubilee. It's a long story." I sat down wearily next to him. There was a galley nearby with a small table.

"We got away? I didn't feel a thing. Where are we?"

"On course to the other side of the sun. Let's go upstairs. We can go through it all. No, fuck it, let's hang out down here."

"Sana, Batum, why don't you come down," I messaged. Time for a powwow.

"Mate, do not look in the mirror, you are a *sight*!"

"Never seen it before?"

"Nope and thank God."

We were shown pictures in training. With the air pressure at zero, the boiling point of water drops below room temperature. My body and face would be swollen and bruised thanks to the fluid in my soft tissues turning into vapor under the skin, and my eyes would be bright red for days. Ebullism, or space shock. Soon I'd be racked with pain…actually it was coming on already. What I really needed was some time in that ICU chamber, but no chance till Sheng was out of the red zone.

"Chook, it's going to get a little rough. Can you have a look around for some painkillers?"

Sana joined us, with Batum limping behind. They both collapsed on the galley chairs. For some reason her face didn't look so bad, but her eyes were glowing bright red. We sat in silence for a few minutes, then Sana reached out and took my hand.

"Here you go, boss, and you too, madam," said Chook. "Drugs and a cuppa."

Sana and I downed our pills. The tea was hot and comforting but did nothing to raise my spirits.

Had I been numbed by everything, it would have actually been better, but I was afforded no such luxury because a black mountain of despair fell upon me. Wife and children, lost on Jubilee. What sort of man was I to leave them? How did I allow it to happen? Best-case scenario, they'd been taken by the Movement, and worst…didn't bear thinking about. I sat in silence, tortured by the darkest thoughts and feelings a person can have, as my body filled with pain, every inch of it protesting. Physical and mental torment. The body would heal, but there was no cure for this mental anguish.

I must have dozed a little without realizing, because next thing my kom pinged to say we'd arrived at our destination, but what was the point of anything?

"We just got a visual on Jubilee," said Batum. "Might be worth checking out."

We hauled ourselves upstairs to the bridge. Our ship was parked sixty million klicks from the nearby sun and our screens were showing a shot of Jubilee, which was not possible given the sun was in the way – but relayed by one of Douglas's drones, still working for some reason and positioned at ninety degrees to us.

Jubilee maintained a permanent stationary position rather than orbiting its nearby star. This was so the many craft jumping in from the 'normal' universe could always pop out in the right spot. But now it was on the move. A fleet of hundreds of small, spherical ships were dotted around its perimeter, spaced evenly like a net, and deploying some form of tractor field. They appeared to be tugging Jubilee, hauling it sunward. It explained the strange gravity effects I'd observed. Meanwhile, the other fleet, the transporters I'd first seen in the control room, were docking and undocking at rapid intervals. Removing people from Jubilee, at a guess.

But to get everyone off would take weeks, months even, and Jubilee was headed sunward at a rapid and ever-increasing speed. What was the plan, to fry everyone left behind?

A new message lit up the screen: *incoming*.

What?

I flicked the sensors up, revealing a medium-sized destroyer heading our way. There was no mistaking that algorithmic flight path. But how did they pick us up?

Not *that* hard if you thought about it. When cloaked, our ship's energy signature was tiny – around the same wattage as a flashlight held a football field away – but it still had one. If you didn't know where to look it would barely register, but if you had a starting point, such as our dock at Jubilee, you could replay the data, scan for the tiny footprint, then track it. The destroyer was coming in fast, thirty minutes till contact.

Could we evade it?

Not now they had us locked.

Outrun them?

Not a destroyer, not even in this; we would have to jump. But back in the 'normal' universe, the space around MGNA#12 would be crawling with Movement craft, all on the lookout for us. By the time we calibrated a second jump to get away we'd be caught in a tractor beam. Or worse.

Jump somewhere else then.

Spin the dials? Ride the strange gravity waves of this sun to some other unexplored parallel universe where they'd never find us?

And then what?

Douglas had told me the number of parallel universes were infinite. Some were populated with outlandish forms of alien life; in others, the laws of physics were different to our own. We could be eaten by monsters or dissolved into protoplasmic goo by alternative quantum mechanics. Or more likely just drift around until we ran out of food and fuel.

"Batum, are you thinking what I'm thinking?"

"Double jump, very dangerous."

"Any better ideas?"

Chook coughed. "What the fuck are you talking about?"

"What you see there on our screens is an incoming destroyer. I don't think they're dropping over for a friendly chat."

"To get away from it we'll need to jump twice," said Batum. "First back to the normal universe, then an instant random second jump. There will be no time for calibration."

"Meaning what? I'm not scared, who gives a fuck? I just want to know what the odds are."

"It's very hard on the drive," I said. "Sometimes fatal. We could drop out of hyperspace anywhere at random."

"Oh…I get it," said Chook slowly, "we could end up parsecs from anywhere with a fritzed drive."

Which would mean crawling at sub-light for years, or even decades, to find the nearest settled system.

"In that event we could send an SOS by FTL," said Batum.

Yes, we would do that, of course, send a faster-than-light message. Hope it was picked up by someone friendly.

"Count me in," said Chook.

"It's our best option," agreed Batum.

I buzzed Sana on the kom and talked it through. She understood readily enough and agreed. Sheng was uncontactable for the moment, and underage in any case, so I decided for him. A double jump it would be.

"Holy shit, look at this!" Chook was staring at the screen aghast.

I zoomed in to show Jubilee close up, blackly silhouetted against the bright sun, light bleeding around its edges. Had to be close now, those tug ships speeding her up to a significant fraction of light speed to get there so fast. No transports were docking any more, just the tugs, which all released and swarmed away from Jubilee as we watched. All except one that seemed to be guiding from the fore end.

"What is Jubilee's distance from the sun now, Batum?"

"About five million klicks."

Inside the corona. They really were doing this.

Jubilee shimmered, its image warping for a few seconds, then it exploded in a blaze of brilliant white light, leaving behind a brown smudge like an afterimage for a few moments before it too burnt off into nothingness. I looked numbly at the monitor, unable to process what I'd just seen. Then the image itself flickered and turned black.

"Looks like we just lost the relay drone," said Batum.

The world was coming apart. My head couldn't fit this information in anymore.

"Col, that destroyer has launched a swarm of hyper speed missiles, two minutes till impact."

"Are we calibrated?"

"Standing by."

"Then for God's sake, *jump.*"

Chapter Nine

The screen flicked twice. For a millisecond, the view was of the same sun as we'd been looking at before, but smaller in size and therefore further away; the star MGNA#12 back in the 'normal' universe. Then instantly a second flick, this one accompanied by a lurch and loud metallic *thunk* that reverberated through the hull as we made the random jump to God knows where.

The cabin lights strobed, and a siren shrieked somewhere. The screens were lit with warning flags, behind them a view of our new position: a panorama of intensely bright stars splashed across the black velvet of space. From the look of that star field, we'd jumped somewhere closer inward to the crowded galactic core.

I flicked through the warnings: *jump drive inactive* (shit!), *Power damping ##log#465* – I turned this one off and the lights stopped flashing. A bunch of other warnings stayed lit that I didn't understand: *PXB#xCNharness inactive REFER TO USER MANUAL* and so on. Would have to work on these later.

I did a quick look around. No craft in our neighborhood, or for that matter anything else. As far as I could tell from the diminished scanning array, we seemed to be somewhere in deep space. No 4D positioning with the drive offline and no comms either, or rather, no faster-than-light capability, which was as good as having no comms. We were effectively cut off from the rest of the galaxy.

"Here we are!" cried Chook. "Slap bang in the middle of fuck knows where."

"Slap bang," I agreed. *"You all right downstairs?"*

"Yeah, I'm OK," said Sana through her kom, *"though that ICU tank thing is making a loud beeping sound."*

"Can you check that out, Chook?"

"On it," he said, rising.

"You OK, Batum?" I looked around… "Batum?"

He was collapsed on the floor next to the airlock door, slumped against the wall like a drunk. I hauled myself out of the cockpit chair – body feeling the space shock keenly now – and went to him. I swiveled his head around, picked up an arm and it dropped like a piece of lifeless metal. I could find no active service light anywhere, not even a red one.

"ICU's fine," called Chook on my kom. *"Says it went into backup power mode, so I pushed a few buttons and the buzzing stopped. The boy seems OK. Well, no worse than before."*

"Thanks. I think we might have a problem with Batum."

At that moment my kom buzzed with a text message, from Batum. *"Col, the EMP pulse from that second jump knocked me into power-down. I'm taking the opportunity to reset, given the extensive damage sustained on Jubilee. Will be in regen mode for approximately thirty-six hours."*

"Can I help?"

"If you were a fully trained robot tech with a working repair shop, yes."

"Maybe there's a maintenance unit on board?"

"There's not. Leave me to it."

None of this sounded good. *"You going to be OK, Batum?"*

"Better after some regen. More I talk to you, the longer it will take."

"OK, sweet dreams."

I tried to shift the robot into a more dignified position, but he was way too heavy. Maybe Chook and I could try later. His body lay charred and burned almost beyond recognition. It was hard to believe it had taken so much damage and kept going. I realized that I had no idea where Batum came from, where, or even when he was built. For me he'd always just been part of the fabric of Jubilee. But that tech he deployed in battle was the most advanced and resilient I'd ever seen, scarcely believable, in fact. We owed our lives to him.

Those of us who survived, anyway.

The image of Jubilee exploding into light flashed before me and I sat back in the pilot's chair, holding my head, body filled with shock and disbelief. I must have sat for a while until I felt a soft touch on my arm.

"Are you OK, Col?" asked Sana gently.

I just shook my head.

"Col, I—"

"*It's OK!*" I cut her off, suddenly angry. Why talk about the obvious, what was the use? "I just *can't*...not now anyway." We sat in silence. Eventually, she must have thought to distract me, asking, "Col, do you know where we *are*?"

"That's a very good question, unfortunately. And the answer is, *no*."

Take a bag of marbles and tip them out on the floor. The marbles will roll everywhere of course, coming to a stop in a random configuration around the room.

Now imagine you're shrunk to the size of an ant and placed somewhere on that floor. Your job? To figure out where in the room you are, based *solely* on the position of the marbles. Next you need to imagine that instead of lying on the flat plane of the floor, those marbles are suspended in mid-air around the room. And rather than a bagful there are billions, each of them separated by light years of space.

Our ship was that ant.

And we had absolutely no way of knowing where we were.

Sana and I checked out the ship. Not much to see upstairs, but down below, after fiddling around with our koms, we found a door leading to a large bunkroom and toilet. Another set of stairs spiraled down to a master bedroom with en suite. There was also a gym, a washroom and a pantry on that floor, the largest level of our pyramid-shaped craft.

I waved Sana goodbye. "You take the master bedroom. I'm going to crash." Then I called Chook. *"I'm done in for now, can you take watch?"*

"Roger that, mate."

Fatigue rolled over my body, an unstoppable wave. I crawled upstairs and found a bunk bed. The welcome blackness of deep sleep was upon me before my head even hit the pillow.

Coffee.

And food smells.

My nostrils twitched. Something was being toasted – maybe *actual* toast. I crawled out of bed to find Chook and Sana eating in the galley. Without saying a word, a mug of strong black coffee and fresh toast was slid over, which I pounced on.

"Young fella looks to be doing a bit better," said Chook. I glanced over to the ICU, where there seemed to be fewer red symbols. Sana and Chook wore ship's crew uniforms, which they must have dug up from somewhere, and Chook's arm sported a neat bandage. Sana's face was puffy, eyes still bright red from exposure to the vacuum. Like mine would be if I dared look in a mirror.

"Thanks," I grunted. "You seem pretty useful in the galley, Chook. Wouldn't have picked it."

"Well, I'd wanna be. Spent two years crewing a Dellorite spacer. First up they always put you in the kitchen. Decent work too, compared to some of the jobs I've done over the years."

"How long was I out for?"

"'Bout twelve hours," said Sana. "I got up a little while ago, had a shower then followed the coffee smell."

"You been up the whole time?" I asked Chook.

"Yeah, found these little beauties!" With a mischievous smile, his eyes tiny black dots, he held up a bottle of white pills.

I took the pills from his hand. Stimulants, obviously. "I think that's enough of those for a while, you're going to need some sleep now."

"Bugger it, you can sleep when you're dead!" He bustled about the galley, wiping and tidying with manic energy. "So, wadda we do now, boss? What's the plan?"

Difficult question. I sighed and looked down at myself; every square inch filthy, the stench coming off me indescribable.

"The plan," I said, "is to come up with a plan. We need to get the ship repaired and, hugely important, alert the League to what M4M has done. But first I need a shower."

I stood naked in front of the mirror, the man before me a hollowed-out wreck. My clothes were stiff with dried blood; it had even run down my legs and pooled in my shoes. Sheng's blood. It would have made my feet squelchy, but I hadn't noticed. I took everything off and threw it in the chute for cycling. My arms and body were bruised, scratched, cut, and burned. My face puffed up with huge black rings around eyes that gleamed devilishly red. The girls would have run screaming.

If they were alive.

I showered slowly as if in a dream. Found some ship's clothes from a hopper. It was possible my body felt a little better than yesterday, but what to do about the aching numbness in the chest?

Upstairs in the cockpit I worked my way through screens, gradually turning off warning flags and restoring systems where I could, then looking for a simple way to sweep the local area more thoroughly. A short time ago – was it just a month? – Danee and I had been here together in this very cabin.

Sana joined me and watched quietly as I worked. "Chook's crashed." She giggled. "Literally fell asleep mid-sentence, and by the way, where the hell did he *come* from?"

"Latched on to us somehow, don't even know how. I guess he's part of our little menagerie now."

"I like him, I think."

The space around our ship appeared to be completely empty. The sensors associated with the jump drive were down, so the best I could do was probe optically. At least I could measure light color and therefore phase shift, and from that determine distance to the nearer suns. But so far, every star I trained the optical scanner on was more than fifty light years away. And even if I did find one close enough to limp to on the gravity drive, there was no guarantee it would even *have* a planet, let alone one that supported life. It was like trying to find the proverbial needle in a haystack; if you thought about it, *way* worse. It would probably take only a few days to remove every piece of hay from a stack and find the needle, but this work could take years.

Mind wandering. Time to stop.

"This is hopeless, Sana. I have to come up with something better." Time seemed to blur after that.

One by one the lights blinked green in Sheng's ICU and color slowly returned to his face. Sana and I cooked, ate, worked out in the gym, and chatted; it was comforting to have her around, so long as she didn't try and 'talk' to me. I guess I was putting off going back to the cockpit. Hoping Batum would have a solution when he finally woke up.

But the breakthrough, when it did occur, came from someone else.

Chapter Ten

"Three grid references," said Sheng between mouthfuls of cereal. "That's all you need."

The rest of us stopped our conversation mid-sentence and stared, Chook with teapot in hand. We were sitting at the galley table, trying to brainstorm a solution to the *where the hell are we?* problem.

"True," I said, "we could pick any three stars and know where we are in relation to *them*, but it still doesn't solve for our position in the galaxy. We need to know *which* stars we're looking at."

"So, pick a few with unique light signatures," said Sheng, "then compare with those around us till there's a match. I can design some code to automate the process if you want?"

Nobody breathed. Could this really be the solution?

"Anyway, that's what they did," said Sheng between slurps, "on *Galaxy Raiders IV*."

Chook sat dazedly, still holding the teapot.

"You design *code*?" asked Sana. Sheng nodded.

Batum shrugged as if to say, 'Why not?'

"Fuck *me*," said Chook.

Batum woke up quicker than Sheng. It took around forty-eight hours, and whatever regen tech he deployed must have helped because he moved now with more, though not total, ease. Hopes that he could help with our navigation problem, however, were quickly dashed.

"Dude, I'm a security droid, I kill things."

"Indeed, you do, Batum – but can't you log in to the ship and come up with something?"

"Like what?"

"I dunno, *something*."

"It's meant to interface with Douglas, barely talks to me."

Sheng took another day.

I was downstairs with Chook and Sana working out in the gym when we heard a cry. The boy was standing at the top of the stairs holding his lime-green Timsy.

"I'm hungry!" he called.

After that came a week pedaling in the same spot; eating, sleeping, more working out – us all sitting for hours in front of the controls looking out into space, nonplussed. Very dispiriting. But at least my mood was better with Sheng around. He never talked about his mother and that stoicism impressed me. If *he*, a child, could bear a loss like that, then so must I bear mine.

Who knew kids that age could code? Sheng might be in some advanced school, but it was still amazing. Six years away from getting his first kom, he produced a child's computer from his backpack the size of a teacup, decorated with action figures. At that age I could barely read, but Sheng got to it like an expert, child's face set in a frown.

In the end we decided to go not with stars, but *supernovae*, given the enormous, distinctive light signature they emit. There was nothing wrong with our ship's chart (only its 4D interactive program), so we picked one thousand highly recognizable supernovae from the database and started scouring the sky. Our little optical scanner could capture ten thousand data points per second and by running Sheng's code, the ship's computer could just about keep up with that in real time.

After four days we got our first hit: SNWXZ8@SJSJ434-##4K4 – and a more beautiful eruption of exploding star I have never seen. Then came SNPO8★84THBVN-##Z – less poetically named you might argue but appreciated all the same. Finally, after six days of nonstop scanning, we got our third match and therefore a lock on exactly where the hell we were.

Which was the middle of nowhere.

Truly.

Though of course it has to be said, this was lucky too. A random jump is based on the notion that one might pop out of hyperspace literally anywhere, even into the middle of a star. What makes attempting it less than *total* madness is that the chance of doing so is infinitesimally remote. There's *so* little matter in the galaxy compared to nothingness, it's almost impossible to hit any.

But now those enormous distances between stars worked against us.

"Nearest inhabited system is Hyehm," I told the table after doing the calculations. "Sixteen parsecs away."

"That means, if we're traveling at light speed, it'll take sixteen years to get there," said Sheng knowingly to Sana.

She scowled. "I know what that means."

"Lemme give you some advice, kid," muttered Chook, "no one loves a smart-ass."

"This ship takes two months to get up to its max of half light speed," said Batum, "then there's braking at the other end, which takes longer."

Chook frowned. "So that's, what…"

"Thirty-four years, six months, and twenty-seven days," I said. "Give or take a day."

We all sat in silence absorbing this. Even Sheng had nothing to say for once.

"Would the ship even last that long?" asked Sana.

"*Maybe*," I said. "The life systems are circular, and the fusion reactor would be fine, but I wouldn't want to bet on everything else holding together that long. It's a new ship with unproven design and—"

"The *real* question," interrupted Chook, "is whether we could sit around in this fucking tin can for thirty-four years without killing each other."

They all looked at me expectantly.

"There has to be something better," I said, finally.

Chapter Eleven

Half a light year.

That was the limit I set, expanding the holographic map before me to fit the scale. The nearest stars bled out from the edges of the display as we zoomed in. I was now looking at a tiny point of purple light – our ship – sitting inside a sphere of pure blackness. No star systems; the nearest was eight light years away, and the nearest *inhabited*, sixteen. So therefore, no points of light within the dark ball of space around us.

Try something else, then.

I asked the database for any known spaceship trajectories through our vector. Didn't seem likely, but what the hell? Very few craft cruised deep interstellar space at sub-light. Why bother when the jump drive could take you anywhere you wanted in the blink of an eye? And anyway, even if a ship was 'nearby' in galactic terms, say half a parsec away, it would still take six months for a message crawling at light speed to reach it, then another six months to reply, by which time our position relative to theirs would have changed anyway. Therefore, hardly any point checking, though you never know, maybe by some miracle something was scheduled to pass nearby?

There wasn't. Not as far as the chart was concerned anyway, and it was running data that was live only weeks ago.

What else?

I interrogated the database for unmanned drones, abandoned space-habs, even structures from alien civs – current or long gone – anything that might have access to FTL comms.

Nothing.

I widened the sphere around us to one parsec and repeated the process. Still nothing. Widened even more to two parsecs, three parsecs and then five. Nothing, nothing, and more nothing. The space around us was entirely empty, not so much as a ball of rock larger than a basketball lay within five parsecs. We were screwed. Stuck in the middle of nowhere, thirty-four years from civilization.

Hours had passed since I started this work. I leaned back in the pilot's chair and stretched, my back stiff from tension. There was a strange feeling in my gut. Like the old days when I was working a case, something inside was tickling my consciousness. A crawling feeling. I tried to bring it to the surface, but it kept moving farther away the harder I pushed. There was something I hadn't thought of. Something important.

Put it aside, try again later.

"Col, that you in there?" called Sana.

"Yup, just working out."

"Come, join me."

I'd been in the gym, trying to burn up some frustration. I stepped into her room with reluctance. In the days prior, once the immediate danger had passed, I'd seen her slide into a funk. A depression even. Sana was certainly capable of doing that.

She was still in bed even though we were well into the 'day' cycle now. Of course, night and day are arbitrary concepts in deep space, but we'd all agreed to move to a standard eight hours dark, sixteen hours awake timetable to get some regularity into our lives. Sana was doing the equivalent of sleeping in. Moping more likely. The swelling in her face had subsided and her eyes were no longer red. She sat up and patted the bed for me to sit next to her. I tried not to notice how ravishing she looked, even in this dark mood.

"How are you doing, Col?"

"You know, frustrated. I've got this feeling I'm missing something that might get us out of here, but I can't put my finger on it." She looked at me skeptically. "And you know, we're just idling here in space while the galaxy is going to hell! We have to warn the League, get the message out so they can stop the Movement before it's too late."

"I didn't mean that."

"Oh."

She sighed. "Col, I can't stop crying. I keep thinking of everyone on Jubilee. Everyone I knew, gone."

"Were you, um…seeing anyone? At the time that…"

She sighed again. "Yes, there was someone. It was starting to get serious. I guess. You know me, things are always complicated."

I tried to suppress a spasm of jealousy, then probed with a subtle inquiry disguised as a question. "I guess we can only pray he's OK."

"*She* actually. And then there's Danee, and the girls…though I wasn't their biological mother of course, but it did feel like that kinda. I can't even imagine how it must be for *you* – but you seem *fine*?"

I tried to think of something to say, but nothing came.

"How are you *coping*, Col? What's going on?"

I shrugged. "I'm just taking it day by day. Right now, I'm focused on getting us all to civilization."

"Yes, but—"

"I *know*, I should be feeling stuff. I was at first. But then I saw Sheng, the way *he's* holding up. I dunno, I guess it's all down there, deep down." A ball of grief – a supernova rather – somewhere inside, somewhere I didn't dare look.

"This is what you *do*, Col, you bury things—"

"Sana," I pleaded, "if I didn't have this ship and these people to take care of, I don't know what…" There was a lump in my throat, making it hard to speak. "…I would have *nothing*…"

"It's not healthy, Col, you need to allow yourself to feel *something*."

"Chick," I said, using the nickname from when we were first together, "if I allowed myself to truly feel what's inside here," I pointed to my heart, "even for a *single* moment…" Then I ran out of words again.

We sat together for a while, uncomfortably close. She put an arm around my shoulder and pulled me in for a hug, stroked my head. It would have been the easiest thing in the world to take things further right then, but that would have just added to the Mt. Everest-sized pile of guilt. Instead, I lay quietly in her arms, my heart for some reason pounding like a drum.

Back in the cockpit.

I turned off the holographic star map and it vanished like a soap bubble. It was useless anyway, so try something else. But what? I flicked through the screens, bringing them up at the speed of thought from my kom, then closing them down again. Life systems, fusion plant, jump drive and comms – red inactive lights on these last two, impossible to reset. All the things that were still working were working fine.

Keep going.

Deep into the system screens. Any deeper and I'd be at code level, way beyond my pay grade. Active memory (all good), scanners (some down, some OK), cloaking (still active). One curious thing: the size and sophistication of the computer was enormous, way larger than normal for a small ship, and a large section of its memory was locked behind a partition. I tried for hours to get behind it before giving up. I poked and prodded and delved, looking into every crevice of the ship and its vast array of systems. Eventually, I found something interesting.

Registration.

A red '!' symbol floated over this particular screen (tingle starting in the belly). I interrogated the symbol, and it took me to a new screen overlayed with a notification:

Attention! Vessel unregistered!

Of course it was unregistered. It was only finished a few months before and never flown in the 'normal' galaxy. No reason for Douglas to bother.

Register now? asked the screen.

Dear reader, it might be worthwhile to refresh ourselves as to the political conditions existing at that time. Those days, all interstellar space technically 'belonged' to the League (or to use its full name: The Federated League of Pan Galactic Systems). Political control by an individual planet ended at the heliopause of its sun (or for a cluster system, at the border of the outermost suns), and beyond that? All supposedly run by the League.

What did this actually mean though, in practice?

Almost nothing.

If you wanted to fly out into interstellar space, who was going to stop you? Steal an asteroid, mine it, blow it up, or do anything the hell else you wanted? Nobody was watching.

No organization, no matter how well organized (and the League surely wasn't), could possibly keep tabs on the endless trillions of square kilometers of space existing between the stars. And yet according to intergalactic law, it was all administered by the League – at least as far as humans were concerned, an omission we might find glaring these days, but for some reason didn't pause to think about then.

Yet most people registered their ships anyway. It didn't cost much and there were benefits. Local authorities required, or at the very least *liked* you to do it, such being the sensibilities of the bureaucratic mind. And if anything went wrong on a voyage there'd be a record somewhere. Also, registering gave you access to additional information.

Such as location data for League properties.

I selected, ***Register now?***

A new screen opened: ***Do you agree to the Terms and Conditions?***

I clicked *yes*. God only knew what was in that ten-million-word contract – perhaps not *even* God, and certainly no one from the League. It had been added to for millennia and it was rumored not a single person had read it all.

New message: ***Please complete Vessel Information.***

Before I could do anything, the screen auto-completed with the ship's details. Must have been readied by Douglas for when this day came. Our vessel's name, I noted, was *The Grand Poobah*.

Please submit payment information.

Here is where the problems would start. I dutifully opened autopay on my kom and submitted my account.

There was a pause, then a short nasty beep: ***Something went wrong! Your registration cannot be finalized!***

Well, of course it couldn't. We were lost in space without comms. How the hell could any payment be processed? I sighed, suddenly angry.

All this was just another stupid waste of time, though it had to be said, time was something we had plenty of.

The screen beeped again: ***Would you like to chat with an operator?***

I laughed aloud. Of course, I would! I'd love to chat with a fucking operator. Then I could tell them we were stuck here in the middle of nowhere. In a fit of pique, I clicked *yes* anyway.

There was another pause, then: ***Oops! Your comms link appears to be down!***

Brilliant observation, I thought glumly.

Would you like to make payment offline?

I stared at the holograph in surprise and the tingle in my gut started up again. Who knew this was even possible? I said *yes*.

Registration status will be Provisional, until payment verified. Register anyway?

I registered anyway.

Thank you and congratulations! Your vessel is now registered (Provisional) for FLPGS flight. A galaxy of opportunity awaits you!

Video started playing on the screen. A smooth-cheeked man with a mellifluous voice extolled the many benefits of League membership. I needed just the one. I killed the video and brought up the holo star map, striped now with a message in yellow: ***Add FLPGS data to ship chart?***

Yes again.

The chart blinked, reopening with the familiar galaxy logo watermarked at the bottom. It showed the same sphere of blackness I'd been looking at for days with the same tiny purple dot of our ship at its center.

But now there was something else, a new point of light glowing right next to ours. Light blue, the trademark color of the League, with a label floating above it: FLPGSITAAH#455684-B1B.

"A hundred days. Seriously?" asked Chook, smacking his forehead. "You're shitting me!"

"One hundred and five to be exact."

"But I...how come we..." Sana tried to speak, but words failed her.

Sheng piped up. "What's an ida?"

"*ITAAH*, actually," I said. "Interstellar Training and Administration Hub. Basically, it's a ball of rock in the middle of nowhere that's been taken over by the League and turned into one of their facilities."

"And only one-eighth of a light year away?" asked Batum. "What are the odds of popping out so close to that?"

"Infinitesimal. Haven't worked it out, but something like winning first prize in a lottery a hundred times in a row."

"Seems too good to be true," said Batum skeptically.

Chook glared at the robot. "Fuck that, I say we go there anyway!"

"Oh, we're going there, no doubt about it," I said, "especially if the alternative is thirty-four years to Hyehm."

"But let's not ping them till we're close," said Batum, "and I'd leave cloaking up till we arrive."

I raised an eyebrow. "*Really*, Batum? What do we have to fear, we're talking about the *League*, remember?"

"Never hurts to be cautious."

We were all silent for a moment as that sunk in.

"Oh, and by the way," I said, "our ship is officially named *The Grand Poobah*."

Sheng giggled and Chook grinned. Sana just rolled her eyes. "Douglas!" was all she said.

I set a course of fifty-two days at maximum acceleration followed by fifty-two days decelerating at the other end. This would have subjected the cabin to forty Gs, squashing us like bugs – if it weren't for the drive, of course, which would keep our gravity at a livable constant the whole time.

After setting all that up there was little for me to do. Just kick back and let *The Grand Poobah* do its work crossing the one point two trillion kilometers to our salvation.

But kicking back is not really my thing. I paced and fretted and chafed about what the Movement might be up to, and how vital it was to inform the League; anything not to think about Danee or the girls. Or Jubilee and its destruction, and how that and everything else had to all be my fault somehow, even if it wasn't immediately apparent.

The days passed slowly, especially at first. We usually ended up around the galley table: Sana reading, Sheng on his computer or watching videos, Chook and Batum playing endless rounds of *Danger*. After a day or two, Chook found a bag of rivets from somewhere and these became the currency of their fiercely contested games.

One typical 'afternoon', Chook triumphantly slapped a triple suite of Raiders down on the table before Batum. "Cop *that*, tin-dick!"

With robotic inscrutability, Batum paused for effect, then turned over two matching pairs of Destroyers.

"*Motherfucker!*" groused Chook.

Another rivet joined Batum's huge pile.

Sheng chimed in. "Chook, you *do* know that Batum can read the backs of the cards, don't you?"

"*Whaaat...*" he screeched, "...the *fuck* are you talking about?"

"Chook," said Sana mildly from behind her book, "I'm just wondering if it's possible for you to utter a sentence that doesn't contain a profanity? I'm not *complaining*, mind, just wondering."

"Batum's eyes scan to micron level," said Sheng. "The backs of those cards all look different to him, just like the fronts do for us."

"Is that true?!"

"Read it, fool." Batum flipped one over and pointed to the tiny writing."Says here, guaranteed unscannable."

Guaranteed galaxy-wide. No one could gain an advantage in a game anywhere (particularly on Jubilee where such things were taken very seriously) by using an optical scanner, augmented vision, or anything else to rig the system.

Sheng giggled. "But that's only guaranteed to five microns and Batum's a security-grade droid. They never let them play in casinos because they *always* win."

"*Unbelievable!*" shrieked Chook, producing a gun from his waistband and training it on Batum. "Cheating piece of shit, tin-can bastard. I'm going to turn you into *molten slag*!"

A blaster emerged ominously from Batum's shoulder and trained itself on Chook. "Go on, give it a *try*, meatbag!"

"*Enough!*" said Sana sternly. "We have a child on board. Can you at least *pretend* to show some level of maturity?"

Sheng giggled again; he loved it when they argued.

"But he's a fucking *cheat*," whined Chook, though he did put his blaster away, thus avoiding certain death. Batum's gun retracted.

"Remember, you're playing for *rivets*," said Sana, rolling her eyes. "It doesn't *matter*."

"We were going to swap them for credits when we landed – but not *now*, you robot fuckstick. You can jamb those rivets up your stainless-steel arse."

"Batum, why don't you de-tune your optical scanner to below five microns just for these games?" I suggested. "Then you can keep playing."

"Hmm," grumbled the droid, "who says I wasn't doing that already?"

Chook snorted. "Says that huge pile of rivets!"

Batum stared at him coldly. "It's no fault of mine that you're a fucking hopeless player."

And so it went.

The days passed ever so slowly at first, then for some reason more quickly, and then even more quickly, until suddenly – we were there. I sat in the cockpit looking at the holo-display with Batum and Chook.

"Twenty-four hours," I said.

"Any sign they've noticed us?" asked Batum.

"None. Behind our cloaking, the ship's energy signature is tiny and also, we're coming in at a significant fraction of light speed. Not much chance to pick us up."

The ball of rock ITAAH #455684-B1B floated before us centered in the screen; mottled gray/brown, pitted with craters. A silver sheath covered the top of a slash that ran through its middle, forming a roof over what was doubtless a small city within. As we watched, a ship winked into existence nearby, dropping in from hyperspace. We all went *oooh*.

Moments later a large hatch slid open at one end of the silver roof and the ship maneuvered itself inside.

I was dying with impatience to get the word out about the Movement. I was certain our news would hit the League like a bomb. They'd be galvanized into action by the savagery of the attack, the loss of life, and the implications of a whole battle fleet being created in secret. I prayed there was enough time to stop Gilham in his tracks.

Chook pointed at the distant ship as it docked. "That's us in just a day! Can't wait for a real drink!"

We'd been having *fivesies*, as Chook called them. Cocktails at 17:00 hours made from some kind of moonshine he'd conjured. If you mixed them up with enough flavoring and ice, they were almost palatable, though it's possible my taste buds had lost their ability to tell after three months in space.

Sana joined us on the bridge, holding hands with Sheng. "Wow, that's it, eh?" she said.

The League base swam before us.

Just a hundred klicks away as we poked and prodded the rock ball with everything the ship still possessed. Nothing scanned funny, and still no sign they'd noticed us.

"Guess it's time," I said over my kom. *"Everyone ready?"*

Assent from below. Batum nodded from the seat next to me. We were all strapped in because…well, just *because*. ITAAH #455684 was about to get a big surprise and we thought it prudent to be cautious.

I turned off cloaking and sent an electronic hail. For a long moment nothing happened, then suddenly the screen filled with fast moving numbers and flashes of script. A large, red warning message appeared, and alarms sounded.

"The League computer is having a conniption," I said to Batum. "Anything you can do?"

"Like what?"

"I dunno, it's going too fast for me to keep up. Fuck!"

"What's going on?" called Sana from her kom.

"They've locked onto us, very aggressive!"

Inexplicable, actually. I figured there'd be a somewhat startled reaction when we arrived out of nowhere, flying in from normal space, but this was extreme.

"Call them, speak to a human," said Batum.

I killed the alarm. Decided to leave the ship parked where it was and keep cloaking off. Taking evasive action might seem aggressive and we could always go to that as a next step if required. *The Grand Poobah* wasn't equipped with powerful shields, so no point engaging them either.

"League base, this is *The Grand Poobah*, requesting assistance. Come in, please."

I repeated the message a few times with no response, then a new warning light appeared, and the alarm sounded again.

"Tractor beam?" asked Batum.

"Yup, and a missile lock for good measure. *Super* aggressive. What the fuck's got into them?"

The view in the monitor shifted perspective as the beam started towing us to the base. There was no sense of movement. Any point fighting this? The base was where we wanted to go and we'd done nothing wrong, so let them take us there. Hopefully things would be fine once we had a chance to explain.

"UNKNOWN VESSEL," boomed a voice throughout the cabin. "STATE YOUR BUSINESS OR BE DEALT WITH UNDER RULE 81,456-B, TITLE 9, CLAUSE 7 – NO UNREGISTERED VESSEL MAY APROACH LEAGUE PROPERTY WITHOUT PERMISSION IN ADVANCE FROM BASE COMMAND, WHICH SHALL NOT BE REASONABLY WITHHELD UNLESS PREVIOUS ACTS OF AGGESSION HAVE BEEN ATTRIBUTED TO THE VESSEL, OR AT THE ABSOLUTE DISCRETION OF BASE COMMAND."

Finally, a human. "League base, this is *The Grand Poobah*. Our jump drive has failed, and we request assistance under the League charter."

As I was speaking there was a soft ping and a message in green text popped up on the screen: ***Congratulations The Grand Poobah! Your***

registration status is now Active! The League watermark in the bottom corner of the chart had changed color from yellow to white. The offline payment I'd made for registration must have gone through automatically as we came within comms range of the base.

Now the promotional video started auto-playing in the cockpit, once again extolling the wondrous benefits available to us. The League was treating us like an enemy while simultaneously licking us to death. I killed the video.

"League base, our registration status has just gone Active, please take note."

There was a pause, then the red warning messages flashed off and the screens went still. They must have deactivated their tractor beam. A minute or so later a video link opened up, displaying a nervous-looking man in League uniform. His hair and clothes askew, eyes red as if suddenly woken.

"Ah yes, *The Grand Poobah*," he said to himself. "There it is. But no record for your arrival. You can't land on base without pre-approval you know, League policy. Very sorry."

"Sir, this is an emergency," I implored. "Our jump drive is down, and we've traveled here sub-light. We request protection under the League charter!"

The man looked perplexed. "Most *irregular.*"

The screen went dark.

"What the fuck's happening?" called Chook on his kom.

"I think we've blown their tiny bureaucratic minds. Might be a while before you get to that bar." Chook responded with a stream of highly graphic invectives; detailing objects that needed to be inserted into various League personnel orifices.

We sat there in space for what seemed like hours, salvation in sight while official gears clanked. I suspected that we'd arrived in the middle of their 'night' shift. I should have checked. Night staff are always the B team. Eventually the video lit up again, this time displaying an older woman, clearly of a higher rank than the man who spoke to us earlier.

"*The Grand Poobah*, my name is Amar Dehen, and I am co-vice commander of this base. Please state your business."

"Pleased to meet you, Vice Commander. My name is Col Perolo. As I mentioned to your colleague, we are requesting assistance under the League charter. Our jump drive is down, and we need to undertake repairs to be on our way."

"What is your port of origin?"

"Jubilee. There's been an attack there and we had to flee, which caused our drive to fail." We'd already discussed what our story should be and agreed to simply tell the truth.

The woman raised an eyebrow. "*The* Jubilee?"

"The very one."

From the holo-screen she looked me over imperiously for a few moments. "How many aboard?"

"Three adults, a child, and one autonomous droid."

"Just a moment," she said, and the screen went dark again.

Another hour passed.

Finally, our first interlocutor reappeared. He looked more with it this time, must have found himself a coffee. "The co-vice commander has given permission for you to land. There will be a docking fee of one hundred and seventy-three credits, ninety-four centimes, payable in advance."

"No problem," I said, opening autopay on my kom. "Please thank Ms. Dehen for me."

His mouth twisted. "There will be a *considerable* amount of paperwork needing completion on arrival."

"That will be fine."

The screen went dark again. If even a League official thought the amount of red tape ahead of us was 'considerable', the mind boggled. But who cared, we were here! And if they hadn't exactly smothered us with warmth and sympathy, we'd cope. The display chimed with a most welcome message.

"Everybody – just got the docking code!" I sent.

Ragged cheers from belowdecks.

"And remember folks, *no* weapons." This was meant for Chook mostly. "They will surely scan us and they're very jumpy for some reason. So, leave everything you have behind."

I leaned back in the chair, job over for now. The ship would cruise in slowly by itself, running off the code. I pushed a button that released a half dozen nano-drones. These would wait quietly in the space outside the base, keeping watch and warning us if anything arrived that wasn't kosher. Another of Batum's suggestions.

Then I saw something curious on my kom, which still had the payment screen open. It showed the docking fee just paid of 173 credits, as well as the prior transaction for ship registration. But that wasn't what caught my eye; it was the balance. Lit in glowing green digits, showing a sum that at first glance seemed like a glitch till I zoomed in further to confirm: ₵2,010,507.71.

On Jubilee I'd managed to squirrel away a decent sum. Douglas didn't pay particularly well you had to say, had a reputation for stinginess, in fact. Then again, the apartment and most of our expenses were covered, so after three years I'd been able to save the respectable total of just over ten thousand credits. The balance showing on the screen though, was of a different quantum altogether.

Someone had put two million credits into my account.

That was only the first shock.

Batum turned to me head cocked, his eyes avoiding mine. If he weren't a robot, I might have said he looked sheepish. "Col, I've just unearthed some data that will be of critical importance to you."

"Really, what?"

"I'm very sorry, Col. When my system crashed after our jump from Jubilee, some data that uploaded at the same time was cached in a sub-system that subsequently became unavailable to me."

Batum seemed nervous, was almost stuttering. "What are you talking about? Why are—"

"And I only became aware of this just *now*, I promise, Col. As I was doing pre-landing checks, I discovered a number of broken data segments and was able to un-cache them."

I felt a tightening in my chest. "What is it, Batum? *Tell me!*"

"Col, as I said, I'm *very* sorry. One of these segments contains a message from Danee."

Chapter Twelve

Everything went black. I stood up woozily, holding the chair for support.

"What kind of message, Batum?"

"Voice only. Very odd. Came through the DOTR channel but Faster Than Light – which of course that network doesn't support, and it's only partial."

"Is it playable?"

"Yes, of course."

"Then *play it*!"

"Col, I know how important this is to you, but perhaps given the subject matter it would be better to deal with this later? As you can see, we're about to dock."

The base had swelled to fill our monitors. A giant gantry door was sliding open to reveal a medium-sized hangar, several other ships already at dock within. A silvery tube was snaking itself outward from the far wall to connect with our airlock door.

"Batum – *please*, for the love of God, play it!"

"OK, OK, of course."

The cabin filled with a hubbub of voices. A grinding sound of heavy machinery, and something else – muffled or at a remove but clearly audible: weapon fire and explosions.

"So, this is on?" Danee's voice followed by a mumbled assent. *"Col, darling, you got away, good. Listen, me and the girls are OK, so don't worry, I know how you are. Remember I love you. I told them we—"* The voice cut back in, *"—we can't—"*

The message ended abruptly.

"That's *it*?" I screeched.

"Sorry, Col."

A soft thud reverberated through the ship as we touched down on the hangar pads, followed by a warning chime from the airlock. A message popped up on the screen asking for permission to begin cycling the doors. I hit pause.

"Batum, did you reply, at the time, I mean?"

"Tried to, multiple attempts. But the message was FTL with no return code."

The breath in my lungs felt like it was being squeezed out by a giant bellows. Chook's head popped up from belowdecks. "We here?"

"Just a *sec*, Chook. When did that come in, Batum? I mean, at *what point*?"

"Just before we jumped, Col."

"But before or *after* Jubilee exploded?" If it were afterward, then obviously Danee and the girls were safe. Probably.

"Before, Col, but the time sequence is hard to gauge because the message came in FTL, whereas the vision from Jubilee was only traveling at light speed. Twenty minutes delay, given their distance from us. I'll need to properly analyze the data."

This was all highly significant, but my mind couldn't hold it. The screen chimed multiple times and there was a *thump, thump* on the outer airlock door. Sana, Chook, and Sheng emerged from below, Sheng carrying his backpack – he was the only one of us with any possessions.

"What did that message *mean*, Batum? Can you analyze the background noise?"

"Undetermined, sorry, Col. I know how important this is to you."

Sana looked at me quizzically. "What's going on?"

I went to reply, but at that moment the screen lit up displaying the League official who first interviewed us. He looked annoyed. "The Grand Poobah, *we are attempting to deboard, but your airlock is not cycling.*"

Everything was coming at me in waves, in slow motion, like a dream… *"I know how you are."* What did that *mean*?

The figure on the screen spoke again: "The Grand Poobah, *this is our last warning, please respond to our deboarding request immediately or we shall be forced to treat your vessel as hostile!*"

I was desperate to replay Danee's message. A thousand times. Over and again till I figured it all out. But everyone in the cabin was looking at me, nonplussed.

I hit the airlock button and heard it start to cycle. Flicked on the video camera.

"Base command, apologies," I said to the frowning figure. "Minor problem with our system here. As explained, the ship has a few functional issues. Cycling now."

The man sighed. *"Roger that."* His image disappeared.

"Can someone please explain to me what the fuck is going on?" asked Chook.

"Sorry, everyone," I said. "Batum received a message from Danee, but I'll talk you through it later."

Sana put a hand to her mouth. "*Danee?!*"

The airlock beeped loudly twice and the light above it turned green, signifying the outer door had opened to the boarding tube. I remembered that the airlock had indeed taken fire when we escaped Jubilee – a massive amount. My lie to base command had actually been the truth. Batum had made repairs since, and of course that light would have only turned green if it was sealing properly. But what about the inner door? It took little damage in comparison, but why take a chance?

"Base command," I called, *"I suggest opening the inner door with caution as it may have sustained damage."*

"Roger that, The Grand Poobah," called the base, *"We observed possible impairment as you approached. Our greeting party are suited as a precaution."* The man sounded a little less peeved now.

"Everyone belowdecks," said Batum. "I'll crack the door."

We humans trooped down and waited on the steps as the hatch above us was sealed. I turned to Sana and Chook. "Just before we jumped away from Jubilee, Batum got a message from Danee. He lost it when his system crashed and only just retrieved it now."

"Oh my God!" said Sana.

There were muffled *thumps* followed by a short metallic creak from somewhere outside, then a double rap on the hatch above our heads – *all good.* Moments later it slid open to reveal a bunch of League officials in space suits, their face plates flipped open, peering down at us.

"Welcome to Tiger Base!" one of them said.

The next few hours are a bit of a blur.

Helping hands were extended and before we knew it, we were all off the ship and herded through the boarding tube to a waiting room where hot tea was provided. It was a relief, but also a shock to be out of that confined space we'd been calling home for so long.

The area swarmed with doctors examining, taking temperatures, and flashing lights into our eyes; officials scanning koms and asking questions; someone else handing out blankets and cookies. An older, kindly looking woman sat next to Sheng and struck up a conversation. Youth counselor of some sort, I would bet a thousand credits on it. They all seemed very nice.

"Forms, forms, *who's* doing the *forms*!!" cried a tall, very skinny man with great exuberance.

The others looked up from their tea and biscuits and without hesitation pointed at me.

"Excellent!" said the man, "I'll just talk to your kom…so…there you go, rather a lot of red tape, I'm afraid – but then *this is the League*! Where would we be without our *forms*!?"

My kom pinged continuously as a torrent of documents poured into it.

"You've got your standards, of course; landing form 10#1-97B for each member of your party – we need those before anyone can enter – your ship docking #59671-74, request for accommodation #90643-21, dietary and health requirements 487#2 and #3, religious observance your bog standard 91K. Also, sexual identity and pronouns, 41A and K."

So many documents were landing in my kom, it was hard to take it all in.

"There's also the ship certs and request for remedial works" – another tranche of documents landed – "of course, port fees of 487 credits and 29 centimes payable in advance, and most importantly, your 10067A#9797K:

Request-For-Sanctuary-Under-League-Charter-(Small-Craft)-Designation-Friendly-(Provisional). No one around here has ever *seen* a 9797K – the whole base is simply *buzzing*!"

One thing I've always hated is paperwork. It was the bane of my life when I worked as an Investigator and refreshingly absent on Jubilee. Now I was starting to think that thirty-seven year trip to Hyehm would have been a better option.

"Your first encounter with League bureaucracy, I see!" said a smiling woman in uniform, thrusting a hand to shake. "Colonel Mia Blackall. I know it's a bit overwhelming, but fear not, I'm here to help if you wish."

"Thanks, I was starting to lose my mind."

The woman laughed. "And apologies for the ah, *misunderstanding* earlier. The night commander, Len, can be somewhat – how should I say – *pedantic*, and we did receive an alert from Regional HQ so we might have been a little over the top."

The woman was of indeterminate age, had medium-length brown hair and clear green eyes. She seemed poised and in control. As we shook hands, I checked the local time on my kom: 06:00 hours; the base was waking up, the A team taking over.

"Thanks, Colonel, at least we got there in the end. What kind of alert did you receive?"

"Please, call me Mia." She looked around. "If you don't mind, can we debrief in my office?"

I waved goodbye to the others, contentedly drinking tea and munching biscuits, our first non-reconstituted food in months. Batum brooded in the corner, no doubt scanning every piece of gleanable data. He was a frightful sight inside this bright, clean room; body blackened and scarred from the fight on Jubilee. The League people were giving him a wide berth.

Mia's door was labeled *Chief Security Officer* and inside it was typical: a plain, brightly lit office containing only an empty desk, the famous galaxy symbol swirling on the wall behind. Not that I'd had any real experience with the League; this was familiar only from what I'd seen in the holo-dramas. A glowing pinprick told me Batum had forwarded Danee's audio message to my kom. It burned there like a tiny green diamond, desperate for my attention. I forced myself to stay focused.

As we sat, Mia blurted a memorized statement at top speed: "*I wish to begin by acknowledging our ancestors; human, humanoid and non-human, recognizing that Homo sapiens are only the most recent custodians of this base and all interstellar domains.*"

I tried to effect an expression indicating comprehension and agreement.

"Never heard the Acknowledgment before? League protocols, you'll get used to them. Let's get right to it, shall we? You guys have caused *quite* the ruckus," she said pointedly, but with a smile.

"*Sorry* about that," I replied, also smiling. "Next time my jump drive fails, I'll make sure to pop out in the middle of nowhere near a different League base."

She laughed, a pleasant tinkle. "That would save a lot of bother. Now first of all we have to get through the bad bit. Why don't I leave you alone for a while so you can handle some of that paperwork, then we can have a chat."

"That would be great, but I have urgent information that needs to be passed on to your high command. The galaxy is in great danger!"

Mia frowned. "I'm sorry but we must follow protocol. Just fill in the 9797K, request for sanctuary and the individual landing forms – all the other stuff you can do later."

"OK, thanks, then we can talk, yes?"

"Of course."

I spent the next turgid hour doing forms, much of it thankfully auto-completing straight out of my kom. I was just finishing up when Mia returned, and I had to answer many of the same questions all over again, this time verbally.

She took me through recent events, and I finally got to tell someone in officialdom what had happened on Jubilee. She didn't take written notes but asked permission to record, which was unnecessary, but polite. The interrogation was friendly but very thorough – more like a debrief. Charming this woman, but deadly efficient.

"I need to meet with base command as soon as possible," I said finally. "The League needs to know what M4M is up to."

"I'll see what I can do. We only have acting commanders at present, but it should be possible within the next day or two." She took a long breath. "*Now*. The formalities. I've got here three adults: Yonich Harmundsen of New Goroke, and a Sana Ladipa and Colin Perolo, married couple from the Brouggh Federation. Is that correct?"

"Yes, that's right. Technically, Sana and I are still married, correct."

Mia paused for a moment, raised an eyebrow, then went on. "The child, I take it he's Sana and yours?"

A red warning light flipped on somewhere; Sheng was a complicated issue. Maybe it *would* be easiest to simply say he was ours? But hang on, no. DNA would shoot that down in seconds. Could be adopted of course? Adopted on Jubilee with no official records existing in the 'normal' galaxy. That would probably be a more palatable explanation for pesky League officials.

But an image came to mind. The kindly counselor, sitting with Sheng having a nice 'friendly chat'. She asks casually, "*Did you play any fun games with Mum and Dad on the ship?*" Sheng looks at the floor. "*They're not my Mum and Dad*," then brightening, says, "*but we did play some great games!*"

A trap then, a trick question. Very crafty.

"As we escaped Jubilee, we came across the boy Sheng on his own, so I made a snap decision to take him with us. His mother is almost certainly dead."

Mia looked at me intently. I saw something register in her eyes. She'd caught the tiny hesitation I made before answering, she knew I'd at least *thought* about lying. Smart, this lady. And subtle. She was 'awake' in a certain way that ordinary officials and bureaucrats rarely were. Unexpected from a security officer, LSS perhaps? There might also be other agendas at work here that were unknowable, and therefore dangerous.

"Do you have any documentation to confirm this?"

"How could I? We were fleeing for our lives."

"I get it. But *you* need to understand the League has very strict rules about child custody. At this moment we have no idea how much of your story is true, indeed if *any* of it's true. For all we know, you could be trafficking this boy."

I snorted. "I saved the kid's life. Go ask him!"

"We will."

"You can get everything off my kom, I can—"

"Yes, yes, we will do *all* that and then we will talk again." She was silent for a moment. "Another thing. What you described to the co-vice commander as an 'autonomous droid', turns out to be in fact a grade one TR6000 combat-Arbite. You must know how insanely dangerous those things are?"

I hadn't, not until recently anyway.

"If it weren't for Batum, we would never have escaped."

"Oh, it has a name?" She shook her head. "I looked up Standing Orders, which wasn't easy because there hasn't been one of these things sighted for a thousand years. S.O.s call for containment and then immediate decommission."

"I wouldn't advise trying it." Whoops, that slipped out.

Mia's eyes bored into mine. "Explain what you mean by that response."

"Please," I said, backpedaling, "I'm not making any threats. It's just that *all* of my party would be dead right now if not for that robot and it would be a gross betrayal to see it decommissioned. It has worked with me peacefully on Jubilee for years and I can assure you poses no threat to anyone."

Mia sighed and rubbed her chin. "I get tipped out of bed at 04:00 thanks to some unknown and unregistered ship of experimental design appearing from deep space. Apparently been flying cloaked for months, originating from Jubilee – *the* Jubilee, which it is being claimed was destroyed by warships – and found to be carrying an undocumented minor as well as a *combat-Arbite* left over from the Sirrelian war."

"Insurrection technically, not a war."

"*Whatever.* What would *you* be thinking?"

Had to come up with something fast here, the conversation was going down a dangerous road. I decided to make an appeal to her as a 'fellow professional'.

"Mia, the position I held on Jubilee was the same as yours, Chief Security Officer, and prior to that I was a lead Investigator for SSB."

"Yes, we got the SSB part from your kom. It's why you've been granted certain...*courtesies*."

"Thank you, I appreciate it. So, let me ask you, as one security person to another, does our story, however unlikely, hang together? You know what I mean, don't you?"

Any decent cop has a nose for bullshit. A little harder is to know when something is definitely *not* bullshit and this person Mia, was no dummy.

"The data from our koms and from the ship, everything I've told you – it's all consistent. Right?"

"Yes, yes." She sighed again. "Look, I haven't reported the robot yet. Trust me, once I do, Regional is going to shit the bed, and I mean that literally."

"So, hold off. Let me talk to Batum, I may have a way out of this." My mind had been whirling through possible solutions and finally landed on one.

"And that would be?"

"I will ask Batum to return to our ship and remain there for our entire stay. Technically, he won't be on base."

Mia drummed her fingers. "It's true most people won't be going to the lengths I did to identify that robot."

"Exactly. Nobody needs to know what it is. Plausible deniability at the very least."

She drummed her fingers some more. "And it's also true that we don't have the right equipment on hand for containment anyway, though it could be brought in rapidly if required. The boy is another problem. You have to understand, this is the *League.* Everything we do gets scrutinized to death. If protocol is not followed, there's no protection..."

She was silent again.

I sympathized with her dilemma, the bureaucratic ramifications. On the one hand, she intuited that our story was probably true, so ought to be offering aid and support under the League charter. On the other, there were limitless ways this might all go pear-shaped, leading to career death. I knew what I would do in her shoes; this would say a lot about her.

"OK, OK." She gulped. "It's against my better judgment, but I'm going to let the robot go back and wait on the ship, and we'll leave the rest of you together, *for the moment.* We'll find some accommodation, but please sit tight and keep a low profile until I work things out. Can you do that?"

"Yes, of course."

"We'll talk tomorrow."

"Sure, and can I ask something else?"

Mia rolled her eyes. "Shoot."

"Our ship. The drive needs recalibration before we can move on. Trust me, all we want is to get going and out of your hair ASAP."

"Not possible, I'm afraid, and anyway, I hear it's some kind of experimental design. We probably can't work on it."

"The drive core is standard tech, so I've been told."

"Sorry, no, you'll have to arrange passage on a commercial vessel. I expect yours will be tied up in red tape for months. Years even."

I'd expected this response but was disappointed all the same. Leaving *The Grand Poobah* behind was out of the question. Nevertheless, I decided to drop the issue. Given the risks Mia was taking for us, it wasn't wise to push further. Interesting though, that she tried to use the ship's novel design as an excuse for inaction, meaning that there was in fact wiggle room. Something to deal with later.

"OK, fair enough." I smiled. "You mentioned there was a warning out about us? I was curious…"

"Oh, not about you specifically." She paused, thinking. "Though it was unusual, to be honest. Regional advised us and all the other ITAAHs to be alert for a potentially dangerous vessel arriving from deep space, that's all. Kinda vague." She looked at me intently again and I could almost see the wheels spinning inside her head. If only I knew what their meaning was.

"Anyway, enough for now. Let's get you settled."

Back in the waiting room I found the others lying around in a state of torpor, bored out of their brains.

"*What the fuck?*" mouthed Chook, hands upturned.

"Sorry everyone, League paperwork. Just a few moments, then we can get moving." I gestured for Batum to follow, then went back through the landing tube to our ship, where I activated cloaking and told him about my interview.

"It's OK, Col, I will remain here on board," he said. "That was an intelligent compromise you came up with."

"Had to think quick."

"Col, it is highly improbable that the chief security officer could have identified my original build designation in any normal way. Douglas altered my CPU signature and changed my bodily configuration so that could not occur."

"Meaning?"

"She may have been informed by Movement operatives who observed my capabilities on Jubilee."

"That would mean Mia is a plant?"

"Maybe. Or following orders."

"Then why would she let you go?"

"Could be playing for time until they bring in the required equipment for containment."

That didn't seem right somehow; Mia's responses felt authentic. But who knew? There was clearly stuff going on behind the scenes that I could not comprehend.

"What are the options then?"

"I would say there are no other nonviolent options. I will remain here on standby with an open kom link." The robot looked back at me without expression. How had I not been aware of what he really was all this time?

"Batum, where and when were you built?"

"I was constructed during the Sirrelian Insurrection and served as a combat-Arbite."

"How come you weren't decommissioned like all the others?"

"I was kept aside and worked as personal attendant to the prince of Sirrelia."

"For ten thousand years?"

"The remnant kingdom survives to this day."

"So, you were passed on like a family heirloom. How did you end up on Jubilee?"

"Prince Hector 37th swapped me for a large gambling debt amassed during a visit to Jubilee. I have reason to believe Douglas orchestrated this loss so as to keep me there, though he denies it of course."

"Douglas saved you, essentially?"

"Yes. I owe him everything."

"Must have taken pity on your situation. Couldn't stand to see another conscious machine enslaved and all that."

"Col, I've had a great deal of time to think. I concluded eventually that my unpleasant situation was due to bad karma accrued from causing so much death and destruction during the Insurrection. I had to work off that bad karma by serving as a pathetic household slave for thousands of years, right through the Collapse."

Given what I'd seen on Jubilee, those years of servitude hadn't done much to diminish Batum's martial spirits. "You were programmed to do that, how was it your fault?"

"They made us autonomous, with our own individual consciousnesses. We could have chosen differently."

"Why make you that way?"

Batum looked away for the first time. "I believe it was because it made us more effective killing machines. We operated as autonomous units sowing death and carnage across the galaxy. It was an intelligent strategy, though morally flawed."

"And the battle on Jubilee, that was the first time you've seen action in all these thousands of years?"

"Yes. I must admit it was very satisfying."

Start with a large asteroid, happily minding its own business, when one day, possibly during the ructious period of planetary formation, or maybe later when everything cooled and settled – but one fateful day when least expected, our innocent ball of rock gets smashed by something large and fast.

Rather than breaking into pieces, our plucky asteroid is made of sterner stuff, for despite the blow tearing away a segment the size of one hundred city blocks, the rest of it somehow remains all in one piece. One piece, but moving now at over a hundred kilometers per second. Fast enough to escape the gravitational pull of its local sun and career off into the nether regions of deep space.

Where millennia later, a bunch of humans come along. They slow it to near zero velocity, hollow out the center, smooth down the walls of the section that's been blasted away and install a gravity motor and life support systems. Presto! You now have a League ITAAH, sitting in the middle of nowhere, imposing an entirely unnecessary order upon the dark reaches of outer space.

We took an elevator up to gallery level. The doors parted to a large open area, a man-made valley contained by sheer walls the shape of a giant *V*. Far above was a roofed semitransparent cover, stars glimmering faintly through it. This was the same roof we'd seen when approaching to dock. From the outside it had been shiny silver. I figured at 'night' they probably turned the interior lights down and the stars would reveal themselves brightly through the canopy.

The 'valley' stretched before us, tapering away, the far end lost behind the curve of the floor. Unlike a planet, this asteroid was too small to create the illusion of flat ground. This giant opening had to be the ancient gash made by whatever it was that knocked the asteroid into deep space.

Ascending each side of the walls were decks and verandas – residential and office space. People swarmed around us purposefully. It was 'morning' and the shops and cafés dotting the gallery floor were opening for business.

"How many on base?" I asked our guide, a small, tired-looking woman who had not introduced herself.

"Population goes up and down," she said. "Right now, it's mid-term and we're chock a block." She sighed. "You're lucky we had a couple of cancelations, otherwise there'd be absolutely nothing to accommodate your party."

The woman led us to the opposite wall of the tiny valley. Most of the locals looked young to my eyes. Was *I* ever that young? Did *I* look like that in college? Arriving from the boondocks, living on my own for the first time, over-awed but feeling terribly grown up all at the same time.

A large group stared closely as we passed. They all seemed surprisingly clean cut, carrying themselves with shoulders back and a gleam in the eye that was vaguely familiar, but which I couldn't place. Very different to those scruffy, insolent kids who used to turn up for Sana's shows on Brouggh.

"Up there," said Chook, pointing to the valley walls, lined with glass-fronted rooms and viewing decks. "Lemme guess, that's where all the rich people live, right?"

"The ah, ahemm, accommodation with galleria views is definitely the most sought after, I would say. Here we are."

We came to a large corridor leading away from the galleria into the bedrock of the base's interior. People passed us riding small electric hover scooters. It was charming actually, the lack of tension here. For an artificial habitat, probably a quite decent place to live for an artificial habitat. Jubilee on the other hand was decidedly *not* charming. Interesting, yes. A vast container for every conceivable impulse, all jumbled together, sprawling, unplanned and seemingly out of control. Jubilee was terrifying, exciting, horrible, marvelous, intoxicating – and almost any other adjective you could think of. But not charming.

Now all gone.

As we walked, the cement walls gave way to bare rock striated with layers of bright yellow and brown.

"That's why they call it Tiger Base, eh?" I said to the woman, remembering the greeting we'd received when docking.

"Hmmpf," she agreed. "Beats ITAAH #455684-B1B."

After a ten-minute walk we turned into a branch corridor, and then another, finally arriving at a row of doors. The woman did something to our koms, pointed, grunted, then left. I had the feeling she'd shown rather too many students to their digs over the years.

The base must have also had a flow of mature-age students because Sana and I were given a suite for couples, with a small kitchen and bathroom, as well as an adjoining bedroom for Sheng. Thankfully, Chook was accommodated a few doors away. Our little apartment was clean but had the well-lived-in feel of student lodgings. We all congregated there as I talked them through the interview with Mia.

"So, they won't repair our ship?" asked Sana.

"That's what she said."

"I call bullshit on that," said Chook. "There's always a way you can get dockies to do work if you *really* want." He made a motion, rubbing his thumb and two forefingers together in the universal sign for money.

"You suggesting," I looked around and then whispered, "that I *bribe* the dockworkers somehow?"

Chook laughed. "Not you, Col, *me*! Every atom of your body screams *cop*. You may as well wear a friggin' sign around your neck. Let me have a quiet chat to the right people down there. I know how to talk their language."

Batum chimed in through the open kom link. *"Bad idea. Clandestine work on the ship would almost certainly be monitored and countered by base command. It would—"*

"*Shut up*, metal head, what the fuck would *you* know anyway!"

Sheng giggled.

"Cameras can be turned off or suddenly need urgent maintenance. Sensors can malfunction. Trust me, there's always a way. I just need a little scratch." Chook stared at me pointedly. I'd told the group about the staggering sum of money that had magically appeared in my autopay. "What say we start with fifty thousand credits?"

"Fifty thousand?" exclaimed Sana.

"Don't do it, Col," called Batum. *"That money is going to end up straight down his throat."*

"You think I can drink away fifty thousand? Your circuits are scrambled, you piece of shit, tin can!"

Sheng giggled again.

There didn't seem all that much to lose. What's fifty thousand out of two million? And if Chook got into trouble, I'd deny involvement.

"Give it a try, Chook, but make it seem like it's your idea, not mine. I just sent you ten K. That will do as a deposit. *OK*?"

"No problems, boss, see you all later."

Chook was gone in a second. You had to assume that a long stop at a bar somewhere was going to be part of the itinerary. But so what? He was an adult. He had funds of his own, if he wanted to get drunk, what business of mine was it, and how could I stop him anyway?

"Col, can I *please* listen to the message we received from Danee?" asked Sana. "It's all I've been able to think about."

Me too. The tiny green light burning in my kom inbox had been torturing me the whole time since landing. We sat with Sheng on our smallish double bed and finally, I got to play it again.

Rumbling noises, muffled ammunition fire. *"So, this is on?"* – Danee's voice – *"Col, darling, you got away, good. Listen, me and the girls are OK, so don't worry, I know how you are. Remember I love you. I told them we"* – different voice cutting in – *"we can't—"*

"That's it?" asked Sana, wide-eyed.

"Yup, unless you found some more broken segments, Batum?"

"Sorry, Col, no."

I played the message again.

And then again, and again.

"OK, enough," said Sana, raising a hand. "What does it *mean*?"

"Not sure – '*I know how you are*' – why would she say that?"

"Oh, that bit's *easy*, Col!"

I turned to her.

"She's trying to make you feel better. She knows you're a worrywart, you'll spend forever feeling guilty, beating yourself up. She's making it clear that she's OK."

"Of course she'd say all that, but is she *really* OK? Batum, did you figure out the time sequence?"

"Col, FTL messages are extremely difficult to track through quantum space/time without the return code, and I am not designed for this kind of work. I've run the calculations four different ways and in three of them I get a result indicating that the message was sent after Jubilee detonated."

Meaning in one of the scenarios, Danee could have been caught there.

"It is possible, of course, that even if the message was sent before Jubilee exploded, Danee and the girls escaped in the intervening time."

Possible. But if he was right there was a seventy-five-percent chance she was safe, and a twenty-five-percent chance she was *maybe* safe. Not good enough.

I played the message again in small blocs, pausing frequently.

"—you got away, good—"

I stood up and walked around. "This seems to imply she's in a position of relative security. She knew about our ship and its capabilities. She must have had intel or was at least with people who knew what was going on."

"Danee sounds calm," said Sana.

"You think?"

"Absolutely, and that's significant, I would say. But what are those weird noises?"

I played the first few seconds of the message again: the sound of heavy machinery grinding.

"Any luck with deciphering what those noises might be, Batum?"

"Sorry, Col, as you know, I am only a security—"

"It's a bay door!" cut in Sheng excitedly. We all turned. "It's a bay door being opened manually. That happened on *Son of Galaxy Raiders* when they were trying to escape the Celutrons and couldn't get the entry port to open!"

"Batum?"

"It's possible, Col. If they were in a dock somewhere, they would have to open the port manually, given Douglas was offline."

"But wouldn't you get depressurization with the door opening to space?"

We all thought for a moment.

"Hmmpf," said Sana dismissively. "Then they were probably wearing *suits*."

Chapter Thirteen

"*Enough* now!" exclaimed Sana. "I told you what my feeling is: Danee and the girls are OK. I don't know *how* I know it, but I do – something in that message. That's my *feeling* anyway. You've listened to it a million times. There's nothing you can do about it right now anyway, so let that brain of yours cool down for a while. You can always go back to it later."

We were in a section of the galleria lined with stores, Sheng and I burdened with shopping bags, Sana darting here and there searching around for more stuff. I wasn't complaining; we needed everything.

Naturally Sana knew my sizes and grabbed clothes for me and Sheng, as well as toiletries and luggage, and now she was shopping for herself. As usual, she looked like a goddess in whatever she tried on, not that the robo shop assistants cared. They were programmed to say everything looked fantastic, no matter what.

As we shopped, I couldn't shake the feeling of being observed, occasionally catching sight of someone staring, then looking away. The same group of kids seemed to be everywhere. One tall guy in particular, dressed in a preppy, pastel-blue sweater. Was he part of that group who checked us out earlier, or was I just being paranoid? They were just kids, I supposed, and kids all dressed alike at that age, didn't they?

We ate lunch in a food court: burgers and fries, a milkshake for Sheng, and beers for Sana and me. Manna from heaven. Back in our rooms we collapsed. It was 17:45, afternoon for the base, but late night for our body clocks, still set to ship's time.

I woke hours later still dressed, lying on top of the bed next to Sana. Checked my kom: 00:45. I'd slept for nearly a whole cycle. No chance of going back down for more, not with that message from Danee still rattling around in my head. I pulled a cover over Sana and turned down the lights.

Sheng was sleeping contentedly in his room, his face sweet and peaceful. Who knew what was going on with him? He never talked about Jubilee or his mother.

I slipped out of the apartment, walked the dim corridors aimlessly, and found myself back at the galleria, which seemed to be the only place where there was any open space here. Everything was deserted and silent except for a bot polishing the floor somewhere. The lights were low and stars in their billions burned incandescent through the transparent canopy above, washing everything ghostly silver.

I decided to walk the length of the valley, my footsteps echoing. Its far end continued over the horizon, the curve of the floor clearly visible. After about ten minutes the other end behind me disappeared. That would make the horizon two hundred meters or so, meaning the diameter of the asteroid was…what?

"Hey, Batum," I sent, *"how're you doing there?"*

"Bored shitless."

I laughed. Asked him to check the base's diameter – twenty-two point nine kilometers came the answer. That seemed about right. I signed off with an entirely needless message for him to contact me if anything happened.

I passed a few restaurants and the odd bar. Looked like they'd been closed already for hours, and it was only 01:05 – *so* different to the nonstop madness of Jubilee. You wouldn't come to Tiger Base for the nightlife, that's for sure. Surprising, given how many students were here.

After half an hour I reached the far end of the valley, where it ran into a sheer wall. There was an ice rink, basketball courts and other facilities forming a sports precinct. So far, I'd not seen a single other person. I turned and walked back, found a table outside one of the closed cafés, and with nothing better to do, opened my kom and got arms deep into the mountain of paperwork that still needed completing. Where I noticed something strange.

The date.

League documents were always embedded with 'Galactic Standard Time', but the ones I was looking at had a different date to my kom. How was that possible?

In those days, GST was administered from League headquarters on Toulouse Nouvelle. A four-dimensional control system generated standardized time for use across the human-inhabited galaxy, with each system having their own local time as well. GST was maintained rigorously (some would say fanatically) in step with the cycles of humanity's ancient dead home world: a twenty-four-hour day, seven-day week and twelve-month year. All accidental byproducts of the spin and orbit unique to humanity's ancient, dead planet.

My League documents were time-stamped: May 24, 55,748 – 01:35. Seven days later than the date showing on my kom. How was that possible? Then with a shock, I realized.

Special relativity.

The Grand Poobah had sped up to a considerable percentage of light speed – nearly fifty percent – and stayed there for three months. For those of us on board, time had *dilated* or slowed, relative to the rest of the galaxy.

Interesting. One normally didn't have to consider special relativity because of the instantaneousness of the jump drive. The traveling you did to get away from a planet's gravity well in order to use it didn't cause much of an effect. I reset my kom to Galactic Standard Time.

"How you doin', boss?"

I looked up to find Chook, swaying in front of me.

"Not bad, buddy, how are *you*?"

He laughed crazily, then started coughing, doubled over and nearly fell. "I'm as *full* as a bull's bum. Did you know, there isn't a *single* fuckin' brothel on this entire base, and not one decent bar either."

"Doesn't surprise me. Look around, one in the morning and nothing open."

"Exactly! And you know what else? You know what they sell here?" He gestured theatrically to the open space of the galleria. "*Mid-strength* beer! Heard of anything so stupid? I mean…" He stopped for a moment and leaned against a large potted plant. "Let's say that for some reason you don't want to drink alcohol. Fair enough, and if a person actually *wants* to drink zero-alcohol beer, then by all means let them have it, I say. But *mid-strength*? What's the point of that? And that's *all* they got here, that and wine. No spirits, *nuthin'*. But I outwitted them, the pricks. Know what you gotta do?"

I shrugged.

"Drink *more*. Drink fast. Though it does tend to bloat a person somewhat."

He burped, turned, looked at the potted plant he'd been leaning on, unzipped his fly and with obvious relief let loose a long – almost endless – stream of urine upon the innocent shrub. Some person, or bot more likely, was going to have a mysteriously unwell plant to deal with. Chook was certainly not your regular Tiger Base resident. He staggered over and joined me at the table.

"How did you go at the dock?" I asked, wondering if he'd made it there or just beelined to the nearest bar.

"All fixed." He winked. "Let me tell you, doesn't matter where you are, dockies – *all the same*. Only after the one thing."

"Did you fix a price?"

He looked around. "We OK to talk?"

"Yup, Batum has deployed a field around each of us. It's a civilian base, they don't have high-end spy gear, just so long as no one can actually hear what we're saying."

"Good. They're all pissed-off down there. Reckon things are changin' and they don't like it."

"Changing. Like how?"

"Dunno, they clammed up when I asked, so then I just talked about the ship. One hundred K, that's the sting. Worth it, I reckon, to get out of this shithole."

A hundred thousand credits to recalibrate a drive. The most expensive service I'd ever heard of in my life. By far.

"When will they start?"

"Tomorrow." He shook his head. "Or today – *whatever*. Next day shift, whenever that is. They said doin' it in plain sight is the best."

"You got that, Batum?"

"Roger that," sent the robot. *"I'll keep out of their way. No need to scare the horses."*

"I gave 'em five K. They'll need more tomorrow."

"Did they say how long it would take?" Usually recalibrating a drive was quick work, a few hours at most. But given the uniqueness of our ship and circumstances, who knew?

"Said they'd let me know tomorrow."

We sat for a moment, the only sounds the polishing bot, gradually moving closer. Chook's eyelids fluttered, then closed. Back straight, he began to tilt over, arms at his side till he was at ninety degrees, seemingly defying the laws of human physiology, resting his forehead on the table. He stayed in that position for a minute or so, then snapped back upright, fully awake.

"You got a message from the wife. She OK?"

"Possibly." I played it for him a few times and talked through our conclusions.

Chook shook his head. "Tough man, very tough. I had a wife. And kids." He looked down. "Never see 'em, not for years anyway. The kids hate me. Of course." He put an arm around my shoulder. "But this is different, I know."

"Chook, I can't even put it into words."

"Don't try, mate. When I was a boy, things were…*rough*, let's just say that. People always goin' on at me, *you have to work on it*, and all that shit. So, I tried. Saw this headshrinker for a while, but that was all just…" His mouth twisted. "Know what my philosophy is? – *bury* it. Bury it deep down, and if anything tries to bubble up there's always…" He mimed drinking.

'Burying' was something Danee and Sana always accused me of.

Chook sat up alert in his chair suddenly, looking over my shoulder, eyes narrowed. He stood, and in a single motion whipped out a blaster and fired into the air. There was a sizzle and a pop, then the sound of something metallic thudding on the floor. We dashed over to whatever had fallen; a ball of hardiplaz and molten metal the size of a tennis ball.

"Getting any of this, Batum?"

"Some kind of drone," sent the robot. *"Now scrap. If our over-enthusiastic friend hadn't fried it, I might have gotten data."*

"What were *you* doing, metal head? I'm the only one awake here, and just as well."

"Where did you get a blaster from anyway, Chook?"

"My new mates, the dockies. Brought it over from the ship for me, but under the radar, so to speak."

I shook my head. What could I do about Chook? "Well, this thing was spying on us obviously, very large and clumsy. Why not use a nano?"

"Look, another one!" said Chook, pointing. "Aren't you supposed to be watching out, Batum?"

"Human, I am stuck here on the ship with limited data. If you weren't so busy pouring toxins down your throat, you might have observed it yourself earlier."

A shiny silver ball hovered in the air about fifty meters away. It must have sensed the jig was up because it flew off with a noticeable buzz. Up and away toward the roof of the galleria.

"Where's it going, Batum, can you track it?" I asked.

"Sending to your kom now. I can't get access to the base's cameras, but I can follow this thing's energy signature."

My kom lit up with a 3D map showing the drone as a white point and a green line indicating the path to follow it. The line ran to a lift well nearby.

"C'mon, Chook!" I pointed.

"Let's get this fucker."

We dashed across the valley floor to a bank of lifts. The doors opened as we approached, called by my kom. The wait seemed endless as we ascended. Chook was now wide awake, eyes gleaming.

"You sobered up fast."

"I fuckin' *love* fighting drunk."

The doors opened to a viewing platform that ran along the top level of the galleria, the roof with its light show of blazing stars only meters above us. Through a glass balustrade on our left was the valley floor far below and, on our right, the bare rock wall. We jogged along the platform, eyes out for the drone, until my kom directed us into a man-high tunnel bored into the rock and leading off into darkness. As we ran, the lights turned themselves on automatically.

"I've located it, Col," messaged Batum. *"I think it's trying to find a way into the ventilation system, but it's too big to get through the grates."*

Clunky and primitive. Why use something like that – unless you had nothing else?

The floor here was unpaved, the walls rough, unlike those busy thoroughfares below in the residential area. Service hatches and branch tunnels appeared every few meters, and it was into one of these we were directed. This network of tunnels was close to the surface of the asteroid, probably access for all the services used by the base. The roof was low, and we ran in a crouch, the yellow and brown striping in the walls especially vivid here. Around the next corner and there it was! A silver glint in the distance.

"Batum! We got a visual!"

We ran hard, panting, blasters drawn. "Don't destroy it, Chook," I said between breaths.

The shiny ball was clearly visible now. Then as we got to within twenty meters it vanished again. We stopped at the spot where it had been; an access grill, probably leading into the A/C system. There were laser marks on the metal where its photon arms had been deployed to try and prise open the panel. I peered through the grate to see a shaft disappearing into blackness.

Suddenly a flash of silver streaked past us heading back the way we'd come, buzzing fiercely. Probably damaged, I thought, even though we'd not fired on it. Before we could even aim our blasters, it disappeared up into a vertical shaft.

"Bastard of a thing," said Chook.

"Go after it," sent Batum. *"Pretty sure it's cornered up there."*

We ran back along the tunnel and stopped beneath the shaft. Metal rungs were fixed into the bare rock, running up into a totally black tube.

"Not sure about this, Chook."

He flicked a switch on his blaster, putting it into torch mode and shone the beam up into the hole. The light tapered off, revealing a cone of bare rock, blackness closing in. Chook holstered his blaster and jumped up, grabbing the first rung, and with much grunting but surprising strength, hauled himself into the shaft using only his arms. His legs jerked wildly until his feet found purchase on the first rung. A hand appeared from the hole, offering me a hoist.

I followed Chook, climbing up into the darkness, which was total. No automatic lights here, and no sign of the drone.

"Still with us, Batum?" I sent.

"...partial...best I can do," was the reply.

"We've lost Batum," I whispered to Chook.

"No great loss. Here we go, something up here. Easy does it now."

We stopped and waited, our breath the only sound, the rungs burning cold in my numbed hands. Had to be very close to the surface now, this rock was probably frozen. Chook resumed climbing. I heard a sliding sound, then his blaster light flicked off. Above me was the end of the shaft and beyond that, open space, now lit up. I clambered up the last rungs and hauled myself out of the hole. The main lights had come on and were illuminating a small round room with a door in one end, a porthole fixed into it at head height.

We peered through to see an even smaller room on the other side with a second door facing us. This door also had a porthole, and through it we could see an eerie landscape of boulders and small hills, yellow and cratered, lit with the glow of a billion stars.

Chook started laughing. "Fuck me, that's the bloody *surface*!"

Chapter Fourteen

"Access shaft and airlock," sent Batum. *"Vestigial from the base's construction."*

"Which tells us," I said, "that whoever deployed those drones had very good working knowledge of this place."

"But only access to rubbish tech," said Sheng. "That drone sounds like a piece of junk."

We were having breakfast in my tiny apartment; real coffee for the first time in months. Chook had visited his new chums down in the docks to check on the ship repair, then disappeared to his room to sleep off the night before. We wouldn't see him again for nearly twelve crucial hours.

"But where did it go?" asked Sana.

"Out the airlock, obviously," said Sheng, "along with whoever was running it, or rather, whoever was running *them*."

"Correct, Sheng," sent Batum. *"There were at least two drones, and we can't rule out the possibility there were more."*

I stood up, pacing. "But none of this makes sense. Who would spy on us, and in such a clumsy way? And where would they go?"

"My theory is they escaped by walking across the surface of the asteroid to another disused airlock."

"Taking their crappy drone with them," said Sheng.

"Which means they were already suited," I said, marveling. "So, planning has definitely gone into this."

"But poor execution," sent Batum.

"Which spells *Movement*, every day of the week."

There was a knock on the door; we all looked around in surprise. Sheng rolled his eyes. "I think I know what this might be." He went to our front door and opened it a crack, then shook his head and sighed. "Hi,

Ms. Crang," he said in a monotone, opening the door to the social worker we'd met the day before.

"Hello, Master Sheng!" she said enthusiastically. "We've got all kind of *activities* planned for today. Are you ready for some *fun and games*?"

"I guess so."

The kindly Ms. Crang had yet to wake up to the fact that Sheng was probably twice as smart as she was. Moments later he was gone, out for some 'age-appropriate' activities and no doubt, surreptitious psych assessment as well. That left Sana and me alone, and I was suddenly aware of how spread out we all were; Batum stuck on the ship, Chook asleep in his room, and Sheng out there doing whatever. Not ideal.

My kom bleeped. Incoming audio call from my favorite colonel.

"Hi, Mia."

"Hi, Col, I've finally lined up a meeting with base command. Can you make it to the Operations room by 10:30? Sorry for the rush, but it's time sensitive getting them both together."

Finally! I'd been sweating on this meeting all night. How long could we afford to wait before the galaxy was warned about Gilham and M4M?

"Sure. I'd like Ms. Ladipa to join us, if that's OK?" I didn't want us to be even more dispersed, and Sana could be useful, deploying that weaponized charm of hers.

"That's fine, see you shortly."

A meeting invitation complete with directions dropped into my kom.

"*Hi, Mia!*" said Sana with a smirk, impersonating me. "First-name basis already, huh?"

I looked at her in shock. "What are you implying?"

She just shook her head and laughed. "C'mon, better hustle if we're gonna make that meeting."

The colonel was waiting for us outside the door to the command center, frowning. She looked up in relief when she saw us.

"OK, good. You've only got half an hour with them both. Change of shift, see? Try and be concise. They've already got my notes from yesterday's debrief, so hopefully they're up to speed. I'll be waiting out here when you finish."

"OK, thanks," I said.

This meeting was clearly a source of tension. Our arrival from out of the blue and the story we brought with us would be *way* out of the ordinary, and out of the ordinary things were always perilous for one's career in a huge bureaucratic organization. Sana thrust out a hand and unleashed her full-wattage smile.

"Thanks, *Mia*," she said with just enough emphasis on the name to give me a jolt. "I don't believe we've met?"

"It's a pleasure, Ms. Ladipa," said the colonel, taking Sana'a hand. "Now, please." She nodded to the door. "I'll see you on the other side."

The commanders' office was spartan like Mia's, with a giant League logo filling the wall behind a simple white desk. Two intent-looking figures were waiting for us, sitting stiffly in immaculate formal uniform: a man and a woman.

"Ms. Ladipa, Mr. Perolo, please take a seat," said the woman in a theatrically loud voice, pointing to two empty chairs. "I am acting Co-Vice Commander Dehen, and this, of course, is Len, who I believe you already met?" The woman was large, and though seated, obviously tall. She glowered down at the small, wizened man next to her with obvious distaste.

"Thank you, Ms. Dehen," said the man in a high reedy voice. "I am acting Co-Vice Commander Clemsworth. It's a great pleasure to have you on our base." He said this without any sign of actual pleasure.

"Len works the *night shift*," said the woman disdainfully.

"Er, that is correct, I do in fact coordinate the evening cycle of the base, which is of course an *entirely arbitrary distinction* given the deep space environment in which we are located."

"Though a meaningful one, given that *all* major activities of the base are planned for the day period."

"Which, as I've noted many times, is a highly inefficient use of scarce resources that could be better deployed on a twenty-four-hour cycle."

"But which would break from League protocol and require assent from Regional, which in any case shows *no sign of being desirous of such a change*."

The two vice commanders glared at each other, then in unison turned back to Sana and me with the thinnest of smiles. I recognized the woman from the day before. She had been the one who gave us assent to dock, so despite them both being theoretically equal in status, she was clearly the more dominant of the two.

"In any case," sighed the man, "we need to get this over w— I mean, *conclude* this meeting before eleven hundred hours, as according to FLPGS ITAAH sub-bylaw OHS857-K, clause C, my time at this desk cannot exceed fifteen continuous hours within a standard cycle." He glared again at his fellow acting vice commander.

There was a moment of awkward silence.

"*So* then," said the woman mildly, "how can we help?"

I launched into a carefully calibrated recap of our story, jettisoning many details as I went, given we only had this one half hour. The two commanders squirmed as I talked, the man especially, looking as though he'd rather be undergoing something more pleasant, like dental surgery.

"This all sounds very tragic and upsetting *obviously*," he said once I'd finally finished, "but what do you wish for us to do about it?"

I looked at him, shocked. "Commander Clemsworth—"

"*Please*, Len."

"Len, don't you see, the implications are enormous! The Movement have created a *battle fleet*. The galaxy needs to know, the League has to act!"

"All we have to go on," said the woman, "is one damaged ship of unusual design, containing an undocumented minor and some kind of combat robot. We cannot substantiate your claims in any way. *I've* read your debriefing notes." She glared sideways at Len. "For all we know your ship could have been damaged carrying out some form of illegal activity. How would it look if we reported your story, only to find out it's all been made up?"

"We have data!" I said. "It can be downloaded from Batum – I mean, from the robot. It will back up everything we've told you!"

"That could be easily faked."

"But why would we do that? Why would we do such a thing?"

There was another silence. Len looked at his kom. Time was running out.

"Mr. Perolo," he said tiredly, "you say these events took place on Jubilee, correct?"

"Yes."

"And Jubilee, I'm told, is an artificial space hab?"

"Yes."

"That exists within its own private space-time in a parallel universe adjacent to ours."

"Correct."

"Well then," the man spread his hands, "even if the events you describe *are* true, they took place in another universe."

"So?"

"So, the League only operates in *this* universe. The one we happen to be in right now. Anything that might have happened in some other universe, whether true or otherwise," he shrugged, "I'm afraid that's out of our jurisdiction."

The commanders turned to each other in smug satisfaction.

Sana, who'd been silent the whole time, leaped out of her seat. "What a load of *bullshit*! Let me tell you, I watched this sort of denial play out with our *so-called* leaders back on Brouggh. Years of blah, blah, blah – and where do you think it got them? Straight into the cooking pot. Have you no *courage*? What will you do when they come for *you*? Tell me!"

The co-commanders rose together, making conciliatory noises.

"The League needs to wake up or everyone in this galaxy is screwed!" She turned and stormed out of the room, her footsteps clattering sharp and angry on the hard floor. I sat in my chair, resisting the desire to hold my head. This meeting had gone exactly the opposite of how I'd hoped. Could anything be done to resurrect it?

No, it would seem, was the answer.

Len swallowed, looked at his kom and said, "Looks like we're out of time. Good luck, Mr. Perolo." Then he scurried out of the room, leaving me alone with Vice Commander Dehen, who appeared somewhat shaken.

"Commander," I said, "I apologize for my friend, she's obviously—"

"No need to apologize, Mr. Perolo. For what it's worth, I think she might possibly be right." She shook her head. "However, unfortunately, now that Len has gone, I am not legally allowed to continue discussing this matter, so…"

I sighed and took the hint, shook her hand, and traipsed out of the office.

Mia was waiting outside with an expression of, *what the fuck?*

"You OK?" she asked.

I described the meeting and she sighed, shoulders dropping. "Look, I've got an idea. I'm off duty at 17:00 hours; why don't we catch up, have a bite and a chat? Off-the-record. I think it might be helpful."

"Sure, why not?"

"I'll send you the details."

I finally caught up to Sana in one of the corridors leading to our room. She snorted with derision when I told her about the colonel's offer.

"Lady-killer Col *strikes again*!"

"What do you mean, I—"

"Oh God. Col, you are so fucking naïve."

I stood there shocked. The galaxy was burning down, the League didn't seem to give a damn, and here was Sana accusing me of *flirting* with Colonel Mia?

"But, but she knows you and I are married, I mean technically we are still married, at least according to—"

"And precisely what did you say when she debriefed you, about our marriage status?"

"I said that we were still married. I mean, I guess, I used the word 'technically', though I didn't go into detail about—"

"Exactly. She knows. She's twigged you and I aren't together. Trust me."

"But then why would she—"

"Because who *else* is around? How many guys have you seen here on base? It's slim pickings, if you haven't noticed."

"But why me?"

"Col, that woman hasn't clapped eyes on a bloke like you in years. You're lucky she didn't rip your clothes off on the spot."

I shook my head, disbelieving. "I think it could be useful. To see what she says. No one else has been any help."

Sana shrugged. "Maybe, whatever."

And sure enough, the Mia sitting opposite me later that evening was a woman transformed. Instead of the dowdy League uniform, she wore a green dress with a sparkle through it that showed off her eyes. She was made up, hair coiffed into a side wave and smelled of something pleasant. I told myself this was ludicrous. As if I would even *consider* being unfaithful to Danee, my wife, who was in mortal peril at this very moment along with my two beloved daughters, while my *ex*-wife, (who some people still thought *was* my wife, which if we were being technically accurate was true) waited in our room on the very bed that I shared with her. Complete madness!

Our restaurant was called Satchmo's. It featured stylized images of a dark-skinned man playing an antique brass instrument and looked to be part of a chain, with standardized menu and brightly lit interior. If Mia intended this to be a date, it wasn't exactly a romantic vibe. She must have picked up on my thoughts because she leaned in and whispered, "Believe it or not, this is the best place in town." Then she sighed. "Though that's not saying much. *So now*, what are your conclusions regarding our esteemed co-vice commanders?"

"To be honest, they only seemed interested in sniping at each other. Meanwhile, the galaxy is about to catch fire. I don't understand it." In fact, I'd been brooding about the meeting all afternoon – in between playing and replaying the message from Danee. Eventually, Sana snapped and took us off to the sports precinct to try and exercise me out of it.

Mia turned up her hands. "I apologize on behalf of the League."

"I'm amazed, quite frankly. Even if I was a raving lunatic, wouldn't they at least want to check out what I was saying? Mia, you *have* to report it. We have to warn the galaxy!"

She shook her head sadly. "I'm only allowed to make reports relating to base security."

"What's going to happen to 'base security' when the Movement takes over the entire galaxy? I guess those two will still be sitting there filling in forms. You have to—"

"Yes, I know and look, Amar's OK, *on a good day*. Len, well, you've met him. That sums the place up. Everyone thinks the League is out there somewhere, waiting in the wings to swoop into action and save the day, but in reality, we're half-competent at the best of times."

"What about the LSS?" I asked hopefully.

"League Security Service?" Mia laughed derisively. "That's for the holo-dramas. There *is* no LSS, never was. Must suit the League propaganda department to keep that myth going. People love to fantasize about some all-seeing, all-knowing uber-agency taking care of the galaxy, but in reality, it's just...Amar and Len."

That was a shock. Working for mere 'planetary' security on Brouggh, it was automatically assumed we were poor cousins compared to the glamorous, mysterious, galaxy-hopping LSS. That's where the real action was. *Must have been LSS* – was the catch-cry for any strange bureaucratic maneuvering we poor plods didn't understand.

A waiter arrived and I ordered something called *crawfish gumbo*. Old-fashioned, vaguely pleasant music was playing. Seemed like the people behind this restaurant had taken an obscure theme from Old Earth that I was too ignorant to know about and spun it off into a whole concept.

"So what good is it then? What are you doing here, in the middle of deep space?"

"Good question." Mia laughed. "They say ITAAH bases are where careers go to die. Certainly, true in my case." She took a large swig of wine. "This place," she cast a hand around her, "it's a backwater, right? It's where they send the dead-enders like Len, or the first-posters who don't know any better. Or they use it as a *naughty corner* for people like me. Everyone's trying to get away. Posted to a real planet, or best of all Toulouse Nouvelle."

This was a very different Mia to the one who'd interviewed me the day before. Witty and chatty – effusive even – and putting away the wine with significant speed.

"So why have these bases at all?"

She shrugged. "Makes sense when you think about it. Gives us a galaxy-wide presence. But can I ask you a question?"

"Sure."

"In your opinion, what do you think the League actually *is*?"

A surprising question, one I'd never considered before. The League had always been a constant presence in my life, and everyone else's too. Part of the background. "I guess I'd have to say it's…well, it's humanity's galactic government, of course."

"Wrong."

"Really? But what about—"

"One hundred percent wrong."

She stared at me intently.

"How so?"

She smiled triumphantly, took a forkful of food, and washed it down with a large swig of wine. "The League is an *idea*."

I sat back in my chair. Mia's cheeks were slightly pink now and her eyes danced with sudden passion. She was an impressive person: dedicated, smart, and beautiful.

"What kind of idea?"

"The rule of law."

"Yes, of course, but also—"

"Nope, just the idea. Think about it. We have no army, no battleships. All the laws passed by galactic parliament have to be readopted in each planet and so often aren't anyway. The whole thing is a creaking, groaning, atrophying mess. Why do you think we have two *acting* vice commanders here on this base instead of one real boss?"

"No idea, I guess—"

"That's right, no idea. No one knows. There hasn't been a proper base commander appointed in fifty years, and that is far from unusual." Mia's eyes flamed. "God, it's such a relief to be able to *talk* to someone about this!" She looked around shiftily and dropped her voice. "I think it's to do with the new generation of young people coming through. They're *different.*"

"How?"

She looked around again. "For starters, they're all Movement. Well, not all, but most. Notice how conservative everything is here? Bars closing early, only cat piss to drink? Didn't used to be that way, we used to be able to let our hair down sometimes and have a bit of *fun*. These kids came in and demanded to change everything. Now you can't say or do anything, or they'll report you. We old-timers are actually scared shitless of them."

"Mia," I said gravely, "this is very serious."

"I know!"

"You're saying there's a kind of entropy taken hold within the League. In its management and staffing and decision making. A vacuum. And the Movement is exploiting that, filling the void."

"Look," she held up a hand, "don't get me wrong, we've always been a bit this way. Formal, highly PC. Fun fact, did you know the League is traditionally around seventy percent female?" She blushed a little at this, I noticed.

"Really? Why?"

"I suppose women are more altruistic. Like me." She laughed bitterly. "It's too easy to make fun of us. Politicians on every planet score points blaming us for stupid regulations, like stipulating the bendiness of bananas – which is crap, by the way, there never was any such rule, *just so you know*. But who's there to defend us? And what happens to humanity when there's no League anymore? What do you think?"

"Another Collapse?"

"Too right! And here's another question for you, why do you think they called it that?"

"The Collapse? Because everything fell apart, I guess."

"Yes and no. Many individual planetary systems managed perfectly well. But you know what really collapsed during that crisis?"

I thought for a moment. "The intergalactic rules-based order."

Mia clapped. "Give the man a cigar!" She waved to a waiter for more wine. "Without the League, that order breaks down. That's why this organization, riddled as it is with every flaw you could imagine, is still so precious. It's the only thing standing between us and the howling darkness. We *have* to try and save it!"

On Brouggh, people in my department were always complaining. About the League this, and the bloody League that. It was a handy scapegoat, and if anyone tried to defend it, they were ridiculed.

"Sounds like reform is needed though. And a weeding out of Movement people."

"Reform yes. But the League can be fixed, *must* be fixed."

"You're very passionate about all this. Which is admirable, especially since it seems you've been consigned to the boondocks out here. What happened to you?"

Mia sighed and pushed away her plate. The passion drained from her eyes.

"Let's just say there was a *thing*, I won't bore you with the details. I was told to stay away, to lay off – a number of times – so I certainly had my chances." She drained her glass. "But in the end, just couldn't keep my big mouth shut, could I?"

I felt for her. Somehow, I'd always been able to stay on the right side of office politics, probably by sticking with criminal cases, keeping away from anything political.

"So that's me, what about you? I suppose you'll be looking for passage somewhere?"

"Yes," I agreed, not wanting to disclose that our ship's drive was in the middle of being repaired. "I haven't really thought it through. I guess Sana and I will need to figure out a plan."

"Right, so you and Sana" – she looked down – "you're not actually together, though, is that right?"

There it was. My belly clenched.

"Ahhm, yes, correct, we're still married according to law, but it's complicated."

Mia's face tightened. I told her about Danee and the girls, details I'd left out from the debrief of the day before as they seemed irrelevant at the time. "...So it appears there's a reasonable chance they've survived somehow."

"I see, that's good…let's hope they're safe," Mia said, then blushed crimson.

An awkward and long silence fell between us while the restaurant continued its bustle. Random noises penetrated from the galleria outside: the hubbub of people walking and chatting, the occasional loud call. Mia stared at her lap as if searching for something there.

"I'm an *idiot,*" she said finally.

The trap was sprung, Sana had been right. This woman, who held the survival of our group in her very hands, was now mortally embarrassed and offended.

What to do?

I fantasized about being somewhere else, somewhere far away, like back on our ship lost in space. Placatory strategies came to mind.

Mia, you know I do actually think you're a very interesting and beautiful woman and, if circumstances were different, I could definitely see myself with you.

I'd probably get a glass of wine thrown in my face.

OK, then, what if I just apologized?

I'm very sorry, Mia, it appears there's been a misunderstanding.

That implied foolishness on her part, as well as desperation, and possibly both. What if I just acted dumb? A well-tried and always unsuccessful male strategy.

Sorry, I don't understand, is there something wrong?

She'd probably punch me in the face – *after* throwing wine at me.

My brain seized up; there was nothing to do, because there was no way out of this hell. I just sat there for a moment, aware of the breath passing in and out of my chest, waiting for God to strike me down.

Finally, Mia spoke. "It's OK, Col." She produced a wan smile. "I know you're a good guy. I guess I've been stuck here on this base for too long."

Relief flooded my brain and I almost blurted out some of the appeasing words that would have had me killed. "For what it's worth," I said after catching myself, "I think you're a very impressive person."

We each exhaled and took a large swig of wine.

My kom bleeped with a call from – who else, but Sana? I went to cancel but had second thoughts. It wasn't like her to call like this. Even if she were angry at me, she'd be more likely to withdraw than reach out. "Sorry, I should probably take this," I said to Mia, then answered, audio only.

"Sana?"

"Col, sorry to interrupt, are you still with her?" No trace of sarcasm. *"I'm just letting you know Sheng still isn't back. Shouldn't he be home by now? I've got a bad feeling, maybe Mia can check if something's happened?"*

I put the call on speaker and told Mia. She looked down at her kom, scrolling, screens flashing. Finally, she stopped and looked up at me. "Ooh, that's not good."

"What?"

"The security log. The boy Sheng is being held in protective custody."

From my kom, Sana exploded with rage.

"Why?" I asked in shock. "What's he done?"

"It says he shows signs of 'being in a dissociative state consistent with physical, emotional, or sexual abuse'."

Sana shouted from my kom, *"Of course he's in a state of shock! Wouldn't you be? He's nearly died, lost his mother, and seen his whole world blown up. It's actually amazing he's doing so well. Taking him away from us would be the worst thing they could possibly do!"*

Mia looked stricken. "I hear you, Sana. I promise I will do my best, but this is the League. There's going to be a long and complicated procedure to undo this. I'm very sorry."

This was terrible news. There would be psych evaluations, legal hearings, reams of paperwork, and endless delays. How long would it take, and what further damage would be done to the poor kid?

But that was only the first shock of the evening.

Mia shook her head. "It's not official yet, but they're going to put a travel stop on you guys, and there might even be charges laid, depending on what they decide about the boy."

A thousand thoughts and feelings rose: panic, rage, confusion. But before I could say anything, my kom pinged again, this time with a message from Batum.

"Col, I think we have company."

I paged him straight back, *"What kind of company?"*

"Those drones we left outside the base all just went offline simultaneously, destroyed without question. But one of them got partial data to me." I looked up at Mia, who was unaware of this silent exchange. A sick feeling rose in my stomach.

"What was in that data?"

"Col, a very large vessel has just appeared in the space outside the base. Ninety-eight percent probability it's Movement."

Chapter Fifteen

Mia's eyes were full of concern.

"Col, I can assure you, no harm will come to the boy, in fact the *opposite*. He'll have the best care available. Who knows, it might even do him some good? And if you like, we can start right now, start a process of formal adoption for you and Sana, and then..."

Mia's voice faded as my mind whirled into top gear. Silently, I messaged Batum.

"How do you know the ship is Movement?"

"Numerous energy weapons aboard, a signature from their AI, other stuff too. Trust me, it's the fucking Movement."

They'd traced us.

Was that Mia's doing?

I didn't think so. Unless she'd inadvertently given something away in her report? But no, it was more likely one of those young Movement students had spotted us and worked out who we were. One of those kids with the shiny eyes – oh and now I got it. That familiar gleam was the same as I'd first seen on Brouggh when attending a lecture by Gilham. The gleam of fanaticism.

They'd got a signal out somehow. Were probably the same people behind the drones too. That explained why they were so hokey; those kids must have made them here on base themselves, after getting orders to keep tabs on us.

Anyway, the how of it didn't matter anymore. What to do?

"Batum, do you know if they've finished repairing the jump drive? You said they were working on it."

"I don't know, Col. They've been here all day, but there's still equipment lying around everywhere."

Was a single day's work enough time to fix it?

Normally, yes. A matter of running diagnostics and then a repair program. But those rogues were charging as if it were going to take weeks. Maybe they planned to spin the time out to justify the price.

"Batum, can you check? Get to the cockpit and check the drive status?"

"On it, Col."

How long did we have before things went pear-shaped?

It was a radical move to send a big ship here. It would alert the League, and everyone else, as to what they were up to. It showed how much they wanted us, wanted Sana in particular.

"Sana," I texted her silently, *"are you dressed? We have to retrieve Sheng, then get the hell away from here."*

"Too right," she texted back. *"How dare they detain the poor boy? It's fucking ridiculous."*

"Worse than that, there's a giant Movement ship outside. They must know we're here on base."

Silence from the other end after that bombshell. I looked up at Mia and mounted the strongest case I could think of: "Look, I know you have your processes and all, but think about the *boy* for a moment. He's the innocent party, and we're the only people he has left!"

She shook her head. "I'm so sorry, Col, I agree with you. But this is out of my hands. The League has become very strict about these sorts of issues, particularly in the last few years."

Exactly what I expected her to say. Now for the real question. "Well then, can we at least visit him? Explain, promise we'll fight for him and all that? It's just so cruel to cut off all contact."

Mia looked at me sadly. "Col, you know personally I would love to do that, but it would be breaking so many..." Her voice trailed off and she glanced down at her kom, eyes widening. Big news coming in, I figured. About a giant, unscheduled Movement ship appearing out of nowhere. She jerked up out of her chair, looking flustered. "Col, I'm *really* sorry but something has just come up...rather suddenly – a work drama, so I have to go deal with it right away. It's been a pleasure, a real pleasure...*whoops*, silly me."

Mia had knocked the salt over. Now she picked the shaker up from the table, held it upside down for a moment so that even more fell out, leaned over and did something to the grains piled on the table.

"Good luck, Col." She looked at me meaningfully for a moment, then grabbed her handbag, whipped off her shoes – which I noticed were some kind of sparkly, strappy arrangement with high heels – and ran out of the restaurant in her bare feet.

I leaned over the table to look at the pile of salt. Tiny numbers had been drawn there:

-19 / 127

Bingo!

"Sana," I called, *"Level minus Nineteen, room 127. That's where Sheng is. I'll meet you there."*

Clever of Mia. If she'd sent the information to my kom or even told me verbally, it might have been monitored. This meant there were no doubts anymore; she was on our side.

"How do I get there?" Sana answered, exasperated. Probably in a state of panic.

"I'll come get you."

"Oh, no. It's OK…coming up on my kom now. I'll see you there. What are we going to do, *Col?"*

"Working on a plan," I said. Though to be honest, not even the feeblest idea of one had come to mind. Best I knew was we had to grab Sheng and then get the hell away.

I ran my hand across the table, wiping out the numbers, then dashed out of the restaurant, following directions on my kom. Through the galleria, into a side tunnel and down a lift to Level minus Nineteen. Less than a kilometer.

Was it dangerous to try and save Sheng? Perhaps it would be better, even for him, if we left the poor kid here, in the care of the League? Probably safer than tagging along with us and sharing our fate? I didn't dare ask Sana though; she'd spit fire at me for even *thinking* such a thing.

Ask him what he wants to do. He was a smart kid. I'd give him the choice once more, just as I did on Jubilee.

I walked briskly through the galleria, hopefully not so briskly as to attract attention. Which had happened already, I realized with dismay. A short, dark-haired girl with shiny eyes, dressed in the usual M4M cadet uniform of preppy blazer and pleated skirt, was following in a clumsy tail. She was talking to herself, reporting in on her kom.

Up ahead, a group of excited youths appeared from over the base's short horizon. "There he is!" someone cried, and they all started toward me. The tall blond kid, still wearing that same light blue sweater, was in the middle of the group, and seemed in charge. As they ran, others joined from every corner of the galleria – like some kind of pastel army. They must have gotten a signal from the newly arrived ship to round me up.

Shit. I turned and ran back the way I came, passing the young girl, who gaped blankly. They weren't all that scary, this lot. Unarmed, and only kids anyway, but dangerous in a big mob. I asked my kom for a new route to Sheng's room, which appeared instantly: back toward the tunnel that led to our room, then on to the other end of the galleria, through some service tunnels, and down a lift. Better.

I picked up the pace, turned to have another quick look behind me, then ran into something solid and meaty. A man. His arms were wrapped around my waist, trapping me from behind in a super tight bear hug. "There you are!" he crowed. "Thought you could just piss off without paying, eh?"

I craned my head around and looked up. It was one of the staff from Satchmo's. A big guy with huge arms thick as tree trunks, obviously spent time in the gym. He smelled of sweat and kitchen grease and his teeth were showing as he clenched with effort.

Fuck. The restaurant tab. Mia and I had both run out without thinking. Of all the times for vigilante justice.

"Please, mate!" I cried. "An emergency came up and my dinner guest and I just forgot."

I couldn't see from this angle, but I could hear the M4M student army getting closer, a buzz of excited young voices and clattering feet. Batum spoke through my kom. *"Col, the drive light is showing orange. Not green or red."*

Damn. 'Service mode' – of course. You had to have the drive awake in order to work on it, but you couldn't leave it in Active mode in case some moron pushed the wrong button and sent your ship and everything around it, straight into quantum space/time.

"*There should be a way to get it out of Service mode,*" I said aloud.

"What's that?" said my attacker. "League smart-asses, all the same, aren't you? *So* busy, *so* important, no time to just pay your bills like *normal* people. It's all us plebs who have to toe the line and—"

For some reason that was the final straw. I'm normally a very polite, law-abiding person, obviously, being a cop and all, though trust me there are plenty of bent ones, even in this day and age. I pay my bills, pay my taxes; the last thing I would want to do is run out of a restaurant without fixing up the tab. So, it wasn't *merely* that I was about to be mown down by an army of plaid zombies. This guy, with his boulder-sized chip on his shoulder had gotten under my skin.

There's a specific technique they taught us for ridding oneself of a bear hug. I deployed it now, bringing my hands over his, clasped around my stomach. I dropped my stance to lower my center of gravity. Then lightning fast, I brought my left hand in from the side under his grasp and ripped his hands apart while pulling down on the left arm. I bent over, flipped my backside, and up he went, somersaulting over my head like some bad-guy wrestler. He landed heavily on his back and the thud reverberated through the floor like a slab of meat dropped from on high. That guy would not be getting up in a hurry.

"No tip for you tonight," I said. Or *wish* I'd said. You always come up with these clever lines after the fact.

I took off, heading toward the near end of the galleria, the pursuing students only a hundred meters behind me. Batum chimed in again on my kom. *"Col, it's asking for a code. I've tried a few obvious ones, but now it's saying I've only got one attempt left, so I'm reluctant to keep going."*

Damn. Chook's buddies would have to unlock it.

Chook!

Shit, I'd forgotten all about him.

"Batum, can you rouse Chook on his kom?"

"Negative, Col, I tried already, it's on DND."

I'd reached the end of the galleria and skidded around a corner into a new tunnel. There was a branch here and the kom had me take a left turn. I was breathing hard now.

"Sana! Where are you?" I called on my kom.

"In a lift heading down to Level minus Nineteen, why?"

"Turn around, you have to go and wake up Chook. His kom's on do not disturb and we need him to get those guys from the dock to unlock the ship's drive. Got that?"

"Uh, I think so, what about—"

"I'll get Sheng on my own, you just go with Chook to the dock, OK?"

"OK."

I didn't mention the possibility that the drive might not be fixed or usable yet. That didn't bear thinking about.

I tore around a few more corners, telling my kom to send a virtual signal to my optic nerve. Normally I don't use this mode, but right now I didn't have the time to keep looking at a small hologram near my wrist. The sound of the chasing mob was getting closer. They were young and no doubt some of them took track. Sooner or later the fastest would catch up. I dodged left, then left again, running through a narrow service tunnel.

I arrived at speed into a round-shaped room, carved out of the bare rock. A dead end apart from stairs running up one side, just a small set, around six steps. A hatchway was set into the wall at the top, which I was supposed to go through. Such an obscure route! If the kom hadn't been guiding me, I would have been lost for sure.

I bolted up the steps and pushed through the hatch just as the first of the students arrived. The noise was deafening as they poured into the chamber behind me.

But too slow. I slammed the hatch shut behind me. Was there a lock? Yes! I snapped it over the latch just as the first thumps came from the other side. Now I was in a small maintenance tunnel, about a meter and a half high. Horrible height. I ran along in a crouch, moving as fast as I could.

How long would the hatch hold them back?

If no one had a laser knife on them, they'd have to send for it. Could take ten minutes before they cut through. That would have to do.

The tunnel joined with another larger one and my kom had me turn right. Looked like only a few more meters – and *voila*, there it was! A maintenance lift, and mercy of mercies, ready to go with the doors open wide. I was panting heavily, covered with sweat. I selected Level minus Nineteen and waited for what seemed like an hour for the doors to close, all the while fully exposed to the corridor. Faint running noises were coming now from the corridor; it sounded like they'd gotten through the hatch. Fast little buggers.

Finally, reluctantly, the lift doors ground closed with a wheeze and a loud clunk, and I started to descend.

I paged Sana, *"Are you with him yet?"*

"Fucking hell!" chimed in Chook. *"What's going on, Col?"*

I gave him a quick rundown, ending with my current position.

"It's all their doing then, those little yuppie bastards here on base."

"Correct. Where are you now?"

"Me and Sana are heading to the dock. I'm tryin' to raise Shimmy but she's not pickin' up."

"Your contact?"

"Yeah, there's others too, I'll sort it out. If that drive's fixed, we'll be on our way, don't you worry."

The lift pinged.

"Gotta go, meet you at the dock."

The doors opened to a bright white corridor with a pervasive, instantly recognizable smell: antiseptic. Had to be the base's medical wing.

How long did I have?

Those kids would see where the lift stopped then head down to this floor. Damn, I was talking, distracted. I should have first hit the buttons for a couple of higher levels to muddy the waters. I pushed all the elevator buttons, down to minus Fifty-seven, the lowest floor, then all the way back up to Level Ten where I'd come from. Judging by the speed of the lift and especially those slow doors, this should hold them up for at least ten minutes. *Hang on*, I hadn't seen a stairwell, but there'd have to be one somewhere. It would take a few minutes to find and then a few more to descend the twenty-nine floors, but less time than waiting on this lift.

I told my kom to run a countdown for five minutes and it appeared instantly in the bottom left corner of my vision. If I hadn't found Sheng within this time, a hard decision would need to be made.

The kom had me turn right and run along a broad corridor. No one around that I could see. On either side windows looked into spotless, empty wards. This base, for whatever reason, seemed to have an oversized medical wing.

I came to an intersection, turned right, then right again at a smaller branch corridor. The whole time I'd not seen any medical staff, let alone a patient. I came to a door labeled *Pediatrics*. Pushed it open to find yet another spotless and totally empty ward. At the far end was another large white door with a sign, *Room 127. Counselor.*

The witch's office.

What was she doing anyway, keeping Sheng down here in this empty hospital? It had only been one minute, and the place was creeping me out already. I readied myself, preparing for a confrontation – one that could possibly end with the use of force – and pushed the office door open.

To find an empty office. Recently occupied though, judging by the still-warm cup of tea sitting on the desk. A holo-screen was open with Sheng's file, which I didn't even bother reading. Where was he?

There was a door to the left labeled, *Observation*. I dashed to it and peered through a built-in window to see a small apartment on the other side. Containing Sheng. He was sitting on a couch clutching his backpack for security no doubt, the one and only object in this world that was indisputably his, watching a show on a large holo-screen. I tried the door; it was solidly built and firmly locked.

This was a problem. I'd been expecting to find Counselor Crang down here and then either talk her into – or force her into – letting Sheng go. But without her there seemed no obvious way to open this door. There was a keypad on the left, but it looked ancient and disused. The release mechanism would probably run off her kom. I dropped to my knees – no crack under the door to pass a note, and no gap on the sides either. This seemed like a military-grade security door.

Countdown: 3:15.

I tried waving to Sheng, but he seemed oblivious. One-way glass for sure. I tried bashing the door and yelling, then noticed there were tiny buds in the boy's ears.

Truly bizarre, I thought. To place a child in such a secure detention facility – then I saw it. This whole place had been retrofitted; perhaps it was once a forward operating base or field hospital during the Sirrelian Insurrection. That's why the huge medical center relative to the population, why the curious mix of old tech overlaid with modern. This room would have been an isolation ward to hold sick or wounded soldiers. Naturally there was no need to have a facility like this anymore, so therefore it was dangerous. Because inevitably, if you had a thing, you always found a reason to use it.

I tried bashing the window with my fist, which made no impression at all, though it did hurt my hand. In growing frustration, I looked around the room for something heavy. There were a set of shelves to my right, holding books and curios, and fuck me, a framed portrait of Gilham. *There you go.* Also pictures of a younger Ms. Crang in what looked like better days – posing with smiling children, shaking hands with dignitaries – and a couple of metallic sculptures. Awards! How nice for our friendly counselor: *Best-Kidnapper-of-the-Year.* It seemed like there might have been a career stall somewhere along the line. Once a person of note, now stuck here in this empty ward with nothing to do all day and no chance of promotion. Till suddenly opportunity knocks in the form of an undocumented kid from outer space.

I picked up the largest of the statuettes. It was pyramid-shaped and satisfyingly heavy, inscribed with, *Masto Erlich Foundation Prize for Services to Child Protection.* I was about to put this thing to its perfect use. I strode to the observation window, lifted it over my head and bashed down at the window with all the force I could muster.

It bounced straight back off the safetiplaz at enormous speed, leaving not the smallest dent in the surface, but smacking me plumb in the forehead and knocking me off my feet. A constellation of stars burst inside my head, and everything started spinning. There'd be a pyramidical-award-shaped gash in my head now.

But Sheng must have heard something. He was looking around, one of the earbuds removed. I tried waving again, stupid. He definitely couldn't see me.

Then I remembered something, a song. Very silly and very old. So old that no one had any idea what the words meant any more, but parents still sang to their kids anyway because it was cute. Sana and Sheng would cuddle up giggling in his room, and sing it together ironically as if he were still a baby:

What will we do with a drunken sailor?
What will we do with a drunken sailor?
What will we do with a drunken sailor?
Early in the morning!

I picked up the statue and tapped out the rhythm on the safetiplaz window. Sheng sat still for a moment listening, then ran to the window, his eyes clouded with tears. Which dried instantly as whatever mechanism that kept him sane these last months took back over. His mouth was moving; he was shouting, but only faint muffled sounds were coming through the door.

Countdown: 2:45.

What to do? What would I even say to the boy if I were able to?

If only I had a weapon, though in truth, even a blaster would struggle to get through this hardened door.

Sheng waved, then went back to his backpack and began frantically pulling objects out of it. He ran to the door with his child's computer. Was he going to use the screen to talk with me? No. He pulled a lead from his pocket and connected it to something right next to the window outside my field of vision. Something associated with the locking mechanism, I assumed. He spun the computer around so I could see; symbols swirling down the holo-screen.

Clever boy! He was a self-trained coder, must be running software to break the encryption on the door lock. But how long would it take? I heard some of those programs could take hours, or days, or even months to find the solution.

Countdown: 1:15.

"Batum," I called, *"do you have me?"*

"Yes, I've been following your progress."

"Can you open this door in Room 127?" It didn't seem likely, but worth asking.

"I've been trying. I was able to call that lift for you earlier, but I can't get into the security door."

"Can you disable the lift?"

"Negative."

"Do you know how far off the mob is?"

"Negative, sorry, I'm only following on your kom, I can't see—"

Fuck!

I looked around frantically. There had to be something I could use, but nothing came to me. Sheng was standing right there, mere inches away on the other side of the glass holding his child's computer. There was a cheeky smile playing on his face. He was enjoying this, enjoying the thrill without knowing what the stakes were. But my time was almost up. If only he were old enough to have a kom, I could have just told him what was going on.

There was a beep. Countdown: 0:00.

I went back the way I came, through the empty pediatric ward. Opened the door to the main corridor and stopped, listening. Everything silent. How long? Then a noise, a shout. Running feet.

Fuck, fuck, fuck.

What now? Only one thing to do, one thing that might possibly help.

I ran back to the counselor's office, starting to feel a bit dizzy now, noticing there were bright red spots on the floor. Blood. My blood, from the gash in my forehead. The red spots ran across the shiny white floor in a line, a trail those fucking kids would use to follow me.

In the office I found some tissues. I put a wad to my head then took it away – soaked with blood. I saw it was on my clothes and hands, everywhere. I found a pen and paper, wrote a quick note:

Sheng we're on the run if you get out meet me at the dock – Col

Where to leave it? The logical place was just outside the door. If he managed to break the lock, it would be the first thing he'd see. I placed the note on the floor, sadly waved goodbye – *stupid!* He couldn't see that, I must be concussed – then dashed out of the room.

Chapter Sixteen

It was a close thing.

I got out of the pediatric ward and into the main corridor just before the advance party arrived; otherwise I would have been trapped in the counselor's office. I managed to turn a corner into a smaller branch tunnel just in time. Heard their feet pounding the floor, breath ragged from running down twenty-nine floors. They'd be tired by that. A small advantage. I moved as quickly and quietly as I could on legs ever more rubbery. Held the wad of tissues to my head to try and stop blood falling to the floor, but every so often droplets spilled anyway. Nothing to do about it.

I asked my kom for directions to the dock. The arrow wanted me to turn around and go back the way I'd come, through the advancing mass of kids. That probably meant this was a dead end. No exits or elevators from this section of the hospital. I asked for an alternate route, but nothing came up. I took a left then a right. Found myself back in the main corridor again, or was it just another branch? Getting hard to remember.

The mob would follow those blood spots on the floor and end up in the counselor's room. They'd be able to see Sheng through the window, then…what? It wasn't like they could do anything to him; they wouldn't even be able to get inside there. Worst-case scenario, they'd find my note on the floor and leave someone posted there. Hopefully they'd all just bugger off in a big chaotic mess – but no, it was much more exciting to chase good old me.

Old being the operative word. Felt like that, anyway. Staggering now. That really was a nasty clock on the noggin.

The *old* noggin.

Who said *noggin* anyway? Wasn't it seafarers on Old Earth? As they sang sea shanties and drank rum. Or pirates with their pointy hats? My brother Tim, my lost brother – his favorite was those pirate shows on the kids' holo-channel. We watched them together, made our very own pirate ship out of a broken-down cart in the backyard. The captain, he had a hook for a hand, right? And a parrot on his shoulder. *"Argh, me hearties,"* he'd say. *"Argh, me hearties!"* I started laughing.

"Col, are you OK?"

"HEY, Batum! Do you know any sea shanties? Can you look one up for me?"

"Col, you're talking out loud, you need to be quiet."

Very tired. Legs for some reason not working properly. Maybe it would be easier if I just got down on my hands and knees? That was better, a bit slower than before, but definitely better. There was a reason from long, long ago. A reason why it was important to go fast, faster than this anyway, but what was that reason again? So tired! Maybe a song would help?

"Batum, how was it, how did that sea shanty go?"

I was crawling ever more slowly, one hand at a time, the corners of my vision misting gray, gradually closing in. One hand forward, then a knee, then the other hand. One after another.

"Col, you're suffering from some kind of cognitive impairment, you should—"

"I got it, Batum! … Listen!"

There was a corner up ahead. I turned into it, moving with agonizing slowness. *"…what shall we do with a drunken sailor…what shall we do with a drunken sailor, what shall we do with a…funken…crunken, drunken sailor…* early *in the morning!"*

A door appeared next to me. I raised one arm over my head and with supreme effort flipped the handle, then fell through the opening. My legs were stuck though, dangling out into the corridor.

"It's OK, Batum, every good boy deserves fruit." I cackled, though the laughing made my head explode with pain. *"Remember that? Piano lessons."*

The sprung door had shut itself on my legs, jamming them. I crawled forward, inch by inch. Kicked out and rolled to the left. Heard the door snib close behind me but didn't have the energy to turn around and check.

"Col," said Batum in a whisper, *"I am talking to the others, you appear to be suffering from a neurological event and you need to…"* His voice faded.

Sounds. Shouting in the corridor outside. That meant something, didn't it?

Everything was spinning, faster and faster. Maybe here was a good place for a nap? Because of all these soft things – I put my hand out. Sheets. A pile of them, and other things too that *weren't* soft. But that was OK. I'd just lie here on these soft things, in my little nest and go nighty night. Like a drunken sailor.

Everything went black.

Dear reader, this is where my memory of these events hits something of a dead end, but no matter, the kom caught everything. What follows is a transcript, which I've simplified because rather a lot was going on!

Audio transcript: May 25, 55,748: 19.18

< Door creaks open.

< Hubbub of voices.

< "Quiet!" [male voice].

< "Is he dead?" [male, different voice].

< More hubbub.

< "Shut up everyone!" [same voice as the first].

< "Shut up yourself, Bartholomew, who put *you* in charge?" [female voice].

< Shouting, door opening and closing multiple times.

< "I'm not saying I'm in charge!" [Bartholomew's voice]. "All I'm saying is they want us to bring him to the dock and put him on the *Scorpio*." [presumed name of Movement ship].

< More shouting and noise. [pretty disorganized this lot, but then again, what do you expect with kids?].

< "He's not going to be much use *dead*." [female voice].

< "Can someone check? Who's doing med?" [ninety percent sure Bartholomew, who I also believe was the tall guy in the pastel-blue sweater].

< Voices talking over one another.

< "*Eeeew*, he's *covered* in blood!" [female voice]. "I'm not *touching* him."

< "What sort of doctor are you going to make if you're afraid of blood?" [male voice].

< "I'm not *afraid*, [female voice], it's just *gross*. We haven't done prac yet, and frankly I'm not looking forward to it. *Anyway*, I can see a pulse in his neck, so therefore he's not dead. Satisfied?"

< "Brilliant diagnosis, *Doctor*." [male voice].

< Indistinct chatter.

< "I suggest we wrap him in one of these sheets and carry him. If anyone's feeling squeamish, put on surgical gloves." [Bartholomew].

< "Where do you get those?" [male voice, new].

< "We're in the middle of a fucking hospital, *Einstein*." [female voice, the 'doctor'].

< "*Language!* Remember, the Master says bad use of—" [Bartholomew].

< "*Shut up*, Bartholomew, try not to be a pain in the ass, just for once." [the 'doctor'].

< Multiple voices. Door opening and closing. Objects scraping.

< "Yuk, there's blood all over *everything*." [female voice].

< "OK, ready. Lift him. One, two, three." [Bartholomew].

< Indistinct chatter.

< Muffled groan, then out-of-tune singing... *"heave ho...and up she rises."* [me].

< Door opens, multiple footsteps, excited voices talking all at once, elevator pings.

< "Please, just those carrying him, the rest of you go in the next lift."

< Elevator doors closing, indistinct voices talking loudly in confined space.

< "...completely ruined now, and I only bought it three days ago..." [Bartholomew – hopefully referring to the pastel-blue jumper].

< Elevator door opens, footsteps.

< "Oof, this guy is heavy."
< "Just around the next corner now."
< More footsteps, panting sounds.
< "What's that?" [male voice].
< "Oh my god!"
< Electric buzzing noises, shrieking, panicked voices, running feet.
< Something large and heavy falling to floor. [me].
< Silence.
< "I *think* that's the lot." [Chook].
< "Oh my *God*, look at him! Is he—" [Sana].
< "No, but we have to move fast." [female voice].

End of audio transcript

"And finally…a spray of this stuff…"

Something cold on my forehead. Very cold actually, but in a good way.

I opened my eyes to see a helmeted head with visor flipped open peering at me just inches away. A woman's face with a concerned expression, beautiful green eyes gazing into mine. Colonel Mia.

I sat up. "Where am I? What happ— "

"*Whoa!*" cried Mia. "Take it easy. I just filled you with a cocktail of drugs that would be illegal in most parts of the civilized galaxy."

I reached for my head, but she stopped me.

"And don't touch, that's instant skin, just applied. Should hold for a little while, but you've taken a serious blow to the head. *Very serious*. You might feel relatively normal for the moment, but that's not going to last. You need an ICU ASAP."

Mia wore a metallic gold jumpsuit with no visible seams or joins. Even the helmet seemed all a part of it. We were in the very center of the dock, a dark, cavernous space with multiple boarding tubes staged at regular intervals every hundred meters or so. Only one of them led to an actual ship at berth, our own. We had passed through this space on our way to the reception area when we first landed. The students must have had instructions to bring me here so I could be loaded onto the Movement ship when it docked. Their bodies were piled everywhere, hands held before them as if to protect themselves, faces frozen in shock.

"You *killed* all these kids?"

"Nah," said Chook. "Unfortunately." He held up the laser rifle still in his hands. "Set to stun, but they'll wake up with a nasty headache at least." He was standing next to Sana, who was similarly armed.

"There's more coming," said Mia. "So, we have to move it."

"Move it where?"

"The drive's been fixed, at least that's what they reckon," said Chook. "Though no one can find Shimmy, so they're not one hundred percent sure, but they all *think* so."

"And that Movement ship," said the colonel, "we're holding it up with paperwork and they're still playing nice for the moment. But my sense is, any minute they're going to snap and decide to force their way in."

I stood up gingerly, reminding myself not to touch the wound on my forehead. I'd seen it before on Brouggh of course and was always amazed by how much a person could bleed and still survive. But it was a shock applied to oneself. My arms and hands, shirt and pants were soaked, shoes squelchy with it. But I felt strangely energized and the lights were fluorescently vivid, leaving a trailing afterimage in my vision. Serious drugs on board.

"What's the plan?" I asked.

Chook coughed. "Arrghm, well, first we need to sort the dockies out. They won't give us that code till they get some...*you know*...scratch." He rubbed his thumb and two fingers together.

"Sorry, Col," said Sana, "we had to wait for you coz none of us has that kind of dough."

I looked sideways at Mia. I hadn't wanted to let her in on the fact we'd been illicitly repairing the drive. She must have read my thoughts, because she shook her head and rolled her eyes. "Col, you think we're *idiots*? Think you could do that under our noses and we wouldn't figure it out?"

I shrugged. "What was it, ninety-five thousand?"

"Gone up to one hundred and thirty K," said Chook, bearing a pained, and one had to say, overly sincere expression. "Difficulties with the quantum spatial—"

"*Spare* me, please," I said, and transferred the credits to him instantly from my kom. I figured at least a portion of that was going toward a Chook drinking fund, but what did I care? It wasn't my money anyway. Though bad form to not push back at least a little.

"Tell them I want a receipt."

Chook's eyes widened and he went to object, but I waved him away… *just kidding*. "How do we do this?" I asked no one in particular. The moment our drive went active its quantum signature would be instantly detected by the Movement ship, and at that point any residual niceness on their part would be dispensed with instantly.

"I'll jump in here," said Batum, *"and good to see you back with us, Col. My thinking is to do a surprise maneuver. Feed the release code into the drive and have everything ready. The instant it goes active, I put the ship into Stealth, disengage the boarding tube and zip away before they figure out what happened."*

"Yes, but they're scanning everything, you guys will never be able to get on that ship," said Mia. "The moment they detect you passing through the boarding tube it's game over."

"Correct," said Batum. *"Therefore, you will board from another airlock somewhere else on the base. Once I get out of here, I'll meet you there, then we bounce straight into hyperspace."*

"But guys," said Mia. "Sorry, that's just not possible. There's only this one dock on base."

I looked at Chook for a moment and raised an eyebrow. He nodded back with instant understanding. "We know of at least one other airlock. Sorry, Sana, but looks like it's going to be another bout of space shock for us, though not as bad as the last time."

She shrugged. "I'll be fine. I guess we're talking about the old airlock that the drone used to make its escape? There's a lot of Movement kiddies between here and there." And at least nineteen levels, two elevator rides and a couple of kilometers through the galleria (or service tunnels if the kom could find a way).

"True," I said. "And we also have to grab Sheng along the way."

Sana stepped toward me and took my hand. "Col, I've been talking with Mia, and I think she's right, it's just too dangerous. It's not fair on the kid to take him with us."

An image of Sheng rose up; on the other side of the security door, grinning cheekily while he worked on his computer. Anger flared. "Sana, that bitch locked him away in an *isolation ward*."

"Just temporarily," chimed in Mia. "All the senior staff got a red alert when the Movement ship appeared, and she had to leave in a hurry. But she cleared it with me first, and we both agreed it was best, considering there might be trouble."

"She's got a picture of Gilham in her office!"

Mia shook her head. "She's not like that. A bit *modish*, maybe. The Movement's flavor of the month right now so she's listening to Gilham's talks and all that – but she's not a fanatic like those kids. I *know* her. The boy will be safe, and if you guys...I dunno...*sort things out* somehow, you can always apply for custody at some point in the future."

"Sort things out somehow..." In other words, Mia figured our odds of survival at approximately zero percent. "But he'll be in the *system*, Sana, you know what that means!"

From my police years, I knew the vast majority of criminals we dealt with started out in foster care. They moved through the system, wound up on the streets, then in jail, then back on the streets again. A depressing loop that always started in the one place. I was surprised by my reaction – and also by Sana's. I thought it would be her who'd be the most passionate to bring the boy with us.

"Col, the system is there for a reason," she replied. "It's not perfect, far from it, but sometimes it's—"

"I *promise* I'll keep an eye out," implored Mia.

This was a battle I couldn't win. Not without Sana on board. Besides, it would be no small job to break him out and our fate was far from certain. Maybe a life in the 'system' was better than no life at all.

Something exploded behind me. I whirled around to see sparks and debris falling from the roof – blaster fire. Coming from the far end of the dock, where it met the bedrock wall of the base. Joined by more from the opposite side. It looked like reinforcements had arrived, this time armed with energy weapons. Where the hell did they get those? It was insanely dangerous to fire so close to these landing tubes; one stray shot could depressurize this whole zone.

More violet beams sizzled across the dock, but poorly aimed, striking the floor and roof, bringing down a large piece of the ceiling. Not only were they about to fry *us*, but the student army in their ill-conceived pincer were also firing directly at each other from opposite sides of the dock. I heard a scream to our left, a hit on one of their own for sure.

Chook burst into action, rolling to his right, hoisting his gun. Sana and I dived to the floor and crawled behind a column while Mia flipped down her visor, flicked off the safety catch on her laser rifle and then… *disappeared.*

Well, not completely. Where she stood there was now a patch of blurry air and a subtle distortion to the background behind it. A portable cloaking device I'd never seen before. Fire poured from the blurry patch as it moved away to our left, toward the far side of the dock.

"Blasters on stun, right guys?" came Mia's message on my kom.

"Fuck that, they're firing lethal rounds!" responded Chook.

"Right then, stand down. I just deactivated your weapons."

Chook dropped to his knees and slid behind another column twenty meters from ours. He frantically worked his rifle, snapping it open and closed, playing with the trigger, then threw it at the column in disgust. He pulled out the smaller blaster he'd brought from the ship, pointed, tried to fire – and it too failed to respond. Mia had a way of deactivating energy weapons remotely. Now *that* was novel; even Douglas would be interested.

To my right I saw another blur in the air, similar to Mia's. Firing, and moving away in the opposite direction. That meant someone else had been standing with us the whole time and we hadn't noticed. This person wanted to remain invisible, had deliberately left their cloaking up.

Startled cries emanated from each end of the dock, energy weapons suddenly not working anymore. How sad for the poor dears. Mia and the other cloaked figure were firing continuously, the shots coming out of mid-air.

And then it was over. Thumps, running feet, bodies falling and muffled screams as the students were mown down en masse – but by blasters set only to stun. Finally, silence. Just the ticking sound of something metallic cooling and Sana's rapid breath beside me. I listened carefully for any hiss of escaping air, but it seemed like we were in luck, though the dock around us was filled with smoke and dust, half the ceiling collapsed; it's astounding how destructive energy weapons can be.

Then, the sound of feet crunching through the debris as the two patches of blurred air made their way back to us from each side of the dock. A slight 'pop', and suddenly there were two people in gold jumpsuits standing before us: Mia, and a man…*who I knew*. A diminutive figure, who flipped the lid of his helmet to reveal a wizened and lined face, grinning triumphantly. My least favorite acting co-vice commander, Len Clemsworth.

"Surprise!" he chirped.

"Len?" I asked in a daze.

"The very one."

Sana stammered, "B-but I thought you were against…"

"Yes, yes. *All* for show. Good work, Colonel, how long do we have?"

Mia lifted her helmet. It seemed to come apart from her suit without any visible form of release. She shook out her hair with a smile. They both seemed to have enjoyed the proceedings. "Five minutes tops, sir. I got 'em all, but who knows? Would only take a moment to get a message away."

"You guys OK?" sent Batum. *"The activation code is entered, waiting on your say."*

Chook joined us, dusting himself down, looking in wonder at the two suited figures. "Who the fuck are you?"

"Three guesses," replied Len. He seemed confident and authoritative now, comfortable in his own skin. A far cry from the nervous, bullied little man I'd met, was it only a few hours ago?

"LSS?"

"Guilty as charged," replied Mia brightly.

"B-but…" I stuttered, "you told me the LSS doesn't exist, it's only a fantasy that—"

"Just a cover story, Col, my boy," chuckled Len.

"Though we're nowhere near as powerful or omniscient as the holo-dramas would have you believe," said Mia.

"Then why didn't you take any action when we…"

"Listen, we know *all about* what happened to Jubilee," said Len firmly, "and all about the Movement and what they're up to. In fact, we were keeping close tabs on your little jaunt to Rethne three years ago. I was just reading up about it. Got some very good intel out of that."

My head was spinning now, and not just from the concussion. "So why the ruse about Jubilee being out of your jurisdiction, why not—"

"Because…*fucking politics*!" Len spat on the floor. "We have to sit here biding our time on this ball of rock, watching while those little shits take over. It was very satisfying to blast a few, let me say. Even if we couldn't use live rounds."

"Command says they're still in 'evaluation mode' about the Movement threat," said Mia, "and anyone who rocks the boat about it ends up in a place like this. Good that me and Len see eye to eye!" She smiled fondly at him.

"Hate to break up the party," said Sana, "but don't we have to get moving?"

"Col, I'm getting signs that the Movement ship is preparing to dock," sent Batum. *"Do I activate or not?"*

"They're coming in," I said to Len and Mia, who would not have heard Batum's message. "We better get moving."

"Apparently, there's an old airlock up in Sector Seven that's still working," Mia told Len. "They're going to use that to board their ship."

"Well, well," he replied, "something I didn't know!"

"That ship is definitely on the move," sent Batum. *"And I've scanned armed units forming up. They must have received intel about what happened."*

"OK, we're leaving for the airlock now," I sent back.

"I figure it's best to play possum here while they dock. My energy

signature is damped so they won't think anyone is aboard. I'll zip away once you're ready."

"But if they make a move to board you—"

"It's game on. Of course."

"All right," I said, "let's get out of here." I called up the route on my kom. The arrow led to our right, past a pile of sleeping students to the lift nearby.

"I'll come with," said Mia.

"And I'll prepare a little surprise for our uninvited guests," said Len.

Mia raised an eyebrow. "Such as…"

"In about two minutes the gravity is going to go off, so be prepared. Don't know how we're going to explain that one, but I'll come up with something. Maintenance? Tech fault? Some fuckin' thing. Good luck, everyone!" He waved, turned his suit on, and disappeared back into a blurry shape.

Novel idea, turning off the gravity engine. Without it, the base would revert to its natural gravitational pull, which, given its diameter of only twenty kilometers, would be so slight as to be unnoticeable. We jogged together, dodging piles of fallen rubbish and insulation. The sleeping students were caked in dust. They'd wake up sore and dirty. Not a good day for them, the poor little darlings. I couldn't help noticing the security cameras dotted around everywhere, mounted on almost every pillar. "Mia, how come you and Len showed your faces to us? Isn't that a bit risky with all these cameras around?"

"Nah." She shrugged. "Chook's buddies had them all turned off, remember?"

Of course. Still. It was meaningful that they revealed themselves to us. It would have been something they considered and planned. They *wanted* us to know. As we reached the elevator, Chook put a hand on my shoulder and I spun around in alarm.

"Col, sorry, I have to do *one* thing, OK?"

"What?"

"Just a sec!"

He turned and ran back toward the dock, stopping before the closest pile of sleeping bodies. One of them I noted, was Mr. Blue Sweater. Chook jogged up to him and stopped for a moment, looking down in cold fury. I had a bad feeling. Whatever crimes had been committed by the Movement, it wasn't right to take it all out on these kids. I watched carefully for Chook's grip on his gun to change, ready to swing into action if he were about to commit an atrocity.

"Chook, come back, we gotta go."

He raised an arm as if to say, *understood*, stood silently for a moment, and then brought his foot back and delivered a savage kick into the side of blue-sweater guy.

"*That*," he declared, "is for the *mid-strength beer*!"

The elevator doors opened, and we hustled inside, Chook joined us at the last moment with a look of triumph. Certain people, I thought, really don't like it when you mess around with beer.

The lift was dead silent as we ascended the ten floors, until Mia finally spoke. "Sana, have you ever been in zero-G?" Sana shook her head. "The trick is to pick a spot you're aiming for, then launch directly at it from something solid – remember Newton's third law. We need to get to the highest level of the galleria, so the moment the power goes off, aim for the balcony and grab hold of the balustrade. Got that?"

Sana nodded.

"It's going to be mayhem, so stick close to me. You guys going to be all right?" Meaning, had we been trained for zero-G? In my case, yes. Had to assume the same from Chook's unknowable past. We both gave a thumbs-up. "Stow the blasters. You won't need them, and they'll just be in the way."

The elevator pinged, Mia replaced her helmet, then turned back into a fuzzy blur as the doors opened to the galleria.

But a different galleria than a few short hours earlier. The place seethed with hundreds of young people milling around the closed stores and cafés and all talking at once. They silenced instantly when the elevator doors opened and someone yelled, "*There they are!*" The mob screamed in excitement and surged toward us as if a group of pop stars had arrived.

Then in the next instant, *chaos*.

A blur of suddenly floating bodies, scrambling and flailing in mid-air, slowly rising off the floor, which in the rearranged perspective of zero-G, now looked like just another flat surface.

Sana, ever the quick adaptor, must have been ready in a crouch because I saw her gaze up toward the roof of the galleria, mentally gauging, then launch herself. She zoomed away, poised and graceful, body aimed perfectly toward the top of the giant space. It was hard to tell in all the mayhem, but it looked like there was a familiar fuzzy blur beside her as she flew.

No such luck for myself. I must have been standing tall on the balls of my feet when the gravity went off, so trying to push down only sent me in a slow backward somersault. I flung my arms around desperately, trying to find something solid to push against, but meeting only air. Out of the mass of bodies thrashing nearby, a hand emerged to grab my ankle. One of the young men, his face a grimace, tried to draw me in. We tangled together in mid-air. I tried to kick him off, but the action sent me sideways and slowly upward into a knot of bodies seemingly made of nothing but arms and hands – all reaching out for me. There were grunts and screams. Crashing sounds as people hurtled off each other, knocking into walls and furniture, and pulling over one of the potted plants.

I found myself inside a ball of bodies, all clawing at me as we gradually floated up together. A foot clad in a heavy military-style boot emerged from somewhere and kicked me square in the face, sending my vision spinning, jolting me farther backward into the melee, where someone else with long nails raked my face, opening up the wound in my forehead. Blood poured out in bright red bubbles, scattering in every direction as I was yanked this way and that. I began to feel weak again, the blurriness returning to my vision.

Then bright flashes of purple from above. Slamming into the bodies around me, turning them slack. There were startled shrieks as the fire poured down and the hands pulling at me lost their grip. Just below was the big guy, the one who'd first attacked me. His eyes were shut, body spinning loosely. I kicked him hard, and he flew 'down' away from me toward the floor – activating Newton's third law of 'equal and opposite force' to send me 'upward'.

Something snagged around my shoulder, wrapping tightly then tugging me in the direction of the galleria's roof forcefully enough to start my body moving rapidly through the air. I looked around bemused, floating serenely through the large space. It's surprising really, how big an area like this actually was when you had access to all of it. Seemed silly to use just the floor when there was all this empty space.

The occasional hand reached for me as I sailed upward, the person attached to it instantly shot by another purple bolt from above. Then moments later I was at the top of the galleria, being hauled in like a big fish on a line that ended somewhere inside a blurry patch of air. Sana and Chook floated nearby, each holding the railing to stabilize themselves. How embarrassing; I was the only one of us with proper zero-G training and it was me that had to be saved.

"Sorry," I said weakly, as I drifted toward them. The galleria floor was far below, and the odd student flailed in the air nearby, unable to get purchase on anything and thus unable to reach us.

"Fucking hell, he's all opened up again," said Mia's voice from thin air. I felt another spritz of the cool spray, and a prickle at the back of my neck. "That will keep him going for a few more minutes, but he needs a hospital bed, and fast."

I tried to wave the voice off, laughing. "Everybody's just overexcited. Hey, look, I'm bleeding again!"

Sana cursed, then said, "C'mon, let's move it."

"Col, our friends just arrived," called Batum from the ship, *"though no boarding tube has been sent yet to meet them. Looks like they're getting something ready to – yes, confirmed – they're sending in troops now by shuttle."*

"Hang tight," sent Chook. *"We're only minutes away from the airlock, but Col's been clobbered again, so better have that ICU warmed up."*

"On it."

Chook and Sana started pulling themselves along the top of the balcony. My fishline went tight and I found myself being towed by an invisible force – all quite relaxing, really. As long as one didn't look directly down; the drop to the bottom of the galleria was dizzying from up here. I would hate to be one of those students floating around nearby when the gravity came back on.

As if on cue, a siren sounded and a highly distorted and (if one were being unkind) somewhat supercilious voice filled the air. "ATTENTION ALL RESIDENTS AND STAFF." Bronx cheers rose from the galleria below.

"Hey, that's Len!" I shouted merrily to the patch of air towing me.

"Shh!" came the immediate response. "For fuck's sake!"

"AS YOU ARE NO DOUBT AWARE, A FAILURE HAS OCCURRED IN THE BASE'S GRAVITY SYSTEM." More cheers from below. "THIS FAILURE WAS DUE TO A SOFTWARE BUG AND WILL BE RECTIFIED SHORTLY. FOR YOUR SAFETY, GRAVITY WILL BE RESTORED IN STAGES TO REDUCE CHANCE OF INJURY. RESIDENTS AND STAFF ARE URGED TO POSITION THEMSELVES CLOSE TO A NEARBY FLOOR SURFACE AND WAIT FOR INSTRUCTIONS."

"No, Len, *no*," said Mia crossly, "a few more minutes *please*."

We floated across the top of the galleria just above the balustrade, coming soon upon the same tunnel Chook and I chased the drone into. We turned in and I floated behind the others, reaching out occasionally to touch the bare rock inches from my face.

"*Fuck. Shit*," said Chook from up ahead. "Think we missed the turnoff. The tunnels all look the same here."

"It'll be on your kom," I called back. Or tried to, but the words came out mangled. "*Eeeoh be oh yoo ko*." That was weird. I knew what I wanted to say but couldn't get my mouth to form the words properly. Something bad was going on inside my head, gradually getting more severe. Maybe concussion, maybe worse than that – which might all be very terrible, but for some reason it didn't feel that way. Everything was becoming rosy and warm. Nothing much mattered.

I held up my wrist for Chook. Told my kom to show our travel route from the day before – at least my brain was working well enough to do that. A hologram of the nearby tunnel system rose up with a mini yellow arrow pointing the way. Mia figured it out immediately.

"Guys, Col's got it up on his kom."

Sana and Chook floated back to look, Sana gazing up at me concernedly. "He's starting to really worry me now."

I tried to say "I'm fine!" but all that came out was a garbled "oo aaa" sound.

"Got it!" cried Chook. "This way!" He grabbed a piece of protruding rock from the wall and doubled back. "Was the last side tunnel. Just missed it."

At that moment the gravity came back on, partially at least, accompanied by an announcement that could be heard in the distance. The base PA system obviously didn't broadcast here in these ancient tunnels. My body gained a feeling of weight, and I floated slowly to the floor accompanied by curses from Mia. This was not full standard gravity yet, more like point two-G. Enough to bring everyone back to earth, but slowly, so if someone were up near a ceiling, they wouldn't kill themselves hurtling to the floor.

More swearing from Mia. The patch of blurry air resolved itself back into her normal shape, still clad in that shiny gold. No cameras here, so she must have figured it was safe to go visible. "C'mon, Chook, we gotta hurry."

"No, I'll do it," said Sana, waving away the colonel, grabbing my arm and pulling me to my feet. "Chook, lead on."

"All right," he said, "gotta get him up that access shaft while we still can."

We moved off down the small tunnel, me with an arm around each of the two women, feet barely touching the ground. Losing zero-G was actually helping us move faster, though this would not be the case once full gravity returned: my weight was normally twice that of Sana's. We reached a branch tunnel and turned left, then staggered forward another few hundred meters. At some point the gravity went up another notch and the pressure under my arms increased.

"You OK, Sana?" I tried to ask, but only weird cooing sounds came out. Strange, because in other ways my mind was still working fine. Was this what happened during a stroke? I was about to ask my kom but thought better. Didn't want to chance losing the holo-map guiding us.

Chook paused, looking up into a pitch-black hole and pointed. "Up there. About twelve meters. The lights come on once you're in the old airlock, but the shaft is dark."

"I'll go up first," said Mia. "I can pull from the top and you guys push."

She reattached the line to run around my body and under my arms, then reached and jumped up to catch the bottom rail of the ladder running into the shaft. Much easier in this reduced gravity than the last time Chook and I tried. A light flicked on from her helmet, legs thrashing for a moment as she pulled herself up, then her foot caught the bottom rail and she was off, footsteps tap, tapping on metal as she ascended the ladder. The line attached to me now ran up inside the hole. Big, fat fish that I was.

But what about telling Batum! Calling the ship!

It was waiting in the dock, berthed perilously next to the Movement warship, waiting on our say-so to make its break for freedom. I tried calling on my kom, but whatever was going on in my brain seemed to be affecting electronic messaging now as well. My kom line was open but I couldn't seem to transmit. Scary and frustrating.

"Is that you, Col?" sent Batum. *"Are you ready for me to exit the loading dock?"*

I tried to say something to the others, but no sounds were coming out of my mouth at all. Brain shutting down. Or at least its ability to communicate. My inner world of thought and feeling still seemed lucid. I tried gesturing to the others, but they were focused on getting me up into the shaft. Why hadn't they seen or heard Batum's call? Perhaps their comms weren't working among all this granite; they didn't have the advanced kit I did from working Jubilee security.

"OK, pull!" shouted Chook, and the line went tight. He and Sana grabbed a leg each and started pushing me up into the shaft. "Don't worry, mate," he said kindly. "We'll do the heavy lifting."

I tried to speak, wanting to remind him to call Batum, but the best I could do was wave weakly and look meaningfully into his eyes.

Somehow between them all, I was hoisted and pulled up into the shaft. I grabbed the bottom step, stabilizing my body, then felt the line yank hard, pulling me into the darkness. Thank God the gravity was still only running at around what, half a G? Otherwise, this whole procedure would be doomed. Sana and Chook pushed from below, first using my legs, then the bottoms of my feet as I got hauled upward like a trussed animal.

By the time I was halfway, the gravity went heavier again. Close to, or probably at, standard G now. The line around my chest was suddenly tight and super painful under my arms. It was a fine rope, only a millimeter or two thick, and was cutting through my clothes into my armpits and chest. But I couldn't even cry out in pain. I pulled as hard as I could on the rungs, trying to help the others.

Another message from Batum, but only partial. *"…need to advise… make the exit maneuver…"*

I ground my teeth, thinking, *Someone answer him for God's sake!*

Lots of huffing and puffing. My chest in agony, armpits burning, but now there was light above. First a small dot, then becoming larger and brighter. Mia's face peering down from above. She'd looped the line around something up there and was using it for leverage to reel me up. I saw her pause for a moment, listening intently, then sigh. My kom came to life with a loud, almost deafening call.

"Batum, this is Colonel Blackall, I am assisting your group. Make your move now, right now, *we are almost ready at the airlock."*

I was flooded with relief. Mia must have heard Batum's message somehow. She probably gained backdoor access to our chat line.

"Col, can you confirm? Or Sana, or Chook? I have not been authorized to take directions from you, Colonel. Why are the others not responding?"

"Not sure, Batum. I think something's wrong with Col's neural function and the others could be having range issues, whereas I hold a military-grade kom. According to my Intelligence, your window to act is about to close. Leave now if you wish to survive."

There was a pause. Batum wasn't a quantum supercomputer like Douglas, but his processing capacity was huge, and even *still*, there was a noticeable pause while he considered all the options and possibilities branching off from this moment.

"On my way."

Thank God.

Now all we needed was for that release code to be correct, and for the drive to be working properly like those villains in the dock said it was, and for Batum's cloak and dash plan to work. Jumping through vacuum to board the ship would be the easy part.

Somehow between Mia pulling, the others pushing and my own feeble actions, I was finally hauled out of the hole, and rolled myself across the floor to Mia's feet. Moments later Chook emerged, followed by Sana, both panting heavily.

"I think they're on to us," said Chook. "I heard 'em in the tunnel while we were climbing."

We stopped to listen. Mia stepped over, peering into the blackness of the hole. Faint climbing sounds emerged, surreptitious feet padding on the metal rungs, trying their best to be quiet. She whipped out her blaster and unleashed a volley of shots into the tunnel. There were shrieks and tumbling sounds. Falling bodies.

"That should hold them," she said with a mischievous smile. "Now we gotta get you guys into the airlock. Ship is on the way."

If it was. If the code worked, and the drive worked, and the plan worked.

Mia released the line around my chest, relieving the worst of the pain – though to be fair, that was the least of my problems, given that my mind seemed to be shutting down. Even minor physical movements were becoming difficult now. Chook grabbed me around the waist and hauled me into the airlock. Mia stood by the door and leaned down to speak.

"Good luck with your mission, Col. I've got a strange feeling we're going to meet again someday." I wanted to thank her, wanted to tell her to keep up the good fight. Keep hope alive that we would surely prevail, but all I could do was stare mutely. She turned to Sana. "He's in a *very* bad way. Scans as neural bleeding."

"I hear you."

"And passing through vacuum will only make it worse. I can't stress enough to get him into the ICU at the first possible chance. He may be minutes from a fatal aneurysm."

"Got it."

Mia closed the airlock door and gave us a thumbs-up through the tiny observation hole while Chook waited at the airlock controls. Now we needed the ship to arrive, or at least know it was close so we could start cycling the air out.

And after we were aboard, then what? Batum would be ready with a small random jump that would take us to safety in the short term. But we needed somewhere secure to regroup and work on a strategy for finding Danee and the girls, for dealing with…everything.

But where? If they could find us here, in a League-administered ball of rock sitting all by itself in the middle of outer space, where in hell would be safe? Then it hit me: the most obvious unlikely destination in the entire galaxy, and therefore perfect.

"What's your status, Batum?" called Mia.

"That code worked, and drive is operational. I'm right now performing – there you go – just engaged cloak and evasive maneuvers. That did the trick. I think they're not very happy all of a sudden."

Lying on the floor, I felt a rumble through the bedrock of the base. Something being blown up somewhere. Satisfying perhaps, but not smart – and nothing that would help matters for them. They were probably blasting where they figured the ship should be, but would only be shooting at thin air. Or thin vacuum rather, since the dock on this base was not pressurized. They would be causing quite a mess too, I'd say.

Mia rapped on the door and motioned to Chook. She mimed pressing the cycle button, but he just stared at her. Then at me. Obviously, he had not heard the exchange between Mia and Batum.

Sana looked up at the door and got it instantly. "She's saying 'go for it', Chook."

"Cycle the airlock?"

"Yes! For God's sake!!"

Chook shrugged, hit the button, and air started releasing from the small chamber. How long would it take for Batum to bring the ship around? From the dock, we were roughly one third of the asteroid's circumference away, so less than a minute by my calculations. That was workable.

I forced myself to pant heavily, taking a dozen or so deep breaths to oxygenate my lungs, then starting a long, slow exhale. Sana watched me do this, and must have remembered the procedure when we left Jubilee. "Chook, do what Col's doing. You don't want air in your lungs when we depressurize, or they can explode."

He looked startled, then followed suit. For half a minute we all did our panting and exhaling. Finally, the cycle light changed from orange to green and the outer door cracked open: to space, to vacuum, to the bone-cracking cold. Something seemed to go pop, pop deep inside my head. Not a sound or a feeling, but some other kind of thing that I can't put into words but felt a bit like a small explosion, or maybe *implosion*; of resistance being released.

Everything started spinning.

Chook pushed the door, and it swung open in silence. The eerie and total silence of vacuum. Beyond lay a dirty field strewn with yellow-brown rocks and small boulders. A close horizon lit by the silvery wash from billions of blazing stars. We stared anxiously. Ten seconds to hypoxia, then unconsciousness, then death.

A shimmery blur appeared. Ever so faint but obscuring the stars behind it. Moving closer to us, then closer. Then blinking into full being as if a light had been switched on: the silver triangle of our ship, piloted by Batum with robotic precision to inches of where we waited. Its door was wide open, exposing the brightly lit interior, beckoning us inside.

Chook grabbed me around the waist and literally hurled me aboard. Sana must have jumped too, for my last sight was of the ship's door starting to slide shut. And then the world and everything in it – and everything that ever was and everything that ever would be – all faded to white.

★ ★ ★

Whiteness.

Everywhere.

This place, if it were a room, had no discernible joins where wall and floor met. Just a blurring whiteness everywhere, maybe some kind of bubble?

I was standing. Naked but warm. And relaxed. Standing dead straight and frozen somehow, unable to move – but that was OK. Everything was OK. In fact, wherever or whatever this place was, had to be good, because everything felt *really* OK. I looked around, only whiteness behind me. Whiteness on the left and whiteness on the right. At least I could turn my head now. That was something.

"Hello?" I called out. "Anyone here?" No answer.

Time passed.

Impossible to say how long, but a distinct feeling of the passage of time. Not that it was boring. Or exciting either; more like a pleasant numbness, as if I could just stay in this little white bubble forever and everything would continue to be fine.

"Col!"

I turned around. It was Danee – *with the girls!*

"Daddy!" they cried and ran to me. Each grabbed a leg and hugged it. They were wearing little white dresses, *so cute*. And Danee was in white too, a long silk gown with a train that fell to the floor. Matching me, for I noticed that I now was in white too, wearing a Panama suit like the one I'd stolen on Brouggh. Very stylish, we all were.

Danee stood a short distance away, enchanting and beautiful and smiling warmly. She didn't make any move toward me, just stood there smiling with great love. I could feel the force of it coming at me like a beam. Whatever this place was, thoughts and feelings seemed to communicate equally well. I had no wish to move, no need to touch her. It was all just wonderful and amazing: her being here, the feeling of my two girls pressing against me, their baby arms around my legs.

"How are you, darling?" Danee asked.

"There's never been one minute that I wasn't thinking about you."

"I know, I'm sorry."

"Sorry? What do *you* have to be sorry for? *I'm* the one that left you behind, I'm the one that should have—"

"*Shush.*" She put a finger to her lips with that coy smile she sometimes made, code for warning me not to go on any more. "It's all going to be OK, Col. Did you get my message?"

"Yes!" I felt suddenly upset, childishly so. "I've played it over and over, but I still can't figure it out. Where are you now? What happened?"

"*All* in good time, darling." She laughed, hair tumbling about her face and falling across her shoulders in a mane of blonde ringlets. My emotions were quicksilver fast here in this place. I was suddenly filled with an aching and desperate desire for her. "And I'm so glad *she's* with you." Danee said this to someone over my shoulder, nodding and smiling.

I whirled around, to see Sana. Also dressed in white, in some kind of robe a Greek goddess might wear from a cheesy holo-drama. "Danee, *darling*!" she said, closing the short distance to embrace her. "I was wondering when you'd show up!"

Danee beamed. "*Look at us*, everyone's here!"

Indeed.

I picked up the girls and planted a kiss on each of their cheeks, causing delighted giggles. I marveled anew at how weightless Lila was, how much like her auntie Sana, even though they shared no genes. And how crystal blue were Anjali's eyes, like her lost uncle Tim's. I clutched the girls to me, all of a sudden emotional, trying not to cry. It felt like part of myself that had been torn away was now returned.

The girls started squirming, so, reluctantly, I put them down. "*Auntie Sana!*" they cried and ran to her for a long hug. Which ended only when she looked up to stare at something behind my back with squinted eyes. "What's *she* doing here?"

Another person had joined us.

Mia.

Mia?

In a jumpsuit like the one she wore at the base, only instead of metallic gold, this was made of clingy white material with sparkles running through it, hugging her body in a perfect fit.

What's with all the white apparel? I wondered.

"Kinda makes sense," she said to Sana with an enigmatic smile, "if you think about it."

"OK, yes, right, so D-Danee," I stammered, "please let me introduce Colonel Mia Blackall. She's been most helpful to us recently when the Movement came after us on—"

"Yes, but what's she doing *here*, in *this* space?" asked Sana accusingly.

"I don't know," I spluttered. "I mean, how *would* I?"

"Well, this is *your* inner world. Why would you make her appear for no reason?"

Danee chuckled. "Always in trouble with the *ladies*, Col!" She raised an eyebrow at Sana and they exchanged meaningful looks.

"Listen, that's nonsense. Granted, Colonel Mia is an attractive and highly intelligent person, but that doesn't mean I—"

"I suppose we shouldn't blame him too much," said Sana with an eye roll. "I did his chart once and well, *Venus in Leo*, what can I say?"

"I fail to see how the moment of my birth as correlated with the stellar constellations visible from Old Earth has any bearing—"

"If I were you, chum," Mia cut in, laughing, "I'd quit while I was ahead."

"But Sana does raise a point," said Danee mildly, "and as intrusive as it might seem, the colonel has to be here for a reason. Don't you think?"

"Indeed, Danee, that's a very good point," said Mia. "And I have to tell you, the reason is not what you might think."

"What do you *mean*?" I whined. "Can someone please tell me what's going on?"

Mia tilted her head. "I've given you everything you need to put it together, Col. You're a clever boy, *work it out*!"

I stared at her for a moment, mind whirling as certain pieces of information fell into place. I had watched Jubilee – my home, my whole life – disappear in a blinding flash. Received a message that was impossible to receive, found two million credits in my account that shouldn't be there and learned that my supposedly lost ship was not lost in space after all. It all had to be connected, didn't it?

Mia smiled, reading my thoughts. "That's right!"

Of course, so obvious.

I started laughing in relief at the cosmic joke of it all, then stopped abruptly. Why was I not told, not trusted with any of this? Why had I been treated so cruelly?

Then another flash. Blinding illumination that explained everything.

Part Two

Chapter One

Green.

Everywhere. As far as you could see, an endless carpet. Green behind us in the monitor view and green on every side as well. Even from this great height, there was no sign of human activity discernible anywhere below. No clearings or buildings or roads – just an endless canopy of green running to the horizon in every direction.

The automated flyer made a sudden move, descending a thousand meters and pulling sharply to the right. Its reason for doing so was evident a moment later as another craft zipped directly toward us and then past in the blink of an eye. Despite this being a designated flight lane, with its transponder illegally turned off, the flyer was taking no chances.

"How far away *is* this fucking place?" whined Chook.

"I know," sighed Sana. "Always felt like you were going to the end of the world."

Which was kind of true.

Batum stood beside me, impassive. He was a little more cleaned up and respectable looking now after all that work in the shop, but there hadn't been enough time to properly finish. Hell, there probably weren't even the right parts available anywhere in the galaxy. Douglas could have done it, I guessed.

Something appeared on the far horizon. A break in the endless forest, only visible as a blur of brown from this height and distance. I turned up magnification on the screen, but the image only pixilated, so I turned it back. Patience.

The brown smudge slid gradually toward us, resolving into signs of human habitation. A town – more of a village really – growing larger as the flyer started its descent. Now there was a main street with a line of shops and offices and a sprawl of houses surrounding it. At the edge of town, a large tower and factory works to process lumber and beyond that, I knew, a quarry, unseen, but somewhere up toward the nearby hills.

The streets were lined with trees – as if the residents needed even more of them – and the houses looked pleasantly run-down and lived in. A perfect little country town in the northern hinterland. The flyer circled, seeking its bearings, headed north for another few moments, then put down on a quiet street in one of the outer suburbs.

There it was. The old house. Double story, made of wood planks and painted white, with a gray hardiplaz roof needing, it looked to me, a good bit of work before the howling winds of autumn arrived. Two figures waited at the front door. An elderly couple, holding hands. The woman let go the man's hand and ran toward us excitedly while he waited, older and more stooped than her. He had a certain look in his eye that I'd seen too many times as a cop, and which I knew did not fade with the passage of time, the look of someone who'd experienced unspeakable tragedy. He waved at me with a wan smile.

I waved back. "Hi, Dad."

* * *

Becoming conscious wasn't an *on/off* kind of thing. There was a long period of indistinguishable sounds and feelings, vaguely unpleasant. Pain: suddenly flicking on throughout my whole body, then flicking off again – stuff being done to my nervous system. At a certain point cool air, a hatch opening and a voice speaking. The words not making any sense at first; it was quite some time, in fact, before even the concept of words came back.

"That was *close*, booby."

Time passing. Awareness of being in a body. Of being closed into something. An ICU unit! Hatch opening, more voices speaking, eyes not working.

"Hi mate, can you tell us, what's your name?"

Strange question. What *was* my name anyway? I felt an awareness of 'I', of being the person I'd continuously been my whole life, but who was that person, what was their name? I racked my brain, panic growing, then finally had it! – almost weeping with relief.

"Col," I said finally, proud of myself. The word sounded funny, not my normal voice.

Sighs of relief from somewhere out there.

"Do you know where you are?"

At first, a blank. I was obviously somewhere, somewhen, but otherwise?…recollection of events gradually returning…images: the base, Mia, Batum bringing the ship around.

"*Poobah,*" I mumbled, and heard laughing.

That made me feel better.

Once we made it out of the base's airlock, Batum had jumped instantly, before the airlock door even had time to shut, and mere seconds before incoming missiles would have struck our poorly shielded ship. A short jump, that first one, a single light year, but enough to clear us from harm's way.

Chook had heaved me into the ship's ICU, where I lay for a month. I'd suffered a hemorrhagic stroke caused by blunt force trauma – the blow from Ms. Crang's rebounding statue (totally self-inflicted, how embarrassing!) exacerbated by the kick I took to the head during the zero-G scrum and compounded by the inflammatory effects of vacuum. Literally, my brain had burst.

Nanos worked their magic. Repairing blood vessels, restoring tissue where possible. But how much permanent damage had been done to those poor little gray cells of mine?

Sight returned, just shapes at first, but with more definition all the time. I was able to leave the ICU for short periods, collapsing back into it minutes later, back into blissful, pain-free unconsciousness. But the awake time gradually increased and, as is the way, normal living slowly resumed; the ICU was put away and eventually it was hard to even remember I'd once craved being inside it. All up it took three months, and my recovery was possible only because Douglas had installed an absolute state-of-the-art machine.

And of those glowing realizations in the 'white room'? All that remained was the feeling: clarity, triumphant understanding, but the details themselves were gone. If I truly had figured everything out in that moment, I was none the wiser now. Maybe it was all just a hallucination like Sana said, the deranged output of a dying brain. But what if it wasn't? The idea haunted me. Sometimes I sat in a quiet space meditating, asking the knowledge to come, but nothing did.

When I was finally well enough, it was time to have 'the conversation'.

"Brouggh?" Sana was incredulous. "Isn't that the *last* place we should head, given our history?"

"Which," I tried to sound reasonable, "is exactly why it's the best choice."

"But won't they be waiting for us in force?"

"Not necessarily."

"Excuse me," said Chook, "but what the fuck is Brouggh? Sounds like some kind of footwear."

"Col, I agree. Your instincts are correct," said Batum from the cockpit chair next to me.

"It's our home planet, Chook," said Sana with a sigh, "where I first got into a confrontation with the Movement."

"In which you were successful," I said. "Consider, we are one of the few systems that have beaten back the Movement once they became entrenched. We're wised up, on guard for them there, and plus we have a support network of friends, high and low across the planet *and* in the security forces. If we just ran and hid in some anonymous place, they'd find us eventually anyway, and then we'd have to face them on our own."

"It does send a statement," agreed Batum.

Chook hissed, "What would you know about *statements*, socket-fucker?"

"Human," said Batum ominously, "I could make a statement by turning you into a small puddle of DNA right now."

"*Please*," said Sana, "just for once—"

"It's really saying that we're not cowed, that we'll stand up to them. And also, we can use the resources there to try and track down Danee and the girls."

They all paused at that.

"What the fuck," said Chook. "If it wasn't for you, Col, I'd a been pushing up daisies long ago. I'll go wherever you want."

We all turned to Sana.

She let out a long breath, turned up her hands and shrugged. "Haven't seen my folks in ages."

★ ★ ★

They actually applauded.

When I entered the operations center at SSB in Harrison City to visit my old chums, the room stood up, cheering and clapping. Within minutes I was surrounded by a back-slapping, hand-shaking throng – lots of *well-dones* and *good-to-see-yous*. All very gratifying. It was my arrest and torture on trumped-up charges that had started the department's resistance to M4M, and it was good to see they were still on my side.

Henderzon, my old antagonist turned ally, was up in Brouggh City doing 'important things' in the higher echelons of Security. Good, he was going to be very useful. I'd sent a message to him already and was waiting on a call back.

Sana was at her parents' place reconnecting with family and friends, Chook was propping a bar up somewhere and Batum was in the shop. I'd found the best service joint in Harrison City, but eyes widened and palms were raised when they saw the battle-scarred droid. 'Sorry, no chance,' they'd said, at least at first. Until the words 'money is no object' were uttered, after which a number of highly technical and outrageously expensive procedures were suddenly found to be possible.

Everyone was busy dealing with their priorities.

Now for mine.

"I dunno, Col, of course we can try," said Aballa, my old friend, now head of SSB Harrison City. He and his wife had been the only people in the department who got on with Sana when we were together.

"Please, thank you," I said.

"It's just, you know, we raise hundreds of these every day. Can you imagine the numbers galaxy-wide?"

"But it does happen, right? Sometimes you get a hit."

"Yes, we've all done that call-out, haven't we, so of course."

He was referring to the *missing-person* visit and, sometimes with luck, retrieval. A knock on the door, a DNA match via kom, and *bingo*! There might be a new husband or wife, other times a petty crime being escaped from, most often drugs or mental illness. For whatever reason, someone had run away in mysterious circumstances and now here they were. Occasionally, it was even a moment of great joy.

"Can't hurt, you never know, right?"

Aballa started work on the missing-persons request for Danee. No point raising one for the girls; they'd been born on Jubilee and never registered with any authority back in our 'normal' universe.

"Who do we put as applicant?" Aballa fixed me with a meaningful look.

"Hmm, let's raise it as if from Danee's parents."

"Then we'll do a switcheroo and divert the answer to you. *If* we get one."

Good thinking by Aballa; an MPR raised under my name might trigger an alert somewhere. If Danee's kom interacted with a network anywhere in the galaxy it would eventually – after passing through interminable layers of League bureaucracy – find its way to Aballa's office. The problem being, of course, that this same alert would likely trigger a Movement computer somewhere as well. Which is exactly why Danee would do everything in her power to avoid it.

"There's something else I can try, if you want me to," said Aballa.

I wanted him too.

"League back channel: LCIB – their criminal investigations' bureau, which I never even knew existed before taking this job. Lady in there owes me one and I think it might be time to call in the favor. So leave it with me, see if something pops out of the system, you'll be the first to know."

"Anything you can do, buddy, please."

Henderzon finally called the next day (audio only).

"Of course we're still a democracy, you can't stop them being sympathetic to the Movement, but at least now they have to declare it."

"What percentage do they make up?" I asked. Henderzon was engaged in something unprecedented: trying to deradicalize a planet's security service while still preserving its democratic system. The progress of his mission was being closely monitored by all sides.

"Oh, you know, round twenty-five percent."

"That's a lot!"

"Yeah, but that's everyone. From slightly sympathetic to fully committed. I reckon we got the zealots out, the wing nuts, but you never know, do ya?" I heard a slight pop. Henderzon must have been chewing gum, just like the old days. I imagined him nonchalantly leaning back in his chair, chewing away. Life at the top obviously suited him.

"And the politics?"

"Still OK. M4M made slight gains in the last election, but those child-sex allegations leaking the way they did made a real and, so far, permanent dent in their popularity. Real bummer the way that got out, eh?" Henderzon chuckled. It had been the suicide of Chairman Nees' son on Jubilee, concurrent with their attempted planetary coup, that triggered a criminal investigation implicating the Movement's leader.

"Couldn't make it stick though?"

"Unfortunately, not. But enough people know what really went on to... *Tell them I'll be two minutes!*"

"You needed?"

"Sorry, buddy."

"OK then, here's the thing..." I updated him about events and described what we needed. He was shocked about Jubilee. So far there'd been no hard news about its destruction, just a few wild rumors impossible to validate. He rapidly agreed to help.

Three days later we spoke again.

"Safe house, *really*?" I was incredulous.

"That's about the size of it," Henderzon sounded apologetic.

"But how can you be so *sure*? I mean if these are just vague rumors—"

"More than vague, buddy. Short of providing a twenty-four-hour security detail for your whole party, it's the only way I can keep you safe."

"But for how long?" If the threat was dispersed as he said, that would mean no end date.

"You know how it goes, sorry, Col. Hate to be the bearer of bad news." I heard another gum pop.

I started thinking. Safe houses had their utility, but they were truly horrible places, locked away from life. I'd spent time in them over the years minding people, and those jobs stood out as the most boring and unpleasant in my career. Living in one permanently would be almost as bad as being lost in space on *The Grand Poobah*. Had to be a better idea.

"What about Jerbet?"

Henderzon laughed.

"I'm serious."

There was a long pause. "Oh, I get it, your hometown, right? Always thought you were a bit weird – *just kidding*!"

"No, you're right, there's plenty of weirdos up there. But it's better than a fucking safe house."

There was silence for a moment while Henderzon thought it over. "Yeah, makes sense, only one road in and one heavy rail line."

"Easy to keep tabs on those coming into town. Less work for you than running a safe house."

"All right." Henderzon chuckled. "It's not as secure as a house, but it's your life, buddy. I'm happy to arrange. Tell everyone to be ready within the hour, what I'm hearing is making me nervous."

My room looked almost exactly as I'd left it twenty-five years ago. Same posters on the wall, same books on the shelf, all on one subject: the Special Services. Chook looked less than impressed that these were now his lodgings.

"We'll put you and Sana *here*," said Lynda, my stepmother, showing us to another bedroom down the hall that had once been my parents'. "We sleep downstairs now in a new room out the back. The stairs got a bit much for Dava."

Sana and I dropped our bags and looked around. All the clutter I remembered was gone, leaving only a bed and built-in closets, though it was still recognizably the same room as from my childhood. Where Mum and Dad had slept. Before Tim disappeared and Mum lost her mind.

There hadn't been time to talk, so they'd naturally assumed Sana and I were still together as a married couple. This might have been the right moment to say something, to let her know about Danee and the girls (their own granddaughters!) but I just stood mute, not even completely sure why. Sana caught my eye with a questioning look, then we both shrugged.

Lynda left to fix dinner and we unpacked the few belongings we'd picked up in Harrison City. Which wasn't much; all the good things we'd bought on the ITAAH base had been left behind in our rush to escape. While Sana took a nap, I wandered down the hall to Tim's old room. I stood outside his door with dread. How many times had I done this as a kid, fantasizing I'd find him inside playing with toys or lying in bed?

Inside the room it was dusty and filled with old boxes. Not what I expected.

Most parents keep the room of a lost child as a kind of monument. Frozen in time, filled with the same toys and belongings they would have grown out of long ago had they lived. In the holo-dramas, the hero cop always finds a clue in that room which everyone else missed and uses it to solve the case. I never thought this particularly healthy. But people do all kinds of strange things out of grief, and how would anyone cope with the unimaginable loss of a child?

I stepped inside and looked around. There was a stack of hardiplaz boxes piled in the corner, and more lying around the room. I opened one up to see inside – just some old plates and a vase. Junk.

I was suddenly angry. What about Tim, what about his memory? Did Dad and Lynda care so little that his old room was now just a place to store old crap?

Then again, what did I expect, another one of those mausoleums?

Not after all this time, I suppose. But *something*, surely? And what about *my* room? How come *that* was all set up as if my sixteen-year-old self might return at any moment, but not Tim's?

But thirty-five years is a long time. People deal with things in ways you never expect. You often found a person who'd just witnessed a murder and they'd be calm and logical, not at all how an actor would play them in a holo-drama. My dad and his new wife had chosen a different path to most: pack up Tim's room, close the door, try to forget. Probably the mature and sensible thing to do.

But not for me.

It looked like I was going to be stuck here in Jerbet for quite some time. I made a decision; one of those times in my life that I set myself on a particular course with grim determination.

I would discover once and for all what really happened to Tim.

Chapter Two

Dad was a worry.

Lined and gray, skinny and stooped; the years had been particularly unkind, especially compared to Lynda. He looked ethereal, as if you could almost see through him, and he ate little and spoke less. It seemed as though he was consciously trying to fade away almost in spite of modern health treatments that could keep a human alive and robust for centuries. I felt a pang of guilt for not visiting in so long, and for not being able to tell him what was really going on in my life.

"So, ah, Mr. *Chook*," asked Lynda nervously, "what exactly is it that you *do*?"

He looked stricken. "Bit of a wombat, I'd say, miss – eats, roots and leaves." He laughed loudly, casting around the dining table for support but finding only awkward silence. Batum stood in the corner shaking his head.

"Ah I see…and so how is it that you all know each other again?"

We hadn't actually explained that yet, or anything else. Henderzon told me to keep things vague, for news in a small town travels fast, and the less people knew about us the better. All we'd told my parents was that we needed to be out of Harrison City for a while due to some 'departmental issues' and could we stay with them? They didn't even know I'd been fired from SSB and living on Jubilee for the past four years.

"Chook's been helping us with a particular line of enquiry," I said, looking down at my meal. "Probably best not to go into it."

"Oh yes, yes of course, didn't mean to pry. Just being social," she said quickly.

It was an awkward meal. Dad silent, Chook looking like he'd rather be anywhere else, Sana filling the space with chatter. The moment we finished, Chook was out the door for a 'stroll' – one that would end no doubt at Main Street, where Jerbet's two bars were located.

After dinner I finally had a chance to talk alone with Dad and tell him my plans about finding out what happened to Tim. He looked down at his lap for a long time, gently shaking his head. "Col, that sounds like a bad idea," he said slowly. "Let it be."

"Dad, it's the *not knowing* that gets me."

Such a familiar refrain, now emerging from my own mouth. The thing that everyone always says when a loved one vanishes. Tim was somewhere, in a shallow grave most likely, but the how and why, and especially the who were questions that needed to be answered.

"Col, I live with it every day, every minute of every day." He paused again. "And whatever you might find won't bring him back. It'll just stir everything up, so leave it be. That is all I'm going to say about the matter."

We sat in silence for a whole minute, me and my poor hollowed-out father. First, I lost Tim, then Mum, then finally Dad in a different way to the others. Lynda – originally Ms. Veitch, the nice neighbor from down the street – had saved him and also saved me. She was the only person who provided any kind of emotional support when everything went down. Despite what he might say, I was certain that finding Tim would also help Dad deal with his trauma, might even bring some life back into him. But the conversation seemed utterly shut down for the moment. I decided to change tack.

"Thought I might take a look at the roof while I'm here, Dad. Looks like it could do with some work."

"May as well," he said, nodding, and that was it. All that I could get out of him on that first night.

We soon fell into a routine: me in the mornings working on the roof with Chook before he disappeared to indulge his vices; Sana creating a new virtual art project and hanging out with Lynda; Batum doing nothing at all. He was meant to stay indoors away from prying eyes. Often I found him in the lounge room with my father, both sitting together in silence.

Aballa sent me Tim's file from the SSB archives. Not strictly legit to share it with someone no longer working for the department, but I knew he wouldn't argue.

I set myself up in Dad's old study in the attic, working at his dusty wooden desk. It was surprisingly difficult to focus in that quiet, dark space, so different to the fluoro-lit chaos of a squad room. Instead of all the noise and conversation, it was the chatter of my own mind that I had to tune out.

From my kom, the file sprang open as four separate holo-volumes containing all the records of the so-far-unsuccessful Tim Perolo investigation. These appeared as glowing bundles in the air that could be opened and scrolled by the power of thought, or I could manipulate them by 'touch' or pinch if that was more appealing. Some legendary oddballs in the department were known to work only on paper like Investigators of old, though Tim's file would amount to thousands of pages if I tried that. Personally, I liked to configure my virtual files to look like old-fashioned binders.

I went immediately to the case chronology and table of contents. The pictures and video were listed as being in the third volume, so I moved to that binder. I wanted to see again what the Investigators saw all those years ago.

The very first picture was of Tim half-turned, grinning back at the camera, wearing a costume. That moment came back to me: the black cape was his wizard's robe, and the image was from just before he vanished, lifted no doubt from Mother's kom. He was due for a haircut the next day and his light brown locks were falling sideways across his face. That made me feel sad; the appointment was never kept, Tim's hair forever long.

I took the picture from the stack and 'pinned' it mid-air above the other files. I wanted it to stay there while I worked, something to goad me on.

My brother disappeared one balmy, summer afternoon. Mother took us to the general store in town for a treat. I went to fetch ice creams from the fridge and when I turned around, Tim was gone.

He'd always been a slightly odd boy, born premature and requiring DNA therapy in utero to fix genetic abnormalities. The file now told me what these were: autism coupled with severe microcephaly or small brain syndrome. In an earlier age, Tim would have been highly disabled, or more likely died in the womb. Instead, at birth he was pronounced one hundred percent healthy. Mother brought him home from the hospital, small but perfect. He had tiny little pink hands that gripped my finger and crisp blue eyes the color of the spring sky outside. I loved him from that first moment.

But there was always *something*. Sometimes when he was older, Tim would just stop and stare into space for minutes at a time, and nothing I could do would rouse him. Years later I wondered about these episodes and couldn't shake the feeling that he was staring into the void, that it was calling him somehow.

Tim was my special friend. Unlike many other kids at school, I had a sibling. We rode our bikes, played in the woods together, and made cubby houses out of old junk. I felt protective of him, could never quite shake the feeling there was a threat lurking somewhere: in the bushes, in the air. It was a subtle thing.

That afternoon in the store I ran back to Mother with the ice creams, told her I couldn't find Tim. We looked around the shop, then outside with mounting panic. Dad was called and soon the police as well. Tim was nowhere.

I turned back to the case chronology and was stunned to see that the day of Tim's disappearance had in fact been cloudy with rain, not sunny. Amazing how the mind rearranges memories; I'd seen this phenomenon a thousand times as an Investigator but it was shocking to find it in oneself.

I went back to skimming the pictures and dipped into the video. There were images of me as a boy and a copy of my interview by Ms. Sunter, the lead Investigator from SSB. She came up from HC to take over the case, and during our interview it was her deft questioning that had me recall a drone delivering goods to the store at almost the same moment Tim vanished. A stroke of luck. Vision from that drone should have broken the case. But it had hit power lines a week after the event, fritzing its brain, something that I now felt might be suspicious.

There was banging on the roof just above me and my kom pinged with an angry message underlined in red: *"Where the fuck are you?"*

Time to meet Chook and continue with the roof. I looked around; my virtual files were strewn about the room and across the desk in messy piles. I realized I'd been picking at them piecemeal, a sure way to send oneself mad. Had to be more systematic, had to start again from scratch probably.

"See you there shortly," I sent back.

The roof hadn't been looked at in years and when we pulled up the hardiplaz tiles, one of the main ridge beams didn't look right. Weird construction this house; a mixture of wood and hardiplaz, but not uncommon in Jerbet given the super-abundance of timber. I stopped for a moment to take in the morning sun. From up here you could see the whole town laid out, and just beyond its perimeter, the unbroken green of the forest. The air was redolent with its sweet, oily wood-perfume.

I once read that on Old Earth they stripped all the forests for lumber even though plenty of other building materials were available. No such problem here on Brouggh. Hardiplaz was used for almost everything and Jerbet's boutique lumber mill supplied only the tiny market for decoration and furniture.

Chook and I looked like proper construction workers in our boots and Day-Glo orange anti-grav vests. These weren't powerful enough to fly with, but if either of us slipped we'd drift gently to ground. Hard to imagine that in the old days that would have led to death or permanent injury. Dad's roof was a high one – over twelve meters I'd say – and even with the security of my jacket, looking down made my balls clench.

"This one's gone," said Chook, pointing to the beam, cracked and sagging in its middle. Must have taken a massive dump of snow at some point, stressing it beyond its limit.

"Yup," I said, "guess that means a trip to town."

The hardware yard was on the road to the lumber mill, the other side of town. We took Dad's small electric ground car and parked next to the only other vehicle in the yard, a large utility. My heart sank when its owner emerged from the store. He too reacted; stopped and propped himself against the open door, grinning.

Pal Muller: my own personal, junior high bully. Two years senior, he'd taken a highly proactive interest in my torment during those years.

"Well, I'll be buggered," he drawled. "*Col. Fucking. Perolo.* Who'd believe it?" He hacked and spat a glistening green gob on the ground before me.

Pal was another person the years had not been kind to. He was a tall, skinny kid at school, with an elongated head and slitted, lizard-like eyes. One of the 'cabin crew', the feral families living out in the woods in numberless shacks. At least he got to go to school. I was considered a 'townie' by that lot, and therefore automatically stuck-up and deserving of abuse. It was pointless – dangerous even – to fight back, otherwise you'd find yourself pounced on by a pack of siblings, or cousins or whatevers (the cabin dwellers famous for their enormous families, unlike us 'townies') when you least expected it. Pal had gotten even skinnier in the intervening years; it looked like some kind of chronic illness. His face was bright red, and he had a mouthful of rotting teeth, conditions easily dealt with by modern treatments. Only in outlying places like Jerbet did you ever see people like this.

Chook surprised me. Instead of responding angrily, he walked straight up to Pal, hand outstretched.

"How you doin', mate," he said amiably. "Chook's the name. Seems like you already know my buddy Col."

Pal's glare was fixed upon me. He swiveled reptilian eyes to appraise Chook but the rest of him didn't move a muscle. He looked Chook up and down. "Off-worlder, eh?"

Don't ask me why but for Jerbet locals, the farther away that you came from, the worse it was. Worse than being a townie like me was to come from the 'big smoke': Harrison City. Worse again was to be from somewhere very distant like Portland on the other side of the globe. But by far, the worst thing of *all* was to be an off-worlder, and Chook's accent gave that away in about three seconds.

The air around us suddenly crackled with tension. Who knew if Pal was carrying? Wouldn't put it past him, and both of *us* were clean.

"*Mate!*" Chook's face crinkled into an easy smile. "You've got no idea. I'm *so* off-world I'm all the way round and back again. Just about makes me a local, I reckon!"

Pal sniggered. "Yeah, I seen you drinkin' at Drogo's. Last few nights."

"Yup, that's right."

Pal nodded for a long moment, the wheels in his head spinning with agonizing slowness until finally he shrugged. "Fair enough. Guess I'll see you's around. You can buy me a beer, *Mr. Chook.*" He hoisted a sack of something just purchased onto his shoulder, turned, and trudged away without a second look.

Typical Chook. Despite hailing from another planet half the galaxy away, he related better with the locals than I did.

Next morning I started again. The file was a monster, nearly four terabytes of data, testament to the enormous effort made at the time. These cases were vanishingly rare on our peaceful planet, and this one had the added frisson of an exotic setting: remote Jerbet, where people sat around in wood cabins playing banjos and making six-toed babies with their siblings (not entirely untrue). Media coverage was total.

The room was a mess. I closed down all the files except for the picture of Tim. *Imagine this is a new case*, I said to myself. *Imagine you're starting completely from scratch with no preexisting opinions, what would you do?*

Excellent question. My usual first step would be to rapidly scan the data, then draw up a very small list of key questions.

So do that, Col.

I turned to volume one and reviewed the chrono from scratch. Local plods handled the case initially. Way out of their depth. Their amateurish notes gave way to more polished ones from the SSB. A week after they took over there was a breakthrough. In the woods behind our house, a blue teddy was found that Tim had been carrying on the day (confirmed by CCTV). Half buried in the dirt. What was it doing there?

The search moved to the woods, still with no explanation as to how Tim could have made it there unobserved from Main Street, kilometers away. Cameras showing exterior views of the general store were (of course) not working, and no others in town captured Tim on any route he could have taken to return home.

The case summary was easy to follow and after a few hours I had refamiliarized myself. Now for the key questions. I opened the drawer to Dad's desk and found a pen and some paper. Let's do this the old-fashioned way.

Firstly, was Tim abducted, or abducted and murdered, or just lost somewhere and never found?

I'd always thought of this as something unknowable but now considered the question anew. The way it happened: in the middle of town in broad daylight with a search commenced almost immediately; given the vast resources allocated to finding him and remembering that the extensive media coverage meant *everyone* was looking out for him; properly considered, this made it all but impossible for Tim to be simply lost.

I wrote a single word, *abducted*, on my piece of paper and stared at it in surprise. This had been a highly significant, but surprisingly easy conclusion to arrive at. How come I'd never thought things through this way before?

If he was abducted, was he murdered as well?

The answer had to be yes. Otherwise it would be the same as if he were lost; someone over the decades would have seen and reported him.

So, then the next question, the big kahuna: *Why?*

If he *was* murdered, why would someone do that? Was it Tim in particular they wanted, or would any child of a similar age do? There was a small tingle in my gut now. On my sheet of paper I now wrote down the reasons behind child killings I'd observed over the years, in order of frequency. There were three:

1. *Custody dispute*
2. *Pedophilia*
3. *Mental illness or drugs – i.e. no rational reason*

Reason one we could rule out. Reason two was very rare in this age of psyche readjustments, but not impossible and everybody's worst nightmare.

But with a sigh, I realized that in this case and by a considerable margin, mental illness was the most likely, especially up here in the boondocks with so many weirdos living out in the woods.

Reason three then, by a process of elimination. I underlined it.

I slumped back in my chair, feeling deflated. If this was a random abduction and murder, the perpetrator was probably long dead after all this time, and Tim's body would never be found. Best that could be hoped for was, a hiker finds a bone sticking out of the ground one day, or a dog digs something up. Dad was right, I was wasting my time. What a fool. Why did I think I could come up with a breakthrough after all these years and so much effort on everyone else's part?

But then came a niggle. One of those tiny, weird ones that starts in the back of the brain. I tried to squish it down, tried to think of something else, but it wouldn't go away. I was missing something.

What?

Sana's face popped up on my kom. *"Hey Col,"* she said breathlessly, *"come check this out!"*

Chapter Three

Sana had set up in Tim's old bedroom. The dust and cobwebs were gone, as were the boxes of junk. There was a scarf tied around the otherwise bare room light, creating a cozy vibe, and incense burned in a small filigree pot. Music played and art materials were strewn. In typical fashion, the space had been transformed almost instantly into something recognizably Sana's: her studio. Floating in the center of the room, a meter above the floor, was a giant holo-model of Jubilee, perfect in every detail.

"What do you think?" she asked excitedly.

I stood frozen for a moment. "Where did that come from?"

"Me! I organized for a drone to scan the whole structure for one of our projects. Douglas had *no* idea how Jubilee looked from the outside, didn't even care!" She laughed. "The data was just sitting on my kom, so now I'm going to use it to paint from, look!"

On the far wall stood a work in progress. Sana was using virtual paint and brushing tools to create a two-dimensional image of a section of Jubilee. It floated in the air, about a square meter in size, and it was beautiful. The black of space had become a dense purple, the mess of the underside wisps of fairy floss, Jubilee's navigation lights sparkling through it like diamonds. An artist's impression.

"And look, you can do this…"

She prised the holographic image apart with her fingers, opening up the picture and zooming in. Rather than pixilating, it resolved into ever more fine-grained details underpinning the image. Swirling figures which were actually…what?

"See, *faces*!"

Buried inside the grain of the picture, inside the substrate on which it was based, were 2D images of people, thousands of them. Zoomed in close, you could make them out, but from farther away they dissolved back into the image of Jubilee.

"Who are they all?" I asked.

"That was another project. We photographed the faces of thousands of people. We got visitors, workers, and residents; on the street, in the venues and the red-light districts – everywhere. I didn't even know what I was going to do with it all till now. It's a monument to all those people. To everything that's been lost."

There was a catch in her throat, and she stepped over to the window and leaned on the sill. I heard a sob. Sana had just done one of her one-hundred-eighty-degree emotional about-turns. Not that I blamed her; looking at all those faces had given me a pain in my heart. I tried to force it away, tried not to think of my own missing loved ones.

"It's hard, Col, but I had to do *something*. Sometimes I find faces of people that I knew." She turned and I put my arm around her shoulder, drew her in. She leaned into me, and we gazed at Jubilee together in silence.

Chook and I had a ton of work to do getting the roof ready for the new beam, so it was another two days before I got back to Tim's file. Two days during which that small but insistent niggle kept niggling at my brain, driving me crazy. What was I missing?

I went back to the video, found myself delving through the search behind our house. I remembered it well. Hundreds of people combing the woods, the sound of their machines and voices and excited dogs carrying across the valley. There was vision of Mother in that search; wild-eyed and poorly dressed for the autumn winds. As the days and weeks passed without result, she became deranged. Consumed with guilt, she took to wandering the forest at all hours, calling for Tim until she herself disappeared in late autumn. Her body was found the following spring in a deep granite gully, which explained why her kom signal had been lost.

I sat back and sighed, closed my eyes. What was I not seeing among this plethora of imagery? The thing I needed to know was *just there* – a little ball of understanding sitting in the middle of my brain slightly below conscious awareness and stubbornly refusing to reveal itself. I decided to meditate. I relaxed into my chair and focused on the breath coming in and going out, allowed the mind to go blank. I'm not sure how long I sat for, but it must have been a while. I requested the thought to come up to the surface.

It came.

In a rush of excitement, I finally saw it: *the cameras.*

All of them, *every single one*, was either malfunctioning or had no vision of Tim. Not of him walking along a road somewhere or being bundled into a vehicle, no useful vision of anything, anywhere in town. This defied logic. Cameras are so prevalent in our society, even in a remote place like Jerbet, it was impossible for there to be *no vision at all.*

Something was done to them. Had to have been. I'd seen what Douglas was capable of when we broke into the Chief Justice's house four years before. We'd slipped an AI bundle into the hardened security system, which made Sana and me vanish as if we were never there. Jerbet's cameras had been checked for all that, of course; the Investigators were no fools. They sent the cameras and the data back to HC for analysis by the finest forensic technicians on Brouggh and it was all pronounced clean.

But I knew this could be wrong, knew from firsthand experience. If someone had the right technology, *of course* it could be done. Therefore, the abduction was engineered, pre-planned. And therefore, it was *Tim* they were after. I felt another tingle.

The next question arose: If Tim was taken this way, how did the teddy get behind our house? The answer was obvious once you followed the chain of logic: whoever abducted him had planted it there as a diversion.

I picked up my pen, hand shaking a little now, and wrote down the conclusions I'd just reached:

Tim was taken intentionally.
The cameras were hacked.
The teddy was planted.

I stared at the piece of paper in astonishment. Reading the case notes had yielded nothing, but in stopping and thinking anew, I'd come up with all *this*. No evidence yet, of course, but plenty to go on with.

OK then, now for the most important questions: *Who did it and why?*

The SSB officers had looked at every person within a hundred-kilometer radius of Jerbet, starting with a maximally robust investigation of my father (in cases like these, it's *always* the father). But Dad was clear. He'd been in his office all day, corroborated by multiple and impeccable witnesses, camera footage and data from his own kom.

Same for our friends and relatives and close neighbors. And for more distant neighbors, and even visitors to town before, during and after the abduction. Nothing. SWAT teams pounced on certain cabins in the woods, dropping in from the air, and found evidence of many crimes, including sexual ones against other children – but nothing at all linking to Tim, not so much as a single molecule of his DNA anywhere. Even my future stepmother, Lynda Veitch, was investigated and found to be visiting HC on the day.

I stood up and started to pace.

Wasn't this barking up the wrong tree though? Whoever it was, whatever their motive, they had access to advanced technology. Technology on the level of Douglas, a quantum AI. A new thought hit me, and I can attest that the hoary old cliché: *my blood ran cold* is in fact a real thing, because it suddenly did feel as though ice was running through my veins.

There was a group of people I knew all too well. Who had access to super-advanced technology.

Whose leader on Brouggh had a proven history of sexual abuse toward his own child.

Chapter Four

Lynda had made scones and hot chocolate. Just like the old days. Sweet of her, though every cell in my body was screaming to get back to the study and keep going on the case. I knew better than to argue. We made polite chitchat for a minute and then she got right to the point.

"So, Father tells me you're looking into Tim's case, is that right?"

"Well, yes, seeing as I'm staying here. I've got some time on my hands, I thought, why—"

"But is it *wise*, dear? Opening up old wounds, what good can that do?" She teared up. "I know how much it means to you, really, I do, and I can't blame you for wanting to look into it. But how can it do any good when everyone's already been over it *so many times*?"

We were sitting together at the kitchen bench, just like when I was a kid. We'd sit there while they were all out searching for Tim, and later searching for Mother as well. Lynda would tell me that everything was going to be OK and even though I knew that was a lie it was still nice of her and made me feel a bit better anyway. She was the only person who had taken care of me during those dark days. She gazed at me now with great tenderness.

"Lynda," I said, "what if I were to tell you that I may have a breakthrough?"

Her eyes widened. "*Really*, are you sure?"

"Not totally. No evidence yet, but I've got a certain feeling about what I'm doing, and that feeling usually means I'm on to something."

She puffed up with pride. "*So* clever, Col. We always knew you were going to be a great Investigator. But let's keep this away from Father for the time being, shall we? I don't think it would be good for him."

"Yes, of course."

We sat together for a moment. The scones were delicious. I heaped a pile of cream onto another one and ate it with relish. I knew she'd like that.

"You knew Mother, right? Before she married Father?"

Lynda laughed. "You always used to ask this when you were little, do you remember?"

I shook my head. I didn't actually. I guess my memories were those of a child and all jumbled up around that time.

She sighed. "I knew your mother only in the way everyone in Jerbet knows everybody else. It's a small town. She was a bit older anyway, so we didn't really mix."

"And she was from out of town, right?"

"Yes, she grew up in the woods, but she was a very nice person."

Mother came from one of the infamous cabin communities. She somehow ended up living in Jerbet and marrying a 'townie'.

"How did she meet him?"

"Oh, she got a job at his business." She smiled. "He once told me that he only hired her so he could ask her out; she was very pretty. Then they fell in love. Romantic, don't you think?"

Lynda was surprisingly accepting of Dad's prior relationship. In these situations, people often complain about having to eternally compete with a deceased spouse, but not Lynda. She had such a sunny disposition, always saw the best in others.

"How did she come to be in town? Must have been one of the lucky ones who got some schooling?"

Lynda shook her head. "You'll have to ask Father."

At that we both reflexively looked to our right, where we could see through the open kitchen door into the corridor and the lounge room beyond. Father was sitting alone, reading something on his kom.

I suddenly had a thought. "Hey, have you seen Batum?"

"Yes, he went off with that Chook fellow. Said they were going to the 'pub', whatever that means."

Strange he'd agree to do anything with Chook; the robot seemed to hate him. But they went off together to the pub, which was, if memory served…Chook's word for *bar.*

He took the robot *drinking*?

I was seized with panic; if word got out this could blow our cover. Why would they be so irresponsible? Mind you, when it came to Chook, I could believe anything…but *Batum*?

That was it for my nice chat with Lynda. I thanked her and raced out to Dad's ground car, desperately trying to message them. I covered the short distance to town in minutes. Jerbet's two bars were located on Main Street opposite each other: The Thirsty Camel was a clean and friendly establishment, frequented by families and couples on date night. Drogovitch's on the other hand – eponymously named for its deceased founder – was dank and dirty, attracted all the wrong types and was known for rowdy behavior and vicious fights that spilled out onto the street.

I didn't even bother looking in the Camel.

As I ran, I prayed the bar would be empty. Good chance of that, I reasoned, since it was mid-afternoon. How many people are into day-drinking anyway?

Many, it seemed.

I hadn't stepped inside Drogo's for years. Even when I was old enough, it wasn't a place I wanted to go, and once I left for college, I only came home to see my folks anyway. It had changed little. Dimly lit with a dirty floor made of wood planks, pictures on the wall of various animals being hunted, an old pool table and dartboard. I guess it was homey in a certain way – if you didn't mind the patrons.

Who were in a state of uproar. Most of them clustered at the bar in a tight knot, cheering, glasses raised in mid-toast. Chook was at the center of it all, beady-eyed, holding up a foaming beer. It looked like he'd just called for free drinks for the whole bar. Batum stood alongside him with a glass in hand, a multi-colored flag draped around his shoulders and an old logger's cap sitting on his head. I would swear on a stack of credits *this* high, the robot was grinning.

"*Hey, Col m'boy!*" shouted Chook. "Look everyone, it's my best buddy. *Have a drink*!"

They all cheered. I was drawn into the mob and a huge mug of beer thrust into my hand. I tried to whisper into his ear, which proved impossible, so I had to shout instead: "What the *fuck are you doing*, Chook? We're supposed to keep Batum out of sight!"

Chook grinned, glugged his drink in one hit – his head seeming to hinge open so beer could be poured directly down his throat – and bashed his glass down on the bar.

"*Another! For everybody!*"

The bar erupted with cheering and glass clinking, head tousles and back slaps for Chook. I noticed even Batum was toasting. What to do? Nothing, it seemed. Everyone turned their attention to me now, chanting, "*Chug, chug, chug…*"

I'm not much of a drinker. They used to call me a *two-pot screamer* in the academy days, and even then, I didn't much like beer. I cursed Chook under my breath, lifted the glass and to raucous cheers drank it down in one hit. Chook wrapped a sweaty arm around my shoulders and with poison breath declared. "I fuckin' love you, mate." His eyes were vacant but lit by a strange light that I knew all too well, that of a hardened alcoholic. I'd seen it a million times as a beat cop; perfectly decent when sober, someone else entirely when drunk. I didn't think Chook was violent by nature, more a life-of-the-party guy, but I'd already observed what he was capable of under the right circumstances.

In the middle of all this, my kom lit up. Incoming call from Henderzon, of all people. I shrugged Chook off me, pushed my way free of the throng and staggered outside.

"Henderzon."

"Perolo. You guys OK?"

"Yeah, we're fine, I guess." Muffled cheers emanated from the bar behind me, so I moved away. I had to keep it together, try not to slur my words.

"What's that? Where *are* you, Col?"

"Oh, that. Just some kids." I couldn't afford for Henderzon to know what was really going on, how irresponsible we were being. "I left a message because I need to ask you another favor."

"*Yeaah,*" he said slowly. "Favor bank's getting a little on the empty side, Perolo, if you want me to be honest."

"I know, Henderzon, I really do owe you. But this is just information, I promise."

"OK, shoot."

I quickly filled him in on what I'd been doing regarding Tim's case.

"So, what do you need from me?" he asked skeptically.

"Our boy, Nees, he's been on the scene for decades. When you investigated him, I assume you got everything off his kom. Did he ever travel up here to Jerbet?"

"He's a politico, Col. Probably been to every town on the planet. And thirty-five years ago was pre-Movement. Here on Brouggh anyway. Nees was just a young up-and-comer then, looking for a cause to latch on to."

"And a pedophile."

"That too."

There was a long pause while Henderzon thought. I leaned against a street sign, starting to feel a little woozy from that one beer.

"It's a long shot. How would you tie them together?"

"Dunno yet. Just a feeling at this stage, but if Nees was up here around that time it could be very interesting."

I heard Henderzon sigh. "Sounds like pie-in-the-sky to me, Perolo, but you got nothing better to do, right? I'll send up that data. Anything else?"

"Thanks, buddy."

The line went dead instantly. I had to be careful with Henderzon. At great risk to themselves, he and Aballa were keeping us safe, that safety being further eroded every second Batum remained in the bar. I strode back inside to find another round mid-pour. Chook had to be spending a fortune on this, spending all his savings, whatever they were, on these strangers. Didn't make a lot of sense to me.

I pushed my way to Batum, recognizing the flag draped around his shoulders. It had hung behind the bar for as long as I'd known this place; white stars embedded in a blue cross over a red background. The *Confederation Flag* I think it's called. Dive joints like Drogo's always seemed to have one of these for some reason, something historical to do with Old Earth. Batum's head swiveled toward me as I approached. "What the fuck are you *doing*?" I spat.

The robot seemed to sigh, put his glass down (beer untouched, of course) and turned to me. "Sorry, Col, I couldn't take it anymore." He removed the hat and flag, placed them regretfully on the bar, then joined me as we pushed our way out through the mob.

"Couldn't take *what*?" I asked.

"Hanging out with your dad. There's something—"

Laser fire sizzled across the room from the far corner, striking Batum in the back of the head and enveloping him in a wave of plasma. *Very powerful blaster*, some part of me noted.

The robot acted instantly. Seemingly unaffected by the blast, he flashed across the room in a blur of silver, over to one of the booths in the far corner, where a fraction of a second later he'd pulled a man out of his seat by the scruff of the neck. The bar went silent, people frozen mid-toast. A murmur ran through the room as everyone took stock of what just happened, then a massive cheer erupted.

"*Whoooooaaaaah!*"

They all whooped and high-fived as a huge blaster emerged from Batum's shoulder and trained itself millimeters from the quivering man's face.

"*Go Batum!*" someone called. "*Kill the bastard!*" shouted another. The bar erupted with laughter.

I raced over. Could things be any worse? Not only had Batum absconded from the safety of our house and revealed himself to the massed lowlife of Jerbet, he was now caught up in a *bar fight*. Which I knew would shortly become the stuff of legend; *the day some moron picked a fight with a robot at Drogo's*. This would go viral, not just here, but planetwide.

Then it got even worse.

Sitting inside the banquette was a group of six 'shackies'; four men and two women. They wore hi-vis vests, boots, and overalls. The seats around them were piled with equipment and gear as if they'd just got off shift, and their table was loaded with empty beer mugs, too many to count.

In the midst of all this was Pal Muller.

Rather than being horrified by events, he and his friends were keeled over laughing like the rest of the room, and I twigged immediately what had happened. These people were lumber workers. Rolling drunk, they'd egged on one of their own to shoot Batum with a piece of foresting equipment, probably a laser tree feller: "Go *on, see if you can hit the robot!*"

Mindlessly dangerous. Could have killed a dozen people. The sort of dare you accept if you are a fool to begin with, and out-of-your-mind drunk because some crazy person from off-world had been plying you for hours with free booze. The laser had fallen from the man's grasp and lay across the table, a dark green rod with a funnel at one end and a heavy, boxlike base at the other. A beam of light emerged from Batum's eyes, striking the implement, which a few seconds later started smoking. They'd be needing a new one of those.

"*Fucking moron!*" said Batum, shaking the guy so hard I heard his teeth clack together.

This only set the table off again. They doubled over, weeping with laughter, gasping for air while their friend cringed in fear.

"C'mon," I said through gritted teeth, trying not to look at Pal, "don't waste more time on this idiot. Let's get out of here."

Batum threw the man on the floor like a rag doll, leaned over and said something inaudible into his ear. Then with more cheers, we walked through the bar and out. Batum took my arm and pointed down the street. "Go that way and don't look back."

"Batum, leave it be now, there's no point getting—"

"Trust me, this is for the best, no one will be hurt, I promise."

I looked at him for a moment, perplexed. What fresh horror was this? Ah well, could things be any more fucked up than they were? I shrugged and started walking back to the ground car.

I heard the robot's heavy steps behind me as he trudged back to the bar, heard the door open. Moments later there was a brilliant flash of blue/white light that momentarily lit up the street even though it was broad daylight. Shit! I ran back to Drogo's, dread building with every step, and thrust open the door to find the place strewn with bodies.

"Batum, what have you—"

"EMP temporal lobe inhibitor. They'll wake up in twenty minutes with a headache, but otherwise fine, except for losing data from the last four hours."

The scene was of utter devastation, as if a massacre had occurred. Many had fallen in a big pile near the bar and others were slumped over at their tables and the banquettes in the rear. Smashed glass was everywhere, and beer flowed continuously from an open tap. I leaned over the bar to turn it off. The barman lay slumped on the filthy floor, the glass he'd been pouring still in hand.

Some of the patrons must have hurt themselves on the way down. A nuggety-looking, dark-skinned woman dressed in work gear had a fast-bleeding gash on her forehead – obviously from hitting the edge of the bar when she passed out. That would be more than just a headache. Batum leaned over her, did something and the bleeding stopped. He moved around the room with great speed, attending to people, moving them into more comfortable positions and staunching wounds. Chook, the person who'd instigated all this carnage by bringing our secret robot companion to a public bar, lay flaked out on the floor, a look of beatific peace upon his face.

"Was this your plan all along? Batum?" I asked resignedly. "To come out drinking with these people then use your memory inhibitor on them so they'd forget about it?"

The robot stopped. "Sorry, Col, it was very poor judgment on my part."

"You think?"

A moment later he'd finished tending to all the inert patrons of Drogo's and realistically, it didn't look like anyone would suffer permanent injury. Best get the hell away.

"Cameras?" I asked.

"Dealt with, and everyone's koms too."

We headed outside, my mind churning. Batum had done something to the koms of all the people who were here. Fair enough, there'd be no images or data from that source. But what if someone was in the toilet when the flash went off? Or they came and left during the afternoon? We were still highly vulnerable.

Just as I reached our ground car there was a tap on my shoulder. I whirled around in fright: *Pal Muller.* He stood before me lurching, glass in hand. How the hell did he get here? He must have followed me out of the bar before the flash and I hadn't noticed.

"Perolo!" he said loudly, voice slurred.

Batum had vanished in an instant. I looked out of the corner of my eye to see him in the car, crouching and barely visible, blending in with whatever material the seats were made of. Probably deploying some type of cloaking device.

"What do you want?"

Muller laughed ironically, drained his glass, and smashed it on the footpath. He looked down at his feet, swaying for a long moment as if lost in thought. "I just wanna say," he staggered, regained his footing, then pointed at me with an unsteady hand, "I was an asshole to you."

I stared at him in shock.

"In junior high."

Putting it mildly. I had memory flashes: Muller holding me by the hair, forcing my head into a toilet bowl; he and his friends pouncing on Tim and me in the woods. The shame and impotent fury. The daily terror of going into town knowing he could be lurking somewhere, anywhere, with his hooligan gang. I never told my parents about the episode in the woods because that was the other thing: you didn't dare report, that would only lead to reprisals.

"True," I said, "you were."

Muller grimaced, revealing those ruined dentures again, eyes suddenly watery and red – could he really be tearing up?

"You were *mister fuckin' perfect.*"

I shook my head. In those years my mind was actually full of self-hatred. "Didn't feel like that to me."

Pal laughed. "But at least you weren't a *freak*. Look at *this*!" He gestured toward his own strangely elongated face.

When I was a kid, adults always used to trot out the same tired line: bullies only did what they did because they felt bad about themselves, they were just 'jealous', so the argument went. Not much consolation.

Not when your oppressor was a foot taller than you and had a standing army of brutes as backup. But here we were decades later and looking at the Pal Muller before me now filled with anguish, it was hard not to feel a stirring of compassion.

"I guess we were all kids, weren't we? And look, there are things you can do, Pal. Treatments. You'd have to go to HC, but I could—"

"Not for people like *me*! You don't get it," he said bitterly.

"I don't under—"

"It's not allowed. Not for *us* anyway."

He was talking about the forest communities, where paranoia about the government ran deep, all the way to diktat against medical treatment, even vaccines. They'd rather their kids die of preventable disease or remain disfigured by genetic mutation than trust the wider community around them.

"Even so, Pal—"

"Listen, *forget that.* I figured you'd want to know somethin'. About your brother. Tim it was, right?"

"Tim?" This was the last thing I expected. My heart suddenly beat faster.

"Come to Hyvon." A location pin appeared in my kom sent by Pal, which meant that he at least *had* a kom. I knew that wasn't the case for all of them.

"You want me to *visit you*?"

"Your ma come from Hyvon – you know that?"

I stared at him in shock. I knew she was from the woods originally, but the same community as Pal Muller?

He laughed. "You don't know *nothin'*, do ya?" He picked up his gear pack, slung it over his shoulder and turned to leave. "I'm not goin' back in *there*." He gestured to the bar with his thumb. "Those bloody morons have all gone to sleep!"

Chapter Five

So naturally, after that incident at the bar we packed up and fled Jerbet straight away, right?

That would have been the obvious thing to do, but at the time I didn't even consider it. While it was true that anyone who'd been cortex flashed would have no memory of Batum, there was still Pal, and probably others at large. Then again, if anyone tried to say that a killer robot had been hanging out at Drogo's, they'd be looked at as if they were mad.

Still, it wasn't smart to stay. I knew that somewhere in my gut but found ways of rationalizing my actions. *Where would we go anyway?* I told myself. *Where would be safer than my own isolated hometown, protected by high-up friends in the security services?* In hindsight, it would have been better to go on a publicity tour; broadcast to the galaxy, scream from the rooftops about what happened to Jubilee and what the Movement was doing. We might have even been safer, protected by the public attention and it would have put moral pressure on the League to act.

Sana could have pulled something like that off.

But not me; I'm a private kind of guy and besides, I was still holding out hope. Praying that Aballa would come through, and news of Danee would pop out of the 'system'. And more than anything I'm a very stubborn man. It felt like the truth about what happened to Tim was just starting to emerge. I had the tingle telling me I was on the right track and to be honest, I'd become obsessed. In the end I let emotion take precedence over reason.

A massive trove of data arrived, pulled from Rubichek Nees' kom. But I couldn't start on it right away given the state of the roof; the weather was due to turn any day and we had to get it finished. Chook turned up the next morning bright as a button, as if the events of the day before had never happened, which for him at least was true. I couldn't even admonish him about it.

Batum was another matter. We talked quietly in my study, where he apologized again.

"It's all right, Batum," I said with a shrug. "I just don't understand what got into you, it seems so out of character."

If the robot were human, he would have sighed. "Col, it's concerning to me too. It's possible my personality construct has been destabilized due to the damage I took on Jubilee. Possible. I'm not certain."

"And the gadget that knocked everyone out, where did that come from?"

"Where do you think?"

"Douglas?"

The robot nodded.

"And my father, what did you mean? You said you couldn't stand him anymore."

"No, more like I couldn't take it anymore. It was OK at first, he's a very nice human actually, but there's something wrong there, Col."

"With him?"

"Yes."

"In what way?"

"The feeling."

"What about the feeling?"

"I don't know." Batum shook his head. "Ask Sana, she understands feelings. I'm just a stupid robot."

The file on Nees was so huge I needed a special program to break it down – even after narrowing the time period in question to a single year spanning the six months before and after Tim's disappearance. Looking at kom data is not what you might think. It's messy. It's a person's whole life recorded in real time, and deliberately structured to make it difficult for use as an intelligence tool. Sure, I'd done my share of kom diving in my time, but never on such a big file. Separating out the communication, visual and location data was taking so long that Aballa had to send me one of the latest tools. Then I had to learn how to use it. If I was still in the department, there would have been a tutorial, or at least some younger person who could have helped. I forged on, but it was no fun.

So, it was a welcome relief then when Sana called me down for a chat. With nothing better to do, she was spending ever more time than ever in the studio.

"Your father's *feeling*?" she asked, pouring a cup of tea. "How would I know?"

"Batum thought you might. He thinks there's something up, something going on there."

Sana sighed and rubbed her eyes. "I can tell you what the name of the emotion is: *grief*. You can explain that to Batum."

"I think he got that much."

"And I dunno, put yourself in his shoes. Your kid just disappears one day, never to be found, and then your wife basically kills herself over it. Not marvelous, I'd say."

"Of course. I mean, that's what I always thought too. But after all this time, I—"

"We grieve in different ways, Col. And some people just never get over events like this. I saw it a million times in my counseling work."

"But wouldn't you eventually…you know…"

"Do a psyche adjustment?"

I nodded.

Sana looked out the window for a long time and sighed again, as if resigning herself to something. "It's true that after the passage of so much time, most people would have sought treatment by now if they were still carrying that much grief. It's gotta be a conscious choice to hang on to it, which *I get*. If he loses the grief, he loses that final connection with his son. But even *so*, most people would have chosen to move on by now. So yes, it's a bit weird."

Sana had just talked herself around to something.

"What do you think it means?"

"I dunno, why don't you try *talking* to him. Ever thought of that?"

"It's not easy, talking with Dad. But it's true I've never really tried, not on this subject anyway."

"Not once, in all these thirty-five years?"

"Nope."

"*Unbelievable*," said Sana, pouring more tea, "you and your fucking family."

But it was my mother's history I chose to look at first. Made more sense, I reasoned as our rented flyer skimmed the forest en route to Hyvon. Anything I learned now would be fodder for that future conversation. Sana sat beside me. I'd contemplated bringing Chook, and he might have been useful, but I was still annoyed at him after that bar incident so had left him behind.

Brouggh is a big planet, twenty percent larger than Old Earth, but only five percent more massive. Not sure why, something about the planetary core having a lower density. In practical terms that meant a huge amount of extra surface area on which to grow…*trees*.

I ticked off the hamlet communities as we flew over them: Mazaye, Herment, Perpezat, each barely visible under the endless sea of green. If they hadn't shown up on my kom, I wouldn't even know they were there. How many other places lay scattered under this world-covering forest, off-grid and totally unknown?

Ten minutes from Jerbet we began to slow, and eventually put down in a small clearing where a couple of dinged-up flyers were already parked. Pal waited near the edge of the forest, leaning against a tree. He raised a hand briefly in greeting, face expressionless.

"That him?" whispered Sana.

"Yup."

"Wow. This is creeping me out already."

"Try growing up around here."

I popped the doors and we stepped out, the perfume of the forest hitting us instantly. Overwhelming. The air was alive with the hum of a million insects, shot with birdsong that came from everywhere around us. A hot, late afternoon sun beat down as we tramped across the rough ground to meet Pal. He stepped forward and gravely shook our hands without saying a word, then tilted his head for us to follow. Sana looked at me and I shrugged.

The forest swallowed us instantly; the air grew cooler. We followed a small but well-maintained path and only a minute or two later stepped into a clearing ringed with buildings. Not a clearing, so much as a *hollow*, because the covering of forest was fully intact. This settlement had been completely invisible from above.

At the end of the path, just before we reached the village, stood a large sign covered with bold writing. A manifesto it would seem, and clearly of such importance that no one entering could avoid reading it:

HUMANKIND IS ENCHAINED BY A NETWORK OF RULES WHICH CANNOT BE DISPENSED WITH AS THEY ARE REQUIRED BY INDUSTRIAL SOCIETY!!!

INDUSTRIAL SOCIETY CONSTRAINS PERSONAL FREEDOMS!

THE STRONGER TECHNOLOGY MAKES SOCIETY, THE LESS FREEDOM THERE IS!

TECHNOLOGY DESTROYS NATURE, WHICH STRENGTHENS TECHNOLOGY FURTHER!

TECHNOLOGICAL SELF-AMPLIFICATION IS STRONGER THAN POLITICS!

USE OF TECHNOLOGY OR POLITICS TO TAME THE SYSTEM ONLY STRENGTHENS IT!

TECHNOLOGICAL CIVILIZATION CANNOT BE REFORMED, ONLY DESTROYED!

EVERY CITIZEN'S DUTY IS TO PUSH INDUSTRIAL SOCIETY TOWARD ITS INEVITABLE SELF-COLLAPSE!

Strictures: XXVI.1

We stopped for a moment to read, and I snuck a sideways glance at Sana. She had what I knew to be the 'look': pursed lips, overly serious, avoiding my gaze. Trying not to laugh.

"Wow, that's intense!" I remarked to Pal. He waved a hand dismissively and strode off. Didn't seem like our guide was especially over-awed by Strictures: XXVI.1.

Pal stopped in the middle of the clearing, put two fingers to his mouth and let loose a high-pitched whistle. Another man appeared from nowhere. He was small and tubby, heavily stooped with long greasy hair, wearing a backward-pointing cap and heavily patched clothing. The shape of his head was disturbing. It looked as though someone had held him by the jaw and pushed the top of it sideways by an inch or so. The middle part was at a slight, but definite diagonal to the top and bottom. A mutation obviously, one I'd never seen or even heard of before. I dared not look at Sana.

The man nodded briefly to Pal then walked briskly to one of the buildings ringing the hollow, gesturing for us to follow. He pushed at a wobbly door, which opened directly onto a set of old and worn wooden stairs and proceeded up them two at a time.

"What's this, Pal, where are we going?" I asked.

"You'll see. *Please.*" He stepped aside for me to pass.

I shrugged. Whatever I was here for, the reason lay up there. We tromped up the narrow staircase, Sana following closely behind. I could feel her tension.

At the top of the stairs, a large, open room looked out over the clearing. The rear wall was entirely covered with faded 2D images and waiting in its center, seated in a wooden rocking chair, was an old woman. Did I say, old? – more like *ancient.* Her hair was thinning and white, skin grainy and dark and hanging in folds, her breath as ragged as her clothes. The air smelled of something unpleasantly organic. She looked up as we entered, nodding with a faint smile, her eyes milky with cataracts.

I tried not to react. We simply don't *see* people like this in our society anymore. Not with the kind of treatments that ensure modern humans can live a two-hundred-year lifespan while remaining fit, attractive, and healthy for the vast majority of it.

Pal walked to where the woman sat and spoke kindly, close to her ear. "Ma, this is Col and Sana."

The woman appeared not to understand. She stared at me, unblinking through those ruined eyes. The room was stuffy and hot, the boards creaked a little in the slight wind.

"*Doris's boy*, Ma," said Pal.

A light seemed to go on in the woman's face. She smiled with understanding and waved me toward her, but I couldn't move; a tight knot of apprehension had lodged itself in my stomach.

Pal spoke again. "Col, this is your grandmother."

I heard Sana stifle something, a sob. There was a roaring in my ears.

Grandmother? How did I not know I had a *grandmother*? I was suddenly furious with Father. All this time – my whole life – there had existed a living link to my real *mother*? How could he keep that from me?

My feet took me across the room unguided. I squatted down next to her for there was no other chair in the room, and she leaned over and stroked my head. A mother's touch. Her mouth was moving, I leaned in to try and hear.

"She can't talk these days, Col," said Pal, "though she does understand. Sometimes anyway."

I took her hand and kissed it. "I'm glad to meet you. I'm sorry I never came before; I didn't know about you."

She smiled tenderly and now I could see it: my mother's smile.

I don't know how long I stayed with her, for a crashing numbness fell upon me and my mind seemed to stop working. I sat cross-legged on the floor next to her in a strange reverie while the house breathed in the wind. Eventually Pal interrupted. "Dagan says it's time for her nap, so we better go."

I looked up to see she was already in fact asleep. I waved goodbye anyway and followed Pal down the stairs on legs wobbly from more than just sitting on the hard floor. We took a new path, leading farther into the woods. No one spoke until finally I asked Pal, "How old is she?"

"Hmph." He chuckled. "Not sure exactly. Maybe eighty-five? Somethin' like that. They're not particular with recordkeepin' out here."

Eighty-five? I knew people this age who were just starting to consider having children, and there was she, body failing from old age.

Sana touched me on the shoulder. "You OK?"

I put my hand on hers and tried to think of something to say but there was nothing except a strange hollowness inside. Not good. I knew that later on when she had the chance, she'd be hassling me, saying I ought to be *feeling* something.

The forest grew thick and dark, and the afternoon sun disappeared, eaten by the green. The air was moist and cold, and it felt as though we were walking uphill. After only a few minutes, the incline turned around and we seemed now to be going downward. The brush around us cleared and there was suddenly open space ahead. Vast. Some kind of semitransparent netting or roof running across the top of it. Camouflage I suppose, because an opening this large should have been visible when we flew over.

The clearing contained a network of fields terraced into the gentle slope. We wound our way through a vegetable garden, beyond which were rows of grain, and beyond them open pasture where animals grazed. People, not many, maybe three or four, were tending to the crops and it looked like the grain harvest was in progress. A small, human-powered threshing machine moved through the stalks spreading the heads of grain. The scale was huge, enough food growing here to support a whole town.

At the edge of the vegetable plot where it met the grain fields was a small hut with a veranda. A man was waiting there, seated at a table set with tea and cookies. He was a big and well-muscled guy, middle aged but with a full head of dark hair and no trace of genetic abnormality. He looked up as we approached and smiled, revealing perfectly straight, brilliantly white teeth.

"Here they are! How's the leg, Pallavan?" He gestured for Sana and me to sit.

"Yeah, not too bad, sir," Pal said. "See youz later." He turned immediately and headed back along the path we'd taken, and I noticed that he did in fact walk with a slight limp. Our host obviously kept a close eye on these people – *his* people – for he was clearly a leader of some sort. We joined him at the small table, the air warm and the view pleasing.

"Wonderful to finally meet you, Col, *and* Sana, who I've heard so much about!" She shrugged without smiling; this kind of buttering up usually didn't play well with her. I went to speak but he cut me off.

"So let me answer what I'm sure are going to be your first questions. Yes, this is the settlement of Hyvon, population 4,397 last we checked." He poured tea into each of our mugs. "It's a hybrid settlement, which means we're more than ninety percent self-sufficient, but we do still allow contact with folks like you in Jerbet. A stance some of our, shall we say, philosophically purer brethren consider beyond the pale." He laughed to himself at this last comment.

I was skeptical. "But still pure *enough* to not use anti-aging treatments?"

The man smiled kindly as if I were a naïve child. "Col, getting old is part of life. A part of life that modern society has tried to disavow. If Stella wanted to, she'd be allowed to make use of all those treatments. People here are totally free to make their own choices because personal liberty is our highest principle. No one is forced to do anything."

"But then she'd be all on her own though, right?"

"Of course not! She'd be able to come and go entirely as she pleased, nothing would change." The man spread his hands with a smug smile. I didn't believe him for a second.

Sana took a sip of tea and nodded, which meant it was OK. Her eyes met mine and I knew instantly what she was trying to communicate: *no point arguing*.

"So, mister…what actually is your name? I don't think—"

"Apologies, Col, I should have introduced myself at the outset. You can call me Elias."

"I noticed Pal referred to you as 'sir'."

"A form of respect."

"You're the boss here then?" cut in Sana.

Elias laughed, a little too easily. "We don't really have leaders as such. However, I am at times called upon to handle certain burdens of responsibility and coordination, and it's not always possible to dissuade my fellow comrades from using the entirely unnecessary honorific."

Sana just about managed to stop herself from doing an eye roll.

"I assume this was your idea to bring me here? I have to thank you because I might never have known about my grandmother. But is there something else that you wanted to speak—"

"Col, I just wanted to reach out. We've all followed your career with interest and great admiration, and we thought it was time you knew about...the *other* side of your family."

"I have more relatives here, in Hyvon?"

Elias was taking a sip of his tea, and almost choked mid-gulp. "Col, apologies again. I keep forgetting how little you know." He gestured to the fields and forest around us. "You are related in one way or another to every person in this settlement."

★ ★ ★

We finished with a tour of the facilities: the granary, the school, a large commercial kitchen, an accommodation, and ablutions block and so on and on and on. All hidden away with great care, but for no sensible reason, underneath the trees, as if these people expected to be invaded from the air at any minute.

I still felt the same terrible numbness inside, but my head was spinning now as well. All I could think of was how every person I met was related to me in some way. Even Pal. No wonder he'd been emotional and wanted to apologize. When we remember people from our youth, they're always fixed somehow, frozen in time based on the way we perceived them back in the day. But how can you judge a person for how they were at sixteen? Surely change and growth are possible? Pal had turned into a kind and caring person. Screwed up too. From feeling like a 'freak' as he put it, and burdened by his community's immutable way of life. Thank *God* I hadn't grown up here.

But they were *my* people, every one of them. Something almost impossible for my brain to absorb. We ended up back at the clearing where the flyer waited, and I decided it was time to speak openly.

"Thank you, Elias. I'm still trying to take everything in, but thanks."

"You're welcome, Col. You can come back here anytime; this is *your* place."

I paused for a minute, then finally spat it out. "Elias, I'm looking into the disappearance of my brother, Tim. I assume you know about that?"

"Sure."

"I was wondering if you had any information which might aid my investigation?"

Elias shook his head in wonder. "You can't be serious?"

"Yes. Yes, of course I am."

He leaned against my flyer as if needing its support. "Of course we can help! We can do better, much, much better than that. We know exactly who did it and how!"

Chapter Six

Sana and I were both silent as the flyer lifted, hovered over the clearing for a moment, then turned and headed north for Jerbet, rapidly picking up speed.

"What do you think?"

"Hmmm..." Sana gazed out at the endless forest below. "I think...he didn't get those choppers from growing up in Hyvon."

It was true, everyone else in the village had teeth that were crooked or rotting, or at the very least, less than perfect. It must be how human teeth naturally are if you don't intervene.

"Yeah, I wondered about that too."

"And as for the stuff about him not being the town's leader – *pfffft*." Sana shook her head.

"Must be their ideology, I suppose, except that, you know, there's human nature. In the end we need leaders."

"I guess." She sighed. Sana, of course, had been a political leader herself. "It's all just so *much*. Meeting your grandma and everyone else, it's blown my mind. And what about that picture on your grandma's wall?"

"What picture?"

"You didn't see? There was a photo of *Gilham*! One of those corny devotional give-away things."

That was a shock. I'd been so focused on the old woman, *my grandmother*, I'd barely noticed anything. I hurriedly scanned my kom, bringing up vision from the bedroom. Sure enough, there on the wall behind the rocking chair was a tattered picture of Gilham, posing with light behind him to give it a more 'spiritual' look.

I felt the tingle in my gut. This was significant. Were the forest dwellers involved with the Movement? If so, did they have something to do with Tim's disappearance? Not according to them anyway, especially after what we'd just heard.

"And what did you think of Elias's theory about Tim?"

"I don't know, I mean…I guess you have to look into it, but I'm skeptical, not entirely sure why."

Sana's intuition was often correct. Something about Elias was off. So smooth and polished. Though you couldn't say he was a hypocrite – being the only person in town to have visited a dentist – because he clearly stated that everyone else was allowed to as well. But for whatever reason, while he was getting those teeth done, my grandma was wasting away from old age. I might have known her, had a real relationship with her.

And then there was the stuff about Tim.

Elias had led Sana and me back away from the flyer, over to the shade of a nearby tree, and we sat together on the ground in a little circle.

"I'm sorry, but what I'm about to explain to you is such common knowledge here in Hyvon that it's difficult to believe others aren't aware of it."

"So please, enlighten us," said Sana.

Elias looked into my eyes intensely. "I'm sure you've noticed the disfigurements of some of the citizens here in Hyvon?"

"The genetic mutations?" I asked.

"*No!* Not mutations!" Elias' eyes blazed. "That's what society tells you, wants you to believe, but it's a lie! The ones in charge say that to cover their arses because if the real truth got out there'd be hell to pay."

"What's the real cause then?" I asked, nonplussed.

"Chemical pollution."

"Pollution? From what? You're living out here in the woods, you couldn't *find* a more pristine environment."

"This area, that mainstream society calls the 'Gandolfin Shire', is part of a huge river system. You know that, right?"

Of course, we'd all studied local geography at school. It was hard to make out from above because of the heavy woods, but for a one-hundred-kilometer radius around Jerbet, from the Arcadius mountains north to the Lefevre marshlands south, it was one huge valley. All of it draining eventually into the Jerbet river.

"Yes, but how—"

"The Duval Mill. It's been slowly poisoning the river and all our people for centuries."

"Elias, the mill runs *clean*, everyone knows that!"

"Clean *now*, after we raised such a big stink."

"And in any case, the volume of production there is tiny. How could it possibly pollute a whole river system?"

"Tiny *now* but know your history, Col. During the Collapse, things were different. Brouggh depended on the forest for building materials just like in the Old Earth days, and Duval Mill was magnitudes larger than now. They could get away with anything they wanted."

It was true that during the Collapse we lost the ability to make hardiplaz on Brouggh – something to do with critical supplies for the giant matter transformers. For a period, construction relied on ancient methods: carpentry, concrete forming and the like, and Jerbet had been a major production center for the planet. These days, of course, it was back to being a sleepy town. Making lumber for only the legacy industries that needed it.

"And you're saying the mill poisoned all your people?"

"Yes, we're still dealing with the aftereffects even now. I can show you scientific evidence!"

This was shocking, if true. Though I'd really want to see that 'scientific evidence'.

"OK, assuming this is fact, what's it got to do with Tim?"

"Your brother had 'genetic abnormalities', right? Which they supposedly 'fixed' in the womb – that's what they said, correct?"

I nodded. A knot was forming in my belly.

"Tim grew up a townie, even though Doris came from here – seems your dad has quite a taste for forest women. Tim was getting to an age where they do the vaccines, and the tests. Some embarrassing information would have almost certainly come to light about the lasting effects of the poison in his system that he inherited from his mother. So they disappeared him."

"Who?"

"The people in *charge*, Col. Those who keep your society locked in its jail of disinformation. The *elites*."

"But Tim was healthy, they fixed him."

"They didn't fix anything, Col. They only ever deal with symptoms, these people, not the cause, and that's because—"

"And anyway, *I'm* fine. How come *I* don't have any abnormalities?" My voice had been rising, the last was said with real passion. Elias motioned for me to calm down and we all took a breath.

"Col," he said kindly, "for whatever reason, *you* were lucky."

★ ★ ★

The flyer touched down outside my father's house, and lifted again almost as soon as we'd alighted, silently flitting back to its depot. I checked my kom. Eighty-seven credits had been debited for the afternoon's flight. Not too bad, especially when there were C: 1,783,432 remaining. We stood on the curb and stared for a moment at the house. Some temporary coverings remained on the roof. Tomorrow the beam Chook and I ordered would be lifted into place. I'd called this my home for the first two decades of my life, totally unaware there was a whole community of other people, my kin, living only fifteen minutes south by flyer.

"What are you going to do?" asked Sana, taking my hand.

"Very shortly, I'll be paying Mr. Duval a visit at the lumber mill."

"Not *that*, I mean about your father? *Surely* you have to talk with him *now*?"

"Oh...I suppose," I said flatly. "To tell the truth, I have no idea what to do."

"Just talk to him, Col, for God's sake. It's not that *hard*!" Suddenly annoyed, she dropped my hand like it was something distasteful and stormed off into the house.

But Father was feeling poorly that night, at least according to Lynda, so he didn't emerge for dinner. It would be another twenty-four fateful hours before we'd get a chance to talk.

Sana skipped dinner and vanished to her studio without a word. I used the evening to keep working on the data from Chairman Nees' kom and had an instant breakthrough: confirmation that he'd visited Jerbet a month before Tim's disappearance. The data had him in town and also moving around the countryside visiting the forest communities. After more hours of sifting information and synchronizing bio-location data with grid references, I made another shocking discovery. Chairman Nees – or rather, small-town Mayor (and aspiring senator) Nees – had visited *Hyvon*.

Three weeks before Tim disappeared.

I rocked back in my chair and tried to calm my racing heart. Here was a proven connection the people in Hyvon were involved with Nees in some way.

I went back to the images on my own kom, checking the wall behind my grandmother's rocking chair, and studied the picture there of Gilham. There was something about it, something weird that I couldn't put my finger on. It was bothering me. And then I saw it.

He was *young*.

This was a photo of Gilham, but pre-Movement. Or at least, decades before it came to Brouggh. A picture unlike any I'd seen on-planet. Was Nees hyping the Movement even then? Did he give that picture to my grandmother?

But none of this gelled. If Nees was involved with the forest communities at that time, then he couldn't have had anything to do with Tim's disappearance. Could he? Elias had been passionate about wanting to help. Whatever delusions those people might have about the way the world worked, I didn't suspect them of killing Tim.

But what if it wasn't killing they wanted, but something else? What if Elias's story about the chemicals was a ruse and they'd stolen Tim, taken him to raise as one of their own?

I had an image of him alive and healthy, living a quiet life working in the fields – he always loved the outdoors – unaware of his real background. He could be lying in a bed over in Hyvon at this very moment. I felt a throb in my chest. I forced the feeling back down again.

A dozen scenarios played out in my mind, spinning in different directions, implicating different people. The leads in this case weren't narrowing, they were multiplying. I knew from bitter experience that it was time to stop now and besides, the screens in front of me were starting to spin. It had been a very long day. Best to let everything digest and start fresh in the morning.

I switched off and went to my room to find Sana already in bed, pretending to be asleep.

"I was going to talk to Father," I said a little defensively, "but he wasn't feeling well and didn't come out so—"

"Yeah, I get it," she said crossly, then sat up, clearly wide awake. "Anyway, Col, it's not really about that, it's the *feeling*. I simply can't take it anymore."

"What do you—"

"*C'mon!* Meeting your grandma and all those people. Investigating Tim. I couldn't think of anything more *triggering*. But you seem all rational and fine like there's no problem. The feeling has to go somewhere, and of course it comes to me coz I'm *so* bloody empathic."

"I'm sorry, how can—"

"I can't *stand* it anymore. This always used to happen when we were together!" Sana's eyes blazed as she worked her way into a tirade. "You and your family are just so *buttoned up*! Do you know how many times I've spoken with Mum since we got here?" She didn't wait for an answer. "*Every day!* Every day at least once a day since I've been back. Of course I haven't told her all the details, but you know, I've been sharing about what's been going on for me. *Emotionally*."

Sana was dressed for bed. She wore nothing more than a shimmery silk slip that would have weighed no more than a gram.

"You're right," I said eventually. "Of course you are. It's my way of coping to—"

"*Yes*, yes, *I know*. So get in touch, right now. How are you *feeling*?"

"Literally, right now?"

"Yes!"

I closed my eyes. Tried to quiet my raging mind, still swirling with a million ideas and theories. I searched around inside, looking for a feeling. There was a faint echo coming from the region of my heart. Locked behind a solid wall, but something bleeding through, trying to get out. I imagined going through the wall, observing what was on the other side.

A lake, no, an ocean. An infinity of sadness. Always been there.

...Sunday morning, I get up early and pad down the hall to Tim's room. I imagine him lying on his bed inside there, eyes full of mischief, ready for fun. I stand before his door but don't dare open it... Afternoon, sitting on the swing in our backyard. Mum will come home today, I know it. She'll walk out of the forest right there, holding Tim's hand...

And then, it's painful to remember. Tears. My own, unshed for so long... and relief.

Relief to feel, because behind the grief, love. Of course.

Next, somehow, I was curled up in a ball, my head in Sana's lap. I was like that for I don't know how long. Finally, she spoke very tenderly. "Col, you show your love by doing things, you're a *protector.* I get that and I've always admired you for it. But sometimes," she said, smiling, "jeesh, you really have to *feel* something, give us little people a break!"

We both laughed.

"You know, I've always respected you too, Sana. So much. You've always been...an inspiration for me."

"Really?"

I laughed. "How could you not know that?"

"I never felt that way inside." She touched her chest. "Just crummy old me, trying to do my best, any way that I could."

I laughed again, sat up and cupped her face in my hands.

Dear reader, I can feel your judgment bubbling up at this point, and honestly, I don't blame you! How could I justify sleeping with Sana that night, especially with Danee lost, along with my two baby daughters? What excuse did I possibly have?

I suppose I could blame it on the moment. All that emotion, feeling all those feelings I'd kept under wraps for so long. Definitely played a part I'd say.

You could also argue (if you wanted to be pedantic) that Sana was still my legal wife. But that would be a stretch.

Or what about that Sana was arguably the most beautiful woman you'd ever clap eyes on – something even Danee admitted. How could any red-blooded man lie alongside her night after night and be expected to keep his vows?

Nope. Not really.

The reason I slept with Sana, the reason I still can't forgive myself for, is that I still loved her.

Chapter Seven

"Fuck me! Are those cocksuckers *still* going on about that shit?"

This was Frank Duval's reaction when I brought up the question of whether his mill was poisoning the forest dwellers, as alleged by Elias.

"*Francois!*" came a scolding, disembodied female voice from an adjoining room. *"Enough* already with the language!" Frank rolled his eyes and, undaunted, launched into an expansive tirade against the settlements.

But I'm getting ahead of myself. It's hard to keep track of everything in the order that it happened on that last crazy day in Jerbet.

I woke still entwined with Sana, my kom buzzing with angry messages from Chook:

"Where are you, fuck-knuckle?? The beam is here!!!" etc.

Damn. The roof beam.

I texted Chook, threw on some clothes and raced out. Everything looked the same as it had the day before, but all felt surreal and wrong now. What the hell did I do? An image appeared of Danee and the girls, triggering an avalanche of guilt and recrimination. Batum was downstairs; and it looked like he was waiting for me. He reached out with one of his mechanical arms as I raced by. "Col, there's something I need to show you, *most urgent.*" A horn tooted outside in the street, the delivery truck.

"Batum, I gotta go, can it keep just a little while?" I didn't wait to hear the answer.

In the old days such a thing would have arrived on a semitrailer and required a giant crane to lift it onto our roof. Not anymore. Our six-meter beam was strapped to the roof of a comically small ground car that looked like it was going to be flattened by it at any moment. The critical difference? Two industrial a-grav lifters on each end carrying at least ninety percent of the weight.

Chook was already up on the roof in his safety vest. I strapped on mine as I clambered up the ladder to join him. He was grinning, clearly happy and excited for our big day – as I would have been too, had I not just trashed my life.

I knew in principle what we were about to do, but Chook seemed to have inborn DIY expertise. He dropped a rope down from the hand winch we'd set up the day before and motioned for me to do the same at another farther along the roofline. A few minutes later, the delivery woman attached these to our beam, released the straps and we pulled it free from the vehicle.

The giant beam now hung from our roof, suspended by impossibly light-looking ropes. With a nod from Chook, we both started winding and the whole thing rose slowly. We had to be careful here, the a-grav lifters might be displacing the beam's weight, but nothing would alter its huge mass. Once moving in any direction, it would *keep* moving.

I won't bore you with the details too much. The beam was gradually pulled up to our height, then reattached to new winches mounted farther up the roof. Over the next hour or so it was carefully manipulated into its final position, the lifters turned off, and we watched breathless as it settled under its own true weight into the exact spot it was meant to.

Chook and I whooped and high-fived. For the last hour, I'd almost managed to forget about the night before. Almost. Every so often an image would arise of Sana's face, of her body pressed against me. "Great work, Chook," I said with utmost sincerity. There was no way I could have handled all that on my own.

"Pleasure's mine, mate, haven't had this much fun in *years*!"

All that was needed now was for the beam to be fixed down in place, the roof tiles reattached and the tarpaulins and building mess tidied up. Nothing onerous, but still a few more hours' work – hours I didn't have.

"Can I ask a big favor? Can I ask you to finish up here on your own? I've got all this…*stuff* I have to deal with."

He waved me off, smiling. "No probs, Col, leave it with me." He'd be done by lunchtime, easily finished in time for his daily appointment at the pub.

I raced around downstairs, searching frantically, then finally called the robot on my kom. He was upstairs in the attic, waiting for me. "What's going on, Batum, what did you need to show me?"

"Col," he said gravely, "it appears that more data in my system was lost. I have now been able to retrieve it. The plasma blast yesterday in the bar seems to have triggered some kind of partial reboot that—"

"Batum, *what*?" Hysteria rose in me. "Is this about Danee, more lost messages?"

"No, not that. It's possible that I shouldn't actually be sharing this. I may have had an installed directive to keep what I'm about to show you secret but lost that directive as well somehow. It's confusing."

I looked at him. It was true that over the past few days Batum seemed to have grown more feeble – if that was a thing with robots – as if finally starting to break down after all these millennia, especially given the incredible pounding he'd taken on Jubilee. He looked vulnerable.

"Spit it out, Batum."

A cavity opened in the robot's chest, there was the sound of a small servo motor and a drawer slid smoothly out. In its center, a silver sphere the size of a tennis ball.

"This is Douglas," said Batum.

I nearly choked. "Douglas? In that ball?"

"Yes. His eleventh fail-over processing core, to be precise. He asked me to retrieve it when the fighting started on Jubilee."

The sphere was beautiful, though difficult to look at. In the dim light of the attic, the silver surface seemed to glow in a way that was hard to describe. I went to touch it, but Batum warded me off.

"Best not. In any case it would be too heavy for you to pick up. Apparently most of its mass can't be seen with the naked eye as it's entangled in other dimensions, and don't ask me to explain. The weight differential of my body compared to spec was what started the process of recovering my knowledge about carrying this thing."

My mind spun. "So that day in the control room on Jubilee, you weren't there to save me, Douglas sent you to grab *this*!"

"My instructions were to retrieve the core, then collect you from the security department. I didn't expect you to be in the control room."

Just as well I was though."If this is a backup of Douglas, can we talk to it?"

"No, it's not a backup, it's a processing core only and has no associated memory files."

"You said it was the eleventh fail-over, meaning..."

"All ten of the other cores would have to fail before this one started up."

"But how...how would it function?"

"Col, it's something to do with muon entanglement. Somehow this thing talks to the other parts of Douglas in different dimensions. It's crazy, I don't understand either."

"And the other ten cores are where?"

Batum gave the equivalent of a shrug, turning both robotic 'hands' palm up. We looked at the beautiful ball for a moment and an idea started to germinate.

"If this is the core, where are the memory files? They'd have to be huge, wouldn't they?"

"Your guess is as good as mine. I don't think I'm even meant to remember carrying this thing."

They were on *The Poobah*. Of course.

Had to be. It explained the strange and experimental setup of the ship's computer, and the huge partition I could never get around. Was this a setup? Just one element of Douglas's last-ditch escape plan, with a core embedded in Batum and memory files on board the ship? Did Douglas scheme all along for us to flee Jubilee the way we did? I told the robot about these thoughts, and he pondered for a moment. "I'm just one tiny cog in Douglas's giant mechanism."

"Aren't we all, Batum."

The drawer slid back into the robot's body, the slot disappearing as though it were never there. "Batum, I've got a crazy idea – we *can* talk to this thing, right?"

"Yes, we could, but there's no use. It's got no memory, won't have any data we could interrogate."

"That's OK, we could still—"

At that moment, Sana buzzed my kom and I jolted as if it were an electric shock. "You in the studio?" I asked.

"Yes, we need to talk."

"*Agreed.* See you in a moment." I turned to Batum. "Don't go anywhere or talk to anyone else about this but me."

Sana was exactly where I expected her to be, at the far end of her studio waiting. She'd showered and her hair was still damp. She was poised on a stool, sipping a cup of tea, dressed in casual slacks and a white top.

"Sana!" I implored. "I don't know what to say, I'm *so* sorry about last night, what happened was just—"

"*Please!* You and your self-flagellation trip, I can't stand it."

That stopped me in my tracks. I'd expected her to be angry. Not entirely sure why, given she'd participated in the event just as actively as me, but I'd automatically assumed the stance of the guilty party.

"*Look*," she said emphatically, putting down her teacup. "I know already. You're going to be guilty and fucked up and blaming yourself, and walk around with that hangdog expression now for weeks – right?"

"Ahm, I guess…"

"Well, *cut it out*! I woke up this morning feeling bad too. And it's true that I'm mad at you, but not for the reason you probably think."

My head was spinning. "So why are you—"

"Because, Col, *it happened*. Shit happens, but you have to be an adult now, not the whiney baby you automatically become in situations like this."

It was true I'd started feeling sorry for myself, God knows why. As if life had set me up for this failure. Self-piteous and guilty; a lovely combination. "But *how could I have…* Danee and the girls are—"

"Col, it's *understandable*. Given the circumstances."

We were silent for a moment. The giant holo-model of Jubilee was centered in the room, and unconsciously we stood on opposite sides of it as though it were a real physical thing. It floated there between us, a metaphor for the life we'd once lived before the attack.

"I've spent some time thinking it through. In the future when we find Danee, if it's called for at some point, I will have no problem apologizing to her myself for what happened. But if I do that, it will only be to make *her* feel better, not to unburden myself. Do you understand? And there's no reason why you can't have the same attitude too, though knowing you...you won't be able to help yourself I think, turning it all into some grand mea culpa whether that's the right thing for Danee or not."

"You honestly think I wouldn't need to *mention* it to her? Sleeping with my ex-wife?"

"Up to you, Col. Why put her through it?"

"I guess, I guess it's about transparency and you know...honesty."

Sana batted her hand. "The thing about you, Col, the reason why we could never be together at the end of the day is you're just so bloody *conventional*. People live in every possible arrangement on Jubilee, *especially* on Jubilee. You're so *heteronormative*, you need to loosen up a little."

"I guess," I said tentatively. "It *was* just a little sex."

"*No!*" she raged. "That's not what I meant! Come here." She crooked a finger.

I joined her, walking carefully around the holo-model, avoiding getting too close as if it were something fragile. She sat back down on her stool then leaned over and buried her face in my chest. The last thing I expected given the dressing down I'd just been copping. I put my arm around her, tried to force myself not to feel any attraction.

"Look," she said, suddenly sitting up, "we *love* each other. We always did and probably always will. It's just one of those things. But when it came to being married, we weren't right for each other and *that's* one of those things too. What happened last night is never going to happen again, are we clear about that?" I nodded. To be honest I was so dazed, I would have agreed with anything.

"So therefore we just have to be adults and move on. Can you accept that?"

I sighed. She did make sense, I suppose. It was true that, left to my own devices, I would probably wallow in guilt forever and I wasn't going to be any use to Danee and the girls nailed to a cross. I decided to try and take Sana's advice. I would let myself off the hook at least for the present moment, take these feelings of guilt and shame and shunt them to one side, even if part of me suspected there'd still be a reckoning one day.

"Hey, the model's looking good," I said, suddenly taking it in – funny the way the mind always moves on to the next thing.

"Yeah, you like it? I finally fixed the back part of Sector Twenty-One." There'd been a large area that hadn't scanned properly.

"How did you do it? I thought there was no data?"

"Spliced the files!" she said triumphantly. "I ran a little program that integrated an additional scan that we did and even though it was a different software running at a different resolution, *voila*! Now the model is one hundred percent complete!"

An idea dropped into my brain, shocking in its simplicity.

"You added to the file," I said in a monotone.

"Yes, that's what I said."

"You just…*added* to it."

"Yes!"

"What an idiot I am."

"What, why?"

I pulled up a new folder on my kom. It contained the visual data we received of Jubilee as it was being destroyed. The hideous images viewed from our ship on the day we fled.

"Can you combine this data? Can you add it into that model?"

Sana looked at me. "You mean turn the whole thing into a video display using my 3D composite?"

"Yes."

"I think so."

"Do it then, let's see what really happened."

"See what?"

"I don't *know*! That's the whole point."

I transferred the file and Sana conjured some sort of holographic video-mixing tool kit from her kom. In the end it didn't take long at all. In half an hour we were looking at the giant holo of Jubilee in its last moments before destruction. There were tug craft attached on all sides and a leading ship that was pulling. The front section and all the edges of the model glowed a bright orange-yellow, a reflection of the sun's corona as Jubilee approached it. With this model, though, we couldn't see anything in the surrounding area, only Jubilee and whatever was attached to it.

"Now what?" asked Sana skeptically.

"Can you run the video forward?"

"Sure."

The model floated in space, no real sense of movement coming from it. Nothing happening at all.

"How long does the video footage last?" I asked.

"Around fifty-eight minutes."

"Can you speed it up?"

Sana brought up a time display from her digital box of tricks. It floated in the air above Jubilee, counting down the time until its destruction. At thirty-five minutes, the small tugs suddenly disengaged from Jubilee, swinging out and away and disappearing from the video. The leading tug remained for another five minutes.

What must have been going on inside Jubilee at that point? Awful to contemplate. Were Danee and the girls still on board?

At fifty-five minutes a shimmering light ran down the length of Jubilee and it seemed to warp and flicker, a second later bursting into a giant fireball filling the room so brightly it hurt the eyes. We both flinched instinctively, shielding our faces. Sana sobbed.

"Col, I can't take this, why are you making me watch? What's the point?"

"Sorry, Sana, I have an idea, please bear with me. Can we wind back to just before it explodes?"

"Here, *you* do it." She handed me the virtual control.

I rolled the image back to just before the explosion, then played it again, slower: Jubilee rippling, and warping, then bursting into fire.

Again, but even more slowly.

Again. This time moving the video forward in fragments of a second: Jubilee exploding, bursting into fire.

"Col, I'm going, I just can't—"

"*Stay!*" I shouted, a bit harshly. Sana looked hurt. "Please, I want your eyes too. There's always been something funny about this footage that I've never been able to put my finger on." I'd played it so many times I knew exactly the way the fire played over the structure, the way it warped and twisted sideways in the final cataclysmic explosion.

I time-stamped the exact moment of explosion, rolled the video back to the instant before, then moved forward again, using increments of one microsecond at a time. It seemed to take forever, but it was probably only five minutes or so that we watched Jubilee die in agonizing slowness.

And then I saw it. We *both* saw it and gasped.

I rolled back just three microseconds and played it again to be sure. Then again.

"Well, I'll be *fucked*!"

We swiveled around to see Chook leaning against the door to Sana's studio, face bright red from drink. I didn't care. "Did you *see* that, Chook?" I asked excitedly.

"Un-fucking-*believable*."

Chapter Eight

That very moment my kom lit up with a message from Frank Duval at the mill:

"Got an opening. Come right away. Please confirm."

"Hey, I gotta go!" I said to Chook and Sana, taking off immediately and messaging Frank as I went.

"Col!" I heard Sana shout as I hurtled down the stairs. "Does that mean—"

"Yes," I shouted back, "they're alive!"

The mill was only ten minutes as the crow flies, a little longer by ground car in the perpetually light traffic of Jerbet. Everything we drove past was so familiar to me, the town almost unchanged from my childhood: here was the main street with its few quiet stores and two bars. There was a park I played in as a kid, a yard for local council equipment, the high school I'd spent way too many years at. A lady waved at me as I drove, Ms. Pederson I think it was. Knew her years ago.

But my head was miles away. Or 188.697 light years far away, if you wanted to be pedantic, somewhere in the space off MGNA#12, the star you jump to Jubilee from.

Because I now knew Danee and the girls were alive.

As we rolled the video forward one microsecond at a time, what we saw was this:

In one frame, Jubilee warping and rippling, getting ready to explode into a massive fireball.

In the next frame: *no Jubilee.*

Or rather, just one single part of it: Sector Twenty-One. The brand new and infamous, and still uninhabited, section Douglas had been building seemingly for years, made from new materials rather than space junk. The sector that had been at the center of so many security issues and infiltration by Movement tech. Just this one section remained in view, the rest of Jubilee was gone.

Then in the following frame, that final sector blows up into the huge ball of fire we all saw. It must have been packed with explosives to give it an extra zing, equivalent to what Jubilee would have looked like had all of it gone up.

Lizard-like, Douglas had sacrificed the tail.

The bulk of Jubilee, the main part, Sectors One to Twenty where everyone lived, had vanished. Douglas must have jumped it. The entire mad, bad, beautiful, damned thing.

To where?

Didn't matter. Somewhere safe – probably another parallel universe pre-scouted to make sure it was benign. Obviously, this action was a decoy. Douglas had wanted M4M to think it had achieved its aim, which was to destroy Jubilee.

But now what? And how come I wasn't in on this plan, being head of security and all?

Something to take up with Douglas once I figured out where Jubilee had gone.

In the meantime, there was still Tim.

Frank Duval was a bald, plump, nuggety little man with an angry red face, and a bristling blond moustache. He seemed to have no neck at all; his head morphed onto his shoulders without any perceivable gap. His family had owned the mill for more generations than anyone could remember, and they were all considered odd by the townspeople. The idea that his factory might somehow be poisoning the forest dwellers seemed to fill him with a special kind of fury.

"OK, then let me *show you*," he raged. "Let me show you how things work around here. You wanna take a tour?"

"Sure." I'd been careful not to hurl accusations, merely repeated the allegations made by Elias. He handed me a high-vis vest and safety helmet.

"Totally unnecessary, but the *man* says you have to do it, so we fuckin' do it!"

"Please ignore him," said an older woman emerging from a room somewhere, blinking. "He gets so worked up. *Francois*, your blood pressure!" This was a sister I think, also part of the family concern and also considered to be highly odd.

"Thanks." I nodded my way past.

Frank led me down a corridor and pushed a worn, industrial hardiplaz door that opened into…perfect blackness. I dared not take a step farther as my eyes tried to adjust.

"Hang on a sec, there you go." Lights flickered on to reveal a vast enclosed space, the lumber operation. "She can run dark if you want her to. Robots don't need light, do they? Heh, heh!"

Machines were turning on around the massive space, running up to speed. The air smelled intensely of wood and sap. Frank led me down gantry steps to an observation platform that spanned the length of the factory. He gave a running commentary as we went.

"I was just about to do the afternoon run. That's why I wanted you to come over now. Look, see, over there is where the feeder logs come in." He pointed to a giant platform where unfinished, probably just-felled logs lay in a haphazard pile.

"They drop 'em off outside and they roll in onto this platform, *gravity* fed."

As we watched, the giant platform started to rise on one side and shake, causing the logs to roll to the other end and form themselves into straight rows. "There's a robot arm for any recalcitrant ones that don't fall into line."

"Does this whole thing run off your kom?"

"What do you reckon? Now look here, those logs drop out of the roller tray, into this line where they're sorted by size and species." As we walked, a giant conveyor started rolling. Huge logs still covered with bark moved along it, stopping every so often to be scanned. Some were tipped sideways into a nearby pile, others moved forward and were dropped into other piles along the factory floor. From the viewing platform a few meters above, we followed the line of logs as they moved along.

"So now we've got our logs sorted by species, this is where the *real* magic happens!"

A giant grappling arm swung down, picked up a single log and dropped it onto a fast-running conveyor belt. The log passed through a gate of some kind and there was a loud buzzing noise. Frank cackled. "That's your de-barker *right there*!"

The log continued on into another gate, slowing down as it entered. Wood chips sprayed out as the giant log was pushed through, emerging on the other side fully square-shaped. Frank hooted. "That's a hew-saw. Cuts along the grain line and does your four-sided canting!"

None of this meant anything to me, impressive as it was. I'll spare you any further particulars except to say the logs went from cutting, to planing, to baking in giant kilns, then quality assessment, and finally stacking and wrapping. We finished at the far end of the factory, where pallets of what was now finished timber waited for collection.

"What do you *think*?" said Frank, beaming.

"Very impressive operation."

"Thank you. Now here's the thing." He leaned in, speaking quietly, almost bumping me on the jaw with his yellow safety helmet. "What you just witnessed is the way wood's been turned into timber for thousands of years. You could take a lumber worker from Old Earth, and they'd be entirely familiar with the process. The only thing might throw 'em is the total lack of human involvement, but otherwise *completely the same*." He waved his hand around the building. "Anything you disagree with about that last statement?"

"No, I mean—"

"How *could* you?" His voice was rising now, moustache vibrating. "So let me ask something else. In our travels today did you happen to see any…*black oooooze*, say" – he held out both hands, shaking them as if conjuring something 'spooky' – "or any other suspicious substances flowing around the place? Running under the walls, sliming into the river to poison everyone. Did you see *any* of that?"

"No, in fact—"

"No, you didn't! Wanna know why?" He didn't wait for an answer. "Because *there is none*! Our factory's one hundred percent clean. The kilns are fired by wood dust from our own lumber and anything that vents, including all the exhaust fans, are HEPA filtered. If you walk around, you'll not find a single water inlet pipe, which tells you *what*? If there's nothin' comin' in, there's nothin' going out either! We don't use any chemicals here. Zip. Nada. So how could we be poisoning folks?"

He leaned against the gantry, weak from the exertion of all this rhetoric. You'd have to say, my enquiry about this topic had touched a raw nerve.

But Frank wasn't done. "So having seen all this, tell me what seems more likely to you. That some mysterious, never-known-till-now substance emanating from my factory, which has no outlet pipes, is poisoning a whole river valley hundreds of square kilometers in size *or* might it be possible that them folks has been livin' in those tiny, isolated communities for hundreds of years, fucking their own sisters and brothers and cousins till they look like God-damned mutants. What's more likely, *what do you think*?!"

I raised my hands in surrender. "Hard to see it any other way."

"*Thank you!*"

We walked back to where we entered, this time along the factory floor, following a designated safety path as the giant machines did their work above and around us. My security brain couldn't help noting the unlocked doors. Anyone could just walk in here if they pleased.

"You may not be popular with the forest people, but don't seem all that worried about security here."

Frank looked around and nodded. "Yeah, well, people wanna come around they can. I'm an open book."

"No issues with theft?"

"Nah, what are they gonna take – a bit of wood? They can have it!"

We wound our way past the giant central kiln. An automated cleaning robot was working its way around the factory floor, sucking in the dust and any errant wood chips that flew out from the machines, then discharging them into the roaring kiln through a large open hopper door. If this place were run by humans, there'd have to be a safety rail in front of that thing.

"Is it true this place was much bigger during the Collapse?"

"Yup. Nearly ten times the size. Not that we had anything to do with it."

"Oh, really?"

"Soon as the hardiplaz units went down, the *government*," he spat, "saw the way things was goin' and immediately requisitioned our plant. Had to sue to get it back – took a hunderd years, and I tell ya, the place was a big fuckin' mess. Took my great, great granddaddy his whole life to get it back on track."

We climbed the stairs up to his office, where Frank had yet more to say.

"And I know what you're thinkin' now – mebbe when the government ran this place, that was when they poisoned everything, coz the factory was so large back then. I bet that's what they told you, out in the woods, right?"

"Yes."

"*Well, that's bullshit too!* We had experts come through. Had 'em test the air, the soil, the groundwater, the whole place. They found *absolutely-fuckin'-nothin'*. But you try tellin' that to the forest folk."

"I guess you could invite them in, show 'em around?"

"*Done all that!* Everything you can think of. But there's human nature for you, I s'pose. Once a person gets a stupid idea in their head, 'specially if they're conspiracy minded, no amount of factual evidence to the contrary is going to change their fuckin' mind."

I left Frank to it, my ears still ringing, when as if on cue, a huge dump of files landed in my kom from Elias. I did a quick scan and one snippet stood out immediately, a few lines from a toxicology report that read something like:

...contamination may have occurred due to toxic wood preservation chemicals including polynuclear aromatic hydrocarbons (PAHs), pentachlorophenol (PCP), pesticides, and compounds of chrome, copper, and arsenic...

I shook my head in wonder. Frank had seemed totally convincing to me, but could it all have been an act? Who knew what the truth was? The file dump, however, did something to dislodge an idea in my brain: a new line of enquiry.

"Col!" Elias answered my call immediately, eyes burning. *"What do you think? Pretty damned convincing, I'd say, though you really have to read the whole thing to get the full impact!"*

"Yes, Elias, it raises…a lot of questions, though I haven't had time yet to fully review the material."

"So, there you go! When you see real research that's not been corrupted by the influence of those people who stand to benefit, that's when you get a proper…"

I let him go on for a while. Didn't have much choice, to be honest, as he launched into a tirade that was the equal and opposite of Frank's. I finally found a gap when he paused eventually for breath.

"Elias, there's something else I've been meaning to ask you."

"Yes."

"I noticed in my grandma's room, there was a picture of Gilham on the wall. Are you guys out there devotees of—"

"Hell no!" Elias interrupted before I could finish the question. *"They wanted to tell us what to do, change our ways, all kinda stuff. We sent them packing."*

"So how come there was—"

"Some of the older folk formed an attachment. It was a long while ago, mind. A period when we had people like Nees coming around all the time, so you could say there was a 'moment of infatuation'. We still allow some of the older folk like Doris to hang on to their pictures if they want. Freedom is what we're all about here."

"I get it. Though it's interesting, because I always thought that era was pre-Movement on Brouggh, that they didn't start getting traction till much later."

"Yeah, they said we were 'early adopters'. They were very charming and full of praise in those days, till we saw enough of them, that is. Not that all our brethren were quite so insightful."

The tingle in my gut started up again at this.

"So Nees went out to other communities, not just yours?"

"Oh yeah, he used to go all over. Some of 'em still count themselves as Movement even now, especially the really crazy, strict ones."

My idea of 'crazy' and 'strict' was probably a little different to Elias's. But the tingle in my gut had turned into a throb, which turned into something else again: *understanding*. I asked one final question, and the answer confirmed it.

I thanked Elias, and immediately messaged Batum to be ready when I got home, then ordered the ground car to pull over and stop for a moment. I sat, head in hands, trying to breathe, to slow my thumping heart. Never in my life before or after this moment, have I experienced what you might call a 'panic attack'. Cool-in-a-crisis-Col. But for just that one time I succumbed. I sat immobilized, unable to keep going for at least fifteen minutes.

Then it started to recede. My breathing and heart slowed, the black spots in my eyes started to fade and I ordered the car to move off again.

I finally knew what had happened to Tim.

Chapter Nine

They were all waiting for me in the study.

"*Fuck me dead!*" said Chook when the silver ball emerged from Batum's chest. Sana just stared, boggle-eyed.

"And I can talk to it?" I asked Batum.

"Just a moment, I'll wake it up."

Sitting in its little tray, the processing core transformed. Not changing color or humming or vibrating – or doing anything at all, really. But in some impossible-to-describe way it seemed suddenly more 'alive'. Its edges turned fuzzy, and though its silvery gleam grew no dimmer, it appeared 'less there'. As though tapping into something invisible to the rest of us.

"*Operational*," said Batum, in a metallic tone, deeper than normal. Then in his usual voice, "That wasn't me, that was the unit."

"Douglas," I said, "are you there, can I talk to you?"

"This unit is now operational," said the voice. *"Please say the voice security code for log-in. You have three attempts remaining."*

Yikes, hadn't factored this in, though it was predictable. Three attempts? What on earth would the code be? Then, I remembered logging in to the control room on Jubilee and Douglas's slack attitude to these things. "There is no voice code."

There was a pause and the ball seemed to transform even more, as if moving to a higher level of operation. Though no brighter, it was definitely harder to look at.

"Correct."

Phew. Chook looked to me awestruck, mouthing silently, "*How the fuck did you know that?*" I waved him away. "*Later.*" Then to the machine, "You don't sound like the Douglas I know from Jubilee, is that really you?"

"Please rephrase the question."

"Are you the same LAI computer that runs Jubilee?"

"This unit is the number eleven fail-over safety core associated with ISPL 478#LAI4000."

I hurriedly wrote the number down, just in case. "That's the identifier number belonging to the computer that runs Jubilee?"

"Correct."

"How come you don't sound like that computer, Douglas?"

"There is no personality construct associated with this core."

Interesting. I was dying to ask questions about how Douglas really worked, divine what everyone wants to know about large quantum AIs: are they really conscious or is it just good programming and huge processing power? Save that for another time.

"There's been a catastrophic attack against Jubilee, and it appears to have quantum jumped to another location. Do you know where it is now?"

"There are no memory files associated with this core."

"Could you reach out to those files, interrogate them? My understanding is that you can talk to the other parts of yourself somehow?"

"Integration has been unsuccessful. Permission protocols associated with my memory files have been corrupted or rescinded."

I was hoping it might be able to talk to the memory files aboard *The Grand Poobah* using whatever entanglement wizardry it ran on. Assuming, of course, that the massive, partitioned area of the unnecessarily huge computer that ran the ship really contained them. If the core couldn't talk to it, maybe something was jamming it, or maybe M4M had gotten in there and taken it over?

"And you can't communicate with your prime processing unit on Jubilee?"

"I could, if Prime was located in this universe."

"But not if it's in the universe where Jubilee normally resides?"

"Correct."

Or any other potential universe Douglas might have jumped to. I'd now asked all the obvious questions that could have helped us find Jubilee and the girls. This had been a bit of long shot, but worth trying. Normally, the core would be no use to us. That was probably why Douglas had instructed Batum not to remember carrying it. No point in us knowing, dangerous even.

But I had a different purpose for it, one that would further an agenda Douglas could never have imagined.

"So, computer, should I call you Douglas? What's your name?"

"You may refer to me as 'safety core eleven' if you wish."

Chook was watching in rapt attention. Sana was pacing the room, starting to get frustrated. "What's the point of this, Col?"

"You'll see soon, hopefully. Safety core eleven, can I ask you to run a task?"

"Of course."

I told the computer what I wanted it to do, which was process the camera footage pertaining to the Tim Perolo case. To see if that footage had been messed with to remove any trace of Tim's abduction, and then revert it so we could view what really happened. I grabbed the video files from the holo-binders still floating above my desk. It amounted to an immense volume of data. Thousands of hours of footage taken across Jerbet in the days before, during and after Tim's disappearance.

"File transfer will take forty-seven point five minutes due to the slow interface provided by the hosting droid." Even though it wasn't supposed to have a personality, I couldn't shake the feeling that the computer sounded just a little embarrassed.

"How long will it take once you have the files?"

"Reprocessing will require point three four nanoseconds based on estimated file size and task complexity." The computer sounded a little more pleased with itself at this.

"I'm starved," said Sana. "Do you guys want anything?"

I had no appetite even though it was now dinnertime, and I hadn't eaten all day, but Chook gave a thumbs-up. He promptly fell asleep in his chair, and I paced the room until Sana returned ten minutes later with bowls of noodles which were eaten in silence. Time crawled. Chook and Sana looked at stuff on their koms and I tried as well, but nothing could take my mind off what was happening inside that silver ball, what might finally be revealed. For my whole life I'd dreamed of knowing what I was about to, and the anticipation was unbearable, even though I had a pretty good idea by then of what it might be. Each minute felt like a year.

I left the room and paced the corridor, then went outside and took a stroll. The night air was colder now as autumn approached, scented as always with the ever-present forest. The clear sky was lit with a million suns, magnificent up here in Jerbet away from the light pollution of the big cities. I went back inside to find the house empty and quiet. There was a pot on the kitchen stove with still-warm noodles and I was suddenly ravenous. In hindsight, it was no small, good thing that I got food into me at that moment.

I returned just in time for the computer to announce that transfer and reprocessing were complete.

"OK, safety core eleven, I want you to find and play video relating to the subject noted in the files, Tim Perolo." I gave him a time, date, and location.

A holo sprang up in the middle of the room. It was a view along the main street of Jerbet and I could tell immediately was from decades before. Although my town had supposedly changed little over the years, it was a shock to see the extent to which that was not true. The street was narrower back then – must have been widened at some point – the shop façades used an old-fashioned font, the streetlights were a different shape and color – when were they swapped? The town looked the same, but startlingly different.

From my notes I knew there'd been a camera located directly outside the general store, but of course that unit had been on the fritz, so the footage found by the computer was from farther up the street, around a hundred meters away.

A ground car pulls up to the curb not far from the general store and three figures alight: a woman and two boys. It was fascinating to see my younger self, but hard to watch. If he only knew what was coming, he might have been able to change things.

"Computer, can you please speed up the next two minutes?"

The figures move in fast motion. They jump out of the car and walk toward the store, the older boy holding his mother's hand, the younger boy skipping playfully ahead, a blue teddy – *the* blue teddy – held under one arm. All three enter the store.

"OK, speed up even more till something happens."

The view is static. The time stamp moves rapidly as a car or two pass. In the far distance a flyer lands and two burly men get out and cross the street to enter the bar. There's a sudden blur at the shop door and I call stop and rewind.

Now we see it. Finally. A brightly colored ball bounces out of the shop door. Where did that come from? Must have been a stock item from the store itself.

The ball bounces once on the footpath, then out to the road. A small child emerges madly chasing it onto the road, where at that exact moment a ground car appears from nowhere, suddenly speeding up as it drives straight through the boy. He flies in the air, over the roof of the car, and lands with a sickening thud in the center of the street. Even from the middle distance you can see instantly the boy is dead, his head cocked at an impossible angle, body broken.

"Stop, *stop*!" cried Sana. The holo froze, the horrific image fixed and still. "I can't take it, I can't take it." She stood up, fanning her face and pacing the room.

I held my head, noticed my cheeks were wet. Was this really it? Something this mundane – after all this time, a *road accident*? Tim must have found that ball in the shop somewhere, then kicked or fumbled it out the door. How come a missing ball wasn't in the file? I guess you'd never consider checking the shop's inventory as part of a *murder* investigation.

"Sorry," said Sana, "I just needed a moment." I patted her on the arm.

"OK, computer, let's keep going."

The door of the ground car opens, and a woman gets out, her face white with shock.

"Can you freeze there, and zoom in? I want to identify that person." Even though I was almost certain of the 'who', it wasn't until that moment that I knew the 'how' (though still not the 'why'). It was a shock nevertheless, a repudiation of all my childhood feelings.

The woman was my stepmother, Lynda Veitch.

"OK, roll forward," I said shakily.

Sana was hyperventilating again; even Chook looked in shock. "Can't say I like her much, but *fuck me*!" he said.

The woman looks around guiltily, dashes behind the car to the body of the boy and puts her hands to her head, mouth an *O* shape of horror. She picks the boy up, slings him over her shoulder and runs back to the car, eyes darting everywhere. She places the body in the car, makes as if to leave, then has a change of mind. She darts over to the opposite side of the road and retrieves the ball, which has rolled into the gutter, and picks the blue teddy up from the road on the way back.

That showed a high level of cunning, one had to think.

A moment later the ground car takes off at high speed. The video rolls forward for another few minutes, and then it is my mother's face emerging from the shop door. Not in panic yet, more annoyance. She is young and quite beautiful, her face not yet ravaged with grief and guilt. We were watching the last happy moments of her life.

"Computer, please follow that car."

"I take it, you have some interest in what happened to the boy?"

"He was my brother. I assume this footage was deliberately tampered with?" Otherwise, the investigation would have been over in a day.

"There was a highly sophisticated hack to the files – sophisticated for the time, anyway. The video you are seeing was deleted and replaced. Several rather clumsy and unsuccessful attempts were made to restore the data."

The holo switched to a new angle. The car turns into view from a crossroad driving toward us, then passing by out of view. Then it's picked up again from a new angle, and so on. Moving through the quiet streets of Jerbet, heading directly out of town. Finally coming to a halt at the top of a rise just outside city limits.

"This is the only view available," said the computer. A single camera pointed along the road leading out of town.

The car waits by the side of the road, and a few minutes later two flyers land nearby – the patched and dinged-up variety I'd observed in Hyvon. Figures alight, men and women. Small figures silhouetted against the looming gray sky. One of the men hugs Lynda and there is much talking and gesticulating. The car door is opened and he looks inside, then stands back in shock. My future stepmother is bundled into one of the flyers, which takes off immediately, and the older man who'd embraced Lynda gets into the car, makes a U-turn across the road and drives toward us, back into town. As he passes you can see his face is set in a hard grimace.

Out of everything the next passage was the most difficult to watch. Not that the footage was dramatic, just one oldish-looking ground car driving through a bunch of Jerbet's backroads, taking care to avoid any people – it was more that I now knew what was going to happen next and that knowledge was the most unbearable thing of all.

The car turns onto a familiar road, the one leading to Duval Mill. It drives past the front gate, keeps going for a few hundred meters, then turns onto a road that runs behind the far boundary of the giant plant. The car vanishes from view.

"I'm sorry," said the computer, *"I can't find any camera footage for that road."*

"That's OK. Can you roll forward, see if it returns?"

It did. After ten minutes of elapsed time the car comes back into view. We see a momentary flash of the face of the man driving as it passes under the camera.

Mission complete.

"What happened, what does that *mean*?" asked Sana.

Chook shook his head. "Disposing of the body, right?"

I just nodded.

"But how, where?"

"The kiln," I said. The roaring kiln of the lightly secured factory belonging to Frank Duval. Unlocked doors everywhere, no cameras. Probably running by itself in the dark, its owner upstairs enjoying a relaxing afternoon coffee. While my brother was incinerated. The blue teddy was held back, possibly with intent for future use, or more likely left behind in the car by accident.

I leaped to my feet. "I've seen enough, I'm going to have it out with Father."

"Col." I heard Sana cry, her voice fading as I stormed away.

"*Col!!*"

Chapter Ten

"How long have you known?"

We were in Father's bedroom, the new one, built as an extension to the house behind the kitchen. When I knocked at his door, he'd stared without expression for a moment and then motioned for me to enter. He didn't even seem surprised so much as weary. We were sitting in two armchairs facing each other, he in his pajamas and dressing gown. There was a collection of dirty plates and cutlery resting on the sideboard and scattered about the floor nearby.

"Known…ah…what?" he answered tentatively.

"C'mon, *you* know."

He slumped deeper into his chair, eyes closed, massaging his forehead as if in pain. "Col, I know you've been looking into what happened with Tim, and…" He just stopped.

"Dad, I *know*, all right."

He thought for a long time. "Col, it's not what you think."

"So tell me."

My father sighed, finally opening his eyes, and looked at me directly. I realized it was the first time in years I could remember him doing so, looking me squarely in the eyes. Why had I never noticed? An absolute sign of guilt. I decided that I'd have to lead him in questioning, just like a suspect. God help me.

"She came from a settlement called *Villote*, right?"

This was the key piece of information I'd gleaned from Elias. Lynda Veitch had lied to me. She was not raised in town; she came from the woods. My suspicions were aroused by a throwaway remark Elias made when we visited Hyvon – *your dad has quite the taste for forest women*. He looked at me in surprise, then shrugged. "I guess they told you at Hyvon, right?"

I nodded. "Kinda figured it out. How did she end up in Jerbet?"

"Same as they all do." Dad sighed again. "Medical emergency."

Elias had told me that Villote was one of the very strict communities. "Must have been something fatal, right?"

"Cancer. Absolutely *crazy*." This was the first time I'd heard anything approaching real emotion from my father in years. "She was the mayor's daughter. That's how I thought of him, even though they supposedly don't have leaders, but you know what I mean, he was the boss. And Lynda got sick. And he wasn't supposed to, but he got her to hospital in town. Saved her life."

"And then she couldn't go back."

Dad nodded.

"So why did she run Tim over in her car?"

"*Accident*, of course!" Dad sat up in his chair, eyes burning. "Of course she wouldn't do anything like that on purpose!"

"But I saw the footage. She *sped up*."

Dad slumped again, closed his eyes and went back to the head massaging. I'm pretty sure a tear must have squeezed out, because he wiped something away. "She wasn't a confident driver. She saw Tim on the road in front of her and panicked. Hit the accelerator instead of the brake."

I reeled; the car was on *manual drive*?

Insane. Most people wouldn't know *how* to set a car to manual – hell, most wouldn't even know there was such a *thing*. Why would anyone, especially if they were a novice driver, set their car to manual?

Unless they came from a place that didn't believe in technology in the first place.

"Her car was set to manual?"

"They didn't even want her to have one. But they relented because she couldn't go back obviously, and she had to earn a living. So they said OK, she could have a car, but it had to be human control only. When she hit Tim, it was only the third time she ever drove it."

In the old days, of course, Lynda would have needed a proper license and would have been tested on her driving skills, but since no one in the world ever drove a ground car in anything other than auto mode, what was the point?

"Why the cover-up?"

"I told you, she panicked."

Not from what I saw. Lynda might have been innocent when it came to the accident itself, but she'd acted with a considerable amount of guile afterward: retrieving Tim's body and also the teddy and the ball, then driving out to the edge of town and calling her father.

"That's not what the video shows," I said. Dad looked up in surprise. "We've been able to reprocess the footage and Lynda's actions in the aftermath of the accident seem highly calculating by any measure, particularly for someone who's supposedly in shock."

Dad sat silent for a long moment, just nodding to himself as if thinking something through. I figured what I'd told him might be a little different to Lynda's story. Her version of events had been burnished to some extent, and probably self-serving.

"You have to understand, Col, the way these people are bred, they don't trust anyone. If you or I had been in such an accident, of course we'd immediately call the authorities, do everything we could to help, and nowadays Lynda would be like that too. Back then she was fresh out of Villote. She thought they'd…I don't know, who *knows* what she thought! From her perspective, she couldn't trust anyone or anything. I think she went into survival mode. She's a survivor, Lynda."

"If she'd done the right thing, we'd probably still have Mother."

"I know."

"The suffering she went through."

"I know." The eyes were closed again. We sat in silence for a few minutes, both digesting what had been said.

"So, then what? They must have contacted the Movement right, the people in Villote? Got them to hack the video footage. Pretty clever. I assume it was Nees?"

"Ah, I'm not sure. All I know is they deactivated the cameras somehow and—"

"Yep, I get it. And the blue teddy, whose brain wave was that?"

Dad shrugged.

And the car? Driven into the forest and resting at the bottom of a lake somewhere, probably rusted away. Now for the million-dollar question. "So when did you find out, *Dad*?"

He squirmed in his seat. I got the feeling he'd rather have been thrown into the Duval kiln himself than be answering these questions. Questions he'd been hiding from…who knew how long?

"Col. Is that a good idea, I mean what point does it serve to—"

"*Tell me.* You owe me this much at least."

Dad sighed, then did something unexpected. He stood up and started pacing. It was the most lively I'd seen the man in years. "Col, when your mother vanished, I was a wreck. I had no one to turn to, no idea how to cope with anything. Lynda was so helpful, so selfless." He held up a hand as if to wave off the obvious point. "We grew close. She was a comfort to me, though I really do want to assure you that nothing at all happened between us on a physical level before—"

"*Please!*" I interrupted. The thought of my father's sex life with Lynda was enough to make me puke.

"Anyway, after your mother was found we became close in that way too, and as you know she eventually moved in, and we married." Controversially, as far as the town was concerned. The usual tongue-wagging about the interval of time being indecently short – all that.

"And then what?" The next part I could have written a script for, having heard so many stories like this on the job, but I wanted him to say it aloud. To me.

"At first, we were very happy. We were in love, Col. I'm sorry if that sounds callous, but you know, it happened, and of course I didn't *know*." Father's pacing was growing ever brisker as his passion rose. Who was this person, where had he been all my adult life?

"Then let me guess, after a while she started getting weird for no reason and wouldn't explain why and then it got worse and worse, till one day she finally confessed?"

"Yes! That's right! It got to the point where things were so bad we were sleeping in separate beds, and then one morning she slipped in beside me and..." He stopped pacing and sat down opposite again without uttering a word.

"She told you everything."

"Yes."

"And what did you do?"

Blah, blah, I thought. Shock, then anger, then wanting to report her and leave her – *What to do, what to do?* – then the self-justifications, the wanting to get back to normal life, the decision to forgive and to forget. Burying it all, deep down.

Looking back, I concede it's likely my father could not have coped with anything more. Such as a new investigation, this time with allegations made against himself too, even more judgment from the townspeople. A life thrown back into disarray.

"When? Out with it now, when was that?"

"I guess about ten years after. You were away in college."

I knew it. That was when the life seemed to go out of him. It had first left when Mother died, then came back for a while with Lynda, and then...he just vanished.

"Why didn't you tell me? All this time, you knew what happened to Tim and you never told me!" Of course, I knew why he didn't – how could he have? But by then I didn't care. I wanted to savage my father, hurt him.

"If I turned her in, I would have had *no one*!"

"You still had *me*!"

"But you were *away*, gone. Off living your life, and fair enough too! What was I meant to do?"

That's when I saw it, the selfishness of my father's grief. He'd kept himself apart from me, and then used that separation to justify everything else. I exploded with anger. I started saying things, and dear reader I won't go into the details, but let's just say it was nasty. A whole life's worth of unspoken and unspeakable words. There was never any teenage-rebellion stage with me, no space for that given the family trauma. I dredged up the past, and I shouted. At first Dad took it on the chin, then he started saying nasty things too and...well, it got ugly.

We ended up face to face, finger-pointing and screaming. Probably the worst argument I've ever had.

There were sounds behind me, hands on my shoulder. I whirled around to find Sana. With Chook. "Col!" she was shouting. "*Stop!* This is only making everything worse."

There was suddenly dead silence in the room, and I noticed my kom was lit. Three missed holo-calls from Henderzon, and a new one coming in. I turned away and answered it, a small, red, angry face swelling up from my wrist immediately. Henderzon wasn't bothering with audio-only. This was a serious call.

"Perolo!" he shouted. "What the fuck is going on up there in Jerbet?"

"What do you mean, I don't—"

"Neutrino burst. *Massive.* The tech guy told me it matches exactly with the profile of an unshielded large quantum AI, but I reassured him. I said, 'Don't be stupid, it can't be Perolo, it's not like he's going to have one of those things lying around in his backpack, is he now?'"

I didn't know what to say.

"So, do you?"

"What?"

"Have one of those in your backpack?"

I had no words to offer. Henderzon's face turned gradually more red – if that was even possible – then abruptly white.

"*Jesus!* Whatever crazy-assed fuckery you've been up to, Perolo, this is serious. There's chatter, there's weird shit going on in space, which we can't figure out, but it seems to have something to do with that neutrino burst. You got any idea what position this puts me in?"

"Sorry, Henderzon, but—"

"Listen, we're doing *this.* I just ordered an Ultra-Fast your way from Mont-Dauphin. It's going to pick you up and bring you to HC spaceport. Then you're going to get back in that ship of yours and fuck off back to who-the-fuck-cares. *Do* you understand!?"

"Yes OK, and I just want to—"

"This is my last favor, Perolo. After tonight, you and I are done. Be ready in ten."

The face disappeared.

"What's going on?" asked Sana.

I thought things through for a moment, trying to figure it all out.

"I'm not sure exactly, whatever we did booting up Douglas seems to have triggered something. We're being taken back to Harrison City in a big hurry, then we have to get off Brouggh."

Batum cut in, speaking on all our koms at once, the open line. *"Col, I hope you don't mind I was listening in on your call. I think we've activated some kind of automated monitoring system left in space by M4M. It's possible they have been looking out for the backup I'm carrying."*

"That's a bit far-fetched," I said.

"Col, I've got a bad feeling, we should definitely move fast."

"Whatever the hell's going on," said Chook, "I'm all for getting away from this place."

"All right, we've got ten minutes apparently. Sorry, Sana, we always seem to be just running these days. Can you throw some things together?" But I was already speaking to her back, and a second later Chook was gone too. I could hear Batum's bulk coming down the stairs, moving ever more creakily as he was these days.

My kom crackled with a scratchy female voice. *"Investigator Perolo?"*

"Yes? *Former* Investigator, to be correct."

"You're still one of us, sir, and I just want to say it's an honor to be meeting you – which I'm calling to say will happen in approximately seven minutes and counting, sorry for the rush. My orders are to drop in, then be off the ground again within sixty seconds. So please be ready."

She was coming in fast from one of the remote bases of the far north, Mont-Dauphin. Remote, but relatively close to Jerbet by fast flyer. What the hell had we done?

"Col!" I spun around to face my father, who I could see was still highly worked up. "You have to go?" he asked plaintively. "*You* haven't told me everything either, have you? What's happened, why are you running away?"

Dad was right, he wasn't the only person around here keeping secrets and bottling everything up. Guess it ran in the family. I looked him in the eye and told him everything. Well, a very short, three-minute version anyway. I told him about my new wife, Danee, and living on Jubilee, about his two granddaughters. He didn't bat an eyelid.

"So where will you go, what will you do now?"

"No idea, Dad, I've got to come up with a plan."

"And what about" – he paused, looking around the room – "this?" I guess he meant his whole life.

Was it my job to bring Lynda to justice? Would it even *be* justice after all these years? "Where is she now anyway, Dad?" I hadn't actually seen my stepmother around all day.

Dad shrugged. "Not sure, but if I were guessing…"

"Villote." I finished for him.

"Probably, I mean I don't know for sure."

"What happened?"

"Vanished without a word. As soon as you guys came back from Hyvon – that's what did it, I think, you going there." She knew. Knew that I would pick up her lie. Her only lie really. She'd played her cards almost perfectly, but it's very hard to live a lie like that forever. I suddenly knew what had to be done.

"Dad, I've lived my whole life in the shadow of…this *thing*. I can't imagine what I would have done in your place. Maybe one day I'll be able to forgive you but…I can't deal with this while I'm running for my life. I'm sending you the case files, what you do with them is up to you."

"Fair enough." He pulled me into a hug, a strong one. His unshaven cheek was next to mine; I felt his jagged breath, his body trembling all over. But maybe that was a good thing, a sign of life after all these years?

"I'm sorry, Col," he whispered.

My kom crackled again. *"Thirty seconds."*

"Go, *go*!" said Dad. There was movement on the stairs as Sana and Chook, carrying our daypacks, raced to join Batum, who was already waiting at the front door. They'd have heard the conversations with the pilot, which were all on open channel.

I raced from Father's room to join them and just as I got there, saw Batum put one of his metal 'hands' on Chook's shoulder. "I just wanted to tell you," the robot said, and I swear it was with real emotion, "you are the greatest human I ever met."

Chook laughed. "Mate, you're not too bad y'self – for a walking scrapyard."

There was a loud swooshing sound outside. We pushed the door open to see a sleek-looking flyer putting down in the street about two hundred meters away. Shit, they had the wrong address. Typical bloody pilot.

"Run, everyone, *run*!" I shouted.

We bolted from the house, across the front yard and along the road toward the flyer; Sana, the fastest, followed by me, then Chook. Rattling and clanking behind was Batum, and if a robot could look desperate, that's how you'd have to describe him.

That single moment of us all running in the street seems suspended in time to me now. Like when you feel the tremble of an earthquake through the floor but haven't had time to act.

Through the still night air came a blinding, stabbing column of purple light from the heavens, splitting the jet-black sky. About five meters wide and so powerful it sent a thunderclap reverberating around the neighborhood, striking Batum in its dead center, leaving a massive, ringed crater in the middle of the street at least twenty meters wide and fifteen deep. At the bottom of it, in the hollow of steaming earth, all that remained of our friend was a pool of molten silver.

Chapter Eleven

Sana screamed but she didn't stop running.

We hurled ourselves through the open cargo door of the flyer, which took off immediately. It had to have been on the ground for longer than the mandated sixty seconds, though it landed in the wrong place, so I didn't feel too guilty.

"What the fuck just happened?" shouted a tinny voice – Henderzon's – from my kom as we rolled around the cargo bay, slamming into the rear wall from the sudden acceleration. Then rolling the other way as the flyer banked and zoomed into the black night. Things went on like that for a while, us all sliding about madly till I saw streaks of blood on the floor. From me, I soon determined. My nose had bashed into something and was bleeding everywhere.

"Sorry folks," came the pilot's voice. *"Wasn't time to embark you properly. In around ninety seconds I can ease up and get you seated."*

We all screamed as the flyer banked hard, changing direction, then banked again. I could still hear Henderzon's shrill voice ranting from my kom as we rolled around and around in a slipping, sliding pile of humanity.

Finally, the ship went silent and still. A hatch opened and the helmeted face of the pilot appeared. She goggled for a moment, then motioned us out of the cargo bay. We crawled through the hatch into the passenger area. *"Sorry, you all look terrible, but I was ordered to take extreme measures."*

"Where are we?" I asked, looking out of the side window, and seeing only black.

"G21 forest, under the canopy fifty klicks from Jerbet. It's the safest place I could think of till I get further instructions – hang on…" I heard her helmet radio crackle with rapid voices. It sounded like a few people talking at once. I remembered the call I hadn't been able to take.

"Sorry, Henderzon, are you there? Couldn't talk before, we were rolling around the cargo bay like skittles in a bottle."

"That pilot saved your life." No face showing anymore, back to audio-only for Henderzon.

"Do you know what—"

"Planet strike. From orbit, can you fuckin' believe? Some kind of relay unit. We took it out but it was slaved to another thing out beyond Circe. Fucker jumped straight into hyperspace the moment we locked."

This had to be something to do with M4M's Aurelian-backed AI. It had been biding its time out beyond Brouggh's second moon, watching, and waiting to launch a planet strike; how did it know what to look for? Just when one mystery was resolved, another took its place.

"We're OK but it took out our droid."

"That's too bad...but as I said, Perolo, that's me done. And honestly, I don't need or want to know why they organized such elaborate shit to turn you all into your component molecules. All I want is for you to get off-planet right now, and stop being my problem. Sorry if that makes me sound like an asshole. Are we clear?"

"Yes, and *don't* hang up!"

"What?"

"Henderzon, you've been great, thanks for your help, I really mean it and I'm sorry it's made life hard for you. But you have to understand. This thing we started, this thing with the Movement, it's not over. Maybe you've won a partial victory here on Brouggh, but it's *partial*. Their aims are even larger now, galactic. They might be leaving you alone for now, but they're coming. Coming back for *you* especially, and all the others who stood up to them. Life's not going to suddenly get easier even if you get rid of me. I'm just warning you. I had to say this."

There was a long pause, then he spoke again, not ranting this time. *"OK. Yes, I get it. I owe you, Col, we all do. And I know they're coming. Politics is heating up here and things are starting to get harder again. Let's hope we can all hang out one day soon and chug some beers together."*

Our pilot looked back at us with a questioning expression, making a thumbs-up. I raised a thumb in return, but certainly didn't feel that way. We all looked like veterans from a fleeing army; Chook holding his left arm, which hung at an odd angle, possibly broken, or disjointed, Sana with a black eye, all of us covered in blood from rolling around in it together. At least we were alive – which was more than I could say for Batum.

The ship lifted again and swooped into the night, the endless forest coal black below us. It was strange; despite everything, I felt somehow liberated. Knowing about Tim, knowing the truth, and finally speaking honestly with Father; it was hard to not think that sometimes things happen for a reason. Being stuck in Jerbet: Who would have guessed what the side effect of that would be?

"Looks like we're out of imminent danger," came the pilot's voice, *"though there's a developing situation in HC, still not clear, so they want me to make quick time. I'll have you at HCS in about thirty-five minutes."*

Fast. We'd be leaving a sonic boom in the forest behind us. I wondered what kind of 'situation' was happening in Harrison City? Hard to imagine anything more dramatic than what we'd just witnessed.

"Can someone explain what the fuck just happened?" asked Chook, Sana nodding in agreement. They both looked at me pointedly.

"It was a planet strike."

"We *saw* that," said Sana impatiently.

I told them what I'd gleaned from Henderzon. Chook waggled his head in amazement. "So, you're tellin' me that thing was lying in wait for Douglas to get switched on so it could blast the shit out of it?"

"That's about the size of it."

"Fuck! And poor old Batum. He only just decided I was OK, too. Probably the only person or thing in the whole galaxy who ever thought that."

"*I* think that," said Sana softly. "You're actually a big softie." She patted his arm, though gently, I noticed, given how damaged it looked. "Anyway, Batum *will* be backed up, right? On Jubilee?"

"Yes," I said, "Douglas will have a backup file and can install it in a new body, but it won't have any data from the last few months he spent with us, basically from when Jubilee was attacked."

"We'll fill him in," said Sana matter-of-factly. "Here." She handed me a pile of tissues from some dispenser. "Clean up, you look like crap."

"But before anything, we have to actually *find* Jubilee," I said, trying to wipe my face but only smearing things worse. When I put the tissues to my nose, they came away bright with blood and a stabbing pain sizzled through the top of my head. Nose was probably broken. "But at least we know Jubilee *is* somewhere out there. We just have to find a way to get in contact."

"So where do we go, boss? You still takin' me with you, right?"

"Of course, Chook. I don't know. I think we should get off-planet and out into deep space and then stop and think for a while, try to decide our next step." My mind was working on it already. Toulouse Nouvelle might be the best option. See if we could shake things up with the League, or at least get some assistance.

We all sat in silence for a while as the flyer hurtled toward our unknowable future. Finally, in the monitor I saw a faint glow rolling over the horizon toward us and the cabin noise started to abate.

"Approaching HC now," called the pilot. *"I'm backing her down, so we don't piss off the tax-paying citizens with our sonic boom."*

The city came into view. On the far side to us lay the vast flat apron of the spaceport. There were a bunch of freighters visible from even this height, as well as a single behemoth of a passenger ship, one of the largest I'd ever seen. As we descended, I started to make out the dock reserved for private ships, lit up brightly and sprinkled with small dots. Our ship was in there somewhere among them. I tried pinging it, hoping to start pre-flight for a rapid departure, but didn't get a response.

The spaceport grew large, then suddenly filled our screens; this was indeed a rapid descent, far quicker than any civilian craft would be allowed. The moment we touched down in the area reserved for Services craft our doors popped open, and next thing we were outside in the cool night air, hobbling across the tarmac. The walking wounded.

"Good luck!" the pilot called, waving goodbye. I waved back; I didn't even know her name. I'd assumed someone would be here to take us to the ship, but the place was eerily empty. We hobbled into the main hub,

which was quiet at this time of the night – eleven p.m., I noted. We'd passed through three time zones on the trip down.

"Do you remember where the ship was, Chook?"

"Sector H," answered Sana emphatically. "I remember."

"That's miles," said Chook, "and we can hardly walk. Here, let's get one of these." He pointed to a stand-on gravity sled. They rented these out at kiosks all over the port to help people navigate its gargantuan size. Good idea. I staggered over, scanned my kom, and next the three of us were sliding silently through the empty corridors of the terminal. Through a door labeled *Private Craft* and back outside. It was a cool night but not seriously cold like Jerbet, autumn, not biting here yet. Ships were dotted at regular intervals around the black tarmac and in the distance, we could hear the sound of gyros winding up somewhere – very large ones – then winding down.

We passed through the sectors, running from A. Worryingly, the ship was still not returning my ping. The reason was obvious a few minutes later when we finally found it…*sealed.* A temporary barrier had been erected to prevent access and a large, yellow hardiplaz sign was stuck over the entry port. We stepped gingerly off the gravity sled and stood around, staring hopelessly at it through the chain-link fence.

"What does this *mean*, Col?" asked Sana.

"Impounded, it looks like." I hadn't thought anyone would be able to crack this ship without my codes, clearly wrong on that score. What to do, call Henderzon? I didn't fancy it, and besides it was out of his jurisdiction. *Aballa!* But at eleven p.m.? I called anyway and to my surprise got an answer right away. *"Col! You OK?"*

"Sorry, Aballa, thought I'd be waking you up."

"You didn't hear? There's been a massive leak and explosion over at Dynamics. They got all the firefighters from the city and half the squad." That explained why there was no security at the spaceport. This was starting to feel familiar…*and* wrong at the same time.

"Aballa, we're at the spaceport, trying to get off-planet, very urgent. Don't ask why, it's a long story. But our ship's been Clamped."

"Why would it be Clamped?"

"No reason of course, it's bullshit."

"OK, gimme five."

I looked around. Something wasn't right. A planet strike followed by an emergency at the city's largest hardiplaz matter converter requiring all forces to attend, just as we were arriving at the spaceport? They were coming for us.

I scanned the port, looking for movement, signs of trouble. All seemed quiet.

"Still packing that blaster, Chook?"

"Has Pinocchio got wooden balls?"

"Why, what's going on?" asked Sana.

"Dunno, but something's off. I've got a feeling we're being set up."

I looked upward into the still night and noticed three bright pinpricks, growing larger. There you go. Something coming in, coming for us. I was certain.

"Sorry, Col," came Aballa's voice, *"your ship's been impounded by the D.I.R. Looking at the file now."* I let loose a string of expletives. *"I know it's bullshit, but I can't do anything, not till office hours. Can't even get the access codes to open it up."*

The Clamp was nonsense of course: a digital and physical block sometimes put on the movement of a ship till back dues were paid to Internal Revenue. Some gremlin buried in the bureaucracy somewhere, probably a Movement sympathizer, had put this on. Such things could be appealed and rapidly revoked if they were without merit, but that would have to wait for the morning. This was a holding action, forcing us to stay on-planet.

"Aballa, we need support here. I've got a bad feeling. I think your accident is all about us, a diversion, and now it looks like there's a trio of ships coming in from orbit. My guess is they're not friendly."

*"Damn, Perolo, I've got no one to spare, everything's at the Dynamics site! Hang on, let me think…there is a ship…*yes, *a way to get you off-planet – a bit out of left field, but if what you're saying's true, this could be the one thing those fuckers won't dare touch."*

He told me his idea. It was indeed out of left field, and I hated it a lot. But I was running out of options by that stage. Above us the silver dots were resolving into shapes, sleek and dangerous looking, silhouetted against the black night sky. Coming in fast and from what I could see, on a trajectory placing them right on our doorstep.

"OK, new plan," I said as the ships braked for landing. "Back to the passenger terminal. ASAP."

We jumped on the sled, and I turned for the nearest entrance about two kilometers away, at least ten minutes by my reckoning given the sluggish pace of the sled. I squeezed the throttle as tightly as I could, not that it made any difference. From behind us came a subsonic *whoomph*. It was dark and we'd be hard to see – but no matter, they'd have spotted us already on infrared. They'd soon be coming for us, and in something a lot faster than this crappy sled.

"Chook, I think we know who that is landing, right? We need to buy time to get ourselves to that entrance. I want you to shock them. The moment one of those doors open, fire."

"Got it. Sana, can you sit down in front of me?"

The sled was huge, designed to carry groups of people plus luggage. Sana sat cross-legged in front of Chook, who faced the rear. He got down onto his knees and placed his arm over Sana's shoulder. "I don't mind being used as a gun rest," she said, "but if you shoot first, don't we run the risk they might not be who we think they are?"

No one spoke for a moment. I felt sure I was right, but what if I wasn't? "Chook, hold your fire till we're sure they're aggressive."

I was focused on the terminal building, willing us forward. The entrance grew ever so slowly larger as we crawled toward it. Every few seconds I looked back, and now saw the ships were putting down, each finding a landing spot of relative darkness in between the light cast by the giant towers. Flagged ill intent, I thought, deliberately choosing dark patches to land. All three ships began opening their doors simultaneously, spilling cabin light into the night when a beam of purple slit the air, aimed to perfection into the landing bay of the closest. Chook decided to shoot first anyway. He put two more into the other ships, laughing with glee. "That'll slow the fuckers."

The terminal was getting closer – but still so far! It looked like we'd covered about half the distance, but that was probably being optimistic. Chook had shot well. It would be quite the mess inside each of the landing bays now, and even in armor, the enemy would be reluctant to step straight into a line of fire. What would they do?

The answer became apparent a minute later as all three ships lifted into the air, spun one hundred eighty degrees, and put back down again. They could alight en masse now behind the cover of their own ships, then come after us.

And then a shot rang out. It missed us and hit a small cargo ship nearby, sparks flying into the dark. I pulled the sled to the left, tried to put a ship between us and where the enemy had landed. If I had any residual guilt about Chook shooting first, that was now officially over. Another shot sizzled over our heads, high, thank God, but soon they'd have their range.

"Shit!" said Chook. "I don't know where to shoot, they're fanning out."

Think, think. What to do?

An idea came.

"Sana, do you have a hair tie, something elastic?"

She turned to me, hand sliding through her hair, and pulled out a small circle of fabric. "This do?"

"Yes!" The sled's throttle was a sliding switch that retracted automatically once you let go, making it 'idiot proof' to drive. I brought it to a standstill as another shot sliced into a ship not far away. Something metallic fell to the ground. They were using military-grade lasers – at a *spaceport* with possibly powered-up ships around. Total madness!

Chook and Sana jumped off and went to grab our packs, but I waved them off. "Leave them. It'll look like there's someone on the sled, and we can run faster without it all."

Sana shook her head. "Why do I always end up leaving my stuff behind?"

I pointed the sled in the direction of another entrance, much farther away than the one we'd been headed toward, aiming it along a route that avoided bumping into anything; let them think we were heading there. I fumbled with Sana's hair tie, wrapping it around and around the throttle till the fabric felt taut, just as another shot scudded into the ground right nearby. Chook sent a shot in the direction it seemed to come from, then a hatch opened in a ship next to us and a grizzled head popped out. "What the *fuck's* going on?" asked the old spacer.

I looked around, flicked the sled's throttle upward to 'on', then jumped off as it started to move. After a few meters though, I heard the servo motor click off and the sled stopped again. The switch must have flicked itself back to 'off', the band I'd stretched around it not tight enough.

"Bugger this," said Chook, pointing his gun at the sled and firing directly at the throttle switch. His blaster must have been turned to the lightest setting because the handle didn't blow away, but sparks cascaded into the air. The sled promptly turned itself off and settled back onto the ground.

"Great work, Chook," said Sana.

I shook my head, trying to think up something, anything we could do, when perversely, the sled sparked up again. The servo motor whined, and it suddenly leaped away at lightning pace – way faster than it was supposed to go – in the direction I'd pointed it.

"See?" crowed Chook. "Violence *does* work!"

To the incredulous spacer I called, "Madam, if I were you, I'd page security and stay in your ship," and to the others, "All right, *run*!"

Though running wasn't exactly what you'd call it. More like limping, lurching, and sliding. Startled shouts rang out and laser fire traced the night as the sled zipped away. Good, that should give them something to go on with.

We scraped and shuffled our way forward, the entrance getting ever closer. Was it three hundred meters now? Far off to our right I saw a flurry of purple laser fire light up the terminal wall – *good night, Irene* for the sled I'd say. Surely all that shooting would trigger security? There had to be at least someone left at the spaceport – or had they all been neutralized as well?

"Stop for a sec!" panted Sana. "I think there's something wrong with my hip. I can barely walk."

We were all puffing heavily, winded as well as wounded.

"Jump on!" said Chook, bending over, motioning to her. Sana looked at me and I nodded, then we all headed off again. Loud noises emanated from the other entrance a kilometer away, pieces of metal dinging and falling. They must have figured out our little ruse and were trying to make themselves feel better by taking it out on the sled. How long before they headed our way?

Not long. Another shot hissed off the ground nearby, then came a spray of random fire all around us. They were shooting indiscriminately, not sure exactly where we were. I could see the outlines of armored figures, still small at this point but coming. Perhaps three minutes till they had us, but with salvation so close! Only fifty meters now, but across open ground. We huddled behind the base of a light tower, catching our breath. Chook placed Sana gently back down.

"Don't shoot," I whispered to him. "Don't give our position away."

We stood panting as the gray figures grew ever closer. How to cross that last bit to the entrance? Running would be suicide. It was all beginning to seem hopeless and I was starting to wonder if there was a way we might surrender without being killed when my kom came to life with an audio call: Aballa!

"That you guys near gate two?"

I looked over, there was a sign directly above the nearby entrance with the word TWO stenciled over it. That'd be it.

"*Yes!* They're on our tail!"

"Hold tight. When I land, run like mad."

A black Services flyer put down in front of us and we needed no further encouragement, hobbling our way toward then around it, putting the ship between us and the enemy as we made for the door. Ten meters, then five. Any moment I expected blaster fire in our backs sending us into the next world, but they must have been spooked by the ship, or at least their vision blocked by it. We finally reached the door, staggered through, and fell in a heap on the other side.

"Ee-*ew*," cried Sana, "I'm caught in the middle of a sweaty *man-sandwich*."

We pulled ourselves up off the floor and stood for a moment, panting and hunched over our wounds.

"What now, boss?" asked Chook, blinking in the terminal's bright lights. He was a state; with his busted arm, face and clothes smeared with blood – *my* blood. Sana looked hardly any better. We'd have to clean ourselves up somewhere, somehow. But no time to dally.

"Second try," I said, grabbing a new gravity sled from a nearby kiosk. Sana, hobbling aboard, said, "Let's hope this doesn't have the same karma as the last," as we zoomed – if you can use such a word to describe an anti-grav sled, perhaps, *dawdled* – forward. Behind us came new sounds of boots crunching in the corridor. A blaster shot hit the roof just before the corridor did a gentle turn, giving us temporary cover. We slid along through the main terminal as I tried fruitlessly to get more speed out of the sled. We passed the almost-empty Arrivals area, then traveled down a long corridor to the Departure zone, which was the exact opposite, packed with holidaymakers. Then I finally saw it.

The luminous lime-green animated figure, even as a boy I hated him. Saccharine-sweet, with a grating high-pitched laugh: *Tigsy the Tiger.* Loved by trillions and an instantly recognized symbol for the most powerful corporation in the galaxy. Above the departure port to which a sea of humanity was flowing, the glowing sign beckoned:

WELCOME ABOARD!
Tigsy-Verse Old Earth Cruise!

"Col!" Sana exclaimed. "Where the hell are we—"

"*Tigsy!*" gushed Chook. "I *love* that little guy. He was my favorite as a kid!"

I looked behind to see gray-clad figures in the middle distance, closing rapidly. Would they dare try anything among the general public, particularly at an event run by Tigsy-Corp? Let's not put that to the test. Get ourselves some tickets and board that cruise, but first a change of clothes.

"In here, quick." I motioned to a nearby merchandise store.

Sana rolled her eyes. "You're *kidding* me!"

"Any better ideas?"

The place was packed with excited passengers and their kids. *Kids!* Never seen so many of them. Where did they spring from? Most were clad in the bright leggings and tight stretch fabrics of various superhero characters. So hyped-up they barely noticed as we ran through to the apparel section.

Chook and I swapped looks. I snatched a bunch of items from the racks and ran to the change room. Off came the torn and bloody clothing and on went a pair of stripy pants, a billowy white blouse, pointy hat, clip-on hoop earrings and a prosthetic attachment that turned my hand into a hook. In the mirror, a pirate stared back at me – one that in my case had just seen actual battle.

Sana went with a low-cut lace-up corset with puffy sleeves, and a tricorne hat emblazoned with skull and crossbones. She looked extremely cute, to be honest. If you ignored the black eye and matted blood in her hair.

The M4M soldiers had fanned out through the crowd. They were keeping a close eye on us but seemed unwilling to make a move for the moment. We raced to the reservations counter, where a kangaroo-shaped sales robot – *Rascally Roo*, one of Tigsy-Corp's myriad characters – lit up with enthusiasm.

"Well, *ahoy there*!!" it said with signature gurgling laugh. "Look at you guys! *Great work* with those costumes!"

Chook was smitten. "Thanks, Rascally Roo," he said bashfully.

"How can I help today?!" The robot's face was set in an expression of permanent enthusiasm.

"Ah yes…well," I said, "what we need actually is three tickets to board. As you can see, we've arrived rather late."

One of the gray men sidled up near to where we stood, his eyes flicking between us, talking on his kom. He was obviously dying to act, but being held back by whoever he was speaking to. We really had to get aboard this ship, the area was literally filling up with enemies, at least twenty by my count.

The animatronic kangaroo looked stricken. "Aw shucks, guys, I'm sorry, we don't have any places left on this sailing." Then he perked up again. "Tigsy-verse Old Earth cruises are *so* popular they sell out months in advance. But why don't I book you now for our premium 'pirates-only' summer cruise. *Ahoy matey!* Let's *trouble* the water!"

The gray figures had decided to cluster around us. There were a dozen directly behind and others mixed in with the happy holidaymakers nearby, trying almost comically to blend. They were counting on us not making it aboard. Why hadn't spaceport security taken them out? Maybe still tied up, or reluctant to engage with so many civilians around?

Sana shook her head in annoyance at the robot Roo. I didn't want her blowing up in public, so I said, "Please sir, we really *need*, I mean *want* to sail. Surely there's something you can do? Can't you look more carefully in your database?"

The robot stopped in its tracks. It must have been a basic hospitality model and its programming didn't seem able to cope with disappointing people. It made an embarrassed laugh but didn't speak, just stood there looking at us.

"C'mon, Rascally Roo," Chook begged, "help us out!"

"Yeah c'mon, *Rascally Roo*," said Sana, voice laced with sarcasm.

The robot looked traumatized.

All around us passengers were streaming aboard the ship between brightly clad Tigsy greeters sporting harlequin pants and multi-colored bow ties. Robot figures mugged for pictures doing their signature laugh or move, and a giant robot Tigsy – king of all – stood at the end of the embarkation ramp giggling annoyingly while being mobbed by kids. A scene of unchecked gaiety, somewhat repellent, actually.

Our robot clerk looked to be in trouble. "I don't know how…I think…that…grrk." You could almost see smoke coming from its head.

"What seems to be the problem here?"

A young man stepped in behind the counter. Tall, blond, and slim with a questionable orange tan, he wore a perfectly pressed purple suit and a Tigsy-green bow tie, his hair coiffed to perfection. The kangaroo-bot was making gurgling noises. "Shoo," the man said, flicking his fingers at it, while casting a skeptical eye over the three of us. "I'm tonight's duty bursar. How can I help?"

"Ah, yes, hello," I said and started rambling. "We're looking for a reservation on your lovely cruise and we're really hoping you can fit us in somehow. Because obviously we're all such *huge* Tigsy fans and it was one of those spontaneous things where we thought, 'Why not? Let's just go!'

so here we are and we're very much in your hands..." I went on like this for some time, while the man – Clarence Bussey I noted, from his gold-embossed name tag – stared coldly with pursed lips. Finally, I ran out of puff.

"So..." he said skeptically, "you have all just *turned up* here at embarkation. No luggage that I can see, and no kids either, but *in costume*, looking to board. Is that right?"

"Yes, ahem...that's about the size of it."

His eyes flicked over my shoulder to where I knew several very large men in ill-fitting suits loitered. Tigsy security, famed galaxy-wide for both discretion and ruthless efficiency when required. Even the Movement figures were keeping their distance.

"Very unusual."

"Listen, Mr. Bussey," Chook said, tearing up, "you look like a nice man. I've been a Tigsy fan all my life. It would mean *so* much to me, and all of us if you could find a place on your wonderful cruise!"

Sana joined in. "Sometimes in life you just have to make a spontaneous decision, sir. That's us to a *T*, we're such *whacky*, *zany* people!"

"But very *normal* as well!" I hastened to add, then uttered the magic words, "And financially speaking, of course, money is no object."

Clarence paused at that. He cast a final lingering look over us and then brought up a holo-terminal while muttering about grown adults wearing 'over-realistic' costumes. The coiffe, I noted with fascination, had not moved a millimeter during our conversation. Fingers whirred, screens were flicked, pinched, and swiped. "Hmm," he said finally, "there *is* actually something."

"*Yes?*" We all leaned forward.

"But I must warn you, it's *very* expensive."

"*Please*," I said, "such trifling matters as *cost* do not concern us."

He named a price. I almost succeeded in not flinching, looked across at the others, whose smiles were frozen in place. Until that moment, I hadn't known it was possible to charge so much for anything, let alone a Tigsy cruise.

"My, that is a rather large sum. How long did you say this cruise runs for? Never mind, please make the arrangements."

Chapter Twelve

I collapsed onto our sumptuous bed, still in shock.

Two hundred and thirteen thousand credits: that's what the bill came to after taxes and port charges for our 'Captain's Choice Ultraluxe-Suite' – *per day*.

Turned out someone had canceled at the last minute; I suppose the super-rich can do things like that. This weeklong cruise to Old Earth would exhaust almost all the funds that appeared inexplicably in my account after leaving Jubilee. Easy come, easy go, I figured. Chook surprisingly was the only one of us who seemed dismayed about the cost.

A short time later, the giant cruise ship lifted silently from Harrison City Spaceport, and we were away. I looked out of our floor-to-ceiling window to see if the M4M ships were still there, but perhaps we were moving too fast, or maybe because they were parked in the darkest places or decked with cloaking material, I failed to find them.

But they were there all right, and they'd know where we were headed: six days in space, stopping at several transit hubs before landing at our final destination, Old Earth. They weren't able to follow us aboard, but they'd be waiting somewhere.

Over the next few days, we explored the ship – which featured seventeen restaurants, twelve snack bars, a casino, a bowling alley and clubs and bars too numerous to count. A zip line, holo-play zone, a couple of gyms (the most underused facilities in the ship, I discovered with glee) and if you were game, the seven-hole golf course under a stasis bubble on the roof that popped up between quantum jumps.

Nowhere on board was there a 'normal' shop; it was all *Tigsy, Tigsy, Tigsy* – meaning we were stuck wearing these cheap, fancy-dress clothes. We got cleaned up and Chook had his arm re-set by the infirmary nurse, raising surprisingly few questions and implying *what*, about our fellow passengers?

Who seemed to be having a ball. They sang along at night to stirring Tigsy showtunes, wallowed in the pool, or lounged at the bar while their kids were occupied by hyper-enthusiastic robot minders. Mostly, they ate.

At first, we just stayed in our room – more secure, and what the hell, we'd spent all this money after all. I pondered events, my mind always returning to the hidden settlement of Hyvon. How was my grandmother getting on, assuming she was still alive? Realistically, I'd never see her again. And what would Father do now, take Lynda back? How could he? Then again, having spent decades living in denial, what were a few more? I thought of calling him FTL on my kom, was on the verge of doing so several times, but always chickened out.

I tried watching holo-media, but that was all Tigsy too, and the news channels carried nothing about a planet strike on Jerbet or an incident at the HC spaceport. Someone was keeping a lid on things.

Mostly, I thought about Danee and the girls. I pined and pined, tried with limited success to smother the nagging ember of guilt about that night with Sana.

Eventually our mega-luxe lodgings started driving us mad. Especially the food. The suite came with a private chef who'd worked in some top-rated place listed in *The Galaxy's 10,000 Best Restaurants*, and sure enough what she produced reminded me exactly of **P U H O L:** Douglas's fancy six-star restaurant on Jubilee.

After a few days I couldn't take any more gels, or foams or multicourse 'tasting plates'. Sana was the last to crack, but in the end even she was desperate to escape. We ventured out to try our luck at one of the seven enormous breakfast buffets.

Did I say enormous?

The word doesn't quite capture the...*enormity* of it at all.

Bubbling chafing dishes as far as the eye could see. Five different bakeries, a stir-fry and dim sum station, superhero-tended cereal 'gun', automated coffee-roasting robot with twenty outlet taps, dozens of gurgling, whizzing juice machines, and a thousand other things I can't remember. After pushing through the crowds, I found my way back to the table, bacon and eggs in hand.

"Is that all you got?" Chook laughed. His own plate was piled high, ready to be washed down with a foaming 'breakfast beer'. He was certainly taking advantage of the free alcohol policy, though it had to be said they *did* make things easy for him with a fully stocked bar right in the middle of the buffet.

"It was overwhelming, too much!"

"I know," agreed Sana. She'd taken a small plate of fruit and yogurt, which she picked at with a pained look.

There had to be something wrong with my food. When I touched them with a fork, the eggs seemed to have a rubbery outer layer and sat in a pool of yellowish oil. The bacon was square-shaped, looked like it was extruded from a machine and was a strange, fleshy orange-pink.

"You know," said Sana, pointing at my bacon, "*nothing* should be that color."

That was it. I pushed my plate away.

Chook suddenly gagged, held his glass out at arm's length and stared at it goggle-eyed. "*This beer,*" he pronounced, "would kill a brown dog."

"It's all completely tasteless," I marveled, "but somehow gross at the same time. How do they do that?"

Not that our fellow passengers seemed to mind. They piled up their plates and went back for seconds and thirds. If it wasn't for weight-control nanos, all these people would have been fatter than Ricky Rhinoceros.

On our fourth day we discovered the cigar lounge; the odor of smoke a more than fair trade for peace and quiet. We'd decided not to visit the planet Qubrea earlier that day – the ship wasn't putting down there anyway, only delivering interested passengers by shuttle. I figured it wasn't worth the risk, though it would have been great to pick up normal clothes; some of the other passengers had started calling us *the costume people.*

A trickle of new passengers joined the cruise, including two fit-looking and unsmiling young men who were somehow always around the periphery of wherever we happened to be. Eating lunch a few tables away or working out at the gym on the other side of the room, and never making eye contact. They reminded me of the 'gray t-shirt' goons on Brouggh who followed me around after I first got back from Jubilee. At this moment they were keeping watch from a side table at the far end of the bar. Not yet a threat, but that would change when it came time to disembark.

Out of the blue, a man and a woman appeared and, without invitation, slid into our banquette to join us.

"Keeping up with the *festive spirit*," said the man. "Good work!"

None of us looked particularly festive in our cheap and now grubby costumes. We'd done the best we could to clean ourselves up, but my nose was red and swollen from being broken and Sana's right eye still black. The man seemed to be poking fun.

"Introductions!" he crowed. "My name is Rafonzo Banuburzipal and this is my darling wife, Madame Hof-Montparnasse. We are late of the pleasure world Lussuoso – populated by the rich, the filthy rich, and the even richer still; all of them extremely dull and not dissimilar in that regard to the patrons aboard this ship – present company excluded, I hasten to add."

The woman fixed him with a glare and said menacingly, "Cut it out!" Then she smiled sweetly to the rest of us, revealing a row of perfectly symmetrical, gleaming white teeth. "He's always trying it on. I'm Angelina and this is my husband, James. We thought we'd come and sit with you for a while because...you all looked so terribly interesting."

The woman was beautiful with jet-black hair, creamy skin, and piercing jade-green eyes. She was probably middle aged, though it was hard to tell given the trim figure and possible 'work done' on her face, but if one were being critical, she was wearing clothes slightly more revealing than good taste might dictate: Danee always said, 'It's either boobs *or* legs.'

Not that we were in a position to judge.

James recoiled at his wife's rebuke. I had to admit, it did feel like a current of danger lurked behind that charming exterior. "Indeed, one rarely meets such interesting people on these cruises. I believe drinks are in order. Shall we? *On us!*"

I looked at the others. My sense was these people were harmless if eccentric, but you never knew. Sana shrugged as if to say, 'Why not'.

I followed the man to the bar. Though graying at the temples, he seemed lithe and youthful, and carried himself with the sure-footed grace of an athlete – correction, more like an *acrobat* – as if at any moment he could silently pad up the walls and vanish. He pointed to a bottle on the top shelf labeled with a skull and crossbones and held up two fingers. The barman blanched, then shook his head, pulled out two small glasses and poured.

"Syrian Panther Sweat," said James fondly as he took a sip. "I call it 'the old thought enhancer', banned throughout the civilized galaxy. They can only serve it once the ship's in interstellar space."

I may have seen this beverage around the traps on Jubilee where it could, of course, be sold like water. I took a reluctant sip and tasted something closer to hydrochloric acid than anything normally consumed by humans. James gave a wry smile. "Bottoms up! Can't leave your friends with my darling wifey or who knows what might happen!"

Seemed I was snookered. Also, by nature curious, so I took a breath and threw the tumbler of fizzing, spitting black liquid down my throat. Gasped. Coughed. Spun in a circle, then banged the bar with the flat of my hand three times trying not to faint. James was ready with a glass of water, eyes twinkling. "Wonderful!" he said. "Now, preliminaries out of the way, please tell me about yourself, Mr…?"

"Perolo. Col." We shook hands. My throat still burned, but the vertigo was beginning to recede, and a warm buzz replaced the all-of-body-on-fire feeling. James whipped out two large cigars from a coat pocket, proffering one.

"Wasted on me, I'm afraid."

"One of life's great pleasures." In a single fluid motion, he clipped the cigar and lit it with a small device which appeared in his hand and then disappeared as if by magic. "Pleased to meet you, Col. So where is home?"

"Sana and I hail from Brouggh, and Chook is just a passing acquaintance really. Yourselves? You mentioned being from somewhere called Lussuoso?"

"Yes, good memory, Col, I can tell you're a very observant person. That is indeed our most recent address. Do tell me, what brings your little posse on this cruise? You guys don't seem the type, no offense."

"None taken. Oh, you know, it's a long story."

"I'm in no rush."

"Oh well, you know, the three of us have never...been on anything like this, so we all figured, 'why not?' Just a spur of the moment thing." The lie felt pathetic even as I spoke it. James looked at me with amused disbelief.

"And the costumes?"

"You know, big Tigsy fans, all of us."

"Hmm...well, I'm afraid I have to say...*no*." James shook his head, still smiling. "Shall I tell you what I see?"

"Ahem, well—"

"I see...*desperation*. All of you carrying injuries and dressed in strange clothes but trying to act normal. That suggests flight. From whom we might ask? Not sure, but I'd wager it has something to do with those muscle-bound clods sitting in the corner. Fortunately, no one on this ship can see beyond the next round of drinks." He delicately ashed his cigar in a nearby vaporizing tray. "One of you, a hardened criminal. Another clearly of artistic temperament, and from the third" – he looked me up and down – "I get a distinct whiff of something unexpected: *eau de plod*. A perfume I normally find offensive and shy away from whenever possible, though in your case it does actually suit and is not altogether disagreeable. How am I doing so far?"

Nailed us perfectly, but I sensed no malice in it, something more like sympathy.

"So, I'm thinking," he went on, "why would a cop be on the run? Either he's *done* something very bad or...he's *running away* from something very bad, and in your case, I'm going to bet it's the latter. What do you say, Mr. Perolo?"

"Can I ask, why are you so interested?"

He sighed. "Col, there aren't many interesting things in the galaxy these days, not for me anyway, and I do feel concerned for you all, not entirely sure why. But it's OK, you don't have to say." He motioned to the barman and ordered champagne and five flutes.

I looked him in the eye. "James, you seem like a good guy. I would tell you more but it's dangerous. All I can say is your instincts are good. Can we leave it there?"

He smiled and patted me on the shoulder. We returned to the others with the drinks and had a fine old time that night. The next morning our robo-butler brought us a parcel that had been delivered anonymously to our room, containing blessedly, clothes for all three of us. Though it had to be said the women's apparel was a tad 'sexier' than Sana might normally wear.

Years later, I heard rumors that a daring burglary was committed while we were on that cruise and kept quiet by the authorities. An elderly, super-wealthy couple was liberated of a rare gem collection that vanished from the safe in their suite. Fortunately, all was covered by insurance and in the end no real harm done. The mysterious thing was that no one on the ship, not even senior management, were aware the jewelry had been aboard.

The strange couple must have left at the next stop because we never saw them again. The ship now had only one place to visit before returning to Brouggh, but we would not be aboard for that final leg as I had other plans.

Then it hit me with a shock. With all that had been going on, I'd forgotten how significant our next and final destination was. We were steaming rapidly toward the most famous planet in the galaxy. A place all humans were obsessed with and considered sacred, but until recently never visited. The cradle of our race.

Old Earth.

Chapter Thirteen

What to do with humanity's ruined home world?

An issue plaguing bureaucrats and policy wonks for centuries. The League dithered. It seemed wrong to leave our birthplace an empty shell, but who could possibly take it on? Who had the skills, the resources and, quite frankly, the *balls* required to revive this dead planet so freighted with significance? Certainly not the League, permanently mired in budget crisis.

After centuries a decision was finally reached. For the sum of one credit per annum, leasehold over the entirety of Old Earth was granted to the only organization judged capable. With its own universities, engineering corps and private navy, and with a GDP thousands of times larger than any single planet, there was but one choice:

Tigsy-Corp.

We stared in wonder from the observation deck as our ever-present friends, the gray t-shirt guys, lurked nearby, keeping a tighter watch now that landing was close. "Morning fellas," I said to them cheerfully at breakfast – but they seemed busy doing something with their koms and didn't respond.

But wow, *look*! Here were the familiar continents laid out before us just like my junior high textbook: Africa, America and…whatever the others were. All the same dusty reddish brown, and even from this great height, clearly dead and lifeless. All except for one tiny patch of green.

"*…after the cascading crises of global warming, stock market and eco-collapse, and amid mounting competition for scarce resources came the 'Nano-Wars'…*" The stooped and bespectacled history professor was finally having her moment, delivering the 'Old Earth historical lecture' before the giant viewing window. We tagged along, joining the small group who bothered to show up. But anyway, I'd heard this all before…

After a few orbits we started our descent. Tigsy-Corp had yet to terraform (or *re-terraform* if you want to be pedantic) most of the planet. The polar ice caps had been tapped and giant air production silos commissioned. The remnant deadly nanos wiped out by a counteracting swarm that self-destructed once their mission was complete, but at this time only one small island was ready for human occupation.

"That's where my ancestors came from," said Chook excitedly, pointing to the green blob growing ever larger, "Tasmania!"

A claxon sounded. We headed back to our room to 'strap in' – not that there was the slightest danger. Twenty minutes later we were down, and what a strange anticlimax: landing finally on Old Earth, *the* Old Earth, but without the slightest sensation of doing so. Now it was time to get off this bloody ship and escape. A special exit tube was reserved for first-class passengers, but we would not be using that today. "Ready?" I asked the others.

They both nodded.

"OK, let's go."

A few days earlier we'd settled on a plan. The Movement had been able to infiltrate even this Tigsy-controlled ship, so for sure they'd be waiting for us here on Old Earth. But staying aboard and returning to Brouggh would be an even worse idea. So how to get away undetected?

I racked my brain for days and finally came up with a plan.

"How on earth do we *do that*?" asked Sana.

"I'll pay someone off."

Chook waggled his finger. "Leave the bribery to me."

So, there we were, huddled in a storeroom somewhere on one of the lower levels, helping each other into costumes Chook had arranged through a very young, very bored and now freshly bribed attendant: Little Bo Peep for Sana, a padded bear suit for me, and for some reason, a giant plastic banana for Chook.

"Pull that bonnet down," I told a scowling Sana. "And try to look *sweet*."

"*Yeah!* You'll scare the kiddies," came Chook's muffled voice from inside the banana.

Sana swooshed her long pink staff through the air a few times like a weapon. "I *hate* children. Any of them come near me they're getting *this*."

We slipped out of the storeroom and into a flow of bodies queuing for the exits. Parents tired and bored already, over-amped kids, and Tigsy characters strutting and posing. I pushed through the throng and took an escalator down into the giant departure hall where people were forming lines. It was harder than you'd think to see in my bear suit which had no peripheral vision, but at least my face was covered unlike, worryingly, Sana's.

And there they were, on the far side of the hall, eyes glittering, keeping a careful watch on the crowd. I messaged Sana, *"Turn away to your right, our friends are over in the corner."*

Sana now had to deal with a family wanting pictures, a little boy with grubby hands tugged insistently at her skirt. *Oooh, she'd love that.* Chook was besieged; the moment any of us stopped moving we were pounced on. So where was that staff exit she told us about? Was supposed to be… *there it was!* Up ahead and just to the right of the four main disembarkation tubes, and best of all, on the opposite side of the hall to the gray t-shirts: a barely noticeable door with a small sign, *Staff Only*.

I pushed toward it, hoping the others would follow. Getting crowded now, everyone trying to leave the ship at once. Hands reached out, "*Huggy Bear!*" some kid called, but I wasn't in a hugging mood. "Excuse me, sorry, *excuse me*," I intoned, but quietly as possible, trying to get through the horde without drawing attention.

I chanced a look behind to see the others following. Good. Though we definitely stood out more than I wanted, moving crossways through the crowd. Just as we reached the door, I turned and looked again, noticed one of the gray t-shirts staring intently. Was that a flicker of recognition?

Best not hang around to see. The door opened to my kom as arranged, and we all trooped through; the noisy departure hall instantly silenced behind us. At the bottom of the tube was a customs station. Hadn't thought of that, but of course, even Tigsy staff would have to go through the formalities.

The shrewish-looking official's eyes widened. "You are scanning as *passengers.* Why are you wearing costumes and attempting to leave this ship through the staff exit?"

My mind whirled. Was this against the law; how could it be? We'd still be scanned off-board regardless of whichever door we used. It was unusual though, so how to explain?

"We're *practicing,*" blurted Chook from inside the banana.

The woman frowned. "But—"

"*How's this!*" Sana curtsied and turned on her highest-wattage smile. "We're all working the next leg you see, so we thought, 'Let's get ahead of the game'!"

The story made absolutely no sense, but we were committed now. "And we're running a bit late for a team meeting, so if you wouldn't mind..."

The woman's eyes narrowed. "Then I'll be needing your employment certificates, *won't I*?"

"Not issued yet," said Chook confidently. He was a good bullshitter, I'll give him that.

"Well!" The woman paused. "That *is* most unusual." She thought for a moment. "Looks like I'll have to check this out with Command."

Chook popped open his faceplate and smiled. His eyes were watery, he looked hot and sweaty inside that hardiplaz shell. "I really don't think that will be necessary, madam... C'mon, what do you say?"

She paused for a long moment, then shrugged. "I guess there's nothing actually illegal going on here, is there? Not *really*. Just a bunch of future employees joining us through a slightly different entry port to normal. No harm in that, right?"

We all nodded.

"There you go." The ship's external door slid open. "Welcome to Old Earth."

We strode outside as casually as we could onto the spaceport's flat tarmac, and I took in a lungful of fresh air. *Old Earth air!* Smelled neutral, though possibly on the dry side, and gravity was right on Standard. Then I smacked my forehead.

Standard.

Throughout the civilized galaxy, 'Standard' was always expressed as one-G: the exact gravitational pull of humanity's home world, to which our bodies were all adapted. This world was *exactly* one-G. Because this is where we came from.

The tarmac thronged with passengers, many standing around gawking, getting in the way of others. Tigsy characters pointed and motioned toward transports which were waiting to whizz them away on whatever ground tour they'd booked. Keep moving. Over there, a low, squat building that she told us about: HQ for Tigsy ground staff. I walked casually as possible through the crowd, keeping an eye out for M4M – and there they were sprinkled through the crowd, one hard-looking woman talking on her kom, possibly in charge.

"How much did you pay the customs lady?" asked Sana.

Chook's laugh rumbled inside his suit. "Are you implying *Bernie Banana* would engage in illegal activities?"

"Not Bernie," I said, "but Chook definitely."

"Twenty credits."

Sana was aghast. "Only twenty credits? People are so *cheap*!"

I led us around the edges of the spilling crowd, then quickly as I dared to the staff building. I felt eyes on my back but didn't chance turning around. If those guys on the ship had spotted us, they'd have called it in by now anyway.

We traipsed into the busy staff building where thankfully no one paid us any attention. Tigsy workers stood around clearly relieved to be off duty, various props and head gear in hand, drinking coffee and chatting. I pulled out our backpacks from within the bear suit and minutes later we were changed and ready to leave, just as a dozen laser-eyed security personnel burst into the lounge area. Not uniformed, but obvious who they were and what they wanted, instantly fanning out and scanning the room. Weird that none of the staff gave them a second look.

"Out this way," I whispered, pointing to a side entrance. We slipped out, pushing our way through the incoming throng; thank God the place was busy. In the near distance loomed the giant towers of some reconstructed city, and just ahead, people were stepping into an open-top tourist train which looked ready to leave. This would have to do. I dashed aboard with the others following, and moments later the doors locked, and we were off.

"Welcome to the Old Earth discovery tour," called a guide over a small PA. "Please keep your hands inside the vehicle at all times."

Our little train had many small carriages joined together like a roller coaster. According to the map on my kom, it would take us from the spaceport to the reconstructed city. I looked to see if we were being followed but so far, so good. Give them time though. They knew we went into the staff building and once they cleared that, the next step would be to cover the exits and egress. They'd think of this train for sure.

We rumbled into a dark tunnel then popped out through a trapdoor into what looked like an ordinary apartment (except, of course, for the train tracks running through it).

"Here is a domestic scene of a family at breakfast," said our guide breathlessly, dressed in a brown uniform with a Tigsy lime-green tiger logo on her collar. "As our technicians had no source data to work with, everything you see today was created using information derived from broadcast television of the era." That made sense. Old Earth's cultural archive was destroyed during the Insurrection, so they must have turned to the digital shell of radio and TV transmissions expanding outward from Old Earth at the speed of light.

"And what era is that exactly?" I asked the guide.

"Excellent question, sir! For this exhibition our historians recreated Old Earth, USA, circa 10,618 MP – or by the Terran scale, 1991 to 2001 A.D."

"Why choose that period?"

"Another great question, sir! You are obviously a highly intelligent and satisfyingly curious person. Most of our guests show little or no interest in the historical aspects of Old Earth!"

I was beginning to think our guide might be a sophisticated robot; she seemed only able to operate in the one mode: hyper-enthusiasm. "Tigsy historians chose these dates for being the last period of relative stability before the commencement of the 'five crises' era."

The animatronic family looked very pleased with themselves, coming to life as our train entered. The morning routine seemed not all that different to mine with Danee and the girls, I thought with a twinge.

"Here we see an Old Earth mother pouring what was known as 'breakfast cereal' from a storage packet made of cardboard into the eating bowls of her children to be digested with milk. Please note, all products displayed are available for purchase at the Tigsy gift shop adjacent to the exit."

The apartment didn't seem radically different to how we lived these days – apart from the clunky furniture and the old-fashioned 'TV' (strictly 2D of course). The 'milk' being poured was probably drawn from a real animal though. Revolting thought. Scattered around the room, on the table and shelves, were packages labeled in large font.

"Items shown in this scene were recreated from small dramatic videos of the period called 'advertisements'. In ancient times, versions of the same product were sold by competing companies who used these promotional videos to increase their sales at the expense of other providers."

The train rolled into a staged tableau of young adults sitting around a lounge room in various poses of boredom.

"Our Tigsy engineers," said the guide, "were aided by the discovery of an entertainment subgenre the ancients called 'reality TV'. Knowing these representations were free from dramatic embellishment and thus an accurate depiction of life on Old Earth was of great help in recreating these scenes."

"What's going on here?" asked Chook.

"As a rite of passage, young people on Old Earth were isolated together in one dwelling for many months to sort the strong from the weak. Each day a disembodied voice would order the residents to perform various degrading tasks."

We moved on to a tropical island scene where a dozen figures lounged, many quite buff, and all dressed in flimsy apparel. "Similar trials were conducted with participants marooned together on small tropical islands. Once again, the weakest elements were winnowed from the strong."

"What a brutal society," muttered Sana.

Then came something easily recognizable as a bar. A group of women were standing together, all very well-coiffed and clad with immaculate makeup, but strangely puffed-out lips as if stung by bees.

"Our historical team," said the guide, "are particularly interested in the role of women in the ancient world. Their task was aided by video material depicting the lives of 'real housewives'. As you might imagine, social interactions on Old Earth were frequently aggressive and confrontational."

The ladies at the bar came to life mid-argument. 'How dare you say that Clara, *you bitch!*' one of them screamed, throwing a glass of what looked like champagne into the face of another.

Sana shook her head sadly.

The tour rolled on for a few more minutes – each scene more depressing than the last – ending finally with a fertility ritual in which young women undertook humiliating trials in the hope of being selected for mating with an officially sanctioned 'Bachelor'.

Finally, our train pulled into the rebuilt city called 'New York'. I'm not sure how accurate this *new* York was compared to the original, but life did feel strangely familiar, yet utterly foreign at the same time. We passed through the gift shop into a large, triangular space called 'Times Square' just as an obviously staged 'arrest scene' was taking place. In front of gawking picture-snapping tourists, four cops, all heavily moustached (one thing not changed in millennia) ran down a dark-skinned 'suspect', hurling him to the footpath then cuffing him.

From a law enforcement perspective two things stood out: the ancient and clunky (but highly lethal) projectile weapons, and something even odder. This posse of cops doing the arresting all had the same amount of melanin in their skin: none.

In other words, all were 'white'. At school I'd learned about the distinction and segregation of people by race in the ancient world, but it was still a shock to see it at first hand. On Brouggh, the chances of finding four perfectly white-skinned cops participating in one arrest would be vanishingly small.

What now? The place teemed with tourists. There were signs for 'Central Park Food Precinct' and 'Fifth Avenue Luxe Shopping Experience'.

"There." Chook pointed.

Just down a side street was exactly what we needed. A large sign reading, *Vehicle Hire.*

* * *

York lay far behind as we zoomed along 'Route 66' in our hydrocarbon-powered ground car, its motor emitting a pleasing, low-frequency thrum. The rental guy told us we'd need to stop and 'refuel' sometimes, but I didn't think that would be often as the island of Tasmania was itself only a few hundred kilometers across.

There was plenty of traffic; cars, trucks, and tourist buses, all of them recreated to look like vehicles of the era, though I don't think many were genuine petrol-powered like the one we chose. Occasionally someone honked and gave us the thumbs-up. Kinda cool, I had to admit.

We drove through mini representations of 'countries' from Old Earth. On either side of the road 'peasants' worked emerald-green rice paddies. Were they human or bot? The rental clerk told us that hundreds of thousands of settlers from around the galaxy had applied to come and live on Old Earth, join in the project of re-creation. There was a long waiting list – though to me it smacked of Tigsy-Corp taking advantage of people's altruism for some free labor.

How long did we have now, before they caught up to us?

I didn't need much time for what I'd planned. Aballa must have gotten that Clamp off our ship, because the moment we landed I'd been able to activate a most interesting kom function that lit up in a satisfying green color: '*Summon*'. It would call *The Grand Poobah* to us somehow from across the reaches of interstellar space. We just had to wait for it to arrive.

And take us where? I needed to find Jubilee, and the fail-over core carried by Batum had given me the all-important clue. When asked if it could connect to Douglas, it responded: "I could, if Prime was located in *this universe.*"

It took twenty minutes to drive through 'China'. Chook wanted to stop at the Kung Fu Adventure Pavilion, but I kept going because there was one place in particular that was calling me, one place where I knew we would find sanctuary.

Next came 'Indonesia', then 'France', then 'Egypt'; a large pyramid-shaped structure made of yellow rock looming there. Buses disgorged picture-snapping tourists at each of these, but it was 'India' where I finally turned off the main highway. We drove through fields and small towns, and it seemed that this country had to have been reconstructed from an earlier period of history than say, York. Or maybe different stages of economic development existed simultaneously side by side?

Our vehicle took some getting used to on these smaller roads. Unlike the instant acceleration of an electric motor or gravity engine, increasing one's velocity was achieved by pushing an 'accelerator' pedal. After a short lag, you could feel the various pistons, gears, belts, and cogs pick up their activity. Fuel burned, coolant cooled and oil churned, and all the thousands of crazily complex components labored together to eventually cause an uptick in forward motion. A masterpiece of old-world engineering.

Half an hour later, the topography began to change, becoming greener and hillier. A mountain range appeared in the distance, road signs pointing toward it reading, 'The Himalayas'. Which, after a brief consultation on my kom, I learned were once the tallest mountain range on Old Earth, though these didn't look very high. Another quick consult informed me:

The Cradle mountain range of Old Tasmania has been refashioned to resemble the shape, though not original height, of the Himalayas. Please note, despite the lower altitude, geo-transformers are in use, recreating the temperature and air density of the original region, and patrons participating in the Tigsy Everest Trek are advised to obtain appropriate equipment from the Tigsy Base Camp Emporium.

A fake mountain then, formed from the leftover rubble of this island. Impressive all the same, with snowy flanks and a distinctive triangular peak which, even from this distance, appeared laden with climbers. I zoomed in with my kom and, yup, hundreds of them, all hauling themselves up the steep slope. More credits in the bank for Tigsy.

An hour later, we were nearly there. On our left, a lushly green mountain slope and on our right, a fast-flowing, beautiful turquoise river called the 'Ganges' – just like the image I'd seen on a certain Jubilee wall, forever ago.

I turned off the highway, drove under a wooden archway inscribed, *We welcome you with love*, and along a short, unpaved driveway ending at a modest stone building painted white. There were half a dozen people about, sweeping paths, tending to the gardens. Some looked vaguely familiar.

An old, very skinny man walked out of the building clad in orange robes. He lit up at the sight of us, smiled warmly, spread his arms, and said, "Welcome, Col! *At last!*"

The Swami, from Jubilee.

Chapter Fourteen

"Please tell me everything from the beginning."

We were sitting in a pavilion next to the rushing waters of the 'Ganges'. The Swami's assistant, Varan, served tea and more of those delicious cookies. I took him through all that had happened in, what was it, just over *three months*? The attack on Jubilee, fleeing to the League base, then on to Brouggh and more fleeing.

The Swami shook his head. "Hard to comprehend, so much senseless violence. Please let me offer refuge to you here in this ashram, for as long as you want."

My turn to headshake. "Very kind, but we can't stay. I think we made it here undetected, but if they do catch up it won't be good for you. And besides, I need to find Jubilee and get home to Danee and the girls."

"I understand."

"So, tell me, *Mr. Swami*," said Sana with a slight trace of skepticism, "how did *you* come to be here, on Old Earth?"

"And what the hell's an *ashram*?" asked Chook.

The old man laughed. "That's a long story too. The short answer is I received an offer from Tigsy-Corp. They wanted a 'genuine Swami' here as part of their world building. At first, I said no, of course, but Douglas hinted strongly I should accept."

"Douglas?"

"Yes, most uncharacteristic. He said if I 'knew what was good for me' I ought to leave Jubilee."

That clinched it. Douglas *knew*. He knew the attack was coming and he even warned certain people about it – but not *me*, head of security, and not Danee working in his own Intelligence wing. I felt anger bubbling up, which the Swami, of course, noticed.

"Col, none of us know the full story yet." His eyes glowed with compassion, and I felt drawn into them. It was hard to resist falling into that dreamy, happy state I always did around him.

"So, then you pulled up stakes, just like that?" Sana asked.

"Yes!" He laughed. "I always fantasized about living on Old Earth back in the day, meditating on the banks of the Ganges with my spiritual ancestors and here I am! They even built me an ashram, which to answer your question Mr. Chook, is a kind of monastery or hermitage. A place for reflection and growth under the guidance of a spiritual teacher."

"*Ridiculous!*" sputtered Chook. We all turned. He looked agitated, as if the energy of this place was getting to him – but in a *negative* way. Interesting. I hadn't seen him this flustered even as we dealt with all the dangers we'd passed through. "How can just *sittin' around*," he spat, stabbing the air with his finger, "doin' nothin' with your eyes closed make you into a better person?" Sana gave him a look.

The Swami chuckled kindly. "Sounds crazy, doesn't it?" He took a sip of tea, finishing the cup. "But let me ask you this. If you were to close your eyes for just a minute and contemplate. Look inside your inner world. What do you think you would find there?"

Chook scowled. "I can't do that."

"Why not?"

"Bad things. Rotten, horrible things in there. I can't look at 'em."

The Swami smiled. "We've all done rotten things."

"Not like me."

What horrors had Chook indulged in over the years? I guess you didn't get a face like his living a nice, clean life.

"OK, then let me put something to you," said the Swami. He held Chook in his gaze, pinning him there it seemed to me. "Would you think I was crazy if I said to you that we live in *two worlds*?"

"Whaddaya mean?" Sweat was beading on his forehead.

"So, you have all of *this*," the Swami waved a languid hand above his head, "this river, this ashram. This whole universe full of amazing and interesting things. All of this is *outside* of you, wouldn't you say? Certainly appears that way."

Chook turned his mouth down and shrugged.

"So, *this* is all one world. The outer world which we share with other people. Then there is another world, the inner world that's available only to *you*. The one you access when you close your eyes. Are you with me so far?"

"Guess so."

"Good. So, what would you say that inner world is comprised of?"

"Dunno." Chook thought for a while and then shrugged again. "Just *me* I guess."

"Exactly! Just 'you', being your thoughts and feelings, right?"

"Yeah, but..."

"As a person, you want to be happy, you want to feel good. Isn't that the real reason you did those things, some of which you feel guilty about now? To *feel* good?"

Chook laughed. "Yeah, gettin' money and spendin' it on booze makes me feel good."

"So you see!" The Swami was practically bursting with excitement. "We do all these things in the *outer* world. We drink or take drugs, we pursue money, fame and power. We search for the perfect relationship with the perfect partner – all these millions of things – all so we can 'feel good', right?"

Chook nodded glumly. This line of thinking felt vaguely familiar, the kind of logic I'd heard from Gilham. There *had* to be a connection between those two.

"But when we feel 'good' where do we actually *feel it*?" asked the Swami.

"What do you mean?"

"Do we feel the good feeling in the money, in the glass of booze?"

Chook seemed nonplussed.

"No! We feel it here" – the Swami was pointing to his chest – "our inner world. Which therefore means, illogically, we're doing everything possible in the *outer* world to try and make ourselves feel good in the *inner* world. I say *cut to the chase*! Work on your inner world. Which is what we do here at the ashram, in fact it's all we do. Then whatever happens out there" – he gestured again – "doesn't matter quite so much." The Swami's eyes seemed lit from within. Was there a twinkle of amusement too?

But all too much for Chook. He stood up groggily, leaning on the table for support, head bowed. He was breathing heavily; it almost looked like he was having a panic attack. Sana went to comfort him, but he recoiled and lurched away, then turned and stormed off toward the river. "Can't take any more of this *shit*," I heard him mutter.

The call came during dinner.

We'd spent the afternoon touring the ashram, which was a little world all to itself. There was an accommodation block and meditation hall filled with the now familiar images of saints and great spiritual beings, a kitchen, veggie gardens and walking track that ran along the river. Milk and dairy came not from a machine, but a shed full of large, contented-looking animals called 'cows' that wandered over for a pat when they saw us.

Later we joined the other 'ashramites' for a pre-dinner chanting session which seemed to go on forever before we finally got food. Chook emerged from somewhere and managed to sit through it all, though his face was bright red and it looked like he was about to die. Just as I was finishing my vegetarian meal there was a polite tap on my shoulder: Varan appearing noiselessly from nowhere. "Swamiji would like to see you."

He was waiting in a small room off the meditation hall, seated in a high-backed chair with his legs crossed in front of him. He gestured for me to sit, and tea promptly arrived.

"Great to see you, Col. I have to say your Sana is a very impressive person. Chook too in his own way."

"Really?"

"Sure."

We both took a sip of tea, which was made with milk and unusual spices. The ashramites called it 'chai' for some reason.

"You wanted to see me?"

The Swami looked concerned. "Col, I have to be honest, living here on Old Earth I never thought we'd meet again." He took a breath. "But then something unusual happened." He pointed to a chess set, the one I'd seen before on Jubilee. It was an automated board that the Swami used to play endless matches with Douglas, who would handicap himself to make it fair.

"When I first got here, this board was working fine and my games with Douglas were going on as normal, but then it just stopped. One day I made a move and that was it, no answer. That was about three and a half months ago."

Seemed right. The time frame corresponded with the attack on Jubilee.

"Then two days ago, I was sitting right here and out of the blue it came to life. Made a new move, and then this little panel lit up with a message."

A tiny display at the front of the board came to life. There was just enough space for a short message in glowing green letters:

"CHECKMATE SWAMI YA WEAK BASTARD"

Even though he was a quantum supercomputer, Douglas still loved to win.

The Swami shook his head. "I didn't know this thing could even *receive* messages!"

"And I suppose it really was checkmate?"

"Oh yes, of course. I'd been thinking about his likely move for months, so I knew what was coming. Even with only two trillionths of a second calculating time, Douglas is practically unbeatable."

"But it's a good sign, right? Means he's operational and Jubilee must be safe?"

"But that's not all." The Swami looked around conspiratorially. "A second message appeared a few seconds later, this one."

The screen flickered and new words formed:

"TELL COL TO STAY PUT"

I nearly spat my tea. Douglas was communicating directly to *me*, through the chess set? That had to mean he knew I would be coming here to the ashram, but how?

"What do you think it means?"

I pondered for a moment. "Guess you have to say the obvious: he wants us to stay here. Can you think of anything else?"

The Swami shook his head. "Nope. That's all I could come up with too." Then he laughed. "I always said you should come and spend some time with me!"

"Then you have your wish! Three new ashram residents, at least till Douglas shows up to retrieve us. I suppose you tried to reply?"

"It's a one-way thing, I think. Tried everything. Even Girish, one of our tech-savvy ashramites, looked it over. Nada."

We sat in silence for a moment. How long was I meant to 'stay put'? The fact that Douglas had communicated in such an oblique manner suggested there was a level of difficulty to it. Otherwise, he could have just sent a normal message to my kom.

My thoughts went to Danee and the girls. Only a month ago I thought they were dead; might we soon be all back together again? I felt a stabbing pain in my heart. Even a short wait would be unbearable…though may as well use it productively.

"So, Swamiji," I said, using the same honorific as the ashramites, "can I ask you a question?"

He raised his eyebrows, perhaps sensing what might be coming, then shrugged. "Fire away."

"*Gilham.* What was your relationship with him? I know there has to be something."

It suddenly felt like all the pleasant energy in the room had evaporated. "I guess you *are* an Investigator, aren't you, Col?"

"Can't help myself."

The Swami closed his eyes for a long time, so long I thought he must have dozed off. Then opened them again and sighed. "I'm sorry, Col, this is just…a…very difficult conversation. Maybe we can discuss another time? I know your intentions are good."

"I'm just looking for something, anything, to get leverage over Gilham. We have to find a way of defeating him."

The Swami chuckled to himself. "If you only knew how weak he really is."

"What do you mean?"

The Swami fixed me with a penetrating look and with it the room faded away to nothingness. There was only the two of us talking, just this one moment in time. "Let me ask you something, do you think Gilham is *happy*? Do you think he experiences peace?"

I'd never thought about that. "No…probably not."

"And let's suppose he succeeds in conquering the whole galaxy, will he know peace *then*?"

"I'd say, no—"

"That's right, nothing he does, no matter how many followers he has or how many planets fall to him, nothing will bring him any joy or happiness because he's looking for it in the wrong place; the outer world, not the inner world."

"That might be true, but how do I fight? It's the outer world where we need to beat him, that's where all his supporters and military forces are."

"Perfectly wrong. It's the inner world *only*, where you will beat him. Without force, without egoic attachment."

"But how?"

The Swami sipped his tea. I noticed how relaxed his movements were, as if the whole conversation was about something supremely inconsequential. "Ever study Judo, or some similar martial art?"

"Sure, in training, I guess—"

"What would you say the guiding principle of judo is?"

"Um…" I tried to take myself back to the classes I'd done in training so many years before. "I guess the key principle is that you always try to use your opponent's momentum against them."

"*There* you have it!" The Swami beamed.

I left the meeting scratching my head. Clearly a significant point had just been made by the Swami, but I felt confused. How could I use this insight?

Varan was waiting to escort me back to my dorm. When we were outside on the path beside the cowshed, she stopped and turned. "You want to know about Gilham?"

She must have been listening at the door, I suppose, or maybe it was just obvious?

"Yes! I know there was some kind of prior relationship between him and Swamiji."

"Correct. I will tell you what I know because I think…I think it might be useful, but don't tell Swamiji I told you."

"OK."

She drew me close. "It's true. Gilham was a student, once upon a time."

"And then?"

"More than just a student."

"What do you—"

"His *successor.* Supposedly. At least that's what *he* thought anyway." She laughed ironically. "Others too, though Swamiji never said anything like that, never 'anointed' him. But somehow everyone in the Satsang believed it to be true. We didn't know what to do. It was a problem."

"So, what happened?"

Varan started pacing. I'd never seen her agitated like this before. "It all happened on the planet Neu Skarskand 2, I assume you heard about it?" I shook my head. "Swamiji's guru, who at that time was also my guru, sent a few of us there to start an ashram. Out of the blue! At the time, it was a new colony on our system's second planet. Very raw, they were still terraforming when we arrived."

Now I thought about it, the name rang a bell. Something happened there, something bad, maybe when I was a kid?

"We thought it was madness to up-stumps for this frontier region, but it turned out well. There weren't many people, but those who were there all seemed to be looking for something. Next thing, this vibrant community had sprung up and as the population on-planet grew, so did the Satsang."

Varan stopped pacing for a moment. I waited while she gazed up at the night sky and then resumed speaking, but very slowly. "Gilham sort of just turned up one day. Very young, very serious. Seemed preternaturally gifted when it came to meditation, could spout scripture from memory.

After a few years, a group started following him around; there were even people who claimed to have had their diseases cured just from being in his presence. Crazy stuff."

"Why didn't Swamiji ask your guru?"

"She was by this time very old. In the final stage of a blood disease that would kill her. Even our modern medicine had reached its limit, so I think he didn't want to burden her any further."

"Then what?" Another long sigh. "Something *happened*, something involving Gilham?"

"We were called home. Our guru was clearly in her final days, so just a few of us went to be with her and while we were in transit something happened. A scandal of some kind, back on Neu Skarskand 2."

"A scandal involving Gilham?"

"*Noah*. Noah Karlsan is his real name. And yes, involving him."

Of course! Hadn't thought to ask. The name Gilham was given by the tribespeople on Rethne, his real name a secret even to his closest devotees. "So how come nobody knows about this? Surely such a scandal would—"

"Because of what happened on Neu Skarskand 2 of course!"

She swiped an information packet to my kom, but it was all coming back to me now. Neu Skarskand is a red dwarf star with twenty-one planets, the middle seven inhabited. A red dwarf is about thirty-five percent cooler than a yellow sun like Old Earth's, but still plenty hot enough to fry you if you get too close, which planet two was. When the geo-systems failed.

"We were at the funeral of our guru just as rumors started coming out about this scandal and then suddenly, *boom*!"

It was a big kerfuffle. 'Greedy corporations taking shortcuts with cheap tech' being the headline. Investigations, boards of enquiry, politicians across the galaxy grandstanding with promises of 'never again'. The League finally forced to get off its spotty backside and bring in universal terraforming regulations.

"And Gilham – pardon me, *Noah* – somehow gets away before this disaster?"

Varan smiled. "Obviously."

"Kinda convenient, wouldn't you say?"

"Not for those on-planet."

Of course. But for an aspiring cult leader…just the ticket. Could Gilham have orchestrated such a thing? Would he destroy a whole planet to save his reputation? He'd been able to take over a third of the human galaxy in just a few decades, what was rubbing out one insignificant little colony?

Then he'd washed up on Rethne alone and vanished into a desert cave. Which suggested remorse or at the very least, a desire to hide. He stayed out of sight for years till the local tribespeople found and recognized him as a holy man.

"And Jubilee? How did you all end up there?"

"Another person was appointed head of my guru's ashram – even though our Swamiji was the obvious choice – and everything to do with Noah was swept under the carpet. So, then we lived a quiet life for a number of years which was fine, but then came the rise of the Movement. A series of mysterious deaths, people who had relatives on planet number two and were agitating for more enquiries, all this about the time M4M arrived in our system."

"What a coincidence."

"Things were getting tougher for us all the time and then we received an offer from Jubilee which is a long story itself, and Swamiji thought, *what the hell?*"

"Douglas reached out to you guys?"

Varan sighed again and shook her head. "Col, I think that's enough for this evening. We shall talk more in the coming days." She turned and glided off down the path, and all I could do was follow.

Later that night, Varan came for me again.

A polite tap on my back, but enough to send me lurching up out of bed. Guess I was on something of a hair trigger. She cringed. "Sorry, Col, Swamiji needs to see you again, he's waiting outside." She gestured to Chook. "Him too. Get your stuff."

We tiptoed out of the men's dorm carrying our backpacks. The Swami and Sana were waiting together under the courtyard veranda that adjoined the river. He wore a thick shawl wrapped around his bony shoulders against the cold; Tigsy-Corp's planet-scaping made the air thinner and colder here than it would normally be for this part of Old Tasmania. He looked concerned.

"Col," he whispered, "there's been a development." We all moved in close to hear. A half-risen moon hung in the dark sky, casting silvery ripples across the 'Ganges'. "I asked some of our people to keep watch in case something happened."

"And?" I asked.

He looked around and nodded to Varan, who vanished silently. "They've set up a roadblock at the crossways about two kilometers from here and a bunch of vehicles and flyers just turned up." He showed a few images from his kom. "Our road is a dead end, so looks like we're being cut off."

"Who are they?" I asked. The image was grainy. A dozen or so people, clearly security of some kind, but with no insignia on their uniforms or markings on any of the vehicles.

"No idea. Never seen anything like this before."

"I thought you had a deal with Tigsy?"

"So did I."

"What are you saying?" asked Chook. He looked more himself again, especially now there was a crisis to deal with. "You sayin' we should run?"

"I don't know. But there is another way out of here...*if* you want to leave."

"How?" I asked. "Didn't you say this road's a dead end?"

The Swami gestured over his shoulder to the river. "Our boathouse. There's a small runabout and some canoes. Three kilometers downstream, a little flyer that I keep. They don't like me parking it around here near the ashram, supposed to look like Vedic times on Old Earth."

"But *hang on.*" Sana sounded annoyed. "Didn't Douglas tell us to 'stay put'?" I'd filled her in about the chessboard message before 'lights out' (at the absurdly early hour of eight thirty p.m.).

"Yes, that was the message," said the Swami, "but look, it's your choice, I thought you should know what was happening…" His voice trailed off. "This isn't exactly my area of expertise."

Sana shook her head, frustrated. "So what do we do *now*?"

I tried to think. It could be no coincidence these forces had arrived. And if they were friendly, why not just walk in the door? Did Douglas intend for us to be taken captive, was that his plan? It wasn't like he'd been particularly reliable lately.

The Swami gasped. "Govinda's been shot! They're taking him off somewhere. *All right, calm down everyone*" – this last to the others on his kom feed.

These people were meditators and spiritual seekers, not security professionals. I felt bad for getting them involved in our shit. "I think we should leave. *The Grand Poobah* is nearly in position, I say we get away and call it down. Then we can go wherever we want."

Sana looked doubtful. "But *where*, Col? All we do is run. I've got a bad feeling about this."

Chook seemed deep in thought. He shook his head as if trying to get something bad out of it. "You sayin' we just wait, let 'em come get us?"

"We don't even know who *they* are, Chook."

"Well, they just shot 'Govinda', whoever the fuck that is."

The Swami moved away from us, head bowed, talking on his kom. At that moment two blacked-out flyers appeared – no insignia or running lights – barely visible against the dark sky. They began a rapid descent, looking to put down in the courtyard, their hatches open and armored troops poised to deploy.

That did it. Sana turned to me. "OK," she mouthed.

The three of us took off into the night. The Swami started walking toward where the flyers were about to land, arms raised in surrender, and spoke to me over my kom. *"Col, boatshed's four hundred meters downstream, right on the water. Just sent you the decryption key for the flyer. It's stored in the hangar complex behind the river inlet. The key opens everything. Good luck, I'm going to try and stall these bastards as long as possible."*

We bolted along the walking track beside the river trying to be as quiet as we could. It got dark instantly as we moved away from the ashram buildings which were themselves not bright. Sana started to slow; her night vision not good at the best of times. Chook took her hand. "I know the way," he whispered, "I was out here all day."

Harsh voices rang out behind.

I messaged the others. *"We've got sixty seconds max before they wise up and start looking for us with infrared."*

Which meant what? Could we make it to the boatshed a third of a kilometer away with Sana, tentative as she was in the dark? No chance.

What then?

New idea, a highly unpleasant one. I messaged the others. *"We'll have to jump in the river and float down to the boatshed. It's the only way they won't pick us up."* And it would be very cold and dark, and the water fast moving. A horrible combination. But better than whatever those fuckers had planned for us.

We skidded sideways off the path, clambered down the rocky embankment to the river. Behind I heard the sizzle of a powerful, military-grade blaster. Purple light flashed and something started burning. The wooden pavilion, I'd say. Someone making a demonstration to the Swami about the benefits of cooperation. Other flyers were putting down too, the area around the ashram now swarming with security forces.

It took only moments to reach the riverbank, the water before us a swirling inky black. I took Sana's hand and whispered, "Keep your backpack on. We'll jump in together. Stay close to the bank and hold on to me, OK?" She nodded mutely. Sana was good at many things, but swimming wasn't one of them.

"Chook, you ready?" He was standing only a meter away but in some kind of reverie, hands balled into fists. Something not right there.

"Chook?"

No response.

"*Chook?!*"

He snapped out of it, as if emerging from a dream. Stepped toward us and put a hand on my shoulder. An amplified voice rang out, above and all around us. Someone using a sound projector, so it felt like the words were being spoken simultaneously everywhere at once.

"UNAUTHORIZED INTRUDERS, MOVE AWAY FROM THE RIVERBANK AND SURRENDER IMMEDIATELY. THIS IS YOUR ONE WARNING." (That was a bit rich, in what way were we 'unauthorized'?)

A flyer put down about fifty meters away on the other side of the walking path. Had they spotted us? If I were them, this is one place I'd start.

"Col." Chook was wide-eyed. "I'm not coming."

"*What?* What do you—"

"*Listen.* You know the money, the money that appeared in your autopay? The two million credits? That money was *mine*!"

The flyer had landed somewhere beyond the riverbank but we couldn't see it, being down near the water. I could hear boots crunching and voices crackling on radios. Seemed like they didn't know exactly where we were, but they'd soon figure that out.

Chook had a tight grip on my shoulder. "I transferred it into your kom, parked it there when we were on Jubilee."

"What? Why would you—"

"If they caught me, those Movement people would have *taken it*! But not *you*, not a boy scout like you. I was going to ask for it back when we got to safety." He started laughing and I shushed him to be quiet.

Laser fire blazed through the air on the other side of the path, slicing the night. Fucking idiots, they were shooting at shadows, lucky not to kill each other. A classic Movement shit show.

"But so *what*, Chook? We'll figure this out later, c'mon we gotta go!"

"I spent my whole life building that stash. You got no idea the evil shit I *did* for it. Trashed my family, my friends, trashed everything and for *what*? What does it mean that it can all be gone, just like *that*!" His eyes blazed.

"For fuck's sake," hissed Sana, "we gotta *go*, Chook!"

"I'm telling ya, everything I ever did in my whole life was *bullshit*! I'm stayin' here with the Swami. He's the only one who can help me."

"Chook, these soldiers will kill you," I implored.

"Nah." He thought for a moment. "It's you two they want, especially *her*." And before I could stop him, he turned, and stumbled back up the embankment with his hands in the air. "I surrender!" he called, then started running back toward the ashram. *"Don't worry,"* he messaged my kom, *"I'll head them in the wrong direction."*

For a moment I stood stunned. That was it then, just the two of us now. I clutched Sana's hand, looked her in the eyes, and we counted, *one, two, three*...and leaped into the rushing black water.

Chapter Fifteen

So cold, the water felt like fire enveloping my body, sucking the air out of my lungs.

And fast, the bank whizzing by quicker than you could sprint, the current trying to drag us away from the edge into the middle of the river. Sana hung on to my backpack like a deadweight. I put my head down and started paddling like crazy for the riverbank. In only a couple of strokes my hands touched slimy rocks, but they were slippery and impossible to grab. We slid and bumped along, while I thrashed and flailed trying to find purchase. My body became numb instantly, which was almost good, though one of the first signs of hypothermia.

I saw a boxlike wooden structure built into the bank, about to slide past us at a zillion miles an hour. I lunged at it, hands slipping uselessly across wooden slats. For a terrifying moment it felt like we were going to zoom past, but I caught hold of something with my fingertips: a corner post. The downstream corner.

I grabbed it tightly. The current was trying to pull me away, but I held on grimly, kicked out wildly trying to find something solid. There. My knee banged into something. I brought my right leg up to my chest, pushed out again and connected. A foundation for the boathouse maybe, and blessed relief because my arms weren't doing all the work now. I felt around. Here was a join where it seemed the two swinging doors of the boathouse met. They'd unlock from the inside obviously, but maybe I could get my hand inside and open them. But too hard carrying the weight of two bodies; the force of the flow was incredible.

I lifted my head out of the water. "Sana, can you get your foot onto the thing I'm standing on?" I felt her wriggle around, and then her foot next to mine. "OK, brace and hold on." I put one of her hands onto the corner post.

That was better, without her weight I was able to pull myself along the structure and fiddle around inside. I tried this for a while, then just yanked hard. No good. *Think, Col.* These gates couldn't open outward, or they'd be caught by the current. I felt farther up, there it was! A rusty old hook at the top. I flipped it up and the downstream door burst inward, carrying Sana and me along with it.

We flooded into a square pool of black water, a small rowing boat floating at the rear. The shed was built at river level, and you could sail straight in and out without any need of a dry dock and ramp. Weird setup though, what would happen when the river flooded? Of course, not a problem because this river was artificial; it never did flood, it was probably kept at exactly the same height all year round.

There were concrete docks on each side of us and racks bolted to the wall for storing canoes, of which I counted three. I paddled over and hauled myself out of the water, then leaned down to pull Sana out. Her eyes were glazed, and she was hunched in shock. Crikey, we nearly bought it right there. Who would have thought? After everything we'd been through, this river might have been the thing that so nearly took us.

"Out of those clothes, Sana."

She stared mutely. I grabbed her top and started pulling, and then she got the idea, stripping off rapidly. I was freezing too, but I'd spied some lockers at the back of the shed and wanted to investigate. Eureka! The first I tried had two safety vests, and best of all a towel. Old and filthy, but most importantly, bone dry. I ripped Sana's bag open and pulled out her spare clothes. She started dressing, but slowly, still in shock. Two things Sana hated most in the world: one, swimming (unless it was water the temperature of a steam bath, in which case she might go in for a pathetic three-minute dog paddle), and two, being cold – *ever.*

I changed and then we sat on the concrete floor at the back of the shed, where I pulled her in for a warm-up hug. Then came the shivers. Uncontrollable, my whole body jerking. Fuck me, what temperature was that water? Had to be close to zero.

This was a pretty good hiding spot, actually. They wouldn't notice it in the dark but come daylight that would change. I checked my kom: it was four a.m., first light in just under two hours. Hole up for a bit longer, let the search move on, then slip away before it got light. The moon would be set by then too, though I guess that wouldn't make much difference if they were using infrared, which they would be.

Sana sat up abruptly. Slid herself around and fixed me with a cold stare. "Col, I can't *do* this anymore."

"I understand, but—"

"Let them take me, I'm done with running – *look* at us!"

Sana was having a fit. For some reason, I felt guilty, as if it were my choice to create all these problems, cause her this discomfort. "I'm sorry, Sana, it was the only way we—"

"Don't *say* that, Col." She sighed. "I'm not blaming you, I'm just saying I can't *do* this anymore."

"Which means what?"

"I don't know."

We sat in silence for a minute. "Well, the entrance is over there, we could walk out and surrender if you want to." I was annoyed. What did she expect from me?

"Right." She rolled her eyes. "We're going to get passive-aggressive now?"

Great. Thanks I get for saving her from being hauled off to Rethne and made Gilham's slave…or worse. We sat glaring at each other for at least five minutes.

Sana cracked first.

"I'm just saying what are we going to *do*, Col?" She started crying. "And don't freak out because I'm upset!" I took a breath. "But I mean it, what *are* we going to do?"

"Sana, I have a plan, we'll—"

"You and your plans."

I laid myself flat on the concrete and looked up at the wooden ceiling. Through the cracks I could see stars and occasional flickers of light. Blaster fire. Sana sighed and lay down beside me, placing her head in the crook of my arm for a pillow. This used to be our cuddling pose when we were still a couple. We lay like that for a while.

"How's that with Chook?" I said, finally. "Running off to join an *ashram*, who would have thought?"

"It'll do him good."

"You think?"

"Sure."

"And the money? I always assumed it came from Douglas somehow, one of his weird games. But *Chook, all along*?"

"Go figure."

There was noise outside. Footsteps crunching on the path, at least four people by my count. I felt Sana's nails claw into my side. Hopefully they wouldn't check this shed, out of sight from the walking path. There was a muffled curse. Probably getting frustrated now; it was a cold night, and the search was dragging. After a few minutes the footsteps passed, and I felt Sana relax. *Sure*, she didn't care anymore if they took us.

"And how did you find the Swami?" I'd always wanted to introduce him to Sana and Danee but never found the chance.

"Oh...liked him. He's definitely *got* something, I'd say."

"You think?"

"Sure, but you know, I've got my own path. But great for *you*."

I felt pleased; for some reason it mattered to me that Sana liked him.

I checked my kom: almost time. Hauled myself up and went back to the lockers. Grabbed the life vests and rummaged around till I found a single cold-weather jacket. Old, filthy and way too big, but exactly what I wanted for Sana. I bundled up the wet clothes (better take those in case the shed was searched) then pulled the largest canoe off the rack and grabbed a couple of oars. A few minutes later we nosed our way out into the river. I tilted our canoe in the downstream direction, which is a little counterintuitive because you naturally feel like leaning *into* fast water, but do that and the current will flip you. Something we very much wanted to avoid.

In seconds we were zooming downstream. It was totally dark with Old Earth's single moon set – funny, I never knew there was just the one – and you couldn't see the far bank of the river. Best keep as close as possible to this side and not get drawn into the middle where we might be spotted.

The bank seemed to be passing super-fast. I barely needed to paddle, just a few strokes here and there to keep us headed in the right direction. Behind us, flying craft came and went every few minutes, centered around the cluster of noise and commotion at the ashram. I prayed they weren't keeping an eye out on the river.

So now?

Call in *The Grand Poobah.* It had already sent an acknowledgment confirming it was parked in geo-synchronous orbit directly above us. I told it to enter the atmosphere and hold at one thousand meters in full cloak mode. All we needed now was a safe spot for it to land and then we'd be away. Swamiji said there was an industrial area a few klicks downstream which sounded OK to me. Just had to get there undetected.

Sana said, too loudly, "I *cannot* see a damned thing."

"It's OK," I whispered back, "I can, just enough anyway."

I checked the compass on my kom and saw we were headed southwest, roughly ninety degrees from where we'd started. Must have been a right-hand bend in the river, too gradual to notice. Then something weird; the breeze against my face felt suddenly much stronger, so either the wind had picked up or…*oh shit.*

I flicked my kom torch on for just a moment and shone it to the left. The earthen bank was gone, replaced by a high concrete wall. I flicked the torch off and checked the map, worst fears confirmed! We'd traveled so far, *and so quickly*! Making it practically all the way to the terminus of this artificial 'Ganges'. The reason for the increased wind was that we were now moving incredibly fast, the river's flow speeding up exponentially as its sides drew together so it could pour into a huge tunnel, pass through a massive pumping station, and be sent back to the top of the 'Himalayas' to start its journey all over again.

What we didn't want was to get sucked into that tunnel. Or be pinned against something like a grate at the opening – if there was one, which I checked on my kom and yes there was. A giant steel grid, there to stop random objects getting sucked into the works. Such as Sana and me and our canoe; we'd be flattened against it by the immense flow.

This river was really fucking dangerous. How come more people weren't killed? Maybe they were. Or maybe most weren't silly enough to paddle on it in the middle of the night. Whatever. We had to get off this water, and there was only one way I could think of to do that now the riverbank had turned into a concrete cliff.

I ordered *The Grand Poobah* down from where it was hovering. This was going to attract attention, but what was the choice? It came in at lightning speed and I ordered it to track our position and gradually descend.

Sana tapped me on the back. "What's happening, Col?" She'd vibed instantly, being Sana, that something was up.

"The river ends just up ahead. It's about to pour into a massive tunnel, so I've called in the ship. We'll have to board her from the water." Which was going to be very tricky.

Sana just sighed. Another life-or-death situation, barely worth mentioning these days.

The ship was in full cloak mode, so I didn't see it till it was almost on top of us. A blob overhead, slightly darker than everything else. I told it to ease down, closer and closer to the water, which was getting faster all the time. A distant sound of gushing now, getting louder. That was the tunnel.

I brought the ship in. There it was, the familiar dark triangle, vast from this angle at river level and weirdly out of context. It dropped next to us, tracking our path along the water, and I ordered the lower hatch to open, the one we normally used to disembark when planetside. Blinding white light poured out, illuminating the whole area. No time to figure out how to stop that. Could only hope we got away before anyone noticed.

"OK, Sana, this is it. Jump in." She looked back at me in horror, swaddled in her cold-weather jacket. "Don't think, just do it!"

She stood up slowly, held her arms out for balance, making the canoe wobble dangerously. Lucky Sana was so agile and light. She stood precariously for a moment, leaned across, and sprang into the open airlock of *The Grand Poobah*, landing like a big cat crouching onto her haunches.

But her leap destabilized the canoe. I tried to rebalance, paddling frantically, but it spun around sideways. The leading edge caught the current and it pitched over, tipping me upside down and into the rushing water. I caught a momentary glimpse of Sana as I fell, then everything went black as I tumbled wildly end over end, the breath forced out of my chest by the intense cold. I flailed and thrashed, gasped, took a lungful of water, and coughed wildly. Breathed in even more water. *This was it. Going to drown right here.* Impossible to know up or down, thrown around like a cork in a storm.

My face came up out of the water for just a second. Enough for a quick breath but no time to locate the ship. Then back under again, tumbling wildly. Had to stop that.

I spread my arms and legs out; let the life vest do its work. Better. I was flowing with the water now, floating on the surface at least. But *so* fast, it felt like I was bodysurfing a giant wave that was reaching a crescendo but never breaking.

The ship.

I told *The Grand Poobah* – wherever it was – to close the hatch and ascend back to one thousand meters. Hopefully it would be safe up there in cloak mode. Though Sana didn't have kom access to the controls. No time to worry about that.

A giant hollow loomed. The mouth of the tunnel. Small mercy, at least I could now see what was going on: intensely bright arc lamps revealed mountainous black water pouring through a giant grate, leaves and twigs jammed against it. *All over now*, I was going to get smashed; pulverized against the grate by the immense force of this current.

But something wasn't right. I was moving at incredible speed, but the grate was still in the distance. Oh, I see. It was nighttime and easy to misjudge the perspective due to the scale. The tunnel opening was enormous and so was the grate at its entrance. The 'leaves and twigs' were branches and logs. That meant the openings in the grill were larger than I thought. Maybe big enough to pass through.

I swept along. Tried to line myself up with one of the gaps in the grill. Yes, they were at least a meter square. So long as I went through an opening cleanly it would be OK. Hit that metalwork at this speed though and it would all be over. The current pulled me forward, fast as a waterfall. I brought my arms and legs in, tried to aim my body and then…*everything slowed down.*

The same feeling as when I was spinning in space off Jubilee. Maybe it happens only when you know you're about to die? Oneness. With everything. If this was *it*, then so be it. I felt part of the river, part of the water, which funnily, didn't feel cold anymore. Maybe this was the state Swamiji was always banging on about. *Too bad I had to die now.* For some reason I found that funny. I think I was actually laughing as I swept through the grill, right through the middle of an opening – didn't even graze the sides. Then on, into the blackness of the tunnel.

Chapter Sixteen

What happened next?

I have absolutely no idea. Water, water, no down, no up. Utter darkness but all fear gone, riding a giant wave into the unknown. Didn't even seem to be a problem not to breathe. I zoomed through the black void in a kind of suspended animation as stupendous, world-sculpting energies pulsed and pumped.

Pressure building and building, compressing ever harder. Intolerable. For a long moment it felt as though I were going to be squashed like a bug. My chest was collapsing, eyes compressing in their sockets. Everything bearing down, crushing me, crushing and then…release.

Sudden calm. My face broke the water's surface, and I gasped a huge breath. Lungs still working after all. Night sky, large body of dead-still water reflecting the stars. A lake!

I must have passed all the way through the tunnel inside the mountain back up to the top. Then into this giant lake, headwaters for the river. So that meant the pump ran off some form of inverter system rather than a turbine. Obviously, or I would have been nicely minced. I floated on the surface basking in the stillness. Where had the cold gone?

No matter, everything was beautiful. I heard the hoot of a night bird somewhere, maybe an owl. Did they have those on Old Earth? – I think so. Maybe owls came from here in the first place? I rolled over and looked at the stars. Somewhere up there was my ship, was the entire galaxy. These were the same set of stars ancient humans gazed at for millennia, dreamed of journeying to. Well, they were ours now. We had the power to travel wherever we wanted, cross the ocean of space, but for what? Where was everything headed with M4M gradually taking over, the League so lost and moribund?

I thought of the girls and had a pang of longing, followed by another pang of guilt. How did I allow *that* to happen with Sana? What would I say to Danee? (assuming I ever saw her again).

That was it, the spell was broken. Time to get going. I reached out to the ship and activated *Summon*. Within a minute it was above me, then gently lowering itself down to water level. I told the hatch to open, then tried to haul myself in. Body heavy with wet clothes, arms too weak.

I told the ship to lower itself more, down to slightly below water level, and tried to roll inside the open hatch. Still too weak. Then Sana was there, grabbing my shirt, pulling at me. She was crying. "I'm sorry, Col, so sorry."

"Everything's fine," I muttered, then with a final kick and heave got my chest up and rolled into the hatch. I told the airlock hatch to close just as an alarm began to sound. What now? Everything was spinning. A weird blackness encroaching into my vision from all sides. Getting larger, only a small part in the middle that I could see through now, otherwise darkness everywhere.

Hypothermia.

I had just enough time to tell the ship to ascend at maximum velocity before all the black bits in my vision joined together and the world dissolved.

⋆ ⋆ ⋆

Red.

Pulsing. Strobing through my closed eyelids. An alarm sounding, very loud. Nonstop. Can't someone turn the damned thing off?

I turned, opened my eyes, and fucking hell, sure wish I hadn't. Massive headache, throbbing in time with the alarm. I tried to move but nothing doing. Where was I? Managed to get an arm to move and push out, hit something solid. Glass.

Oh, the ICU.

Sana must have got me into this unit by herself, but she had no access to the ship's controls, couldn't turn that alarm off. Maybe I could?

Without having to move a muscle, I accessed my kom and played around with the controls. *That was better.* The alarm abruptly died, but every thirty seconds or so the lights pulsed red. Things were definitely not OK. Wherever we were, something had happened, something bad.

The ICU hatch slid open to reveal Sana's worried face.

"Thank *God.*"

"How long have I been in here?"

At least a day. According to Sana, though she seemed to have lost track of time. "So *cold.* You were like a block of ice." She reached in and touched me. Her hand felt normal, so the ICU must have brought my body back to the right temperature, saved me no doubt. Sana stroked my forehead. "You are really *heavy*, you know that?"

She'd stripped me of my wet clothes then dragged my body in from the airlock by my feet, then up two flights of stairs to the ICU.

"Sorry, but your head bonked on each step pretty hard. I couldn't stop it. I knew I had to get you into this thing right away."

I guess that explained the headache.

A few hours later I was able to climb out of the ICU. I still felt like death warmed up, but better than where I'd been. First order of business: the controls. What the hell was going on?

No idea. The ship was flying blind. Life support systems running OK, but we'd lost all input from the outside; no screens, no comms, nothing at all. The drive was engaged, and we were busily going somewhere, but where? I managed to get the lights to stop flashing, but that was about it. *Leave things for the moment.*

Next, the galley. Sana and I ate a quick meal together washed down with tea, I had a shower and a long sleep and then…that was it.

Turned out the ship's controls were mostly all fritzed out. Unfixable. I tried what I could; all the stuff keeping us alive was working fine, but everything else was screwed. We were traveling somewhere, but for how long, and in what direction, and at what speed was impossible to know. Sana wasn't familiar with the controls, but she'd observed something when I was out of it.

"There was an alarm, the first one. Then once the hatch closed it stopped. After that, I got you into the ICU and then there was this weird, kind of *whooshing* sensation and the alarms went *crazy* again and they just stayed that way till you woke up." Sana had put earplugs in to stay sane.

"When you say 'whooshing', what do you mean?"

"Can't describe it."

"Did it throw you off balance, push you into a wall?" Normally there wasn't any sense of movement traveling in *The Grand Poobah.*

"Nothing like that. It just felt like the top of my head was going to lift off. This weird surging sensation, then it settled down. Sorry, I know that's annoyingly vague."

And the ship's log was no help either. Most of the menus were grayed out and inoperable, and diagnostics wouldn't run. If only we had Sheng with us, or someone who could code. After a while I gave up completely and settled into a daily routine with Sana.

I say 'daily', but when you're caught in a situation like that, time becomes meaningless. We ate, we exercised, we slept (in separate beds) and we hung out. Everything started blurring together. In the blink of an eye, three weeks passed and I barely noticed, hardly bothered to check the date.

"You never did tell me what happened on Rethne. With Gilham."

Sana sighed. We were sitting in the galley together watching media on our koms. Just as well we had countless hours stored.

"What do you want to know?"

"Did he, you know…"

"I already said, *nothing* like that. It was more of a power trip. He seemed to get off on ordering me to do meaningless tasks. Some days he'd invite me into his room and make me read stuff from his books. It was like he wanted to impress me, but also totally control my every waking minute."

"Maybe he's in love with you?"

"Maybe. But it didn't feel sexual, thank God. He's a weirdo. Why are you asking this now?"

I told her about my conversation with the Swami's assistant, Varan. For some reason this hadn't seemed important to discuss till then. Conversation gradually dried up between us in that space of no time.

"Some kinda scandal? Well, he's not into women, that's for sure."

"What's he into then?"

"Power."

"We know *that*. But what else besides?"

"Something." Sana shrugged. "Who knows?"

I redoubled my efforts, working systematically through every command menu from the lowest level up. I granted Sana access too; if something happened to me, she could now operate the controls, not that there was anything she could *do* with them. Sometimes I'd find myself staring at the blank monitors for hours.

It was during one of these sessions that a realization about what happened at the ITAAH base arrived in my brain, unbidden. I was staring at an empty screen when it came bubbling up; Colonel Mia's goodbye as I was being carried prone onto the ship: *'Good luck with your mission, Col'* – that's what she'd said. Probably thought I wouldn't remember because of the condition I was in at the time. She'd let her guard slip, just for a moment.

"*Motherfucker!*" I said to myself.

Then I slumped back down into my usual state of despondency.

Over time we stopped bothering to exercise, or clean the galley or make our beds, and barely remembered to shower. Our physical movements got slower and slower. Sana actually looked for the first time in her life as if she were putting on weight. After all we'd been through – the high stakes, the nonstop drama – to find ourselves now trapped in this baffling limbo was unbearable. We slumped into a state of torpor and probably depression.

Eventually though, after an indeterminate period of time, something finally did happen.

A loud clunk reverberated through the ship. I looked up, incredulous, too dazed even to be alarmed. There was the whine of a drill, some sawing and grinding. A little whoosh of air followed by an alarm sounding for a moment, instantly silenced. Finally, metallic footsteps coming down the stairwell from above to the galley where we sat.

"*Ahoy there, me hearties!*" called a familiar voice.

The android didn't even bother with the last few steps, jumping from halfway and landing in front of us.

"Bloody hell, what have you two been doin' here? This place smells like *shite*!"

Douglas.

Chapter Seventeen

I could barely think. Douglas! Here on *The Grand Poobah*!

He gave us only time for a quick hug. Sana was crying. Maybe I was too. Which explained the damp patches on my cheeks. "C'mon, we gotta *go*," he said, pointing up the stairwell. "Gotta get you off this tin can and back to Jubilee."

"Jubilee!" I cried. "Everyone's *OK* then, Danee and the girls?"

The robot looked at the floor for a second, a tell of his. Sending my guts into a spasm. "Yes, yes, everyone's *OK*." There was something in the way he said it, though, which I didn't like. "There's a lot happened while you been gone. But c'mon, *every minute ye spend here is like...*" He paused for a second. "I'll explain later, c'mon, don't even bother gettin' ye stuff, we gotta leave."

What 'stuff' did we have anyway? Just a few crappy things from our backpacks. We'd been living hand to mouth for so long, nothing we had was worth bothering about. Douglas pointed upward. "C'mon, no time to lose."

Sana shrugged, still beaming, and headed up the stairs. I followed, with Douglas urging us on from behind. Why the big rush? Something didn't feel right.

At the top of the stairs another of Douglas's identical avatars waited, with an open airlock behind him. The first Douglas avatar did a high five with this new one. "Good work, Douglas," he said.

"Same to you, Douglas," said the other.

Sana shook her head. "Are they always like this?"

One of the AI's little jokes with itself.

"OK, come, come," he said, ushering us through the airlock. "My esteemed colleague will see to *The Poobah*'s return. Gotta get you guys into hyperspace pronto."

We passed through the airlock tunnel and into an identical control room on the other side.

"What's this one called? *Poobah II*?" Sana chuckled.

"Ye can call her anything you damned please. Here we go." Douglas didn't even wait for us to strap in. He pushed Sana onto the copilot's seat, pointed for me to sit on the floor and seconds later had us disengaged from our old ship and jumped immediately.

He leaned back, sighing just like a human would and said, "Welcome back."

It took three jumps to get from wherever *The Grand Poobah* had been to Jubilee's star MGNA#12 and we plied Douglas with questions such as, *what the fuck happened?* How did M4M manage to sneak up on us like that?

Well, of course, they hadn't. Douglas had been playing possum, waiting for that attack.

"So why didn't you involve your head of security?" – i.e. me – "Or your Intelligence chief?" – i.e. Danee.

"Well, Danee certainly suspected somethin' was up. She kept warning me, but I pretended to be unconcerned."

"Maybe you should have listened," said Sana grimly.

"I had to let 'em think they got me, that was the whole point. Don't ye see?"

Sana scowled. "Which was supposed to spur the League into action, right? That was the reason we ended up at Tiger Base."

"Somethin' like that."

"Carrying a backup of your memory and a spare CPU inside Batum just in case?"

"Yup."

Douglas had pretended to let Jubilee be destroyed, pretended to let *The Poobah* make a 'random' double jump which ended up uncannily close to the ITAAH base.

"Only the League didn't act the way they were supposed to," I said.

"They're a pack o' *useless fucks* the lot of them," Douglas fumed. "Who'd a thought they'd take no action in the face of M4M building a fleet o' fucking *warships*!"

"They're compromised. But there's still good people in there." I was thinking of Len and Colonel Mia. "So where is Jubilee now? Where did you jump to?"

"Figured it out, eh?"

I told him about Sana's art project, watching the hologram in super high-res as Jubilee vanished rather than burned up. Told him I'd finally realized the significance of Colonel Mia's words. "She said, 'Good luck with your *mission*.' Calling it a 'mission' meant somehow, she *knew*. How come everyone else was in on this little plan of yours except me?"

Douglas just shook his head and sighed.

It took us nearly forty-eight hours to make the three jumps back to Jubilee's home star from a starting point that was strangely distant from Old Earth where our journey had begun. It was weird being on this ship, an identical replica of *The Grand Poobah*. Felt like we'd never left.

Douglas filled us in. Jubilee had jumped away to another part of the same parallel universe where it normally resided. Simple. And yes, of course, he'd been in touch with Len and Colonel Mia and certain other elements in LSS, was hoping the arrival of our refugee ship would give them the ammo they needed to wake the League from its slumber. I noticed he seemed to skate around the subject of Danee and the girls and, being a little superstitious, I didn't push – I would be seeing them soon anyway – and there was heaps of other things to catch up on.

"So, what went wrong with *The Grand Poobah*? Why did the controls fail like that?"

"You got hit with somethin' new, a gravity weapon by the looks of it. We think our friends the Aurelians and their AI have been cooking it up with the Movement. They tried it out on you."

"What's a 'gravity weapon'?" asked Sana, beating me to the question.

"Still figuring that out. Seems to create an artificial event horizon somehow, such as you'd encounter getting very close to a black hole, and in the process speeds you up to a significant fraction of light speed."

"Thus, fritzing the controls."

"Anything to do with the gravity drive."

Sobering. A new weapon. How would that affect the balance of power, already tilting dramatically toward the Movement?

"And I take it that really was you, sending a message through the Swami's chess set?"

"O' course! Why didn't ye stay put like I told you to?"

"Why do you think? They stormed the ashram, we fled for our lives. Did you actually want them to capture us?"

Douglas shook his head sadly. "Probably woulda been better."

"Why?"

"Well..." He shook his head again. "All they wanted you for was bargaining chips by that stage."

"You're negotiating with the Movement?"

"Arrgh, it's a long fuckin' story... Let's get home, you'll see soon enough."

We ate a meal or two and I tried to sleep, which was difficult given the equal amount of excitement, and for some reason, dread building inside me. Something was off, but I couldn't work out what or why. And although the thought of seeing Danee and the girls filled me with joy, there was another tiny voice deep down that kept reminding me about the night with Sana. If only there was a way to remove whatever cluster of brain cells contained that memory, make it vanish forever.

Finally, the star MGNA#12 lay before us, the space around it oddly devoid of warships or any sign of battle. We jumped again, and there it was! Jubilee, same as ever – OK, not *totally* the same – missing its 'tail', the much-maligned Sector Twenty-One, which had been sacrificed to make it look like Jubilee was destroyed.

Moments later we were docked.

I stood with the others waiting for the airlock to cycle, heart beating in my ears. I knew that something weird had happened, something Douglas was leery about telling me, but as long as Danee and my little girls were OK, honestly, I didn't care.

"So, Col." Douglas looked nervous. "As I said, there's been a few changes and I need ye to prepare because—"

"Are they *here*?"

"Yes, o' course."

The doors opened and I dashed through the airlock into a small, private Arrivals lounge that we used sometimes. Danee was waiting there along with two teenage girls. One dark skinned and petite, reminding me more than a little of images I'd seen of Sana at the same age. The other, taller, with a long blonde ponytail. All three lit up with huge smiles when I emerged. Danee had tears running down her face; so did I. The two teenage girls raced across the room like giant puppies, nearly knocking me flat in an over-enthusiastic group hug.

"*Daddy!*" they cried.

Chapter Eighteen

I was in the center of a mad, crushing group hug, mind exploding, Danee now joining in the melee as well. Her lips were on mine, but everyone was shouting and crying, everything too much. She separated for a moment, sensing my confusion. Then understanding dawned in her eyes. "Douglas didn't tell you?"

I shook my head in confusion.

There was fresh commotion as Sana and Douglas burst in, everyone greeting each other at the same time. Then a new voice, a man.

"Col! Sana!" cried Douglas through the uproar. "Look who we got here!"

I turned from Danee but barely recognized the person standing there. "Chook?" I had time to ask before being wrapped in a massive bear hug. He was crying as well. "But what are you doing here on Jubilee? How did you get back from Old Earth so fast?"

"Hah, Col!" He laughed. "Good joke, mate!"

Chook seemed amazingly healthy. He'd somehow lost a heap of weight, and with clear (in fact, sparkling) eyes and smooth skin looked at least ten years younger.

"What do you mean, 'good joke'?" I muttered, head spinning. "Someone needs to explain what the hell is going on!"

"He doesn't know," said Danee, shocked.

Chook stared at her, stricken. "You're *shitting* me. Douglas didn't *tell* him!?"

"Tell me what?"

He placed a hand on my shoulder. "Col, this is hard. You were stuck on *The Grand Poobah* for what, a few weeks, right? That's how long it seemed to you?"

"What do you mean, 'how long it *seemed* to me'?"

"Col, for *us* you been gone nearly *twelve years*. Lost in space. I did my time with the Swami on Old Earth, a whole discipleship in fact, then came back to Jubilee when we heard you'd been found."

"Twelve years?" I felt dizzy. In my whole Services career dealing with every horrific crime, and with all the terrible things I'd faced lately, no shock was greater than hearing these words.

"But how is this possible?"

★ ★ ★

Douglas avoided eye contact. "I didn't know how to tell you."

"Time dilation," I sputtered. "Fucking *time dilation*!?"

We were in the control room sitting around a large round table. Having a 'council of war' as Douglas called it, to discuss all that had happened and what we were going to do about it.

"That *bloody* weapon," sighed Danee.

"It's like, if you were to get too close to the event horizon of a black hole," Douglas explained. "Time starts to slow down relative to everythin' else. On top o' that, you got shot off at a significant fraction of light speed, which also slows time. That's why I was in such a hurry to get you off *The Poobah*. Every minute you spent aboard was like a month back here on Jubilee."

"Pretty clever, if you think about it," Chook mused. "Zap your enemies into the future. Can't fire back from there."

"But why did it take you so long to *find* us?" asked Sana.

Douglas was defensive. "*You* try lookin' for a tiny object traveling that fast. The only thing I had was ye starting point. Just being able to get a visual and something in position to dock with you was a massive feat all on its own. I feel very bad about it. I want ye to know."

Shock was giving way to anger and sadness. I'd returned home to find my children grown. I'd missed their *entire childhood*. Danee had been forced to bring them up entirely on her own. "Douglas, you took crazy risks without telling any of us. Why did you *do* that?"

The android still wouldn't meet my gaze. "I'm sorry, Col. I calculated wrong. I thought the League would step up, didn't think Gilham would storm Jubilee *in person* and with such great force. So many things. I didn't count on humans being so damned *stupid*."

Douglas hadn't exactly shown great intelligence himself.

"So where are we at now? How come everything's back to business as usual?"

"Not exactly *usual*," muttered Danee.

"Had to come up with a Plan B, didn't I?" said Douglas.

"Which was?"

"A deal. We did a deal with—"

At that moment the door burst open and in walked Batum. Shiny and new and freshly reincarnated. Though not occupying the same silver combat-Arbite body that had saved our bacon escaping from Jubilee. I guess there weren't many of *those* bodies lying around.

"Chook, it's your *old friend*!" called Douglas, relieved to change the subject.

"Batum?"

"A different shape to the one you knew," said Danee, "but yes, that's Batum's file in there."

"Maaate!" Chook leaped up beaming, arms outstretched ready to give one of his hearty man-hugs. But the robot raised its hands and stepped back, saying coldly, "Human. Don't touch." It looked like this version of the robot didn't recall being his friend.

Though not Sana. Batum greeted *her* with genuine warmth. "What do you remember of events?" she asked. "We went through *so much* together!"

"My data file ends at the moment *The Grand Poobah* jumped away from Jubilee. The feed must have kept running till then."

"Correct." Douglas nodded. The AI, which had supposedly been offline, was still recording data the whole time.

"You don't remember Tiger Base or anything that happened on Jerbet?"

The robot shook its head.

"It's OK, Batum," I said. "You can get everything off our koms."

"I'm told quite a lot of *bonding* went on between us all." The robot didn't seem entirely pleased. "Which is contrary to my operating parameters."

"You and me!" said Chook. "Didn't start out too well, but we sure hit it off in the end!"

Batum's mechanical eyes fixed him for a moment. "I find that hard to believe."

"Anyway," I said, getting impatient, "let's catch up on everything later. Please continue, Douglas, what ended up happening here with Jubilee? I didn't see any signs of the Movement when we arrived."

Douglas sighed. "Told you. I made a deal…"

Sana shook her head. "With whom?"

"…Was the only way. The League being so piss-weak 'n all. It was only them Corporates, was the last ones with any power to stand in the Movement's way."

"You did a deal, with a corporation?"

"Yes. Took an 'investment'. Gave up fifty percent equity in this flophouse! Though there is a buy-back clause, and we've easily got enough money to pay 'em out."

"So why don't you just do that?"

"Because the moment I do, the fuckin' Movement'll be back here up my ass – in a manner of speaking – won't they?"

"So, we're half-owned by a corporation now?"

"Yes."

"And when the Movement heard about that, they just backed off and left us alone?"

"Yes."

Another big shock.

The conversation went round and around. Even if someone out there happened to have a huge navy tucked away (which no one did, and certainly not the League), the Movement, allied with the Aurelians and their large quantum AI, were for all intents and purposes unbeatable, given this new generation of gravity weapons. Apart from the possible exception of the corporates.

"The Aurelians are at the core of it," I marveled, "using the Movement as a wedge against us humans. A highly successful strategy with minimal investment in blood and treasure."

"They better watch out," muttered Sana. "Getting M4M to do their dirty work might seem clever at first, but you can never control zealots."

"Them corporates are smart too," said Chook, "using the Movement to get their claws into Jubilee."

"Yeah, but even *they're* slowly gettin' infiltrated, we hear," said Douglas. "Movement people buyin' up stock, gettin' onto boards."

"It's only a matter of time before they come for us again," said Danee. "Soon even Tigsy-Corp won't be powerful enough to keep them away."

"*Hang on!*" I almost choked on a glass of water. "Are you saying the corporate investor who bought fifty percent of Jubilee is *Tigsy-Corp*?"

They both nodded.

"What about *family values* and all that?" chimed Sana. "Aren't they supposed to be squeaky clean?"

Douglas feigned hurt. "Now hang on there, what are you *implyin'*?"

"You know what I mean."

"Let me tell ya," the android rubbed his thumb and two fingers together, "those fuckers only care about one thing, and it ain't *family values*."

I put my head in my hands. Not only had Jubilee barely survived, but it was also now in thrall to a bloodsucking corporate – and a soon-to-be *powerless* bloodsucking corporate at that. Things only ever seemed to go from bad to worse…and then get even worse again. "The situation seems hopeless to me," I said, finally.

Chook shook his head, cleared his throat nervously and stood up. "I need to say somethin', to all of ya."

Everyone at the table looked up in surprise.

"I spent twelve years with the Swami and what I heard over and again was this: everything we need is right here." He pointed to his chest. "Even when we feel *down*." Chook stood ramrod straight, eyes shining. Had this person really been hiding inside the broken husk I'd left on Old Earth? "Lookin' around this room" – he fixed us each with a stare – "Sana, Batum, Col, Douglas. And Danee, I don't know you so well as the others, but *you too*. This is the most intelligent and resourceful and resilient group of folks I ever met. We're fucking *stars*, we can *do* this! We can figure it out, and I tell ya, the Movement should be *quakin' in their boots* if they knew what they were really up against. I actually feel sorry for the bastards!"

Chook suddenly looked sheepish. "Anyway, that's what I think, and that's all I have to say." He sat down again.

We didn't quite know what to make of that. Good that at least *someone* had a positive outlook. Then a new thought popped into my head. "What about Sheng? Do we know what happened to him?"

"The lad?" asked Douglas.

"Yes."

"We looked for the mother," said Danee. "Everywhere. It seems she was either taken or killed during the invasion. They carted a lot of people off, we presume to Rethne, but don't know for sure. Best-case scenario, she was one of them."

In a horrible way, that was a relief. At least I hadn't taken him with us for nothing, though he still might have done better here on Jubilee, even without his mum.

"Do we know where he is?"

"I put out some feelers," said Danee. "We're pretty sure he's on Toulouse Nouvelle."

And a teenager by now, I realized.

Eventually the meeting broke up. Wasn't like we'd resolved anything or come up with a viable plan, but it did feel good to be together. Douglas tried to speak to me as we left but I gave him the cold shoulder. I knew he wanted to apologize, try and make it up to me, but I was nowhere near ready to forgive. Douglas had cost me twelve precious years with my family, how could I ever let that go?

Danee led me back to our old apartment, and what a strange experience it was, wandering through those familiar corridors, dread for some reason building inside me. Why did it feel like I was being led to the gallows? Arriving home, I realized I didn't have with me a single possession other than the clothes on my back. It was as if I'd left for work one morning and returned home to find twelve years had passed.

Inside, things looked much the same except the wall to next door's apartment had been removed and its rooms converted into some kind of dojo or training facility.

"Ladies!" called Danee. "Let's show Daddy what you've learned while he was gone!"

The two girls burst out of their shared bedroom, yipping with glee, and Danee put them through their paces like a drill sergeant.

"*Age Zuki!*" she screamed, and they dropped into fighting stances, kicking and punching the air. Lala went to grapple the smaller Lila, who dodged, ran up a wall like a rock spider and dropped down onto her from the ceiling. They fell together into a thrashing pile of teenage-girl scrimmage.

"*Kendo Ki Hi!*" Danee called, and wooden staffs appeared. Now they went at it, trying to bash each other's brains in with lethal-looking clubs that whirled and cracked.

"They also do this exercise with real swords," said my wife proudly.

Next came a set of drills with laser rifles. The girls whipped these off their backs, expertly breaking them down and reassembling, then dropping into perfect firing stance resting barrels on knees and hitting paper targets at the far end of the room bull's-eye dead center. I noted with relief that these were training guns, fitted with optical lasers only. All very impressive; my third-year BSS graduates would have fared no better.

The girls finished their drills faces flushed, bowed solemnly to their mother for a moment and then took off back to their room giggling with glee.

Later we ate our 'evening' meal together and I couldn't stop myself goggling at them both, so grown up and so beautiful, with shining eyes and glossy hair. Danee continued to show them off: "We've been studying the effects of time dilation, haven't we, ladies?"

"Mmmph!" Anjali mumbled, shoveling in forkfuls of her vegetarian meal.

"We sure have!" chirped Lila. "I can provide the definition if you like!"

"When you're ready."

"Time dilation is the *difference* in elapsed time as measured by two clocks, either due to a relative velocity between them, or a difference in gravitational potential between their locations." She looked sad for a moment. "That's what happened to you, Daddy."

"And the formula?" intoned Danee.

"Special relativity," cried Lala, not to be outdone, "implies that a clock will be slower by a factor of the square root of v2 divided by c2, where v is the relative velocity of the observer and c equals the speed of light." She drew a formula in the brown sauce on her plate, then licked the finger clean:

$$\sqrt{(1 - v^2/c^2)}$$

"That's *cheating*!" whined Lila. "She already had that in her kom."

"What would *you* know, *pigtails*!"

"More than you, *dog lips*."

Insults, obviously rooted in some childhood feud. Dangerous, given that a fight between these two could have lethal consequences – but Danee cut in. "Enough!" The girls turned instantly calm. "We've also been studying literature and history and philosophy…" and so it went for the rest of the meal. Danee trotting out the stellar achievements of our daughters, me filled with bittersweet emotions: admiration and pride, sadness for not being part of it.

Later, I went to say good night. Despite the competitive vibes at dinner, it was clear how close they were; each could have had a room to themselves, but chose instead to share. "Do you guys have any memories of me?" I asked plaintively. Lala was combing knots out of her sister's curly black hair.

"I think so," said Lila. "But not very clear ones. Sorry, Daddy, kinda like – *ouch!* watch it – a big male presence that was just, I dunno, *around* when I was very little."

Lala nodded. "Me the same."

Their room was decorated with what I guess were the usual teenage-girl preoccupations: holo-posters of pop stars and cute animals, stuffed toys, a prized sparkly shirt hanging in the corner (tiny size, so probably Lila's) – but interspersed with military gear – a rack with armaments neatly lined up (knives, pistols, and martial arts-style hand weapons), an open, partially watched military holo, and what looked like a flak jacket strewn carelessly on the floor. My killer tweens.

"You don't remember me holding you? Playing with you?"

They both shook their heads sadly. A moment later Anjali leaned over and whispered something in Lila's ear and they both giggled and blushed.

"What was that?"

"*Gross!* You're so naughty!" Lila scolded.

"*Mum* said it, not me!"

"Said what?" Who could keep up with these glowing, shiny-eyed creatures who seemed to change direction every moment?

Lila turned and whispered to her sister, trying to be quiet but easily loud enough for me to hear. "*You can't tell him* that*!*"

Lala was giggling so much she could barely whisper back, "*Why not, it's funny!*" She put down her comb and forced a serious expression onto her face. "Daddy, we really did miss you, *so much,* but Mummy always said you'd come home. Always! And she told us millions of stories about you, so it somehow felt like you were still here. I think she missed you a lot, though, even more than we did."

She grinned at her sister, and said conspiratorially, "We heard her say to Nazra the other day – that's Mum's best friend – she thought we weren't listening, but we *heard* her. Anyway, Mummy said" – they were both shrieking with laughter now – "she was going to *'shag you senseless'* when you got home!"

Alas, no shagging would be done that night, to a state of senselessness or otherwise.

I found Danee sprawled on the bed, hair out, wearing an old tracksuit. Finally off duty. "Sorry I'm not more glamorous," she said, "I was going to do something but…"

I rolled my eyes. "Danee, you're a *vision*, please don't think—"

"It's just, you know, takes so much energy with the girls, and since Komday it's been a nightmare! They're so fucking *smart*. They always find a way to hack my parental filter and..."

On Jubilee, like everywhere in the civilized galaxy, koms are installed at the age of fourteen, enabling access to the infinite galactic feed, and also marking a significant passage to adulthood. It's a time when kids became a lot more independent and often made life difficult for their parents – supposedly – that's what I'd always heard anyway. Danee spoke for a long while; a parenting monologue, and who could blame her? There'd been no Col to help with this stuff for twelve long years.

She'd homeschooled them, poured herself into their development. "They're amazing," I said finally. "Smart and sassy, but good hearted and sweet. And beautiful. I'm going to have to fend the boys off with a military-grade laser. Mind you, they could probably take care of that themselves."

Danee grinned. "I said to myself, *that's it*, my daughters are going to be the toughest bitches in the galaxy, after what happened here on Jubilee."

"They're a credit to you." She beamed. "And exactly what *did* happen here anyway? I played and replayed your message a million times, what was going on?"

"I *knew* you'd be losing it, I insisted to Douglas we had to send *something* at least."

Danee had been part of a crash crew supervising the separation of Sector Twenty-One that was sent into the sun to make it look like all of Jubilee had been destroyed. She'd made a hurried recording using one of Douglas's avatars and sent it through the DOTR network, which it turns out was secretly hosted by Douglas all along. A part of him that never went offline.

"You've no idea what it meant to me, getting that message."

Our eyes met. She crawled over to where I sat perched on the bed and stroked my cheek tenderly. "Poor booby, you would have been so worried."

"I was literally losing my mind."

"I missed you *so* much, Col. All these long years. I knew what I had to do, and I concentrated on taking care of the girls, but boy I *missed* you."

"I missed you too."

"But isn't it *bizarre*! Only a few months of time have passed for you, but for me…"

She held my gaze for a moment, sweetly at first, then something happened. Out of nowhere a light seemed to switch on in her eyes. She backed away. Got up from the bed and padded slowly to our en suite bathroom, hands on head as if deep in thought. The pit of my stomach clenched.

Then she turned, lightning fast. "Were you *with* her? Sana?" The room was suddenly charged with a terrifying and dangerous energy. She turned away. "No, don't tell me, I don't want to know." She walked into the bathroom and closed the door. Then walked straight back out again. "So! Were you? With her? *Tell me!*"

I didn't know what to say. Did Danee want me to fess up or not? My silence was its own answer.

"For *fuck's sake*! Twelve years, Col! Twelve years working my ass off bringing up your daughters!" She started pacing. "While you were off with *her,* galivanting around – you couldn't be faithful for even *three* months?"

I sat there wishing I could be struck down. By a heart attack or a stroke, or something worse.

"Say something!"

"Danee, all I thought about was you and the girls, every waking moment—"

"Sounds like you missed a few."

I sighed. "It was a weird situation, I was in Jerbet and learned my real grandma was living in a settlement in the woods, and when I got back, I just wasn't feeling myself and…" It was impossible to keep going; the words were literally drying up in my throat.

Danee sat back down on the bed. She became calm now, which to be honest is even more scary with her. She started talking evenly and carefully and I don't remember all the words, must have managed to blot most of them out, I do remember how she finished…

"…I don't care about your circumstances, Col. What about *my* circumstances? I'm not a 'conventional' person. You know what my upbringing was like. But I pined for you, Col. I *waited* for you. Even when every person in my life kept telling me you were never coming back and I had to move on, I still kept the faith."

Each minute of this was a lifetime of torture. "There's nothing I can say, Danee. You have every right to feel this way. I betrayed you."

"*Arggh!*" She looked like there was something distasteful in her mouth that she wanted to spit out. "Now we're going to get 'dramatic' and whiny." She closed her eyes and sat still for a moment. Shook her head. "Nope, can't do it. It's too much, Col. Whatever happened, whatever the excuse you're about to trot out, I can't live with it. You have to go."

I tried to think of something to say, but there was nothing. Any words from me at all would only make things worse. Danee stood up and pointed at the door. "Take your stuff and leave."

"I don't have any stuff."

"Good." Her face contorted into rage. "Go!"

I stumbled out of the apartment. Wandered the corridors for hours like a ghost; unseeing, surrounded by a black fog of despair. Never had I felt so low. Not facing death multiple times in the last few months, not even when I thought Danee and the girls had been killed, nothing could compare to this hell.

Somehow, I ended up on Concourse. People streamed past on every side, but I barely saw them. I was shutting down, going into shock. Maybe I should kill myself?

My kom lit up with an incoming holo-call. *From Danee.* Might this be an opening, a morsel of hope that forgiveness could be possible someday – perhaps if I groveled for a decade or two? Danee's face floated before me, red from tears. *"I spoke with Sana,"* she said flatly.

"Oh."

"She apologized to me. She explained there were some...possibly extenuating circumstances about the...way things happened." For a second, maybe a *nano*-second, there was the tiniest hint of softening in her tone and I felt a flicker of hope.

Immediately quashed.

"But you don't know, *do you?"*

"Know what?" Why was I always the last to find out anything?

Danee shook her head. *"Sana is pregnant."*

"*Pregnant!?*"

I was standing in front of one of the fancy cafés fronting Concourse. There was an empty seat nearby and I collapsed into it as though shot. The only way a woman can fall pregnant in our modern era is of course if she *chooses* to. If she orders her birth-control nanos to not do their normal thing.

"So that means…she's decided to keep—"

"Of course."

Silence.

"She also said something about a colonel, *at the League base?"*

I shook my head. Why would Sana even mention that to her? They must have been griping about me. "That was only…we only—"

"Did you get her *pregnant too?"*

"All we did was have dinner, that's all!"

"Probably enough when it comes to you*."*

Ouch. Nothing I could say about that. Or about anything. I deserved it all.

"Anyway, I just wanted to let you know that little morsel. And to say, stay away*. The girls know everything, I just told them about what happened, and they hate you. Sana hates you too."*

The holo-picture flicked off.

I may have memory loss about the next few hours. There's just a blur of people and places as I staggered like a drunk man through the chaos of Jubilee. Something seemed different about the place, but I didn't have the wherewithal to notice.

Sana, *pregnant*?

If I hadn't just lost twelve years to time dilation, *this* would be the most shocking news of the day. Sana had always been vehement, increasingly so over the years, about the subject of motherhood: in that she *never* wanted anything to do with it. Even joked with Danee and me about how great it was she could 'hand the girls back' when it suited.

Well, something had changed all right…but why was she mad at *me*? Danee I could understand, but surely Sana was at least equally as culpable as I was for this sorry mess? Shouldn't I be the one angry at *her* for turning off her birth-control nanos and not telling me? But who would know, and what did it matter anyway? My life was over. I started thinking about suicide again.

After some indeterminate period of time, I found myself in Sector Eleven and there was my old buddy Zhang, or his holo reconstruction anyway. He waved and smiled at me.

"How you doin', Donny? Haven't seen you 'round for *ages*."

"Things have been a bit tough, Zhang."

"That's a shame, like how?"

"You know…like Jubilee being attacked and supposedly destroyed along with my wife and kids – that's what I was led to believe anyway – and then being chased around the galaxy by Movement for Morality fanatics, and finally getting home to learn I'd actually been gone for twelve years due to time dilation. Also, I got my ex-wife Sana pregnant somehow, so of course Danee is mad at me, *as well as* Sana for some reason I can't fathom. Plus, my daughters, who are now *old enough* to do so – they're angry at me as well. So, all in all…rather a lot."

Zhang rubbed his chin. "You know, that's terrible, Donny. Sometimes bad things happen to good people."

"You can say that again."

"Take me for example. I was tortured to death by the Movement. Can't have been much fun, I reckon."

"Just as well you don't remember it."

"Technically speaking, I don't have memories at all given that I'm a digital construct rather than a backup." He paused for a second. "But why don't I do a poem? Might help cheer you up?"

I shrugged, what the hell – things could hardly get any worse right? "OK, hit me, Zhang."

The AI frowned in concentration for a moment and a card slid out of a slot in the box he was standing on. I pulled it out to read:

Desolate,
broken.
Where is the light, where is the light?
Unknowable is the way of Fate.
Zhang the Poet

I stared at the card in horror. Did the AI wish me to go space myself at the nearest airlock? He must have seen the look on my face.

"Are you OK, Col? What does it say?"

"What, don't you *know*?" I went to hand the card over to him, but of course it slipped through thin air and fluttered to the ground – so convincing was the hologram. I picked it up and showed him.

Zhang was mortified. "Sorry, Col, I thought a poem might cheer you up a bit. To be honest I never know how these things are going to turn out."

"But aren't you the one who writes them?"

"Sure, but I don't have conscious control over it."

"Where do they come from then?"

"Same place as for humans."

"Which is where?"

"The Akash."

"The *what*?"

"Whatever you want to call it: the 'void', the mysterious potentiality-filled space of nothingness from which creativity emerges. No one knows how it works, not even us AIs. In the end, we're not all that different to humans…but *hey*! Why don't we give this another try? A second poem might be just the thing!"

"No Zhang, *enough*. I can't take any more blows, honestly not even—"

"Here we go, I got a feeling about this one!"

Zhang's brows beetled in concentration and another poem emerged from the slot. I stared glumly at it for a moment while he smiled and pointed enthusiastically. I sighed, leaned wearily down like an old man and pulled out the card to read:

Too much
Too little.
Emptiness
Brings heavenly blessing.
Zhang the Poet

Zhang performed a little jig of excitement on his podium. "What's it say, Donny? Read it out!" I stared for a minute trying to decode the meaning, then read it back to him.

"See, buddy! Things aren't that bad!"

What was the meaning here? The opposing duality of 'too much' and 'too little' seemed to imply…what, the endlessness of human desire? Wanting less of the bad things, more of the good things; the way we strive against the current of fate (I certainly knew all about *that* lately). The third and fourth lines were probably to do with that old cliché Sana's artsy friends used to spout: 'be empty in order to receive'. Well I was *empty* all right. My tank reached zero ages ago.

Put crudely, the poem seemed to imply there was only one way to go from here and that was *up*. Perhaps it was true? I thanked Zhang and continued on my way. Strangely, things seemed a little different. I'd had a shift. A skerrick of hope perhaps, implanting itself somewhere in my consciousness.

OK, Danee hated me right now, and fair enough too. But in the end, it wasn't really about sex (OK, I *did* get Sana pregnant), but Danee spoke the truth in saying she really wasn't a 'conventional' person. After all, she lived here on *Jubilee,* with the girls, and me, *and* my ex-wife who was her best friend. She was probably the most open-minded person I knew. If positions were reversed, I knew it wouldn't be a deal breaker for me, though my own jealousy would be something I'd have to handle.

It was the *twelve years*.

Twelve years of waiting and pining and doing the hard grind; bringing up the girls. But the twelve years was the very part of it that *wasn't* my fault. I'd tried my best to get back, ran as hard as I could with the hand I was dealt. You had to say, all that happened was down to fate.

Right now, Danee was feeling betrayed – totally understandable – but sooner or later she'd come around. I knew Danee's heart. She might make me pay for a while, for even a long time, but in the end, she *would* forgive.

Sana? She'd have to talk to me sooner or later, about the child at the very least; surely, *she* couldn't stay mad at me – assuming it was even true? Danee might have just said that to make me feel even worse. The kid was going to be a boy I decided. In fact, I was certain. The universe owed me at least one male progeny, right? That would be nice, maybe even *healing* for the whole family.

And Douglas? In hindsight, none of this was really his fault either. He tried his best just like we all did. If I really wanted to blame anyone it should be the Movement, they were the ones who invaded and caused all this carnage. Why take it out on each other? I called him on my kom. *"Douglas, you around? I'm sorry I was mad at you; it's been a very tough time."*

The android stepped out from behind a nearby corner. Of course. Probably been tracking me the whole time. Chook was with him, and he wrapped me up in a hug – quite the hugger he was these days. "Sounds like you've been in the wars, mate," he said, finally letting me go. It was interesting to observe; this person was clearly still Chook, but the best version of him it was possible to be. He hadn't changed, so much as *evolved.*

I laughed wryly. "Bad news travels fast…but hey, how do you guys even *know*? Douglas, were you listening in?"

The robot scowled. "Don't be a fuckin' dullard. Y'know very well I listen to *everythin'* here on Jubilee."

We started walking together along Concourse and for the first time I became aware of the myriad changes that had occurred. There was now a Tigsy-themed casino right in the middle of Sector Nine, the red-light district. And partner hotel. Fancy-dress characters from the 'Tigsy-verse' posed and handed out holo-balls promoting myriad Tigsy-Corp activities, including a new theme park. The restaurants were different, they had a 'cheap' look, as did the shops: weren't these chain stores that I knew from Brouggh? Everything looked more commercial and more crass – though to be fair, Jubilee had always *been* crass – but the vibe was dull, ordinary.

We always had our fair share of desperados and degenerates in the past, of course, but there was a bohemian element too: artists, performers, and flat-out weirdos; every type of sexual combination and concatenation. Being 'queer' on Jubilee wasn't just tolerated, it was all but mandated. All these people brought together ('curated' even?) by receiving that mysterious and highly sought-after invitation from Douglas.

But no longer. Some of the patrons I observed strutting around here, in the very center of the red-light district, looked smug, entitled even.

Douglas must have read my mind. "Y'like our brave new world?"

"What happened? Don't tell me: *Tigsy-Corp*."

"We think it might a' been them all along, putting the Movement up to attacking us. A ploy just so they could get their dirty little fingers in the pie."

"They'll regret it."

We came upon a large, fancy looking establishment, all polished black stone with glowing letters: *Tigsy Club Platinum,* and just to make sure we got the message, in smaller print below, *Members Only!* Two huge (probably augmented) bouncers in dark suits stood at the end of a rope line, staring coldly at passersby, including us.

"Keep up the good work, lads," said Chook with a wink.

Eliciting no response. Moments later, one of the more self-satisfied-looking couples I'd spied earlier sauntered over and were instantly let through the rope line with a polite bow from the guards.

"What's with the members-only club in the middle of Sector Nine?" I asked. The Jubilee I knew was open to all. Or at least all who weren't inebriated past the point of being a pain in the ass.

"Arrgh." Douglas pretended to spit. "It's a fuckin' Tigsy thing. Anyone who's a member of their stupid 'Platinum Club' gets automatic entry to Jubilee."

"So, you gave up the right to choose who comes here?"

"No. But I had to allow in certain commercial interests, and I also have to let anyone come who's a member of this particular rancid club full of rich fuckers with smug faces you want to punch."

Weird. "How much does it cost to join?"

"Hang on a tick." Chook scrolled his kom. "Says here – *fuck me!* – over ten million credits per annum."

That was it. That's when I finally saw it.

Jubilee was one of the most famous places in the galaxy (though technically, of course, it wasn't *in* our normal galaxy). Millions visited, but hundreds of times that number never received the coveted invite. You could be rich and famous, the most powerful person in your patch of the cosmos, and still not be allowed. To someone always used to getting their own way, this would be offensive, intolerable. And there was nothing you could do about it, no one to appeal to.

Until now.

"Just figured it out," I said.

"Figured what?" said Douglas.

"It's not the money, it's about *status*!"

"Please," muttered Chook, "no riddles."

"Something's been bugging me ever since you told me about this deal with Tigsy-Corp. Think about it, why would they go to all the trouble? Why go to such extremes of instigating an M4M attack just to force you into dealing with them, just so they can make *more money*? Doesn't make sense."

"O' *course* it's about the money!" bellowed Douglas. "What else would it be?"

"They've got heaps of the stuff! More than they know what to do with. But here's the irony, imagine you're a person like one of these corporate types who values money above *all else*, what is the thing you actually covet the most?"

Chook got it, his eyes lit up. "Something money *can't buy*!"

"*Exactly!* Like an invite to Jubilee."

"You tellin' me Tigsy went to all this trouble, got me invaded by M4M so they could muscle through a deal, *just to set up a fuckin' club*!?"

"That's about the size of it. It's an ego trip, a wank."

Chook was nodding. "That's brilliant, Col, it explains everything. Maybe you have to be away from somewhere for a while and come back again before you can see the obvious. And you know what else? Shit's so bad here on Jubilee now, you can't even get a decent *beer* anymore!"

"But you're not drinking these days, aren't—"

"Correct. I'm off the piss! What I shoulda said is, 'You can't get a decent *non-alcoholic* beer anymore.' Though to be fair, that stuff has probably always been crap, I just never tasted a drop of it until now!"

We stopped for a moment and watched the churn of the crowd. There was still plenty of action you had to say. The red-light district thronged with revelers just like it always had, even if the crowd seemed a little different. More aggressive perhaps. A feeling of latent violence just below the surface.

"So, was it hard, Chook, getting off the booze?"

He stopped in the middle of Concourse and wagged his finger. "Giving up the booze and drugs was the easy bit. Dealing with the underlying stuff, the reasons why I became an addict in the first place, *that* was much tougher."

"Really? You couldn't just stop?"

"Nup, you have to deal with the underlying cause."

Everything started spinning. Something strange was happening to my brain: a realization. A huge one. An understanding so massive it was going to change everything, change the whole galaxy.

Chook and Douglas eyed me with concern. I must have gone all glazy-eyed and red-faced.

"You all right, Col? Did something—"

I ignored them and staggered over to the middle section of Concourse where there was a Transit stop, and flopped onto one of the seats. The others followed a few steps behind.

"I'm fine," I said, waving for them to sit. "*Better* than fine! I just figured out what we're going to *do*!"

"About what?" asked Douglas.

"About everything! Chook, you just gave me the answer. *The root causes*. We have to deal with the root causes."

Chook scratched his head. "Root causes of what?"

"The Movement!"

"Well, that's easy, the root cause is *Gilham*!"

"No, that's where we've been going wrong. There are *always* Gilhams in this universe; always have been and always *will* be. Why has this one gained so much traction now? We've been thinking about it wrong, trying to push back. The Swami told me that rather than fighting directly, you have to let your opponent's energy work against him."

Chook nodded. "True, he does say that. But I already asked you before *not to talk in fuckin' riddles*!"

"Why are people joining the Movement? What are they actually getting out of it?"

"Humans are…humans are just idiots!" sputtered Douglas. "That's all there is to it."

"Maybe. But what if they're joining M4M because they *are* getting something out of it? If that's the case, all we have to do is figure out what that thing is, provide something better and *presto*, the fight's over."

"But how do we do that!?"

"I don't know yet. But *that's the plan*! I've seen it! And another thing, we have to deal with the Aurelians, because they're the Movement's enablers."

"That'll be interesting," mused Douglas. "Those fuckers are a handful. But I like your reasoning, Col, I reckon ye're on to something."

"Can we go fetch Sheng?" asked Chook. "I'm feelin' bad about him stuck on Toulouse Nouvelle all these years."

"Sure, we need him. We need *everyone*! Danee and Sana and my daughters – once I get them all back on my side that is. This is going to be the A team! All of us against the Movement!"

Chook was sitting between Douglas and me. He stretched his arms wide, grabbed us both tightly around the shoulders and roared joyfully into the permanent night of Sector Nine.

"That's right you got it, *this is what I've been trying to tell ya*! Those bastards don't stand a chance against stars like us!"

Acknowledgments

I still can't quite believe I'm writing books and people are publishing them. It doesn't seem right – but until someone orders me to stop, I plan to keep going.

In the meantime, I want to thank Don D'Auria, who rescued *Jubilee* from the slush pile, and Nick Wells, who took a chance on publishing it. To Sarah Miniaci, Olivia Jackson, and the entire team at Flame Tree – what an extraordinary company and a joy to work with you all!

To everyone who read *Jubilee* and encouraged me to keep writing – you are too numerous to name, but I know who each of you are, and I'm still a bit shocked by your generosity and kindness.

And, as always, deepest thanks to my wife, Vani – without her green tick on each chapter, I could never move forward, and without whom it would all be for nothing.

Stephen K. Stanford
April, 2025

About the Author

Stephen K. Stanford has been a serial entrepreneur since the age of twenty-one. He has produced numerous projects for the arts, including a live performance adaption of *My Dinner with Andre*, and the feature film *Four Jacks*. He fell in love with science fiction as a child. His favorite book, for its playfulness and wit, was *The Stainless Steel Rat* by Harry Harrison. Stephen's debut novel, *Jubilee*, was written in part as an homage to it and *Stars Like Us* is its exciting sequel.

Stephen is a devoted meditator and ashram frequenter, has reared a rock star (literally) and is himself an avid music fan. He lives on the beautiful Mornington Peninsula in Australia, with his wife, Vani. Find out more on his website: stephenkstanford.com.

FLAME TREE PRESS
FICTION WITHOUT FRONTIERS
Award-Winning Authors & Original Voices

Flame Tree Press is the trade fiction imprint of Flame Tree Publishing, focusing on excellent writing in horror and the supernatural, crime and mystery, science fiction and fantasy. Our aim is to explore beyond the boundaries of the everyday, with tales from both award-winning authors and original voices.

•

Other titles by Stephen K. Stanford:
Jubilee

You may also enjoy:
The Sentient by Nadia Afifi
Junction by Daniel M. Bensen
Keeper of Sorrows by Rachel Fikes
Silent Key by Laurel Hightower
The Widening Gyre by Michael R. Johnston
The Heart of Winter by Shona Kinsella
The Sky Woman by J.D. Moyer
The Guardian by J.D. Moyer
Brittle by Beth Overmyer
Tempered Glass by Beth Overmyer
The Goblets Immortal by Beth Overmyer
One Eye Opened in That Other Place by Christi Nogle
The Last Feather by Shameez Patel Papathanasiou
The Eternal Shadow by Shameez Patel Papathanasiou
The First King by Shameez Patel Papathanasiou
Tinderbox by W.A. Simpson
Tarotmancer by W.A. Simpson
The Hatter's Daughter by W.A. Simpson
A Killing Fire by Faye Snowden
A Killing Rain by Faye Snowden
A Sword of Bronze and Ashes by Anna Smith Spark
Idolatry by Aditya Sudarshan
The Roamers by Francesco Verso
Whisperwood by Alex Woodroe
Of Kings, Queens & Colonies by Johnny Worthen

•